MORE THAN A THIEF

BEVERLY PATT

OWL HOLLOW PRESS

Owl Hollow Press, LLC, Springville, UT 84663

This book is a work of fiction. Names, characters, places, and incidents are products of the author's imagination. Any resemblance to actual people, living or dead, or to businesses, companies, events, institutions, or locales is completely coincidental or used fictitiously.

The Adventures of Sherlock Holmes and *The Sign of Four* by Sir Arthur Conan Doyle are quoted throughout this work and reside in the public domain.

The newspaper articles quoted throughout and the images contained from newspaper reports also reside in the public domain and sources are cited at the end of the book.

More Than a Thief
Copyright © 2023 by Beverly Patt

All rights reserved. No part of this publication may be reproduced, distributed or transmitted in any form or by any means, without prior written permission.

Library of Congress Cataloging-in-Publication Data
More Than a Thief / B. Patt. — First edition.

Summary:
In 1892, in the bustling town of Fall River, Massachusetts, 16-year-old Victoria Robbins feels trapped by her high-society, pre-debutante life. When her next-door neighbors are murdered and her friend, Lizzie Borden, is accused of committing the acts, Victoria begins her quest to *not* become Lizzie Borden.

Cover Design by Pocket Hollow Designs

ISBN: 978-1-958109-38-0 (paperback)
ISBN: 978-1-958109-39-7 (e-book)

To Jer, aka J.Paul,
who makes me laugh every single day.

LYMTTCT

Lizzie Borden took an axe
Gave her mother forty whacks
When she saw what she had done
She gave her father forty-one.

—Anonymous

CHAPTER ONE

"How sweet the morning air is! See how that one little cloud floats like a pink feather from some gigantic flamingo. Now the red rim of the sun pushes itself over the London cloud-bank. It shines on a good many folk, but on none, I dare bet, who are on a stranger errand than you and I."

—Sherlock Holmes in *The Sign of Four*

Victoria turned her back on the motionless form of her mother in bed to pick up the breakfast tray, careful to keep it level so as not to disturb the dishes and utensils. But once she was downstairs in the kitchen, she set it down with a clatter.

"Mother is not getting any better, Penelope. Five weeks now and she still hasn't moved a muscle."

Penelope stopped rolling dough long enough to push her droopy maid's cap up her forehead. "Actually, miss, it's six."

"Six?" Victoria scraped her mother's uneaten creamed rice into the bucket of food scraps. Before this, her longest spell had been twenty days. As she washed the bowl and spoon in soapy water, she refused to voice the one thought circling her mind: *What if she doesn't get better this time?* Her eyes began to burn.

Abandoning the dishes, she wiped her hands on her apron. "I'm stepping out for some air, Pen." As she hurried onto the back stoop, she caught sight of Miss Lizzie's uncle just leaving the Bordens' home and quickly stepped back, waiting until he was out of sight. He was a frequent guest of her neighbors, but his dour personality and dead eyes always made her feel uncomfortable.

Letting the door close behind her, Victoria breathed in the fragrances of summer—cut grass, dusty hay, horse manure, fried bacon, and, even from three houses over, the sweet aroma of the Borden's pear tree. Her mouth watered. Nothing was more delicious than a Borden pear.

As if summoned by Victoria's thought, Miss Lizzie came into view, walking towards the pear tree, basket in hand.

"Miss Lizzie!" Victoria waved. Miss Lizzie turned, startled, then put her finger to her lips before pointing to her home's second-floor window. Her elderly parents must still be sleeping. She motioned for Victoria to come over.

"Sorry," Victoria whispered a minute later, stepping carefully around fallen pears and the bees that swarmed them. "I know it's unladylike to call out, but I was so happy to see you."

Miss Lizzie studied her. "I take it your mother's condition has not improved." How like Miss Lizzie to cut right to the chase.

Victoria shook her head, shoulders sagging. "The paralysis has never lasted this long. She's getting frightfully thin, and I'm really starting to worry." The burning in her eyes returned.

Miss Lizzie snapped a pear from its branch and added it to her basket. "It must be particularly difficult with your father away, as well." Her deep voice was soothing, like a cool hand on a hot cheek. "Quite a lot for a sixteen-year-old to handle."

Victoria's throat knotted. Somehow, quirky, gruff, unmarried Miss Lizzie understood Victoria better than anyone else. One tear escaped. Two. Three.

"Oh, come now, Victoria." Miss Lizzie searched her waistband, then her cuffs. "Ach, and here's me, with no hanky to offer."

Despite her tears, Victoria laughed. "I never remember mine either!"

Miss Lizzie smiled. "Well, chin up. School will be starting soon and will keep your mind occupied." She selected the best pear from her basket. "Here. A sweet pear never fails to improve my mood."

Victoria pressed the pear to her nose and breathed in. *Heavenly.*

"And now, I'm afraid, I must check on my household. We've all had sour stomachs as of late. But perhaps we can do one of our backyard picnics when the sickness has left?"

"Oh, yes, please!" She smiled and wiped the last tear away.

Miss Lizzie placed one fingertip on Victoria's wrist and looked at her intently. "You will get through this, Victoria. You are stronger than you know." With a nod, she turned and strode back toward her house. "Give your mother my regards."

By the time Victoria arrived at her own back door, she'd eaten the pear down to its core. Miss Lizzie was right. She was feeling a little better already.

AT THE SOUND of her maid's footsteps stopping outside the parlor door, Victoria looked up from her magazine and the Sherlock installment she'd already read five times. "Penelope, when is your sister due to arrive? Soon, isn't it?"

"Oh, yes'm, in a little over a week's time." She twisted the dusting rag in her hands.

Victoria gazed dreamily out the window. "What an adventure, traveling all the way across the Atlantic. Miss Lizzie said her European tour was grand."

"An adventure, to be sure, but I don't think Olive will be traveling in the same style as your Miss Lizzie." She gave the door panel a half-hearted swipe with her rag.

"Oh, goodness." Victoria felt her face redden. "I'm sorry. I just..."

Penelope offered a brief smile over her shoulder. "Ah, miss, I know what you meant. I'm just grateful to your father for the full day off, with pay no less. But I can't be leaving you all by yourself to care for your mother, so I hope he comes back from the farm in time."

Or comes back at all, Victoria wanted to say. Apparently, even Penelope had noticed his prolonged absences.

"I'd hoped to take Olive to High Street for tea," Penelope continued, moving to dust the mantle. "Then spend the day moseying through the shops. She's a keen seamstress and can't wait to see all the fabrics our own 'Spindle City' offers. It will be quite a shock coming from our little town in Connemara."

"Well, you and your sister shall have your day out together, whether or not Father returns. I will cover for you, Pen. And perhaps Mother will be better by then, too. She'd insist you go."

"That's very kind of you, miss. And speaking of your mother, I was thinking she could do with a healthy dose of my peach pie."

"Oh, yes, wonderful idea! Maybe with some whipping cream? Mother loves that."

Penelope quirked an eyebrow. "Thing is, I'm fresh outta peaches and I've still got more ironing to do. Care to add a little interest to your mornin' with a trip to town?"

Victoria tossed the worn magazine aside. "You know I do!"

Racing up the stairs, she could already smell the cool sawdust air of the shops and feel the camaraderie of her fellow shoppers bustling by. A wonderful chance to pretend she was on a clandestine mission, just like Sherlock himself, on the hunt for clues on his latest case. She grabbed her purse and, after a quick glance over her shoulder, removed a small bundle from her tufted writing bench and shoved it beneath her coat.

She was just opening the front door when Penelope called out from the kitchen. "Don't you be going without Mr. Pottersmith, now. You're not one of them mill girls, remember, trouncing about without a chaperone. With yer debut this year, you got a reputation to uphold."

"I know," Victoria called back. Then added under her breath, "But mill girls have a great deal more fun."

VICTORIA STOOD on her front porch, straightening her lace gloves, drinking in the lush summer arbor of greenery against the bright blue sky. The neighborhood was abuzz with activity: stable men jawboning outside the livery across the street, top hats leaving for work, women shaking out rugs, the Bordens' maid washing a window in the front of their house. She saw Victoria and waved and Victoria waved back, remembering Miss Lizzie's comment about sickness in the house. Bridget must be feeling all right if she was out in this heat. And here came Mr. Borden shuffling his way down the sidewalk toward town, taking his sweet old time.

Pretending to check her coat buttons, Victoria glanced sideways at him, wondering why men his age thought a chinstrap beard was attractive. Like a long, ugly caterpillar, crawling along his jaw line from ear to ear. And, what's this? The left side of his beard was uneven. *Probably right-handed?* As he got closer, the shiny spot on the right rim of his top hat all but confirmed her theory.

"I see it, I deduce it," she whispered, quoting the Sherlock Holmes story she'd just been reading. *A Scandal in Bohemia* was her favorite, the only story in which Sherlock was bested by anyone, and a woman to boot. She'd pretend she was that woman, with Sherlock as her admirer.

Mr. Borden passed without a hello, making Victoria wonder for the hundredth time how someone so grumpy could raise someone as kind and thoughtful as Miss Lizzie. Once the rest of the neighbors dispersed to carriages and houses, Victoria hurried next door to Mr. Pottersmith's overgrown yard. Ducking behind the bushes, she exchanged her day jacket, gloves, and hat for the bundle beneath her arm. With a pinch of dirt rubbed on her cheeks, Victoria stepped back onto the sidewalk dressed as a maid, a large cape covering her gold-embroidered dress, and an oversized cotton cap hiding her coifed hair.

Now I am free to do as I wish.

In town, four- and five-story buildings huddled along Fall River's Main Street, their stone and brick walls pushing out dry heat and ricocheting the din of clattering horse hooves, bakery cart bells, factory whistles, and cursing drivers. There were plenty of scruffy individuals on which to keep an eye, and a variety of conversations on which to eavesdrop. Every unfinished exchange suggested a mystery:

"…he really ought not have…"

"…nothing like I pictured..."

"...with a rope and hammer…"

Victoria's mind swirled with plots rivaling the most lurid penny dreadfuls and mysterious Sherlock Holmes tales. As she stopped to let a flower seller pass, she felt a hard shoe scrape her heel. She turned, half-expecting to see the beggar from *The Man with the Twisted Lip,* only to find two vaguely familiar pink-cheeked boys from her neighborhood, jostling each other like playful puppies.

"Sorry, miss," said one, barely stifling a snort. "Wasn't me. Say you're sorry, Brownie."

Brownie smirked. "It was all Thomas's fault, miss. You can rat to his granny and make sure he gets a whipping." He giggled as he blocked Thomas's smacking hands, and then they took off across the street, whooping as they dodged carriages, wheel ruts, and fly-covered horse droppings.

What a ridiculous world we live in, where everyone but girls of my age and station can go wherever they want, by themselves. Even children! She checked her reflection in the nearest store window and straightened her cape. *Quite convincing,* she imagined Sherlock remarking.

As she came upon her father's bank, the door opened and Mr. Borden, of all people, came out. Victoria fussed with her hat to block her face, though it was likely unnecessary. He never acknowledged her on her visits to Miss Lizzie. Still, could she not get away from him this morning?

"Andrew!" A voice called to Mr. Borden from across the street. Mr. Borden's usually severe expression broke into a chuckle and he waved his cane like a flag as he hastened between carriages and horse carts toward the owner of the men's hat shop.

She exhaled and continued on, taking mental notes of unusual details: uneven shoe heels, coal-smudged gloves, misbuttoned jackets, suspicious stains. As she approached Benson's Fancy Goods and Notions, a familiar sparking, whirling feeling started up in her chest. *No, no, not here! It's much too public.* Her little game of scooping up useless doodads was reserved for home and schoolyard. Not for stores. But once the feeling came upon her, it was near impossible to push it away.

Trying to regain herself, she focused on the back of a young man in front of her standing just outside the store. He was tall and slim, his hair a mop of unruly dark curls. The bottoms of his pants bore two faint lines, indicating they'd been let out twice as he grew, probably by a frugal mother. Not of the gentry class, then. Something about his posture and the tilt of his head told her he was attentive and smart. Coming upon him, she saw he was engaged in conversation with an even taller man in a top hat and... a police officer.

Stopping abruptly, she was nearly knocked over from behind.

A heavyset woman, smelling of soured milk, pushed her aside. "Watch it, girlie."

"S-sorry, ma'am."

Noticing the disturbance, the policeman leaned past his acquaintances. "Any trouble, then?" He squinted at Victoria. Heart pounding, she ducked her head and dropped into a low servant's curtsy. When she rose, the beautiful green eyes of the dark-haired young man locked on hers in a friendly, interested way. A warmth spread through her chest, like a long drink of hot chocolate. The top-hatted man scowled over his shoulder, and the policeman adjusted the lid of his cap. "Miss?"

Victoria blinked and looked away. "I'm... jest fine," she mumbled, leaning on her false Irish accent. Without allowing herself another glance at the handsome boy, she yanked the maid's cap further down her brow and burrowed into the crowd of pedestrians. In front of the milliner's, a clump of elderly ladies stood blocking the sidewalk, loudly commenting on the brashness of the latest styles, while passers-by streamed around them. Victoria was wedging herself into a spot to catch her breath and peek at the offending hat styles when a slight movement caught her eye. Like a lightning bolt, her hand struck out, clamping onto a bony wrist, the fingers of which gripped a small, beaded coin purse.

"I'll take that," Victoria muttered, yanking back one of the offending fingers, making a young man in baggy-sleeved shirt yelp in pain and release the purse. In the second it took the old ladies to turn around, the young man had disappeared into the crowd and Victoria held out the bulging coin purse. The shortest of the ladies gasped and reached for it, her arm shaking unsteadily.

"Why, thank you!" the woman said, a look of shock on her face.

"Ain' nothin', ma'am." Victoria tucked her chin and dropped a quick curtsy before she, too, disappeared into the crowd. After she was safely out of sight, she smiled to herself.

Wouldn't Sherlock be proud?

By the time the bells of the First Congregational Church chimed eleven o'clock, the day had grown quite warm, and the beautiful gold stitching in her chambray dress was itching her back, the discomfort intensified by her oversized shawl. She found the fruit man and purchased a sack of peaches, then headed toward home. Approaching Benson's, the swirling in her chest started anew. It *had* been quite a while since she and Mother had been to the store. Perhaps she should pop in, for just a moment? Mother would certainly enjoy hearing about the summer displays. Yes, she'd stop, but only if that policeman was gone.

Which, it turned out, he was.

CHAPTER TWO

"My dear fellow," said Sherlock Holmes, as we sat on either side of the fire in his lodgings at Baker Street, "life is infinitely stranger than anything which the mind of man could invent. We would not dare to conceive the things which are really mere commonplaces of existence. If we could fly out of that window hand in hand, hover over this great city, gently remove the roofs and peep in at the queer things which are going on... It would make all fiction with its conventionalities and foreseen conclusions most stale and unprofitable."

—Sherlock Holmes in *A Case of Identity*

M rs. Benson's Fancy Goods and Notions, "a general store for the discerning woman," was filled stem to stern with buttons and baubles, hat pins and hairnets, kitchen utensils and garden tools, and myriad cloth items. Fussy saleswomen buzzed about, dusting, re-stacking, and re-folding. A woman in a blue feathered hat discussed copper pots with Mrs. Benson in the kitchen aisle; a circle of elderly ladies peered and pawed at lace doilies on a table near the front window; two young girls near the cash register sniffed perfume under the watchful eye of a dark-haired saleswoman; and beyond them, another clerk dusted boxes along the back wall.

Victoria's mother loved Benson's, loved having a store in town in which she could find most everything on her shopping list. Victoria loved the beautiful displays, with housewares, dry goods, laundry, sewing notions, handbags, and accessories each having their own sections down the aisles. There was always something new to admire.

She strolled the row with measured care, swinging the bag of peaches by her side, trying to ignore the uptick in her heartbeat. But it only got worse. Maybe she shouldn't have come in, not while feeling like this. *But what could it hurt?* said another side of her. *You're just looking.* As she dragged a finger along a stack of bumpy washboards, the familiar metallic tang filled her mouth and the throbbing in her eyes began. *Oh dear.*

Magpie—Mag for short—had arrived.

Heart racing, skin flushing, Victoria's vision began to narrow as she stood rooted to the wood floor. The ordinary items before her suddenly throbbed with incredible allure: the straight pins gorgeous in their silver unity, stacked with military precision; the sock darners, each with its unique woodgrain polished to perfection, true works of art; spools of thread in colors so beautiful it made her heart ache. But one—and only one—item would be claimed.

She gripped her skirt to dry her palms, then took a step closer.

A rustling in the next aisle preluded Miss Parker, a salesclerk, poking her head up over boxes of Borax. "Can I help you find something?"

The throbbing pulse in Victoria's neck pressed against her windpipe, making it hard to breathe.

Miss Parker's smile flickered. "You look… dazed."

In her dizzy fog, Victoria managed to curtsy. "I'm a bit... woozy, 'tis all," she rasped. "From the sun."

Her legs shook. *So close now,* Mag whispered.

No, she countered. *I shouldn't!*

"Perhaps," Miss Parker continued, her eyebrow arching, "you'd be better off returning home?" She began making her way down the aisle, the clacking of her heels on the wood floor counting the seconds Victoria had left. "If your mistress is about, I'd be happy to call you both a carriage. We have one at our disposal—"

"Ach, no thank you." Victoria tracked Miss Parker like a cat with a mouse while shaking fingers extended toward the shelf filled with thread, the folds of her shawl blocking her projected deed.

A few more heel clacks and Victoria would be in full view. Fingers fumbled against the spools until they found the one they wanted. The moment she snatched it, her chest exploded in white-hot sparks, a glorious feeling of relief and achievement.

Miss Parker turned into the aisle just as Victoria stuffed the spool into her purse.

"I'm fine," Victoria murmured, straining to stay composed as her body rang and her scalp tingled. "I-it was jest for a moment there that I felt... ill." Her lips pressed into a tight smile as she pulled her purse strings shut.

A hand gripped her arm from behind. She whirled to find Mrs. Benson, the storeowner, close enough to see the cracks in her face powder.

"So ill," Mrs. Benson murmured, keeping her voice low, "that you just had to *take something* for it?"

The roaring in Victoria's ears fizzled. Her elation drained. Mag retreated.

Stomach lurching, she thought of her parents. The shame. Why had she done it?

"Please, ma'am," Victoria said, ducking her head. "My missus... she'd..." What was she going to say? She could just

pay—

At that moment, the shop door slammed open, knocking a broom to the floor with a sharp crack. A man in a butcher's apron stood outlined in sunlight.

"There's a killer on the loose!" he yelled. Behind him, a police carriage careened past. "Lock your doors and stay inside!"

BLAZING SUNSHINE and a horrible stench greeted Victoria as she swung open Benson's back storeroom door leading to the alley. Momentarily blinded, she grabbed the door jamb to steady herself, the sounds of panic echoing in the store behind her. The customers had rushed to the window, and the girls by the counter whimpered for their mother, who, in her hurry to get to them, knocked over a stack of papers. The dusting clerk started blubbering, throwing all traces of poise and decorum to the wind, while Miss Parker hurried past, calling, "Stand aside! I will fasten the door!"

It was then Victoria felt Mrs. Benson's grip on her elbow slacken, and she twisted around just in time to catch the fainting old woman about the waist and, with some difficulty, lower her considerably large and limp body to the floor. Grabbing a neatly folded pile of finger towels from the shelf, she'd shoved them under Mrs. Benson's gray head and, with a quick glance over her shoulder, dashed to the back room and its rear door, where she now stood, gaining her bearings.

As the fuzzy blindness lifted, a line of store backs came into view, each with their own teetering stacks of shipping crates, waste bins, metal troughs, and wood barrels—a dreaded "back alley." A movement to the right, near the alley's mouth, caught her eye. The tall, curly-haired boy she'd seen earlier in front of the store, plus his friend, the policeman, rummaged through the greengrocer's bins, tossing aside rotten cabbages and tomatoes.

Her nausea grew, considering her only two options: go back inside and risk arrest, or stay out here and risk running into a murderer. Frightened shoppers hurried past in the road beyond the alley, their ranks already thinning as the news spread. Being questioned by the police was a new risk, but there was nothing for it. At this point, her reputation was more at risk than her life. And if she lost her reputation, her life would be over anyway.

Holding her breath, Victoria closed the door behind her and began tiptoeing through the alley.

Hurry. Hurry.

Her skirt caught a board and knocked it into another, making a loud *clunk.*

Both men looked up.

Don't stop. Keep going.

"Haven't ya heard, missy?" the policeman called, prying the lid off a large barrel. "There's a murderer runnin' loose!" He peered over the splintered edge of the barrel, nose scrunched.

"Yessir," she called back, continuing to pick her way through the maze of splintered wood. "I heared!" Though she'd remembered to imitate a maid, her voice sounded unnaturally high, as if responding to good news. Clearing her throat, she added, "Turrible!"

"Not just terrible, miss." This was the young man who, she could tell even from a distance, was disarmingly handsome. He took a few steps in her direction. "It's dangerous, too."

Don't I know it, Victoria thought, approaching from the far side of the alley.

"Maybe," he added, "you should wait in one of the shops, until things are safe?"

"Thank ye," she said, "I'll be fine."

"That's probably what the Bordens thought jest this morning," the policeman called.

"Bordens?" Stunned, Victoria looked up, and in her lapse of attention, her foot caught on the splintered remains of a table. The sack of peaches flew and she pitched forward, tiny rocks piercing her palms. She tried to scramble to her feet, but her skirts kept getting in the way. It couldn't be *her* Bordens, surely? Fall River was filled with Bordens. She'd just seen that Mr. Borden a few hours ago. The mother and older daughter Emma were bland as tapioca and Miss Lizzie was a Sunday School teacher. Hardly targets for murder, any of them.

The curly haired young man was suddenly at her side. "Here," he said, reaching for her elbow.

Instinctively, she snatched her purse and bag of peaches to her chest.

"Easy, miss," he said, chuckling. "I'm one of the good guys!"

Blushing, she allowed him to help her to her feet, and then found herself staring at his lopsided smile and teasing, green eyes one beat too long.

"W-which Bordens?" she finally asked, recovering her senses.

The young man bent forward.

Taking it for a bow, Victoria dipped a shallow curtsy. But the boy had only been picking a leaf off the fringe of her shawl. She hoped he hadn't noticed the dismissiveness of her curtsy—a sure sign of her class—but the way he regarded her as he rose, now through squinted eyes, made her think he hadn't. Her legs shook as she watched his studied gaze travel from her disheveled cap to the rest of her outfit.

He frowned. "Those are very nice boots," he said, pointing at her feet. "Kidd leather, are they not?"

"I... I dunno." She yanked the skirt hem from where it had caught on the top of one of her boots, revealing their fine workmanship. She took a few steps toward the street. Any minute now, Mrs. Benson could open up that back door, looking for her.

"Come on, junior," the policeman yelled, moving down the alley. "We got a murderer to find!"

The young man held up a hand of acknowledgment but kept

pace with Victoria.

"They're kidd leather, all right." He nodded. "My mother wishes she could afford a pair."

"My… missus…" Victoria said, sidestepping a broken bucket, "gave `em to me. Didn't fit her no more."

"Really?" He moved sideways, blocking her. "Did her feet grow?" The corners of his mouth twitched, as if fighting off a smile.

"Junior!"

Victoria shot a look at Benson's. The door was still closed. "Sh-she's," Victoria stammered, "with child! And… all swelled up. But you said Bordens—which ones?"

"And I suppose," he said, ignoring her question and tugging a piece of puffed sleeve sticking out from her cloak, "your missus gave you this fine dress, as well?"

Victoria shrugged his fingers off her dress. "I don't see why my clothing is any of your concern." She pulled the cloak more tightly around herself. "Aren't you supposed to be helping your policeman friend?"

"I am helping him," he said, his gaze steady, unblinking. "He's just not swift enough to realize it."

As if on cue, the policeman yelled, "Fer Pete's sake, boy, this ain't the time to be courtin' the alley gals!"

Alley gals? How dare he!

Ignoring his friend, the young man leaned forward and whispered, "Next time you want to pose as a maid, miss, I suggest you change your shoes. And leave that ring at home as well—it's a dead giveaway."

Victoria's face felt so hot, she thought she might faint. "I don't know what yer talking about," she huffed, "and my missus is expectin' me."

Lifting her skirts, she rushed down the dusty alley, not giving a tinker's cuss how clearly she exposed her ankles.

CHAPTER THREE

As she rushed through the crowded streets, away from the alley, away from the impertinent young man, Victoria flipped through the Bordens she knew. *There's a mill owner, a colonel, a railroad president. There's Principal Borden at Lindsay Street School. Pretty sure there's a Borden who's a tool sharpener and one who works in Father's bank. There are hundreds of them! It cannot be our Bordens.*

Why hadn't the boy in the alley told her which Bordens instead of talking about her boots? *Leave your ring at home... it's a dead giveaway.* Her thumb spun the jade ring on her finger—her birthday gift from Miss Lizzie. She'd die if anything had happened to Miss Lizzie.

Clutching the bag of peaches and her purse closer to her body as she weaved between slower walkers, Victoria felt the outline of the spool. Shame washed over her. *Stealing from a store, Victoria! And getting caught! That's taking Mag's game too far. You cannot, will not, do that again.*

That decided, she turned down Second Street. Her steps slowed as she took in what seemed was the entire town converg-

ing towards her house—or, more specifically, the house where
Miss Lizzie lived with her sister and parents. With a small gasp,
Victoria dashed behind Mr. Pottersmith's bushes, snatched off
her disguise, plucked her pheasant feathered hat from its spot,
and grabbed at the jacket between the branches. An image of
Miss Lizzie's smiling face hovered in her mind. *You can get
through this,* she'd said, just that morning. *You're stronger than
you know.*

Victoria's hands shook, and she was unable to free the jacket. *If anything's happened to her...* She began to yank it one
way, then the other. Tears burned.

A memory flashed of fishing up in Swansea, Miss Lizzie
sitting on the grassy bank, skirts hiked up, boots unbuttoned in a
manner Victoria's mother would call scandalous.

"You're not going to tell on me, are you?" Miss Lizzie had
joked. "Wouldn't want to ruin my reputation!"

Victoria had never breathed a word of it, for who tells of
secret jokes between friends? She would never want to see Miss
Lizzie in trouble.

But now, much worse trouble seemed to have found Miss
Lizzie.

With an extra hard yank, she was rewarded with a loud rip
and the jacket came free. With the maid's clothes tucked inside
the torn jacket, Victoria ran to her house, where Penelope practically fell over the front porch railing when she spotted
Victoria.

"Thank the Lord you're alive," Penelope croaked, meeting
her on the front walk and enveloping Victoria in a rib-cracking
hug. Her breath was hot and wet on Victoria's neck. Over the
maid's shoulder, Victoria saw a line of policemen on Miss Lizzie's lawn, directing the crowd to stay back on the sidewalk.
Victoria swallowed, her stomach a bowl of oily river water.

"Yer jacket!" Penelope said, holding her out for inspection.
"Why aren't you wearing it?"

Victoria could not take her eyes off the Bordens' house.

Any minute, Miss Lizzie was going to walk out on that front porch, wave to the crowd, tell them it was all a mistake.

"Miss Lizzie," she said, her throat tight. "Is she…"

"She's alive! Miraculously. It was the parents. Both of them…" Penelope's voice wobbled. "Killed."

"The parents?" Victoria repeated. "Both of them?!"

Penelope sniffed, nodded. And then the Bordens' front door did open, but it was Mrs. Churchill that came out. Of course it would be her, sticking her nose right into her neighbors' business! She said something to one of the policemen and then went back inside. Penelope led Victoria toward the porch, away from the crowd which, Victoria realized, had not been running for safety, but rather running straight toward the scene of the murder.

"What about Miss Emma?"

"Out of town, thankfully."

"But this can't be," Victoria said. "I… I just saw Mr. Borden, Pen. Just this morning." She gripped the railing as she walked up her porch steps, remembering hating Mr. Borden from the shadows, him and his chin-strap beard. She thought of Miss Lizzie, of how fondly she spoke of her father. Of the gold ring she'd given *him* years back that he'd worn ever since. How proud Miss Lizzie was of it. How horrible this must all be for her.

"It can't be," Victoria breathed, squinting at the white clapboard house. "He can't be… gone. I just saw him!"

Penelope sighed. "Oh, he's gone all right. There's no arguing with an axe in yer skull."

AFTER DOUBLE-CHECKING all the doors and windows, Victoria ran upstairs and shoved everything under her bed to sort out later. Then she dashed to her mother's room and found her lying in the exact same position as always. Her mother's paralyzed body all angles and elbows, eyes closed, mouth clenched to one side, grimacing as if she'd just heard one of Victoria's flimsy excuses. Victoria stood motionless, heart thumping, feet cemented to the braided rug. Her ankles burned from where her kidd boots had rubbed the skin raw from running, the boots the boy in the alley noticed. Her thoughts were a jumbled mess, and she had the strangest feeling of being in an immense, open field, vulnerable and utterly alone.

Get up, Mother! she wanted to shout. *Get up and take charge like you used to! Tell me what to do!* But those words lodged in her windpipe, making her throat ache. She imagined shaking her mother's shoulder and telling her the awful news—*the Bordens have been murdered.* But that would be cruel and selfish. A vision popped to mind of a man with an axe standing over her mother, while she blinked in wild fear, unable to defend herself. Victoria shook away the image and thought of her father, off on his beloved farm, having no idea that his wife's and daughter's lives were at risk. She should send for him! After all, farming was just a hobby. He should come home and attend to his real job at the bank, and to his household. But then again, who would be keen to deliver a message while a murderer was on the loose?

So that was it. She was on her own. She and Penelope.

With a shaky sigh, she gave one more sweeping glance around her mother's room and then crept out... nearly crashing into her maid in the hallway.

"Penelope! You scared the life out of me!"

"I'm so sorry, miss." The tea tray Penelope was holding rattled. "I just... thought you might need a cuppa?" Her voice cracked.

Seeing her maid's red-rimmed eyes, Victoria's heart softened. "That would be lovely, Pen." Glancing at her mother's closed door, she again imagined a man with an axe standing next to the bed. "Hold on," she whispered and, opening the door a few inches, reached around and removed the key from the lock, then closed the door and locked it from the outside. "Okay," she said, beckoning Penelope down the hallway. "Let's take it in my room. You can have Mother's cup."

"Oh no, miss," Penelope weakly protested. "I couldn't."

"You could," Victoria answered, opening her bedroom door. "And you will. I insist."

It was not like her to boss Penelope, but she had a feeling the poor thing would not put up a fight. Though it was unheard of for a maid to take tea with her employers—and in a bedroom, no less—these were unusual times, and they both needed the company.

The two took their tea at the bay window, Victoria on the padded seat, Penelope on a ladder-back chair pulled close. A swarm of activity poured in and out of the Bordens' yard, mostly policemen and reporters, talking, pointing, writing notes. The two puppy-dog boys from town were there, too—Brownie and Thomas, was it? One atop the other's shoulders, trying to peek into the Bordens' kitchen window.

"Goodness," breathed Victoria. "This is not at all what I pictured a crime scene to look like."

"What do you mean?" asked Penelope.

"Well, in all the stories I've read, Sherlock and Watson, perhaps the Inspector, were the only ones present, and they seemed to have endless uninterrupted time to look for clues. Why, if Sherlock were out there," she said, pointing, "lying flat on the ground as he'd normally be, studying an inch of dirt with his looking glass, he'd have been trampled to death in the first five minutes."

Penelope shook her head. "Real life's messier, that's for certain."

Victoria scanned the crowd for Miss Lizzie but did not see her. She must be inside, Victoria thought. *With the bodies?* A shiver ran through her, sending a splash of tea onto her saucer.

Reaching for a napkin, she asked, "Are you absolutely positive Miss Lizzie is unharmed, Pen?"

Penelope's watery eyes did not leave the chaotic scene and her voice was low and monotone. "Yes'm. Sissy ran over and told me herself. That's how I found out about it. Sissy heard it from Bee, who saw Bridget running for the doctor, who asked her what was wrong. Bridget was in a state, crying that the Bordens had been killed while she was upstairs taking a rest."

"What about Miss Lizzie? Where was she when it… happened?"

Penelope swallowed. "It seems she was in the barn, looking for somethin'. And when she came back in the house, Sissy says…" Her lip quivered.

"Did she…" Victoria said, bracing herself. "See it happen? Or have to fight him off?"

"Neither." Penelope swigged her entire cup and then set it on the tray, giving up her charade of good manners. From her bodice she produced a small bottle and, with shaking fingers, filled her cup and took a gulp. Coughing, she held the bottle out to Victoria. "Spot of tonic? Desperate times and all that."

Victoria finished her tea and held out her cup. She'd never had Penelope's Buckfast tonic before.

"Go easy now," Penelope advised, pouring the dark red liquid. "Little sips."

But even the tiniest sip burned the back of Victoria's throat and made her eyes water.

"Okay," Penelope said, taking another gulp. "Anyway, accordin' to Sissy, when Miss Lizzie walked into the kitchen, she heard a groan and she went into the sitting room and there was her father, with blood all over. She called for Bridget and sent her to get help. They found the mother later. Upstairs in the spare bedroom."

Victoria pictured Miss Lizzie, screaming at the sight of her father. Rushing to his side. Crying. Grabbing a tablecloth to try to stop the blood, her hands and dress stained red. Yelling for help. Not wanting to leave her father's side but then realizing the killer could still be in the house. Arming herself, perhaps.

With her father's cane? Guarding his body until help arrived.

She took a second sip of Buckfast, which burned less than the first. "I just can't believe it, Pen. When I left this morning, everything was fine, normal! I saw Mr. Borden leave for town." Her stomach swam with guilt, remembering how impatient she'd been with his presence, how sarcastic she'd been under her breath.

"Sissy says after the doctor came for the father, he told Bridget to go upstairs to look for the missus, but she wouldn't go. I don't blame her. I wouldn't either!"

Victoria thought of Bridget, waving to her that morning, bucket in hand. "I saw Bridget before I left, too. She was just starting to wash the windows. She waved and I waved back and…"

"Doin' the windows?" Penelope's tone changed, sounding offended. "In this heat? And being ill on top of it? I saw her yesterday and she looked positively green, poor thing."

Victoria frowned apologetically, as if she'd put Bridget to work herself. "I know. But maybe it's one of those lucky things, Pen. Maybe because she was in and out of the house so much, she saw something. As well as escaped death herself!"

"Humph," Penelope said. "The only lucky thing is that she didn't fall off her ladder from heat stroke."

The noon whistles at the mills hooted their discordant cry, startling them both. How could the mills be running and people be going about their day? She wrapped her icy fingers around her lukewarm teacup and shook her head. *It can't be,* she kept thinking. *It just can't be!* She pictured Mr. Borden again as she'd seen him in town. Had someone followed him home? If only she had watched and not been in such a hurry! If only she had crossed the street after he'd been called by the hat maker and "gathered information," as Sherlock called eavesdropping.

If only…

Mrs. Benson's accusing face flashed in her mind.

She squeezed her knees to her chest.

If only she had just stayed home.

"Ach, there's that spooky uncle a' theirs." Penelope pointed with her chin.

Uncle John Morse, accompanied by a man in a brown bowler, had just come from around the far corner of the house. They were stooped over, swiping at the grass and bushes for possible clues left behind.

Victoria sat up straighter. "I saw him leave out of their back door this morning." She frowned. "And now he's back?"

"Somebody must have fetched him." Penelope leaned over the tea tray to get a better look. The gaunt uncle and the man in the brown hat talked and pointed to a basement window. With long, bony fingers, he pushed on the window, but it did not budge. They moved on to the cellar door and yanked on it, but it stayed shut. Locked. Kicked a few rocks aside. Sherlock would be horrified at their brutish ways—"like bulls in a china shop," he'd say to their tromping, pushing, yanking, "seeing but not observing." Why weren't they taking their time? They must be missing all sorts of details, tiny clues the murderer didn't know he was leaving behind. It was the small things, she'd learned, that oftentimes proved the most important.

"Oh, those men look like they maybe know something," Penelope said, scooting her chair forward, all traces of nervousness gone. The Buckfast tonic had done its job.

Victoria followed Penelope's gaze to the yard directly behind the Bordens' where a policeman stood with two workmen, one with black hair and the other with a red hat. The black-haired man spoke excitedly, pointing to the heap of wood scraps and shavings at his feet, then to the fence, then over his shoulder toward Gwyne's, a few houses over.

Penelope leaned forward. "Good! You tell 'em, mister," she said, cheering on the workman. Then, noticing Victoria's troubled expression, Penelope gave her hand a gentle squeeze. "Oh now, Miss Victoria, don't you worry. They'll catch him. With all these people about, somebody had to see something. They'll grab him and toss him in jail."

She rubbed her wrist where Penelope had touched her, thinking of how Mrs. Benson had held her there, and took a gulp of tonic.

"After all," Penelope continued, "it's hard to miss a man running out of a house carrying a bloody hatchet."

SHOCKING CRIME.
A Venerable Citizen and His Aged Wife
HACKED TO PIECES IN THEIR HOME.

The community was terribly shocked this morning to hear that an aged man and his wife had fallen victims to the thirst of a murderer, and that an atrocious deed had been committed. The news spread like wildfire and hundreds poured into Second Street. The deed was committed at No. 62 Second Street, where for years Andrew J. Borden and his wife had lived in happiness...

It is supposed that an axe was the instrument used, as the bodies of the victims are hacked almost beyond recognition. A HERALD reporter entered the house, and a terrible sight met his view. On the lounge in the cozy sitting room lay Andrew J. Borden, dead. His face presented a sickening sight. Over the left temple a wound six by four had been made as if the head had been pounded with the dull edge of an axe. The left eye had been dug out and a cut extended the length of the nose. The face was hacked to pieces and the blood had covered the man's shirt and soaked into his clothing. Everything about the room was in order, and there were no signs of a scuffle of any kind.

SEVEN WOUNDS

Upstairs in a neat chamber in the northwest corner of the house, another terrible sight met our reporter's view. On the floor between the bed and the dressing case lay Mrs. Borden, stretched full length, one arm extended and her face resting upon it. Over the left temple the skull was fractured and no less than seven wounds were found about the head. She had died evidently where she had been struck, for her life blood formed a ghastly clot on the carpet.

No weapon was found and there was nothing about the house to indicate who the murderer might have been.

Miss Borden was so overcome by the awful circumstances that she could not be seen, and kind friends led her away and cared for her…

CHAPTER FOUR

Victoria woke early the next morning to the smell of ripe peaches. *Penelope must be baking.* Rubbing her eyes, her thoughts drifted back to buying the peaches from Mr. Red the day before, the way his gray stubble reminded her of a Scottish thistle, and then how she decided the sack of peaches was too big to fit into her drawstring bag and...

She sat up quickly, blinking, the rest of the day's events exploding in her chest like a fiery comet: Mrs. Benson's accusing face, the boy in the alley, the murders. Penelope couldn't be making the cobbler because she'd never given her the peaches.

The sky was a pre-dawn purple and tree leaves were black with night. A westerly breeze brought in the fresh salty smell of the ocean, and as she sat on her bed, drinking in this hushed scene, she could almost pretend it had all been a terrible, complicated dream: there were no murders, no blood, no incriminating bundle hiding beside her dresser.

Yet the smell of peaches was a dead giveaway: it was, in fact, real.

A dead giveaway. Isn't that what the boy had said about her ring?

Tossing off her blankets, she hurried to the window and peered across to the Bordens. Black silhouettes of policemen were spaced like fence posts around her neighbors' yard, the glowing red dots of their cigarettes blinking on and off. Did that mean they hadn't caught the killer yet? How was Miss Lizzie faring, to be both grieving for her parents while also fearing for her own life? Had she stayed in the house last night? Had Bridget? Or that spooky uncle? Maybe Miss Lizzie stayed with her friend Alice. They were very close.

From the ceiling came the squeak of floorboards—Penelope in her attic bedroom. Even with Father gone and Mother ill, the maid got up before the sun to start her work. Victoria knelt beside the bed and pulled out the tangled bundle of clothes and bags, the peaches filling the air with their fruity smell. Opening her purse, she pulled out the small spool of thread and again felt the zing of excitement.

"So foolish," she whispered. Her fingers squeezed the spool tight against her palm. She hadn't wanted to steal it. Not really. She'd even said no, hadn't she? But that voice of reason had seemed so tiny against Mag's brash one.

Of course, Mag was not real. She knew that. But Mag had been such a comfort to her in years past. A clever, secret playmate. However, it was one thing to squirrel away her father's extra mustache comb, or slip the teacher's chalk into her apron, and an entirely different thing to steal from a store. And though the trappings and rules of high society life didn't fascinate her like they did her dear friend Gwyne, she certainly did not wish to be banished from it. For her sake, but even more so for her parents' sake. Having a thief for a daughter would surely destroy their reputations as well.

"I will add this little spool to my collection and that will be the end of it. From now on, Mother's care will be my only concern. I shall double my efforts and put this all behind me."

Outside, purple dawn bruised tree trunks and grass, and tiny dewdrops blinked from the rose bushes like pairs of watchful eyes. Standing just inside the kitchen door, Victoria hesitated, fingertips tracing the rough mesh of the screen. As far as she knew, the Bordens' killer had yet to be caught. She remembered Sherlock instructing Dr. Watson on the criminal mind, how criminals often come back to the scene of the crime to gloat. A shiver tiptoed up her spine.

To her right, shadowy hats glided above the top of the Bordens' fence as the policemen patrolled the yard. She focused on the old potting shed tucked in the corner of her property, half hidden by lumpy shadows and quivering branches. She could not wait. The sooner she stashed the thread, the sooner she could move on. Make a fresh start.

And so she ran, steering clear of trees and bushes, keeping herself as un-grasp-able as possible and did not stop until she was at the door of the shed. Panting, she swept a handful of vines aside and gripped the wooden door handle, its cold dampness biting into her palm.

An image popped to mind of a grinning mad man crouching behind the door, an axe raised in anticipation. Her eyes watered. Taking a deep breath, she yanked open the door and peeked inside. No killer. A faint hint of smoke in the air reminded her that Penelope would be lighting the stove soon and she had no time to waste.

Squatting on the dusty floor, she groped under the workbench until she found the trowel, candle, and matches. It took several tries with shaking fingers before candlelight flickered beneath the shelf, highlighting where to dig. Years of protection from the elements had rendered the dirt fine as face powder. A minute's worth of scraping revealed the faded pink hatbox with the words *Magpie's Treasure Nest* written in childish print across the lid. She smiled at her younger self, so proud of the items she'd been able to take right from under people's noses. Now this part of her life had to be over.

She lifted the box out of the hole, pulled off the lid, and allowed her fingers to plunge deep into the pile. Waves of blinding happiness crashed behind her eyes as she scooped up handful after handful of treasures, letting them sift like sand between her fingers. One by one, she said good-bye to her treasures: a wrinkled hanky from the equally wrinkled Mrs. Medill at church, hair ribbons slipped from schoolroom pigtails, assorted buttons, pen nibs, checker pieces, James the Cobbler's bent shoe horn, half a dozen hat pins, a cuff link bearing the initials JKP, two thimbles from two different visiting dressmakers, five pieces of classroom chalk, and the first treasure she ever stole: Father's nail clippers, taken the day Mother had her first attack of paralysis. She'd just turned eight and could still remember the sight of Mother's twisted, frozen body before Penelope shooed her away. The nail clippers had been on the washstand and she'd taken them on her way out, the slight heaviness of them in her apron as they tapped against her leg strangely comforting, like a friend telling her it was going to be all right.

Outside, far off, someone coughed. She had to hurry.

Victoria found the chain from her great-uncle's pince nez, whose disappearance had prompted Penelope to blame "one a them pesky magpies," who were known to steal shiny objects with which to decorate their nests. Victoria had decided Magpie—Mag for short—was the perfect name for this secret side of her.

And since this would be the last time, Victoria felt compelled to perform the closing ritual: draping the pince nez chain around her neck, lifting the flickering candle to eye level and whispering, "Mag and Me, sworn to secrecy." Then, with a lick to thumb and forefinger, she pinched the flame until it sizzled out, enduring the pain without complaint.

VICTORIA SAT AT the small chopping table in the kitchen eating her breakfast, just like she had as a child, using the step stool as her chair. The morning paper lay limp on the table, its headline reading, "Borden Murderer Yet to be Found: Police Following Hundreds of Leads."

According to the article, nothing was taken from the house. Mr. Borden's billfold was still in his jacket, the gold ring still on his finger. Authorities were looking at former employees of Mr. Borden's and tenants in the buildings he owned, thinking perhaps one of them might have had a score to settle with Mr. Borden, who was either a shrewd businessman or a tightwad, depending to whom you spoke.

Penelope, joining Victoria at the little table, dropped three sugar cubes into her empty cup, then reached for the flowered teapot. "If ya ask me," the maid said, "the fact that they were whacked fifteen or so times with a hatchet says it was personal. One or two would have done the job nicely. Somebody had quite the bee in their bonnet with those two."

Victoria looked up from her oatmeal. "But not with Miss Lizzie?"

"Dunno," Penelope said, leaning in to sip her tea. "Maybe that. Maybe she just got lucky. Or maybe the good Lord spared her on account of all her good works, teaching Sunday School and all a that."

As a young girl, Victoria had been so excited to finally be in Miss Lizzie's Sunday School class, fully expecting the other students to be jealous of her special friendship with their teacher. But the girls snickered about her low voice and the boys made fun of the way Miss Lizzie's eyelids fluttered when leading them in prayer, rolling their eyes back into their heads and letting their mouths hang open as if they were dead. Victoria hated those boys, Dickie Houndsworth especially, as the instigator of the eye-rolling craze. It was cruel to make fun of someone who kindly dedicated their Sunday to saving your soul, but all that mattered to Dickie was getting the big laugh, and he was good at it.

A loud rapping at the back door brought Victoria back to the steamy kitchen, to the present, where her neighbors had been murdered in their own home a day ago. Victoria and Penelope stared at one another, wide-eyed.

"Dear Lord," Penelope whispered. "Not another murder…" The words hung in the air like shirts on a laundry line.

"Victoria. Open up!" Gwyne's voice was high-pitched, out of breath.

Victoria and Penelope were suddenly up and out of their chairs, struggling to undo the latches. Victoria flung open the door to a beaming Gwyne, decked out in a gorgeous mint green dress.

"Goodness," Gwyne said, laughing, "I had no idea you both would be so excited to see me."

Penelope heaved a sigh and went to the stove to start lining up her irons.

"Gwyne." Victoria pulled her friend inside. "We thought something dreadful had happened! You have heard about the Bordens, haven't you?"

"Of course," her friend said, closing the door behind her. "It's all everyone is talking about. Why else do you think I was in such a hurry for you to answer the door? Can you believe the crowd over there?" Pulling off her gloves, she went on. "My Bridget is an absolute wreck. She insists on carrying the fire poker around the house as she does her chores. It's driving Mother crazy, claiming Bridget's going to end up clunking one of us over the head by mistake."

Gwyne's cheerful babbling, even about something as serious as a murder in the neighborhood, lightened Victoria's mood. She gazed at her old friend, bubbly as a phosphate, eyes glittering, creamy skin brushed pink from her holidays. Oh, how she'd missed her. Unable to stop herself, Victoria hugged her friend tightly, knocking her slightly off balance in the process.

"Tory!" Gwyne laughed.

"I really shouldn't be hugging you," Victoria said, pulling back but still holding her friend's shoulders. "I should be giving you the silent treatment for abandoning me for so long. It's been terribly boring without you. I've had no one to talk to."

Penelope snorted as she squeaked open the heavy stove door.

Victoria glanced toward her maid. "Other than my family, of course."

"Well, I have missed you just as much," Gwyne said. "More even! Which is why I've come to invite you to my Great-grandma Cora's house for a visit."

Victoria gasped.

Penelope straightened. "The one on The Hill?"

Gwyne nodded, the curls around her face bobbing. "Yes, GG! She lives in—" Gwyne stretched out her arms in a dramatic stage-actress pose "—Chateau D'Usse."

"Hmmm." Penelope nodded, looking thoughtful. "Yes, I think I recall your mother mentioning it once or twice through the years."

Gwyne rolled her eyes. "Once or twice a week, you mean. Mother is a terrible braggart."

Victoria smiled, knowing it was true. But Mrs. Jacobsen had also been a trusted friend to her mother, guarding her secret and fending off inquisitive friends with ease and diplomacy.

"Oh Gwyne, she's just proud of her heritage," Victoria said.

This drew another eye roll from Gwyne.

"And generous, too," Victoria continued, "if she's allowed you to invite me to GG's. When?"

Gwyne gave her a quizzical look. "Today, of course. This afternoon!"

Victoria caught the shocked raise in Penelope's eyebrows as her maid abruptly turned back to the stove. She couldn't help feeling the same.

"Today? With all this"—her hand waved in the direction of the Bordens—"going on?"

"That's exactly why Mother wants to go, Tory." She soured her face and imitated her mother's high vibrato voice. "*It's all so unpleasant and low class. And after just coming home from our holidays, too.*"

Victoria couldn't help but laugh at the spot-on impression.

"Of course, all I wanted to do," Gwyne continued in her regular voice, "was to spend my first day home with you, and find out who you saw and any parties you went to while I was gone, but Mother is insisting I go. So I asked if you could come with us, saying you could use the pleasant distraction, what with you being such a close friend of Miss Lizzie's."

The idea of sipping tea in a beautiful mansion while the Bordens' bodies had barely chilled did not seem right. And hadn't she just promised herself to redouble her efforts in caring for Mother? Her fingers worried at the hem of her apron. "I don't know, Gwyne…"

"I know it seems insensitive, Tory, but honestly, Mother is so funny about bringing visitors to GG's, and with school starting soon, I don't know how many other chances you'll get. Plus, we never stay very long, so you can still come back and help with the mourning food or whatnot. And GG is getting hard of hearing so we'll probably get some time to talk, just the two of us. I'm dying to know what you've heard about all of this. And about anything else, too."

Boys, Victoria thought. Of course she wanted to talk boys. "But your mother. Are you sure she doesn't mind?"

"Of course! You know Mother's very fond of you."

It wasn't true—Gwyne's mother hadn't had a high opinion of Victoria for years, ever since catching them in the pantry sneaking lumps of brown sugar—but Victoria didn't wish to argue.

Gwyne placed her palms together in prayer, fingertips touching her chin. "Please, Tory? Would you ask your mother if she could spare you?"

Victoria blinked, then exchanged glances with Penelope.

"Oh." Gwyne blanched. "Is she still...?" Her words trailed off.

There was a light whooshing sound from the fire in the stove as one piece of wood gave way to another. The air around the irons shimmered with heat.

"Yes," Victoria said, dabbing her forehead with a hanky. "Mother is still... infirmed."

"I'm sorry," Gwyne murmured. Her sorrowful eyes suddenly brightened. "But all the more reason for you to get away for a bit. I know how devoted you are to her care, putting her needs before your own. I am certain you could use a break. Am I correct?"

Penelope clanked the stove door shut. "Go on, Miss Jacobsen," she said, making a shooing motion. "You run on home. Victoria'll be along straight away, after she freshens herself up."

"What?" Victoria stared at her maid.

"Miss Jacobsen's right," Penelope said. "You've barely left your mother's side since she fell ill and you're lookin' a little peaked. It'll do you some good to have a little social time."

Gwyne clasped her hands to her chest, grinning. "Yes? Victoria?"

"Well, I suppose if it's just for a short time, and if Pen doesn't mind listening for Mother..." She looked to her maid, who nodded her assent. "I shall be honored to go."

CHAPTER FIVE

When the Jacobsens' carriage finally creaked to a stop, Ferguson opened the carriage door. The sweaty Second Street air flowed out, quickly replaced with fragrances of flowering hedges, spicy junipers, and bountiful rose gardens. Not one wisp of cotton mill smoke dared sneak up The Hill.

Taking Ferguson's hand, Victoria stepped down from the carriage and stared at Chateau D'Usse, a three-story brick mansion that sat back from the street like Cleopatra on her throne, in no hurry to greet her visitors, allowing them to come to her. Enormous shade trees served their mistress, branches bowing submissively overhead. Tall Greek columns flanked the oversized door. Even the birds sounded more melodious on the upper side of town.

From this vantage point, Victoria could see the entirety of Fall River fanning out along the Quequechan: cotton mills with their churning water wheels and belching smokestacks; shipyards crowded with workmen, crates and travelers; neat checkerboard neighborhoods giving way to sprawling rattletrap tenements, lumber yards, smith shops; and even a house being moved down the middle of Bond Street. Somewhere within this messy conglomeration, a murderer hid—or maybe even walked among the pedestrians—holding his secret dear. A cool breeze fluttered Victoria's sleeves, chilling the damp skin beneath. Shivering, she turned away, and followed Gwyne and Mrs. Jacobsen to the grand house.

Timms, the bulbous-nosed butler, walked them through a beautiful, vaulted foyer toward the parlor. Their footsteps echoed, floating up the luxurious staircase and playing among the chandelier's dangling crystals. Victoria gave a secret look of wide-eyed amazement to Gwyne, who replied with an *I told you so* lift of her eyebrows.

"Lady Cora," the butler announced. "Your guests." When he bowed, Victoria noticed a tan smudge on the edge of his collar before turning her attention to the room.

The parlor, easily five times the size of Victoria's own, was a mass of cream and gold fabrics, gleaming walnut tables, intricately carved chests, oriental rugs, overflowing flower vases, and art pieces from around the world.

"So lovely," Victoria whispered. Her gaze swept the room, snagging on all the pocketable items. *Stop. That's done.*

She forced herself to focus on Gwyne's Great-grandma Cora, a tiny bump of a woman in the middle of all the splendor. "Really, Timms," she said, her voice crackly as a dry leaf. "You needn't call me Lady Cora anymore. Lord Thorton is long gone and he was the only one who cared about such things."

"Oh, but you must keep your title, Grandmama," Mrs. Jacobsen insisted, taking a seat on the Chesterfield sofa next to her. "Out of respect for your dear husband." She gazed at the Chesterfield's elegant cushions and ran her hand lovingly across the fabric.

"Stuff and nonsense," Great-grandma Cora said, waving an age-spotted hand. "The title I'm most proud of is great-grandmother—GG! At least I've earned that one. Gwyne, introduce me to your friend and you two sit here." She indicated a pair of matching tufted wing chairs to her right.

"GG, you know Tory, er, Victoria. She's been my best friend since we were in short dresses!"

Victoria took extra care with her curtsy, making sure to not "bob up like a cork," as her mother so often corrected.

"The Victoria I remember," GG said, "was a good deal shorter, with scrapes on her knees and a bow in her hair." Her smile was warm, instantly putting Victoria at ease.

"So nice to see you again, Lady Thorton," Victoria said, returning the smile. She and Gwyne took their seats.

"Oh, Grandmama," Mrs. Jacobsen said, taking her grandmother's wrist. "We've been worried sick about you, up here in this big house all alone. We just had to see you and make sure you were all right."

Victoria hid her amusement as she recalled Mrs. Jacobsen chattering away in the carriage, talking about GG's husband's father being a duke and somehow related to the queen of some small *but very important* island in the Pacific and so on. The issue of GG's safety had never been raised.

"Worried about me?" That got GG's attention. "But my dear, it was all of you who were in danger! You shouldn't have risked your safety just to pay an old woman a visit."

"But GG," Gwyne said, "we now live on the safest block in town. It's absolutely crawling with policemen."

Victoria suppressed a shiver, recalling her morning's outing to the shed.

"Blue suits," Gwyne continued, "as far as the eye can see! And the crowds, they—"

"I think," Mrs. Jacobsen interrupted, widening her eyes at her daughter, "it would do us all good to change the subject, Gwyndolyn. Certainly, we can come up with something more pleasant to discuss?"

GG patted Mrs. Jacobsen's hand. "You're so right, my dear. All this murder business is quite unsettling. Timms?"

The butler, standing next to the hallway door, hands clasped behind him, straightened to his full height. "Yes, ma'am?"

"Some tea and biscuits, perhaps? Ask Bridget if she has any of those fig drops left."

"Yes, ma'am."

Another Bridget. Victoria's family was one of the few she knew who called their Irish maid by her real name.

"So, tell me, Victoria," GG said, clasping her hands together. "Will you be making your debut this year like our Gwyndolyn?"

"I... I'm not sure." Victoria thought of her crumpled mother. "We... haven't had the chance to discuss it."

She and Gwyne had fantasized about their Coming Out party for years—the venue, the theme, the color of the flowers, each changing as they aged. But lately, the thought of being center stage, with hundreds of eyes upon her, made Victoria slightly nauseated. And dancing with boy after pompous boy, pretending to be charmed with their manners and enthralled with their talk of politics and land ownership. Truly, she'd rather stay at home and clean the hearth. The one positive offshoot of her mother's continued illness was the very real possibility of having to forego her public debut. After all, Miss Lizzie didn't have one. Then again, Miss Lizzie never married, and Victoria would prefer to marry than live with her parents for the rest of her life.

"Not discussed it yet?" GG's heavily-lidded eyes widened. "Well, my dear Victoria, don't you think it's time?"

There was a second moment of uncomfortable silence as Victoria tried to formulate a polite answer that did not betray her mother's privacy.

Mrs. Jacobsen placed a hand on the older woman's wrist. "GG," she said, her tone urgent. "You must tell us about Aunt Frieda—has her goiter receded?"

As GG, unknowingly derailed, launched into her sister's latest maladies, Mrs. Jacobsen sent a knowing glance towards Victoria. Though Victoria knew Mrs. Jacobsen didn't much care for her—Victoria was too impulsive, too adventurous, too non-

conformist for Mrs. Jacobsen's taste in friends for Gwyne—
Victoria was grateful for the kindness she bestowed upon her
mother.

"So," Gwyne whispered to Victoria. "Tell me everything
that went on while I was gone."

"First answer me this," Victoria countered. "Is Timms in
the theater? Does he sing? Or act?"

Her friend's eyes widened. "On his off days he does a bit of
Slapstick. How did you know? We just found out ourselves!
Mother wanted GG to fire him but GG wouldn't have it."

Victoria suppressed a smile. "I thought I saw a trace of pan-
cake makeup on his collar."

"You notice everything, don't you? But enough about old
Timms's secret life—what about the Bordens? Were you home
when it happened? Did you see anything?"

"Believe it or not," Victoria admitted, keeping her voice
low, "I saw Mr. Borden twice that morning, the last time probably only an hour or so before he was killed."

"Where?" Gwyne glanced at her mother and great-
grandmother before adding, "Was anyone with him?"

"The last person I saw him with—well, on his way toward,
anyway—was Mr. Clegg, the hat maker and—"

"In town?" Gwyne interrupted.

Victoria nodded. "I feel terrible. I had some very mean
thoughts cross my mind about him and then he was murdered."
The now-familiar lump lodged in her throat again. "Gwyne, do
you think…" Her eyes began to burn.

"Tory?" Gwyne whispered, a shadow of worry crossing her
face. "What is it?"

Victoria pictured Mr. Borden, smiling and waving, and remembered Miss Lizzie instructing the class on "loving your
neighbor as yourself," which for years she thought meant just
the people on her block. "I know it sounds mad, but I feel as
though I may have caused the murders by my unkind thoughts."
She felt better having said it, but there was more—something

else eating at her.

Gwyne reached out and took Victoria's hand. "Oh Victoria, don't be ridiculous. If people dropped dead from others' mean thoughts, the human race would be extinct. Mr. Borden was a mean old sod, building that fence so his pears could rot on the ground instead of being enjoyed by the occasional hungry neighbor girl."

There it was, the old neighborhood complaint about the fence.

"Well, they *were* his pears, Gwyne," Victoria whispered. "And we were stealing." The word opened a hole inside her, a cold dark well. Not only had she had unkind thoughts about Mr. Borden just before his death, but she'd also stolen the spool—there was no other word for it. She'd stolen and Mr. Borden died—perhaps at the very same moment. *What if one had caused the other?*

"Oh for goodness' sakes, Tory, everyone helped themselves to a Borden pear—even my father. Yours too. Mr. Borden could have put up a sign. He didn't have to make his home a fortress with that fence."

"I know, Gwyne, but still." She gave her jade ring a turn. "Miss Lizzie must have seen good in her father."

Timms came in with a tea tray, which he set before the older ladies. Leaning to try to see Timms's stained collar, Gwyne almost fell off her chair, eliciting a scornful look from Mrs. Jacobsen, mostly directed at Victoria, the "bad influence."

"Would you pour?" GG asked Mrs. Jacobsen. "My hands are not as steady as they used to be."

Gwyne leaned closer to Victoria. "Father says you reap what you sow, Tory. Not that Mr. Borden deserved to be murdered for hoarding his pears, of course, but..." She lifted a shoulder in a half-hearted shrug. "I think God rewards the good and punishes the bad."

Victoria's mind went straight to her mother, paralyzed.

"I mean, just look at GG," Gwyne continued. "Kindest

woman in the world, widowed so young, but then swept off her feet by the son of a duke. And now she gets to live here, in luxury, for the rest of her days."

"Yes," Victoria agreed, "but then this husband died as well. Did she deserve that?"

Gwyne wrinkled her nose. "Hmm. I hadn't thought about that."

"And what about Mrs. Borden? She was meek as a mouse."

"True, but—"

"Gwyne, my dear," Great-grandma Cora interrupted. "Have you found your young man yet?"

Accepting a cup of tea from her mother, Gwyne gave her great-grandmother a pouty look. "Oh, GG, you know I haven't. Are you sure your prediction is correct?"

The old woman chuckled, her face compressing into a series of wrinkles. "Of course I am! Plain as day in my tea leaves. A dark-haired man with a suitcase. Clearly from out of town. Now what about your visit to Boston? Did you meet any good prospects there?"

As Gwyne chatted with her great-grandmother about possible husband candidates, Victoria sipped her tea and gazed around the lavishly appointed room, thinking she could describe it to her mother during one of their endless afternoons. Elaborate vases carved from gourds, mythical winged creatures in bas-relief, mosaics of abalone and jade and, on a nearby etagere, a collection of brightly enameled snuff boxes—all gifts brought home from all over the world by GG's second late husband, a big game hunter. One snuff box in particular, a robins'-egg blue, caught Victoria's eye, and immediately her heart began to race.

No, she told Mag. *Not here. Not now. It's over.*

Her dress felt tight and hot. The ladies' voices meshed into a thick hissing tone, filling her ears. All she could see was the blue box; the rest of the room blurred to nonexistence. Her palm ached to hold it, to feel its smooth corners resting against her fingers, to brush its blueness against her cheek, down her neck.

These are not penny items. They're expensive collectibles. One-of-a-kind pieces of art. More importantly, they're GG's.

Victoria shifted to the other side of her chair, away from the etagere, and tried to focus on the adults' conversation.

"Very wealthy... with fifty people working.... them and..."

The image of the blue enameled box shimmered in her mind. She gripped the arms of her chair, her nails digging into the heavy material. She tried to think of something else. Her mother getting better, the Bordens' murderer being found...

Victoria kept her eyes on the women, forcing her lips into a polite smile, trying to keep track of their words, but the ringing in her ears made it difficult to hear. Pearls of sweat trickled under her arms, down her ribs. She could not make her heart slow.

The conversation went on interminably. Laughter. More tea. More gossip about family members Victoria did not know.

She allowed herself two glances back at the snuff box, but it only made her pulse race faster.

Finally, Mrs. Jacobsen stood. "I'm afraid we have worn out our welcome, Grandmother! Your eyes are beginning to droop."

Victoria, as if poked with a stick, hopped to her feet. She did not have to look back to know the exact position of the snuff box. It was as clear in her mind as what she was seeing in front of her.

The older woman's fingers plucked at her dress. "I am sorry, darling. It's not the company, I can assure you. Girls?"

Victoria's smile was tight. "Yes, ma'am?"

"Don't get old. You'll end up needing a nap in the middle of the day like me!"

As Gwyne went to give her great-grandmother a kiss on the cheek, Victoria glanced over her shoulder. The box glowed a luminous, heartbreakingly beautiful blue, practically waiting to be claimed.

Victoria turned then, looking up and around the room, as if trying to commit the grand parlor to memory. Cocking her head, she pretended to notice the boxes for the first time. Dread and excitement battled in her chest. A drop of sweat trickled down her spine. Behind her, Mrs. Jacobsen made plans with GG for another visit. Victoria took one step closer to the display of boxes. She tried to tell herself no, but the roaring in her ears drowned it out. Gwyne laughed at something GG said. Another step, nonchalant. She was now an arm's length away and looking through a long telescope, seeing only the box through the lens. She felt her arm lift. Fingers extend. Breath held. And then...

A warm hand took hold of her shaking one. "Pretty, aren't they?"

Gwyne's voice was like a splash of cold water. The parlor shimmered back into focus.

Her friend was smiling at her. "We better go," she said, rolling her eyes in her great-grandmother's direction. "Before she starts snoring."

"Oh, of... course." Turning, Victoria saw Mrs. Jacobsen staring at her. Deep creases went straight down from the corners of her mouth, the face of a ventriloquist's dummy.

A clock, somewhere, quietly chimed the hour.

GG stifled a yawn. "Good-bye, girls. Come visit me again soon."

Victoria curtsied low, shame pressing heavily upon her heart. That had been a close call. Thank goodness Gwyne had been there to stop her.

CHAPTER SIX

A s the Jacobsens' carriage pulled up to Victoria's home, she could barely see her front porch for the crowd of people on her lawn. The solid wall of humanity stretched to the Bordens' and several yards beyond, all staring at the plain white clapboard. The guilt of her actions—what she'd almost done at GG's—weighed on her, and the sight of this ghoulish crowd made her feel even worse.

"Atrocious," Mrs. Jacobsen declared, glaring out her little window. "Blood thirsty gossips, all."

The tip of Gwyne's nose actually touched her window. "Looks like some are even from out of town, judging from the valises and traveling clothes." Victoria couldn't help but pick up on the hopeful lilt in Gwyne's voice. Could she not stop thinking about marriage prospects for even one moment?

The carriage door snapped open, startling the three of them. Ferguson held out his hand to Victoria.

"I'll help ya to your door, miss. I've got my horse switch to clear us a path if need be."

Victoria gratefully accepted and they pressed through the

crowd. The smell of stale cigars and powder-covered perspiration stirred an unhappy memory of standing in a circus tent, surrounded by townspeople laughing and jeering at the scaley-skinned Allie, the Alligator Boy.

And this crowd, she thought, following in Ferguson's wake, was exactly the same. She wasn't sure exactly what they expected to see—Miss Lizzie walking a tightrope? Miss Emma riding an elephant? Surely Miss Emma had been contacted by now and was home with Miss Lizzie. The sisters were very close and were bound to become even closer through all this. They were all the other had now.

After thanking Ferguson, Victoria rapped on her front door, throwing irritated glances at the crowd over her shoulder as she waited. How could they be so insensitive to someone as kind and good as Miss Lizzie?

Penelope peeked through the window, her look of alarm changing to relief. There was a *thunk* of the bolt sliding out and the door opened.

"Goodness," Victoria said, bustling into the vestibule. "The crowd out there is positively horrid."

Penelope took Victoria's cloak and hung it up. "Everyone's trying to get in for the viewing, seeing as the funeral's going to be private."

"Could you cook something for the Bordens, Pen? I'd like to bring it over as soon as possible. Miss Lizzie needs to know there are those of us that truly care about her."

"Well, I had a bit of a time with those peaches, bruised as they were, but I managed to get two pies out of 'em. I hope Red didn't sell them to you that way."

The peaches. The alley. The thread.

"I dropped the bag," Victoria answered, keeping her eyes on her gloves as she removed them, tugging at each fingertip. "Everyone was in such a mad dash when they heard about the murders. I was jostled and lost my grip."

Penelope mumbled something about replacing Mr. Pottersmith with a younger escort. Victoria wondered if she should have a story at the ready about how he couldn't go with her but decided the less stories to keep track of, the better.

HOLDING THE BASKET containing the peach pie aloft, Victoria threaded her way through the crowd. "Excuse me. Pardon me."

At the gate, an arm shot out in front of her.

"Sorry, miss, family and close friends only."

"I *am* a close friend. From just down the block." She turned a glaring eye at the blocker and her face went slack. *The young man from the alley.* Same green eyes, same foppish dark hair and cocksure grin... with a dimple?

He tilted his head. Squinted. "Haven't we met before?"

"No, I think not," Victoria answered. She looked down at the basket, the embroidered R on the napkin covering the food, her shoes. *Her shoes.* She fluffed out her skirt hem to cover the toes. "Now if you'll excuse me—"

"Ah!" The boy snapped his fingers. "From the alley! The maid with the deplorable Irish accent."

"Me?" Victoria adopted the insulted tone her mother used when arguing with Father. "A maid? I beg your pardon!" She lifted her skirt and tried to push past him, but his arm was an iron bar.

Leaning forward, he ducked his head and said quietly, "Congratulations, miss. I see you've come up in the world."

She held her face taut—she would give nothing away. Behind her, a woman snorted and whispered to someone, "Tried to get in pretending to be a neighbor."

Victoria twisted around. "I am a neighbor! And a dear friend." Then she turned back to the young man. "Excuse me, but what is your official position here?"

The young man bowed. "Forgive me, miss. I am Declan

Dempsey, apprentice detective."

Apprentice detective? Victoria's heart, which was already racing, doubled its speed. Dempsey? She knew that name.

Master Dempsey straightened, and just like in the alley, one dark curl remained dangling over his forehead. "My father," he continued, "is Detective Cyrill Dempsey."

Fall River's senior detective. Oh dear. Her sweaty palms made the basket handle slippery. She tightened her grip.

"And you are?" The young man extended his palm.

"Well, Master Dempsey," Victoria huffed, ignoring his question and his hand, "I will assume the heat and the demands of your position as gate-keeper have muddled your senses, for you obviously have mistaken me for another." She raised the basket. "Now, rest assured I am a neighbor and a friend of the bereaved, and I deserve to be shown in immediately."

Master Dempsey, sliding in front of her, crossed his arms. Though he looked quite stern, a smile played at the corners of his mouth. "I'm afraid you'll have to give me your name, miss," he said quietly, "so I may check it against our master list."

Victoria's head throbbed. Did she want a detective's son knowing her name? What if he went back to Benson's and asked about her? He could tell Mrs. Benson her identity and she could be arrested. Was a spool of thread really worth the risk to her reputation?

He cleared his throat. "Well?"

Victoria's mind whirled. He couldn't really prove it was her at Benson's, could he? And would anyone take an Irish cop's word over that of a gentleman's daughter? She really needed to see Miss Lizzie, but if she made up a name, it would not be on the master list.

"Robbins," she finally said. "Victoria Robbins." She hoped she wouldn't regret it.

The young man smiled. Placing his fingertips to his temple, he closed his eyes. "Vic-tor-ia," he said slowly. "Rahhh-bins." His eyes blinked open. "You're on the list." He took a step back and held out his hand. "Right this way, Victoria Robbins."

Victoria's jaw dropped. He'd tricked her, the devil. The very handsome devil.

One side of his mouth lifted, accompanied by that charming dimple. "Better hop to it, Miss Robbins," he whispered, "before one of these vultures swoops in to take your spot!"

AS VICTORIA SET foot into the Bordens' crowded front hallway, the stench of death, like rancid meat, caught in her throat. A line of people queued at the parlor door and snaked around inside the very small, very crowded, hallway. They squished together to allow Victoria and her escort to pass, then filled in behind like quicksand. Victoria's nausea inched up her throat. What would she do if she became sick?

She glanced at Master Dempsey and he seemed to read her thoughts, for he quickly relieved her of the hamper and presented his hanky. Without hesitation, she pressed it to her nose. Its scent of soap and something earthy, like freshly turned garden soil, calmed her quaking stomach. If she was breaking some sort of societal rule by accepting a stranger's handkerchief, then so be it; better to break etiquette than to empty one's stomach in public.

Navigating through the tight hallway to the end of the line, Master Dempsey following, Victoria nodded to the familiar faces behind hankies—Dr. Chagnon and his wife, the church organist Mrs. Kettleson, nosy Mrs. Churchill, and other neighbor ladies, who exchanged subtle eyebrow lifts at Victoria's escort. In spite of the large number of people present, the hallway was surprisingly quiet, with the sounds of crying from the parlor easily heard over nearby whispers and shuffling feet.

Picturing sweet Miss Lizzie in tears made Victoria's own eyes sting. Blinking quickly, she turned and held out her hand for the basket.

"Thank you, Master Dempsey," she murmured, hanky still pressed to her nose.

He shook his head. "I don't mind," he answered, his voice low. His gaze was direct, and his green eyes studied her.

She swallowed. Did he know what she had done? Was he waiting for something?

"Oh, of course." She took one last deep sniff of his hanky and then thrust it out. "Here. I'm sure you have other things to attend to." Instantly, the odor in the hallway filled her nostrils, smelling twice as horrid, twice as nauseating.

She wished she could grab someone's flowers or breathe through her cuff, but neither were socially acceptable options, and she could only hold her breath for so long. Then she felt his fingers around hers, folding them over the soft cloth, sending chills up her arm.

"I insist," he whispered. "You don't look so good."

"I beg your pardon?"

The young man grimaced. "I meant you don't look well. Which is understandable. You said you were close with the family. And this is…" He shook his head. "Quite unsettling."

"But what about you? How do you… manage it?" she asked, indicating the hanky in her hand.

He shrugged. "I'm used to it. Besides, I'm holding this." He raised the basket. "Which smells top notch, by the way."

Victoria cracked a smile. "Yes," she said, replacing the hanky to her nose. "My maid, Penelope, is a wonder with peach pie."

"Your *maid*, did you say?" He smirked. She gave him a dark look, to which he held up his hand. "Sorry. Neither the time nor place."

Straightening her shoulders, she huffed, "I should say not." Then she turned and stared straight ahead.

Slipping her calling card from her pocket, Victoria placed it on the silver tray with the others, each with the hand-written *To Inquire* at the top. Directly above, on the hat rack, hung Mrs.

Borden's spoon bonnet, the tip of the ribbon dangling just a few inches above the pile of cards like a goal to be reached, a carnival strong-man bell to be rung. Mr. Borden's top hat—the one Victoria had seen him wearing yesterday—hung on an opposite branch.

Master Dempsey leaned close to her shoulder. "As you can probably imagine," he whispered, "there was a great deal of blood."

Continuing to stare at the hat, Victoria breathed deeply through the hanky and nodded.

"That's what you smell," he continued. "Blood. On the walls, the carpets, the sofa—all of which cannot be cleaned until we are through with our investigation."

The word "investigation" brought to mind an image of Sherlock Holmes crawling around next to Bordens' bloody bodies, sniffing, poking, prodding.

"Funny," she whispered around the hanky. "There's no mention of this sort of odor in all the murder mysteries I've read. Those crimes actually seem rather tidy."

"You read murder mysteries?"

Victoria felt her cheeks warm. *The only book a woman should read is the Bible*, Mother was fond of saying.

"*The Strand Magazine*? Sherlock Holmes?" He looked hopeful.

Victoria's heart jumped. No one she knew understood, let alone shared, her passion for Arthur Conan Doyle's stories. She noticed Mrs. Churchill stop her whispered conversation with Mrs. Kettleson to steal a glance at Victoria and Declan.

Victoria, turning slightly away from her nosy neighbor, scrunched her nose at him and nodded. "I'm afraid so," she said, keeping her voice low, "but don't let that get around. My mother would be horrified." After a quick glance back at Mrs. Churchill, now stretching her neck toward the Chagnons, Victoria added, "Unfortunately, I'm quite behind because I have to wait ages for my uncle to send his copy from London. By the time I get them, they're months old and reek of sausage grease."

The young detective bowed his head. "Being a Sherlock Holmes fan, then," he said, his voice barely audible, "you would appreciate the fact that the doctor actually performed the preliminary autopsies here. On the dining room table, to be exact. Removed a few of the organs for testing."

Mr. and Mrs. Borden, laid out between Wedgewood plates and pewter candlesticks, on the very table at which they'd eaten their breakfast! The thought sent a chill down her arms. But why perform an autopsy? Wasn't the cause of death obvious? As Penelope said, there's no arguing with an axe in your skull.

"Master Dempsey, what—"

He raised his hand, interrupting her. "I'm sorry, miss. I have no idea what prompted me to share such coarse details with you." He shook his head. "I'll take this food to the kitchen." He gave a quick embarrassed bow and disappeared into the sitting room, closing the door firmly behind him.

Victoria frowned. She wasn't one of those frail types who fainted upon hearing a gruesome detail or two, for heaven's sake. And though it might be sinful to be fascinated by her neighbors' murders, she couldn't help it. When he returned, she'd let him know she was no shrinking violet.

Minutes passed and Master Dempsey did not return. As she came closer to the front of the line, Victoria began to worry what she would say once face to face with Miss Lizzie. No one close to her had ever died, and she did not know what one said in such a situation.

More people arrived, many of whom Victoria did not recognize, reminding her of Sherlock Holmes in *A Study in Scarlet,* in which the murderer came back to the crime scene disguised as a drunk in order to retrieve a gold ring he'd mistakenly left behind. Any one of these could be the murderer: the man whose top hat seemed to be balancing atop of his enormous ears, the scruffy one who'd apparently misplaced his razor, the fashionable woman with the black crepe hat. Outward appearances, she knew, were not to be trusted.

Victoria turned and stared over the tops of hats and heads at the closed sitting room door. Now that she welcomed the detective's presence, he was nowhere to be found. Turning back, her elbow bumped the banister and she dropped Declan's hanky. Stooping to pick it up, she noted the flowered rug was slightly worn and had a burn spot about the size of a cigar ash next to her left foot. She brushed it with her fingertip but nothing rubbed off. Knowing Sherlock, one sniff would tell him the exact type of cigar burned the hole, and it would be a rare brand, which would lead directly to the killer's identity. She was no Sherlock Holmes, but certainly there must be some observations she could make while waiting.

Glancing up the stairwell, she recalled Mrs. Borden had been killed in the guest room, on the left as one went up the stairs. Miss Lizzie's and Miss Emma's tandem rooms were on the right. The only other space upstairs was a large dress closet. The parents' bedroom and Bridget's attic room could only be accessed by the rear staircase. With Mr. Borden being killed in the sitting room—her gaze slid to the door through which Master Dempsey had disappeared—that meant the killer must have stood in this very hallway, perhaps in this very spot. Mrs. Pepperidge and Mrs. Adolpho, two women from church, swished out of the parlor, their expressions more troubled than sorrowful. Victoria strained to hear their whispered exchange but was cut short by a pointed clearing of the throat behind her. It was her turn. Heart racing, she looked down the hallway one last time, hoping Declan would emerge from the crowd. When he did not, she took a deep breath, lifted her chin, and strode into the parlor alone.

CHAPTER SEVEN

"Do you know, Watson," said he, "that it is one of the curses of a mind with a turn like mine that I must look at everything with reference to my own special subject. You look at these scattered houses, and you are impressed by their beauty. I look at them, and the only thought which comes to me is a feeling of their isolation and of the impunity with which crime may be committed there."

—Sherlock Holmes in "The Adventure of the Copper Beeches"

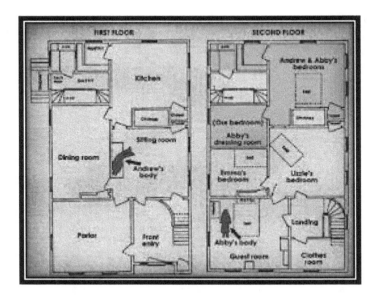

The parlor overflowed with summer flowers, sickeningly sweet in this morbid affair. Victoria found Miss Lizzie sat among them, her back ramrod straight. She looked up at Victoria with glassy eyes, her face utterly expressionless. Victoria felt chilled for a moment—her friend resembled a grim gravestone angel. Where was the welcoming smile, the friendly glimmer?

Victoria pressed her lips into a smile but then felt foolish. She shouldn't have come. She was not a contemporary of Miss Lizzie's; she was not in her inner circle. What should she say? What *could* she say? Suddenly, she remembered what Declan had told her, about the parents being examined on the dining room table. Glancing at the closed door behind Miss Lizzie, she pictured the two lifeless bodies lying amongst the dishes, skulls smashed and bloody, and shivered.

"Miss Lizzie," she said, kneeling in front of her friend. "I am… so sorry." That *was* what people said, wasn't it? If only

Mother were here to guide her.

Miss Lizzie blinked, once, twice, her eyes neither red-rimmed nor puffy. Finally, one corner of her mouth lifted, but it was brief.

"Yes," she finally said. One finger picked at the cuticle of her thumb, which was red and bleeding. The sight of it turned Victoria's stomach. She lay a hand over Miss Lizzie's fingers, stopping the carnage, and this seemed to bring Miss Lizzie back from wherever she'd been.

"My dear," breathed Miss Lizzie, placing her other hand atop Victoria's, trapping it between her own. "How good of you to come." The words poured out all connected, like black molasses from a jar. "Of course," Victoria murmured, surprised and relieved at this show of affection. Surprised, too, at how thick and calloused Miss Lizzie's hand felt on top of her own. Funny how one could be friends with someone for so long and have no idea what their hands felt like. In a corner of the room, Alice Russell finished her conversation with Dr. Bowen and came to sit beside Miss Lizzie on the love seat. Unlike Miss Lizzie, Miss Alice's face was puffed and blotchy and as she fought off further tears, the pouch of skin under her chin quivered like a turkey wattle. She nodded a greeting to Victoria behind a wadded-up hanky.

Victoria nodded back. Her knees were beginning to ache and she wished she could extricate her sweaty, cramped hand from between Miss Lizzie's.

"I am so sorry for... all of this, Miss Lizzie. I know how much you loved your father. And your mother too, of course."

Frowning, Miss Lizzie wagged her head side to side, her stiff collar digging into the soft folds of her neck, leaving a line of chafing. "She's not my mother, she's my stepmother."

"Is that so?" She had never seen Miss Lizzie this way. It was almost as though she'd been drinking too much sherry. Mrs. Borden being her stepmother was news to Victoria. Come to think of it, Victoria had never had much interaction with Mrs.

Borden, who always seemed to be busy with the maid, cleaning or cooking. Chores which Miss Lizzie and her sister never seemed to partake in. Behind them, Dr. Bowen, in his vest and shirt sleeves, sorted small glass bottles into his medicine bag.

Miss Lizzie gave an exaggerated nod. "I was two when Mother died and four when Father re... re-married. To *her.*" She tilted her head towards the dining room door, then wrinkled her nose. "Emma didn't like her much," she confided. "She liked being my little mother. Fourteen years old, she was." Frowning, Miss Lizzie looked around the room. "Where is Emma? She should be here with me."

Miss Alice dabbed her red nose. "She went upstairs to rest, remember?"

"Oh. Yes." Miss Lizzie released Victoria's hand to unceremoniously scratch her ankle, and Victoria quickly stood, placing her hands behind her back, surreptitiously drying them on her skirt. Her feet tingled.

"Victoria, have you been fishing lately?"

Victoria blinked. Fishing? Shouldn't they be discussing the parents, their merits, their joining God and the angels in heaven?

"I'm afraid not," she answered. Miss Lizzie had taught her how to cast her fishing line up in Swansea. After what must have been a hundred attempts, Victoria finally got it right, and Miss Lizzie had called, "You're a natural!" How patient she had been, putting worm after worm on Victoria's hook.

"I haven't been to the farm in ages," Victoria continued. "Mother says it's no place for..." Blushing, she stopped before saying *young ladies* because she knew Miss Lizzie still visited their farm.

But Miss Lizzie did not seem to catch the slip. "That's what I was doing in the barn, you know. Getting lead for my fishing line. Then I came back to find my father. Gone."

"Lizbeth!" Miss Alice whispered. "You told me you were out getting screening for the back door."

Miss Lizzie rubbed her temple, confused. "Yes, I believe

there was that too."

Miss Alice threw a worried glance over her shoulder at Dr. Bowen, who did not appear to have heard the exchange.

Miss Lizzie's gaze wandered across Victoria's face, as if searching for something she'd lost. "Did I ever tell you," she said, dreamily, staring into Victoria's eyes, "that you remind me… of me? As a young girl, I mean."

Victoria smiled at this familiar phrase. "Yes, and I've always taken it as the highest compliment."

As Miss Lizzie slowly nodded, Dr. Bowen leaned close to Miss Alice and whispered in her ear. Victoria caught the words "calmer now." He patted his leather bag.

"Thank you, Doctor." Miss Alice sniffed. "It has been helping her." Tears clumped her eyelashes, which she continued to pat with a balled hanky. "And thank you, Miss Robbins," she added, "for coming."

"Oh! Of course." Though Victoria did not feel it was Miss Alice's place to dismiss her, she couldn't help but feel relieved.

"Yes, just like me," Miss Lizzie continued. "Only, I hope..." Her brow furrowed. She blinked a few times before finding the rest of her thought. "Hope that your future, Victoria, will be brighter than mine."

Dr. Bowen placed a hand on his patient's shoulder. "Now Lizzie," he said, "you've had a terrible blow. But you still have your dear sister, and all your loving friends. And you are only thirty-three! Rest assured, you have a full life ahead of you."

Miss Lizzie turned and gave Dr. Bowen a sad smile, patted his hand. "Thank you, Doctor." Then she sighed and added, to no one in particular, "But I am afraid the worst is yet to come."

LATER THAT HUMID afternoon, sitting in the ladder-back chair next to Mother's bed, Victoria tried to exorcize the memory of her unsettling visit to Miss Lizzie's by reading aloud from Emily Dickinson's *Poems*. Mother ranked poetry second to the Bible, and though Victoria found it equally as dull, she preferred it to the Good Book. However, as hot summer air stirred the pages of poetry, the recollection of Miss Lizzie's dazed behavior and eerie prediction trampled over the poetic words and caused a wave of nausea to creep up Victoria's throat. *The worst is yet to come.* She removed Declan's hanky from her waistband and breathed in its earthy smell, like smelling salts, then used it to blot her damp forehead.

Mother coughed, and Victoria realized she'd stopped reading.

"Sorry, Mother." Laying the book aside, she poured fresh mint water into the white toile basin, the black festoons painted along the rim contrasting prettily against the crushed green leaves swirling about the water's surface. The ice chips had long since melted, but she rinsed a rag in the tepid water anyway and wiped her mother's flushed face. Mother's coughing continued, so Victoria swapped the rag for an old hanky and put it to her mother's lips.

"Here you go. Cough away."

Waiting for Mother to expel the sputum, Victoria stared at the trellis wallpaper, whose mismatched pattern she'd memorized, and considered treating herself and Mother to a second piece of peach pie. A knock from downstairs jolted Victoria from her thoughts. Then a muffled voice called, "Let me in, for Pete's sake."

"Father!" Victoria laughed and hurried down the stairs. "Hold on," she called, undoing the latches. Then she threw open the door to see her father in his brown striped sack suit, his tanned face almost matching his clothes, and she felt a great weight lift from her chest. Father was here now. He would be in charge.

"Pigeon! I was starting to think I had the wrong house," he joked.

"Oh, Father!" Victoria hugged him tightly, breathing in his

farm smell. He was an outdoorsman at heart, he was fond of saying, and tinkering on the little farm was his antidote to the stifling bank he'd inherited.

"It's been so frightening here. You've heard about the Bordens? We've kept the doors and windows bolted night and day."

"News travels fast," Father said, removing his hat. "I came as soon as I could."

A warmth spread through Victoria as she pictured her father driving their carriage at breakneck speed, cracking his whip at Admiral's flanks, shouting, "Faster, faster!" Maybe the thought of losing his wife and daughter was just the kind of wakeup call he needed. Maybe he would be more solicitous, more appreciative—more present. Maybe they'd be more of a family again.

"I'll take that." Smiling, she held out her hand for his coat. When he took it off and handed it to her, she saw a line of white skin outlining his sideburns and neck. "Father! Did you really stop at the barber's before checking on us?"

Frowning, he put a hand to his head. "How did you perceive *that*?"

"Your tan stops a half inch from your hairline," Victoria answered stiffly, hanging up his coat. "Even Watson would have caught it."

He rubbed his hand across his neck and gave an embarrassed laugh. "It was a matter of self-preservation, really. A farmer spotted a madman in his woods, jabbering about the murder, and the way I looked, the police might've mistaken me for him. That, and I couldn't let your mother see me looking so scruffy."

"A madman?" Victoria momentarily put her irritation aside. "Did they catch him?"

Father shrugged. "Just one of the many reports they're getting, I expect. I wouldn't put too much stock in it. So, tell me, how is your mother?"

Victoria took his hat and hung it on its usual hook. "Unchanged. We thought it best to avoid telling her anything about the Bordens."

Father flipped through the small pile of letters on the receiving table. "Mmm. Yes, good thought."

"I imagine your bank employees will be happy you've returned."

He gave a low snort. "I'm not so sure about that, Pidge. While the cat's away, the mice will play, you know."

Hearing him use his old nickname for her reminded her of happier times. She moved to the staircase, expecting him to follow. He didn't. She climbed a few stairs and stopped. "Mother will be so happy to see you."

Father nodded and opened one envelope, peered at the note, harrumphed, and moved on to the next.

"Father, can't you do that later? You haven't seen Mother in weeks!"

He glanced up at her and smiled. "Of course." He put the mail down and came to the stairs, but then, his hand on the banister, he hesitated. "You know," he said, tapping a finger against the wood, "a man at the barber's mentioned a doctor who was treating his aunt with a similar-sounding condition to Mother's. I jotted down his name. Now where did I..." He patted his suit pockets, then started on his pants pockets.

She sighed. Father was forever putting things in pockets and misplacing them.

"Aha!" He pulled a torn slip of brown paper from his rear pant pocket. "Dr. Appelbaum. On Sixth Street. If I leave now, perhaps I could catch him before he leaves for the day."

"Now?" Victoria stared as her father turned and grabbed the hat she'd just hung up. "But you must be exhausted! Have a rest first."

He shrugged his coat back on. "I can when I get back."

Victoria's throat tightened. "But what about the Bordens' killer? And keeping us safe?"

"Well, I feel much better now that I've seen you, and I know Goliath himself couldn't get in that front door." He laughed.

When she didn't respond, Father's smile lessened. "Pidge, if I don't do it now, we'll have to wait until Monday. Sooner is better than later, don't you think?"

She studied her father, who she used to think was the most handsome man in the world. Was he truly putting Mother's health and cure before his own comfort? Or was this just another way for him to avoid spending time at home? She turned and ascended the stairs. Behind her, the front door shut with a final thump.

CHAPTER EIGHT

The next morning, sitting on her window seat in her nightdress, Victoria brooded over her father's late-night return from his supposed visit to a doctor for Mother. Surely it didn't take until the wee hours of the night for Father to describe Mother's condition and for the doctor to check his appointment book? Perhaps the doctor had been hard to locate and Father had to track him down. Or perhaps the whole story was just a ruse to get out of spending time at home. Even when Mother was perfectly fit, he seemed to spend more and more time at the farm. And even when he was home, he seemed restless and twitchy, like a caged cat.

The sound of Father's heavy footsteps scraping up the rear stairs brought her out of her musings. When she heard the tinkle of silverware, her heart lifted. Father was bringing Mother her breakfast tray! Goodness, he hadn't done that in years. They used to do it together on Mother's birthday: toast, jam, soft-boiled eggs, poached pears. It was Victoria's job to pick the perfect flower for the bud vase. She smiled at the memory and snuggled back into the nest of embroidered pillows. She'd stay put for the time being, give them some privacy and time to catch up.

Her window seat was the perfect vantage point from which to view the goings-on in her neighbors' backyards. Even at this time of the morning, crowds lined the Borden's fences, chatting, pointing, straining to see something pertaining to the murders. Police patrolled the yard, a few chatting with the onlookers. One man in a flat cap called from the barn loft window to another man, then tossed down what looked to be a glass canning jar. No sign of Miss Lizzie or Miss Emma, nor Declan or his father.

A knock on her door sounded, then her father's voice. "Victoria."

"Yes?"

"I've brought up Mother's breakfast tray for you. I'm taking Admiral to get reshod."

Frowning, Victoria went to her door and opened it. "Father," she whispered. "Aren't you going to visit with her? She hasn't seen you in weeks."

Father tilted his head and gave her a quizzical look. "Seeing as I've been married to your mother for eighteen years, I think I know a little bit about her. Like how she is extremely modest and does not care to be seen, even by me, when not looking her best."

Anger simmered in Victoria's breast as she stared at her father's freshly trimmed sideburns. "Twenty," she muttered.

"What?"

"You've been married twenty years."

"Oh, for Pete's sake, Victoria! Feed your mother and get her cleaned up and then I'll—she'll—feel better about seeing me." The dishes and silverware clattered as he thrust the tray into her hands. He walked away quickly before she could protest further. There was no bud vase and no flower.

Later that morning, Victoria noticed the guest room bed covers mussed, Father's tie and cufflinks on the nightstand. Irritated, she set the bed to rights, and was halfway down the hall before feeling something sharp digging into her palm.

Father's cufflinks.

She'd done it again.

She hurried to her bedroom and shoved them into her pillowcase for safe keeping.

VICTORIA FOUGHT OFF the heavy sense of failure as she changed her mother's sheets and sponged her stiff limbs. She'd thought putting extra effort into Mother's care would cure her stealing habit, but Father's cufflinks said otherwise. She couldn't go on like this. Something had to change. Maybe she just wasn't trying hard enough.

She dug a flowered silk peignoir out of Mother's drawer and shook it out, sweetening the air with fragrances of the rose and lavender sachets tucked between the layers of finery. Mother blinked no when she saw it, but Victoria insisted.

"You deserve to wear something pretty, Mother. And you want to look your best for Father, too, I know. He's just come home!" Putting it over Mother's shrinking figure was easy, the silk sliding down with one gentle tug.

I could change her every day, rather than every few days. The sheets too. Just the laundry alone should keep me busier. I could trim her hair. Massage her feet with oil. Hands too. Maybe that would help loosen up her muscles. And keep my fingers occupied.

Penelope poked her head in. "'Scuse me, misses, but there's two gentlemen come to speak to Miss Victoria."

Victoria blinked. "Me? About what?"

"Didn't say, miss. But they asked for you by name."

WHEN VICTORIA ENTERED the parlor, her heart surged at the sight of Declan Dempsey and his father, both in ill-fitting tweed suits, the father's too tight around his middle and Declan's hanging loosely about his shoulders.

"Good morning, miss." The heavyset detective, bowler hat in hand, bowed, revealing a perspiring bald spot in the middle of his thinning reddish-blond hair. "Forgive the intrusion. I am Detective Dempsey and this is my son, Declan. I believe you've met?"

Butterflies fluttered in Victoria's chest at Declan's bow. Inside the cramped parlor, he appeared taller and broader than she'd remembered, but he had the same grass-green eyes and endearing curl dangling over his brow.

"We have." Victoria gave a shallow curtsy, and, remembering his hanky in her waistband, fumbled to tuck it out of sight. She prayed she did not reek of her mother's illness. She hadn't even thought to change her dress before greeting her visitors— Gwyne would be horrified. At least she'd had the sense to remove her apron.

"Miss Robbins," Declan said, nodding formally, his secret smile sending off fireworks in her chest. Detectives-in-training really had no business being so terribly attractive.

"Right, well," Declan's father gruffed, "if you don't mind, miss, I'd like to ask you a few questions."

"Oh, of course," Victoria answered, flustered. "Please, sit. Both of you."

Victoria sat on the edge of the sofa, knees together and back straight, hands resting loosely on her lap. Declan sat opposite Victoria, on the edge of Father's wingback and Detective Dempsey dragged over Mother's delicate desk chair and, before Victoria could object, plunked his large frame onto it.

"My son, here, Miss Robbins, as you may or may not know, is training to be a detective, and he's brought some things to my attention."

Declan, head bowed, elbows on his knees, frowned as he

picked at a fingernail.

Victoria felt sick. She must have said something to offend him and he'd told about seeing her in the alley on the day of the murders. What in the world would she say about dressing up as a maid? And stealing a spool of thread? Leaving Mrs. Benson in a dead faint?

"My son tells me," the detective continued, "and I don't know why this would be true, but he claims..."

It's not true, she practiced. *I was nowhere near that store.*

"...that you were a friend of Miss Lizzie's?" Detective Dempsey gave her a doubting look.

It took a moment for his words to sink in. Relief bathed her staticky nerves.

"Oh, yes," she said, nodding. "That's true. I was. I am, I mean. I *am* a friend of Miss Lizzie's." Her gaze flitted to Declan, who was now nodding at his folded hands. Behind him, the grandfather clock ticked off the seconds.

Detective Dempsey's expression did not change. "There is quite an age difference between the two a you, miss, if you don't mind my saying so."

"Well, not friends in the sense of going on holiday together and such. More like older sister or favorite aunt type of friendship." She knew she was babbling but couldn't seem to stop. "We both love animals and the out-of-doors. I'm dying to travel and she's traveled quite extensively, and, oh—" Victoria presented her hand to the detective. "She bought me this ring on her time abroad, to commemorate my sixteenth birthday. I'm sixteen but have not had a Coming Out party yet." She flushed, trying to think of something smart or witty to follow up such a ridiculous statement, but her mind was a thick chunk of lard.

Detective Dempsey glanced at the ring and Victoria saw a flicker of something cross his face—jealousy, perhaps, or disgust. *Suspicion?*

Declan squinted at her hand. "I feel like I've seen a ring just like that somewhere before."

He shook his head, as if mystified, but Victoria could see the tug of a smile on his lips. *That boy.*

Quickly she withdrew her hand. "All I'm saying, Detective, is that your son was correct. Miss Lizzie and I are indeed friends."

"All right, then, as her friend…" Detective Dempsey took a pad of paper and pencil out of his breast pocket. "Can you tell me how she got along with her parents?"

Victoria blinked. She glanced at Declan, but he did not meet her eye. "Detective," she said, her tone cooling, "please tell me you aren't insinuating Miss Lizzie had anything to do with…" The image of Miss Lizzie, dazed, flashed in her mind. *She's not my mother, she's my stepmother.*

Detective Dempsey leaned back in the little chair and folded one ample leg atop the other. "I am a detective, Miss. It is not my job to insinuate; that's the prosecutor's realm. My job is to ask questions. Now, again, can you tell me how she got along with her parents?"

Lifting her chin slightly, Victoria replied, "They got along just fine. Very loving."

"Was she loving toward her father and her mother? Both equally? Or perhaps one more than the other?"

Declan finally looked up. His gaze was direct and unblinking.

Victoria hesitated. "A bit closer to her father, perhaps."

The detective licked his pencil and scribbled on his pad. His chair creaked. "And what about the mother? Did you ever witness an argument between them? Or hear Miss Lizzie complain about her?"

Victoria's heart pounded, for while Miss Lizzie doted on her father, there had been an occasional brusque remark or dismissive tone toward her stepmother. "Detective, I really do not see—"

"Did you ever hear Miss Lizzie call her mother names, like"—he flipped back a few pages and squinted—"*a mean old thing?"*

Victoria put a shocked hand to her mouth. Her friend would never say anything so outright rude.

"No. I never heard Miss Lizzie call her mother such a name. Detective, Miss Lizzie's considerable good works are well known. She's spent years teaching Sunday School, helping the poor, and even serving as an officer in the Christian Temperance League. In fact," she added, her voice rising, "Miss Lizzie's dedication is so great, she gave up a trip to the country with friends just so she could fulfill her duties at the Temperance meeting. By all accounts, she shouldn't even have been here last week." Smiling, she gave him a righteous nod.

"Ahh!" Detective Dempsey looked pleasantly surprised.

Seeing Declan's eyes widen, Victoria's soaring triumph faltered.

"She had plans," the detective said as he wrote, "that she cancelled. So she could stay home. While her sister was out of town." He put the final period on his note with a flourish, then tucked pad and pencil into his pocket. "Miss Robbins." He stood up.

Declan, looking confused, stood as well.

"You have been most helpful. I think we have all we need." He bowed. "Come, Declan." He began walking toward the door.

"But Father," Declan said, "we were going to ask about the neighbors and the fence and the uncle."

Detective Dempsey turned. "You will learn, boy. When you get the answer you are looking for, you stop asking questions."

Victoria jumped up, staring at the red-faced detective. "You've got it backward, Detective! You ask all the questions to lead you to the one, true answer, not the other way around." Anyone who read the Sherlock Holmes stories knew that.

Penelope appeared in the doorway with a tray of tea and shortbread. "Oh! I'm sorry. I thought you might fancy a cuppa tea."

"No time, little lady," said Detective Dempsey, "but I will

help myself to a few of these." He grabbed several cookies and popped one in his mouth. Over his shoulder, with his mouth full of shortbread, he added, "We'll show ourselves out."

"But Detective—"

Declan, looking grim, gave a quick bow and followed his father. When the front door shut, Victoria felt sick. Maybe Miss Lizzie had been right. Maybe the worst really was yet to come.

THE NEW YORK HERALD

MRS. BORDEN KILLED FIRST

[T]he results of today's investigation satisfied Medical Examiner Dolan that Mrs.
Borden was killed at least an hour before
her husband. This appears from the statement of Dr. Bowen, that when he arrived,
Mr. Borden's body was warm and the blood
was flowing, but Mrs. Borden's body was
cold and stiff. During the hour that
elapsed, where was the murderer? He must
have been concealed somewhere about the
house. But it would have been impossible
for an outsider to know when Mr. Borden
would come home.

The murderer must therefore have stayed upon the very scene of his first crime, not
knowing what moment it might be discovered
and he with it, though immediately after
his second murder he disappeared so amazingly that no one can guess how he went.

CHAPTER NINE

The morning after Declan's visit, Victoria pushed her plate of half-eaten toast to the side and re-read the latest troubling article concerning the Bordens. Leaning on the table and rubbing her temples, she mulled over the phrase *concealed somewhere in the house.* The cellar was a possibility, with its dark corners and divided rooms, where the slam of the front door and creaking footsteps overhead would be easily detectible. However, to get to the sitting room to kill the father, the killer would have to creep up the basement stairs and pass through the kitchen, always the busiest room in a house. Had he just gotten incredibly lucky that Bridget was resting instead of cooking and Miss Lizzie had left her ironing to go out to the barn? A smarter hiding place would be closer to the sitting room and front door, which would mean the closet at the base of the stairs, but could a grown man fit inside?

She remembered being in that closet as a little girl, sitting on the floor and holding a coal-black kitten, its pink fleshy belly soft against her wrist. Miss Lizzie had rescued it from the streets and was hiding it from her father until she could take it to their farm. The closet had been roomy enough for her, but she'd only been about seven.

"Good news." Father strode into the dining room and kissed the top of her head, bringing Victoria back from the past. "The doctor I mentioned earlier is coming after lunch to examine your mother." The irksomeness she'd felt at her father's kiss melted. Maybe he did care after all.

"That's wonderful! Will he be able to tell us what she has?" She lifted her teacup only to realize it was empty, so she set it back down.

"He is supposed to be an expert in these types of illnesses." His chair scraped as he sat down at the head of the table. From the kitchen, Victoria could hear another chair scrape, and a moment later, Penelope swished in with the teapot.

"Good mornin', sir. Tea?"

"Please. And two soft boiled eggs and some of that ham from last night's dinner."

Penelope nodded as she poured, the tea a steaming brown ribbon.

"I'm going to need you, Penelope, to help Victoria get Mrs. Robbins cleaned up as best you can. I've got a specialist coming to examine her."

"I've already taken care of her washing up," Victoria said. "First thing this morning. Sheets, bedclothes. Gave her hair a good wash as well. You *have* seen her since you've been home, haven't you, Father?"

"Of course, Victoria." He gave an indignant little huff. "She is my wife, after all."

Victoria was tempted to give a little indignant huff of her own but held back.

Penelope placed her employer's steaming tea before him. "I'll make sure she's freshened up for the doctor, sir. Hopefully this 'un will fix her right up. Poor thing's wasting away to dust."

Father picked up the morning paper and shook it out. "Best not to count your chickens, Penelope. He hasn't cured her yet."

Victoria refused to allow her father's pessimism to douse her hope. This doctor could change everything: Mother could be cured, Father would be happy, and soon they'd be planning her Coming Out party, leaving no time for Mag and her childish game. Scooting out her chair, she said, "I think we're overdue for something good to happen around here, and this has my vote. I'll go check on Mother and air out the room."

DR. APPELBAUM, AN older gentleman with silver hair and a pointed beard, arrived shortly after midday. Neither a chatterer nor a charmer, he got straight to work, prying Mother's limbs out of their clutched positions, peering into her ears and nose and throat, bending each toe, separating each finger, and stopping occasionally to jot down a note.

The room was silent but for the doctor's self-agreeing *mmmm-hmm, mm-hm* as he tested each part of Mother's body. Nothing about Mother's condition seemed to surprise or confuse him. Father had said he was an expert, and he certainly seemed to be. Victoria's hope grew. After what seemed like hours, the doctor carried his various instruments to the wash basin and rinsed them off.

"Well," the doctor said, lathering up his hands. "It is right in line with the other cases I've seen, although this is the most impressive to date."

"Impressive?" Victoria took a hesitant step forward and rubbed her mother's bony shoulder. "Is that a good thing?"

Dr. Appelbaum rinsed his other arm and began drying off with the hand towel lying beside the basin. "Your wife, Mr. Robbins, is what we in the medical profession call 'malingering.' I said it was an impressive case because I've never seen one so pervasive throughout the body. Most malingerers pretend to be weak in just one hand or foot, or blind in one eye, just enough of an impairment to get them out of doing work or garner a little sympathy. But this, this paralysis, well, it's..." He shook his head.

"Pretend?" Father said. "You think my wife has been pretending?"

Victoria looked down at her mother, who was madly closing and opening her right eye. Her cheekbone glistened with tears. A small white clump of food—potato or oatmeal—clung to the hair by her ear and Victoria carefully brushed it away.

"Personally, yes, that's what I call it, Mr. Robbins." The doctor began unrolling his shirt sleeves and refastening his cuffs. "There's a quack named Freud who calls it 'hysteria' and blames it on 'repressed memories,' but it all amounts to the same thing: a paralysis of no physical cause. I'm of the mind that the sooner the rest of you stop catering to her every need, the sooner she'll tire of it and make a miraculous recovery."

Victoria watched in horror as Dr. Appelbaum walked to the end of the bed and shook the small mound that was her mother's feet. "ISN'T THAT RIGHT, MRS. ROBBINS?" He patted them roughly. "You've had quite a long vacation, but it's time to get back to taking care of your family now. Enough is enough!"

Mother, half of her face frozen in a grimace, continued her blinking pattern. Two blinks, pause, two blinks, pause.

"And these spasms with your eye, Mrs. Robbins," he said, chuckling. "They are truly—"

"She's saying no, Doctor," Victoria interrupted. "Two blinks mean no, one means yes." Her throat was so tight she barely recognized her own voice. "She's saying no, she doesn't agree." Her voice rose in volume. "*No,* she's not faking. *No,* you are not correct!"

Mother made a small noise like the yip of a puppy. Her eye gave one watery blink. *Yes.*

Dr. Appelbaum shrugged into his suit coat. "Believe what you wish, young lady, but your father is paying me for my expert opinion, and I have given it."

There was no way her mother would choose to lie in her

own odors than do a bit of dusting and ironing, no way she would choose to be the humiliating subject of endless speculation and condemnation.

"Tell me this, Doctor," Victoria said, stepping forward and lowering her voice. "If she is malingering, as you say, how could she keep it up in her sleep?"

"It's complicated, young lady," Dr. Appelbaum grumbled, brushing past her dismissively. "You wouldn't understand." He grabbed his bag. "Now, Mr. Robbins? If you will show me out…"

Father, who had seemed almost lost in thought, startled upon hearing his name. "Why, yes." He looked around, as if surprised to find himself in his wife's room, the room they used to share together. "Yes," he repeated. "Right this way."

BOSTON DAILY GLOBE
The Adams-Nervine Asylum

"A man's work is o'er at set of sun; a woman's work is never done," runs the old couplet, and these women verify it. Baking, brewing, sewing, scouring, mending, milking, washing, sweeping, working late and working early, bearing babies, nurturing sick folks, that's the recipe for the life of the average farmers' wife, whose husband takes far more care of his cattle than of his better half, and whose "folks" would be scandalized to hear that Sairy Jane was being killed by hard work.

But Sairy Jane doesn't go to the asylum. She can't spare the time. She can't spare the time to go anywhere except to her grave and when she quietly slips into that, it never occurs to the "mourners" to think they have buried, not to say, murdered, a martyr.

CHAPTER TEN

For the next several days, Father was in "a mood," as Mother used to call it: irritable, fidgety, unwilling to engage in conversation about anything, much less Dr. Appelbaum's diagnosis. It didn't help matters that the crowds from the Bordens continued to spill over onto their lawn, trampling their grass, using their flowerpots as garbage receptacles, and barely acknowledging Father as he tried to disperse them. Victoria's mood wasn't much better, for even doubling up her efforts with Mother did not silence Mag's pull, and the effort of constantly resisting made her edgy and snappish.

When she finally pressed the matter of Dr. Appelbaum one morning at breakfast, Father gave a terse shrug and spat, "He's the doctor, Victoria. He's the expert on your mother's condition."

"But *we* are the experts on Mother! We both know she would never fake such a condition. Every time I feed her or wash her, I see the humiliation in her eyes."

"People can fool you," Father mumbled, unfolding the day's paper. "You can never truly know someone." Then he grunted and turned the paper so she could read the headline. "Case in point."

Victoria dropped the spoon she'd been holding as she saw "Miss Borden Arrested: Charged with Murdering Her Father and His Wife." "No," she breathed. Jumping up, she hurried to read the short article over her father's shoulder.

"Gotta hand it to her," Father said, turning the page. "This murder has put us on the map. People as far away as California are following the story. Puts our little Fall River police department in the hot seat."

Returning to her chair in a daze, Victoria sat and blotted at the drops of marmalade beside her plate. *Miss Lizzie, in jail.*

And it was her fault. She'd given Detective Dempsey a reason to arrest her.

"Always knew there was something odd about her," Father said dispassionately. "Didn't seem to have much of an eye for men." He ran his thumb and forefinger down the two sides of his mustache, smoothing it once, twice.

"Father! What a thing to say." Victoria's eyes burned as she pictured Miss Lizzie in the public jail cell, squeezed between the madams and the drunkards, trying to maintain her dignity. Her linen napkin did a poor job of absorbing her tears.

Tipping down the edge of his paper, Father stared at his daughter. "Victoria, are you feverish? What is wrong?"

Had he always been this oblivious to her feelings?

"Father, Miss Lizzie—the godliest woman I know—is in jail."

Father's brow knit in puzzlement. "For Pete's sake, Victoria, save your tears for the Bordens, not the deranged daughter who killed them."

Frustration gripped her chest. "You speak of my friend, Father." A sliver of doubt—how well did she know Miss Lizzie?—flickered through her, but she pushed it away.

"Yes," Father said, speaking to his newsprint, "a friendship which has always troubled me. Why on earth would a grown woman want to spend her time picnicking and tea-partying with a silly little neighbor girl? Didn't she have better things to do?"

"Silly?"

"Oh, don't get your hackles up. You know what I mean."

She didn't.

"And now she has butchered the hands that fed her. Apparently, the money and property her father gave her were not enough. She wanted it all and couldn't be bothered to wait till the old sod died."

Shaking, Victoria replaced her teacup in its saucer with a clatter. She was furious with her father, yes, but equally as furious with herself. If her words were what put her behind bars, she'd never forgive herself. Detective Dempsey's words rang in her head: *When you get the answer you are looking for, you stop asking questions.* What would Miss Lizzie say? She'd probably never speak to her again.

"Father, may I remind you Miss Lizzie was my sole supporter when that horrible Edward Pottersmith claimed I pushed Dickie Houndsworth down the stairs at church? Not even Mother or you believed me!"

The memory, years old, still smarted whenever she thought of it. Dickie and she had been picked to deliver the Sunday School offerings to the deacons when Dickie, clowning as usual, caught his boot heel on the stair edge and fell backwards, the money from the basket flying into the air. Victoria had lunged to grab him but missed, and his head cracked on the fifth step as he tumbled to the base of the stairs. Edward Pottersmith, her neighbor's grandson, had appeared beside her, shouting, "You pushed him! I saw you!"

Father, frowning at the reminder of the incident, took a sip of tea, swallowed. "Well, you did have a bit of a temper, and we couldn't very well call a Pottersmith a liar—"

"Goodness no," Victoria sarcastically interrupted, "but you had no qualms saying the same about your own daughter!"

"Don't be so dramatic, dear." The newspaper crackled as he

straightened it. "That boy woke up a day later and said what happened and the whole thing was resolved."

Victoria pushed her empty plate away and stood. "That doesn't change the fact that Miss Lizzie was the only one to say she believed me." She had never felt so grateful to anyone in her life, as if she'd been drowning and only Miss Lizzie had thrown her a line.

"Meanwhile," she continued, "you and Mother rushed after the Houndsworths as they carried Dickie out, apologizing, not listening to me saying I didn't push him."

Father heaved a sigh. "Goodness, Victoria. Mr. Houndsworth was my employer at the time. I couldn't very well tell him his son was a chowderhead. Back to our original conversation, all I was saying was I am not surprised by your *friend's* arrest."

"Well I am, and I look forward to saying I told you so." Her first instinct was to storm out of the room and leave her father speechless, but since he had just accused her of being dramatic, Victoria took pains to calmly fold and lay her napkin on the table before walking out. She could not resist, however, closing the door behind her with a bit more force than was truly necessary.

Later that morning, Victoria received a note from Miss Lizzie.

Dear Victoria,

I have been meaning to write a note of thanks for your visit after the death of my parents but hadn't had the time nor energy. Now, as you must have heard, my circumstances have changed and time is in abundance. Emma brought a few amenities from home, including the stationery and pen I requested so that I may finally, properly, thank those who have supported me. Your kindness, and that of a few others, is what keeps my spirits up in this lonely, dim cell.

How are you? And how is your mother? I hope she has recovered and that you now have plenty of time to plan your debut as well as read your beloved mystery stories. I'm ashamed to admit, once arrested, my first thought was to secure Sherlock Holmes for help—that is how real you have made him to me over the years. It is a shame he is fictional, as I believe only someone with his superior intellect can save me from my current predicament. I am not sure my lawyers, Andrew Jennings and George Robinson, are up to the task, as I have heard District Attorneys Moody and Knowlton are quite gifted prosecutors.

Please thank Penelope for the peach pie. Its sweetness was a reminder of your family's friendship, especially comforting in the wake of others' abandonment.

Very sincerely yours,

Miss Lizzie

Victoria lowered herself onto the bottom stair and reread Miss Lizzie's note. She imagined her friend sitting alone in a dank cell, writing by a sliver of light cast through a tiny, barred window. *Abandoned.* Was she writing to everyone who came to pay their respects? Surely not the ones who came out of curiosity or stood in morbid fascination in front of her house, craning their necks to get a glimpse of her. The more Victoria studied the letter, the more her pity for Lizzie morphed into something deeper: a need to help an old friend who had been wrongly accused. The letter itself seemed a plea for help—little faith in her lawyers, and friends and family dropping away. And her mention of Sherlock Holmes. Was she suggesting Victoria try solving the case herself? Little did Miss Lizzie know it was partly Victoria's own words which helped swing the jail door shut behind her!

Bitter tears clogged Victoria's throat as she held the note, her thumbs stroking the parchment. What would Sherlock do? Where would he start? The thought of it was overwhelming. It was then she noticed a slight unevenness as her thumbs passed across the page. Holding it up to the light, she saw why.

Two of the words were written with such force that the paper had become indented:

Save me.

MISS BORDEN ARRESTED
CHARGED WITH MURDERING HER FATHER AND HIS WIFE

She Appeared Calm When The Warrant Was Read to Her

FALL RIVER, Mass., Lizzie Borden is under arrest charged with murdering her father and stepmother last Thursday morning at their home on Second Street. She was brought into the Second District Court room about 3 o'clock this afternoon, presumably to give further evidence at the inquest. Miss Borden was accompanied by her sister and Mrs. Brigham. As was the case yesterday, all the proceedings were carried on behind locked doors.

When Miss Lizzie returned from the third inquiry, she was a physical and mental wreck and was conducted to the matron's room. The inquest was adjourned about 4 o'clock. District Attorney Knowlton and other officials went to the Marshal's private office, where they remained closeted for two hours. Shortly after 6 o'clock City Marshal Hilliard and District Attorney Knowlton drove to the home of Andrew Jennings, who had been the family's attorney for some years. They returned at about 7 o'clock, and went into the matron's room, where Lizzie was lying on the sofa. The reading of the warrant was waived. The lady took the announcement of her arrest with surprising calmness. Two women who were with her were much more visibly affected.

The excitement on the street was very great when the news of the arrest became known, although some hours previous it was generally understood that Miss Borden was soon to be made a prisoner. Miss Borden was searched by Miss Russell shortly after she was formally placed in custody.

Marshal Hilliard said today, in answer to questions as to whether or not the police had given up all hopes of locating a murderer outside of the Borden family, that three clues were already being run down and none of them would in any way implicate a member of the household. He said he had not been stinted in money nor men by the City Government because of political complications.

CHAPTER ELEVEN

Soon after her father left for the bank, Victoria stood outside the Jacobsens' back porch, knocking hard on the screen door. The sound echoed in the still of the morning, which struck Victoria as odd until she realized the crowds previously lining the Bordens' fences had been replaced by an empty strip of dirt. She was considering their departure when Gwyne answered the door.

"Victoria," she admonished, bringing her friend inside, "we are not school girls anymore. We need to start coming to each other's front doors and calling on one another properly. We're almost debutantes, after all."

Victoria gave her friend a quick hug. "I know, I know, but you will be pleased to learn we are going on just such a social call, front door and everything." She waved her lace gloves at her friend. "So hurry up and get your hat."

Gwyne narrowed her eyes. "Calling on whom? I was just working on my hand towels. Have you even started yours?"

Victoria strode past her friend, right out of the kitchen.

"Tory!" Gwyne hurried in her wake.

Once in the front hall, Victoria threw open the closet and pulled out her friend's things. "I have to go to town," she whispered, "and therefore, you have to come with me."

"Why?"

"Didn't you see the paper this morning, Gwyne?"

Gwyne frowned. "I read Miss Elba's Etiquette column..."

"And missed the front page? Honestly, Gwyne, what am I going to do with you?" She fished inside her drawstring purse, then thrust the folded newspaper article at her friend, who took a moment to read the first few lines. Victoria thought about showing her Miss Lizzie's note as well but thought better of it.

"Oh," Gwyne breathed. "This is not good, Victoria."

"Exactly." Victoria swapped the newspaper for Gwyne's jacket. "Which is why I need to find Declan."

"Who?"

"Detective Dempsey's son. He's helping with the Borden investigation."

Gwyne clutched the jacket to her chest. "I know who he is! Oh, Tory, I'll admit he's good looking, but—" She wrinkled her nose. "He's Irish!"

"Goodness, Gwyne," Victoria said, flopping a hat atop her friend's head, "I want to talk to him, not marry him!" Although just the thought of Declan sent a strange ripple under her skin.

Gwyne hesitated. "Well, Mother is out for the morning..."

"Perfect." Victoria waved her hand in a hurry-up motion. "I promised Pen I'd be back by noon to help with Mother, so hurry."

"Fine." Her friend took her hat and then smiled at her reflection as she adjusted its slant in the hall mirror. "But what about the man you will marry? He'll expect you to have a full trousseau."

Victoria peeked into the empty parlor, then headed to the front door, unlatching and opening the door as quietly as possible so Gwyne's Bridget wouldn't hear. Victoria let out a breath as she closed the door behind them.

"Whoever marries me, Gwyne, will have to forego cross-stitched towels and learn to wipe his hands on his trousers."

TURNING DOWN THE disreputable Granite Street, home to the Fall River Police Station, was like crossing into a dark and wretched world. Ragged men hung in shadowy doorways and squatted against the sides of buildings; a few equally ragged children held out matches or pencils to sell. Bony-ribbed dogs sniffed through gutters ripe with human and animal waste. Gwyne tightened her grip on Victoria's arm.

Victoria, however, was filled with steely resolve. Miss Lizzie's arrest was a terrible mistake, and she was determined to right it. She would find Declan and explain how her words had been misconstrued. She'd demand to know what evidence they claimed to have against her and refute it, just like Sherlock did, point for point.

Patting Gwyne's hand, she realized this was just what she needed to put Mag behind her. A puzzle to solve. A victim to save. Just like Sherlock. What was he always saying? "My mind rebels at stagnation. Give me problems, give me work!" Ever since hearing of Miss Lizzie's arrest, she hadn't once had the urge to pocket even the smallest thing.

She only wished it wasn't her dear friend that needed saving.

Closer to the station, they saw barred prison cells with shutter-like doors open to the outside, probably for fresh air, but also putting prisoners—in all their misery—on display. The crowd formerly lining the Borden's fence stood on the footpath, pointing and gossiping. Did they see her?

"Tory!" Gwyne held her hanky tight to her nose as they approached the jail, making her sound like she had a head cold. "Are you sure Declan will be here?"

Victoria didn't answer, trying to see around the gawkers to

the figures in the cells, hoping—and not hoping—to catch a glimpse of Miss Lizzie. Her letter had mentioned being alone in a cell.

"My mother," Gwyne continued, "would die a thousand deaths if she knew where we were. Couldn't we have gone to his house?"

With the crowd milling in front of the jail cells, the walk to the front door of the police department was relatively empty, so at least they did not have to fight their way in. Victoria yanked open the heavy door marked with the brass letters FRPD and said, "Declan has a profession, Gwyne. He does not sit around his house like we do, hoping for someone to stop in for a cup of tea and meaningless small talk."

Gwyne huffed. "You make our lives sound so petty."

"Sorry," Victoria said, though in truth she thought petty seemed a perfect description of their sheltered lives.

The station consisted of one large, high-ceilinged room with wood paneling and gas light sconces, and off to the side, a long, shadowy hall to the holding cells. Small bunches of men in blue uniforms stood around the big room, talking, laughing, writing, and smoking. As the girls made their way toward the front desk, however, the male voices dropped, one by one, until the only sounds were the girls' clicking footsteps on the white tiled floor.

The officer at the front desk tipped his hat and smiled at Victoria. "Well, now, ladies, what can we do for you? A little out of your neighborhood, aren't you? Cat up a tree or some such thing?"

Victoria cleared her throat. Swallowed. One of the officers snickered.

"Or perhaps," continued the large-mouthed officer, his tone placating, "cat got yer tongues?"

Lifting her chin, Victoria said, "You can do two things for us. First, we would like to visit one of your... someone you've arrested. Miss Lizzie Borden."

He frowned. "I'm afraid only immediate family—what's

left of 'em, anyways—and her lawyers allowed."

Victoria was half-expecting this. "Well then, secondly, we would like to speak to Master Dempsey, please." Then she added, "Detective Dempsey's son."

The man raised his eyebrows, then exchanged an amused look with someone behind Victoria. "Well, miss," he said, "I'm sure he'd love to speak with you too, but he's not... receivin' at the moment. Perhaps you'd like to leave your calling card?"

A few officers chuckled.

As Victoria fished in her bag, Gwyne leaned close to whisper, "He's mocking you."

"I know that." Victoria pulled out her card and a note she'd written to Miss Lizzie, pledging her loyalty and assistance. She addressed the officer. "I trust there's no rule against a prisoner receiving mail?"

"None at all."

"Fine." When she went to place both in his outstretched hand, she saw that he was missing his last two fingers. A messy clump of skin sat tied up in their place, creamy and bulbous, like chicken fat.

Victoria's breath caught—and she could hear Gwyne gasp as well.

The officer grinned. "S'alright, girly," he said, "the other three work." His two fingers and thumb opened and closed like a crab's claw.

The roomful of men erupted in laughter.

Victoria glared at the man and slapped the card and envelope into his disfigured hand.

Slowly, the laughter died. Gwyne nudged Victoria's side but Victoria did not move.

"Was there something else we could do for you, misses?" the officer said. "A crumpet or two?"

"Well, Officer Fenley," Victoria said, reading his name plate, "now that you have so masterfully established where Master Declan is *not*, perhaps you could tell me where, in fact, he is?"

There was a beat of silence, then a few more snickers. The three-fingered officer glanced around, giving his comrades dirty looks. "I'm not at liberty to say."

"Please," she said, now regretting her snippy tone. "It's important I speak with him."

"I'm sure it is. I'll let him know an invitation to tea is awaiting him. In the meantime, Officer Lupin"—he jutted his chin toward a fragile-looking officer standing near the front door and raised his voice so Officer Lupin could hear him—"would probably jump at the chance to attend. He could even bring his own plate of tea cakes, couldn't you, sweetie?"

Two policemen close to Victoria and Gwyne guffawed while the skinny Officer Lupin shifted his feet, the glowing red tips of his ears visible from across the room.

Gwyne gripped Victoria's forearm. "Let's go," she whispered, giving a tug, and Victoria grudgingly allowed herself to be led away. If Declan wasn't in the station, he'd probably be out in the city, investigating one crime or another. In a town of over seventy-five thousand, even Sherlock Holmes would have difficulty tracking him down.

Officer Lupin, still pink-faced, held the door for them.

"Thank you," Victoria said, giving him a sympathetic smile as she passed.

He tipped his hat, his lips barely moving as he murmured, "Oak Grove Cemetery."

Victoria stopped short, then reached for Gwyne's elbow. "Come along, Gwyne," she said, but her eyes were on Officer Lupin.

He put his fist to his mouth, pretended to clear his throat and added a whispered "Autopsy."

The two girls made their way to the sidewalk and as soon as they heard the door clunk shut, Gwyne grabbed Victoria's arm.

"Did I hear him right?"

Victoria grinned. "Oak Grove Cemetery. Come on!"

Gwyne became a block of marble, immovable. "Have you lost your mind, Victoria? We are not going to an autopsy."

Victoria shaded her eyes and peered at her friend. There was a light crease across Gwyne's forehead she'd never noticed before. It was disturbingly similar to the one crossing the brow of Gwyne's mother.

"Of course we are not going to the autopsy, Gwyne. We're just going to find Declan and talk to him. Did you see the way that horrible Officer Fenley acted? As though we didn't have a full brain between us."

"Well, perhaps he's right, if you're actually considering going. Have you forgotten, Tory? The funeral was almost a week ago! Wouldn't they be buried by now? Maybe Officer Lupin is trying to pull one over on us."

Victoria considered the scrawny policeman, obviously the brunt of many jokes by the meatier, cruder officers. She shook her head. "Miss Lizzie is in jail right now. I need to talk to someone about her. Someone who will actually listen."

"And you think that's going to be Declan?"

"Yes," Victoria said, hooking her arm through Gwyne's. "I do. Now let's hurry."

Give me problems! Give me work!

OAK GROVE CEMETERY was the exact opposite of Granite Street—a picture of serenity, with its steeple-shaped archway and large marble benches, tall oaks and bushy willows towering over sun-dappled hills of gravestones, parcels of chickadees chattering amicably overhead. Somewhere amid all that beauty, however, the week dead bodies of Mr. and Mrs. Borden were being examined. Victoria stood at the entrance, surveying the vast stretch of land, wondering where such an autopsy would be taking place. A special building where the caskets with bodies awaiting burial were stored, perhaps? Holding up a hand to block the sunlight, she squinted into the distance. Probably near the rear, she thought, tucked out of sight.

"Victoria," Gwyne whimpered, huddling next to her, "I really don't think this is wise." She took off her gloves and fanned herself with them. "And," she added, "I'm starting to feel unwell."

Turning to say something dismissive to Gwyne, Victoria was suddenly struck by how small and vulnerable her best friend looked. Her large yellow-and-orange flowered hat overpowered her face, casting gray shadows beneath her eyes.

"Oh Gwyne," Victoria said, softening. "I'm sorry. I've been selfish dragging you here. But it's not for me, it's for Miss Lizzie."

Gwyne glanced around, eyebrows knit with worry.

Headstones in various shapes and sizes dotted the lush grass, many listing sideways, weary from their years at attention, with names and dates long erased by the elements and replaced with a coating of soft green moss. One stone angel, palms raised, smiled disconcertingly, a chilling likeness to Miss Lizzie.

Victoria focused back on her friend. "Don't you feel any allegiance to Miss Lizzie at all, Gwyne?"

Still eyeing the headstones, Gwyne whispered, "She never liked me and forever scolded me in Sunday School."

Victoria smirked, trying to keep things light. "That's because you were forever *talking* in Sunday School." Leaning closer, she poked Gwyne's side and added, "And you don't have to whisper, Gwyne. Dead people can't hear you."

Gwyne did not laugh. She wrapped her arms around her waist. "I don't like this, Tory. Not one bit."

"Goodness, Gwyne, Granite Street was much worse."

Her friend nodded. "Yes, but at least you could see the dangers. Here…" She gave a worried glance over her shoulder. "There are spirits. Of dead people."

As if on cue, a gentle breeze stirred the grass and sent a few

faded leaves rolling over the gravel path. Gwyne's eyes widened, and immediately Victoria thought of the Bordens, their
dissected bodies somewhere close by, their souls restless, mute-
ly calling out the name of their murderer.

But that was stuff of penny dreadfuls, and she was after
facts. With a cleansing sigh, Victoria surveyed her surroundings.
The entrance arch they stood beneath extended on both sides,
dropping into long, low stone walls on either end, and not far
from the left wall stood a small building with arched windows
and a sign on the wood-plank door reading "Ladies Waiting
Room." She knew from Great-grandma Grace's burial—or so
the family story went—that Aunt Frieda fainted at the first drop
of dirt on the coffin and woke up in the Ladies Waiting Room
screaming, convinced she'd been buried in someone's mausole-
um.

Victoria pointed at the small building. "All right, how about
this? You rest in there where it's cooler while I go find Declan."

"I'd rather just go home."

"We've come all this way, Gwyne, and I'm sure it won't
take me long to—"

"You always do this, Tory—march us off into some... unsettling situation, and I'm stupid enough to follow you."

Did she really? Well, if so, Gwyne should be grateful!

"Don't you need a little excitement in your life, Gwyne?"
she asked, urging her friend forward. "Before you marry Mr.
Mysterious and become as boring as our mothers."

Gwyne flushed. "Fine. But where will you be?"

Victoria peered into the sunny greenness. "I'll look for the
groundskeeper—he'll direct me."

"Okay," Gwyne said, "but please don't dillydally. I'll be on
edge the whole time you're gone."

Victoria patted her friend's arm as they walked toward the
little stone house. Her thoughts raced ahead. How could she
convince Declan that the police had arrested the wrong person?
That no matter how convenient a suspect Miss Lizzie made—

104 · BEVERLY PATT

yes, she'd been home during the time of the murders, and yes, she'd supposedly disliked her stepmother...

A sudden gust blew a broken honeysuckle branch across their path, making Gwyne jump. Victoria pulled her closer.

Miss Lizzie is the picture of piety, Victoria imagined explaining to Declan, *helping her father with his record-keeping, sewing clothes for the poor, serving as Secretary and Treasurer of the Christian Endeavor Society.*

They reached the door. A breeze whispered through the leaves, making a hushing sound. In the distance, a steamship whistled its mournful groan.

"I'll be back as soon as I can." Victoria gripped the wrought iron handle and gave it a yank.

But she did not have to go anywhere. For not five feet in front of them was Declan.

And Dr. Dolan.

And Sergeant Harrington.

And the bodies of Andrew and Abigail Borden. Without their heads.

CHAPTER TWELVE

"I could hardly imagine a more damning case," I remarked. "If ever circumstantial evidence pointed to a criminal, it does so here."

"Circumstantial evidence is a very tricky thing," answered Holmes, thoughtfully. "It may seem to point very straight to one thing, but if you sift your own point of view a little, you may find it pointing in an equally uncompromising manner to something entirely different."

—John Watson and Sherlock Holmes
in "The Boscombe Valley Mystery"

Three lanterns hung from a beam in the Ladies Waiting Room, lighting up the Bordens' dissected bodies. Sergeant Harrington had his hands spread out in a useless attempt to shield the girls from the horrific sight, and to his right, Dr. Dolan—Victoria's family doctor—stood, wide eyed, scalpel in one hand, measuring stick in the other, rolled-up sleeves showing slick, bloody forearms. And there was Declan, standing at the Bordens' feet, pencil poised on his notebook, mouth gaped in shock.

The corpses were the color of dirty bread dough—except for the deep purple spots where the blood had pooled. Though headless, with private parts discreetly concealed under cloths, it was still obvious who was who: Mr. Borden's bony midsection lay sliced open like a soggy, unwrapped parcel, while his much heavier wife lay face down, her fleshy back and shoulders covered with deep brown, V-shaped wounds.

Victoria could not move, speak, breathe.

Gwyne screamed and fled from the shadowy room.

"Victoria!" Declan sprang forward, his notebook making a dull thud as it hit the dirt floor, and Dr. Dolan fumbled with the blood-stained sheets, trying in vain to cover the lifeless bread dough.

"Young ladies!" Sergeant Harrington yelled. "What is the meaning of this? Leave! *Immediately*."

Declan, glaring, said something to her—a question, Victoria thought. But her head and ears felt stuffed with pillow batting. He widened his eyes and lifted his palms in a "Well?" kind of manner.

"I... " she whispered. "Their heads... " She lifted one finger toward the corpses. "Where..."

Then something glinted in the lamplight, by Mr. Borden's side, and Victoria saw the gold ring Miss Lizzie had given him, still on his pinky finger. The skin on either side of the band was swollen and puffy.

"Declan!" Sergeant Harrington roared. "Get her out of here!"

Victoria snapped to life and rushed out, wondering if she would ever get the image of those two bodies out of her head.

"I told you we shouldn't have come," Gwyne whimpered, lowering herself onto the low stone wall.

Victoria, knees shaking, sank down next to her. "I'm so sorry. I had no idea they'd be in there."

"I'm just thankful you were in front of me," Gwyne said, "because all I saw was Dr. Dolan with his knife. That was enough for me. Were the bodies… covered?"

The clay-like slabs of Mr. And Mrs. Borden's headless torsos floated in Victoria's mind. They looked unreal, devoid of all likenesses to the living, breathing people she remembered. Except for that ring. Letting out a long, shaky breath, Victoria answered, "Only parts of them."

At the sound of crunching gravel, Victoria looked up to see Declan in front of her, bucket in hand.

He fished a rag from the bucket and held it out, dripping. "Here." The word was short and hard, like the small chunks of mortar at her feet.

Silently, she accepted the rag, wrung it out, and pressed it to her forehead.

"What," he whispered, bending closer, "were you thinking of, coming here? To an *autopsy*? Are you mad? Are you trying to get me kicked off the force?"

"Oh Decl—I mean, Master Dempsey, of course not!" She handed the rag to Gwyne. "I just wanted to talk to you. About Miss Lizzie. Because—"

Gwyne cleared her throat.

"Because she's been arrested and I thought—"

Gwyne cleared her throat a second time.

Victoria sighed and lifted a limp hand toward Gwyne. "I'm sorry. Master Dempsey, my friend, Miss Gwyne Jacobsen. Gwyne Jacobsen, Master Declan Dempsey. Gwyne was kind enough to accompany me."

Gwyne offered Declan her hand. "Charmed." Declan hesitated before bowing awkwardly.

Before Victoria could continue, Gwyne rushed in. "It was never our intention to interrupt your work, Master Dempsey. We came out of deep concern for our dear neighbor, Miss Lizzie."

Victoria stared at her friend's cherubic face—suddenly

bright-eyed and pink-cheeked—and had to admire her resiliency when faced with a handsome young man, even one she'd deemed ineligible. Gwyne was hardier than she acted.

"Declan," Victoria whispered, glancing toward the little stone Waiting Room. "Were my eyes deceiving me or"—she swallowed—"or were the Bordens' heads..."

"Yes, miss," he said. "Removed."

Gwyne gasped. "But it didn't say that in the newspaper. It said their heads had been crushed, not cut off."

"Goodness, Gwyne!"

Gwyne blinked, then shook her head. "I think you must be rubbing off on me, Tory."

"The decapitation," Declan said, giving a worried glance over his shoulder, "was the doctor's doing. Boiled 'em up in a pot in his own kitchen."

Victoria felt sick.

"Boiled them?" Gwyne fanned herself with her gloves once more. "Why ever would he do that?"

Declan reached a hand toward Victoria's shoulder but stopped short of touching her. "You okay, Miss Robbins? We don't have to talk about this."

The heat of the day seemed to have doubled and her gown clung to her torso like a damp second skin. Still, Victoria nodded. "I'm fine. Please, go on."

Declan took the rag from Gwyne, rewet it in the bucket, squeezed it out, and handed it to Victoria. "Dr. Dolan wanted to compare the gashes in the skulls to the blades of the axes found in the Borden's basement, and he figured it was easier to do without the scalp and hair getting in the way."

"And what did he find?" Victoria asked.

"A perfect match—the Kelly hatchet head found in the basement fits perfectly into the cuts in the skulls."

"A Kelly?" Victoria peeked up from under the damp rag. "We have one of those."

Gwyne nodded. "We do as well."

Declan sighed, kicked a small pebble. "That is one problem. It's a common brand. The other problem is that the hatchet in question had no handle, and none could be found."

Victoria sat up straighter, the hard stone bench unforgiving on her backside. "That's hardly conclusive evidence, then."

"True, but it lends credence to the—"

"Declan," Victoria interrupted, "you have to believe me. Miss Lizzie is kind and thoughtful and generous. She's active in the church; she's on the Christian Temperance board, for Pete's sake. She loves animals of every kind—she even kept pigeons in her barn loft as pets—"

"Until her father killed them," Declan broke in.

"What?" Those pigeons were like Miss Lizzie's children, and he'd *killed* them? Victoria's old hatred for Mr. Borden bubbled to the surface. "But why would he do such a thing?"

Declan shrugged. "Seems he thought they were a nuisance. Something about attracting neighborhood boys with slingshots. Wrung their necks, every last bird. Oh, hey, watch it." He pulled away the rag Victoria had clutched to her chest. "You're ruining your dress."

Victoria looked down to see a deep red soggy mark on her pink sateen. Flushing, she checked her cuffs but found no hanky. She'd left in such a hurry, she'd forgotten to retrieve Declan's from under her pillow.

He pulled a neatly folded square from his pocket and held it out.

"I'm using up all of your handkerchiefs," Victoria said, dabbing uselessly at the wet stain on her chest.

"Declan!" Across the yard, Sergeant Harrington filled the doorway of the Ladies Waiting Room. "If you're quite done playing nursemaid, we could use your help in here."

Declan colored. "Yessir!" He ran his fingers through his hair, but the one curl refused to cooperate and bounced back over his eye.

"Please," Victoria whispered. "Surely her love of animals

says something about her character?"

"I'm afraid it does, miss," Declan said, taking a step backward. "But not in a good way. We detectives look for motives, and when it comes to instances of overkill, a very common one"—his shoulders eased into a reluctant shrug—"is revenge."

Wide-eyed, Victoria jumped up. "Surely you can't think she'd kill him over a few birds! She forgave her father, I'm sure. She—"

Sergeant Harrington bellowed Declan's name again.

"Sorry, Miss Robbins, Miss Jacobsen," he whispered. "Just leave the bucket and rag—I'll collect 'em when you're done." Then he turned and jogged away, back to the bodies with no heads.

THE FOOTPATH OUT of the cemetery was strewn with dusty gravel and sun-burnt rose petals, filling Victoria's nose with an acrid smell.

"Goodness," Gwyne sighed, walking beside Victoria. "When you said I needed a little excitement in my life, that was not what I had in mind."

Victoria gave a rueful laugh. "I am so sorry, Gwyne. That was not the kind of excitement I'd intended either." She shook her head, trying to clear the images of dead bodies, both human and bird, from her mind. Severed heads, wrung necks. And the real-ness of it, not in a story, not made-up. It was all too gruesome. Meanwhile, Miss Lizzie was sitting in a cell somewhere, alone, with these images and worse, swirling around in her memory. Guilt pricked at Victoria's conscience as she remembered asking Miss Lizzie a month or so ago why she didn't keep pigeons anymore. No wonder she hadn't answered.

"And what a shame your Declan is an Irishman," Gwyne continued, kicking her skirts as she walked to give her ankles some air. "Because you two would make quite a match."

Victoria stopped in her tracks and gave her friend an incredulous look. "You amaze me, Gwyndolyn Jacobsen!"

"Why, thank you." Gwyne dipped a shallow curtsy.

"No, truly, Gwyne! Headless bodies, murdered pigeons, and your first thought is that the detective's son and I make an attractive couple?" She laughed again.

"Of course it was not my *first* thought," Gwyne whispered as they stepped aside to let a woman pushing a baby pram to pass. "It was *a* thought. One of many. But, honestly, Victoria, you have to start thinking of your future. I want us to be in each other's weddings, have children at the same time, go on family picnics and holidays together. And in order to do that, you have to put in at least a little effort in finding a husband. You don't want us to be separated, in two different worlds, do you?"

The thought of being without Gwyne made Victoria feel hollow. She slipped her arm through Gwyne's. "Of course not."

"Good. Then I have a proposal for you."

Victoria frowned. "What kind of proposal?"

Gwyne pulled Victoria off to the side of the boardwalk, out of the way of the busy shoppers clomping past.

"*I* will accompany you on your errands to help Miss Lizzie…" Gwyne said.

Victoria eyebrows raised. It would be lovely to have her best friend with her and not have to suffer through Mr. Pottersmith's snail pace, or be forced to sneak about. "If?"

"If *you* agree to a joint Coming-Out party. At GG's." Gwyne smiled widely. "GG and I worked it all out. She and her best friend were presented to the Queen, along with a handful of other girls debuting that season, and says it is her very favorite memory."

GG's grand parlor swam before Victoria's eyes, the glowing bit of blue on the shelf filling her with dread.

"Of course, our debut will be a thoroughly modern affair," Gwyne continued. "No queen kissing our foreheads, no feathers in our hair, no reversing out of the room so as not to show our backsides. We shall invite only the most handsome and eligible young men, as well as our girlfriends from school. We will employ the grandest musicians in Fall River, offer the most scrumptious and elaborate spread, and it will be the most magical night ever!"

Victoria hesitated. "My mother…"

"Has always planned on you making your debut," Gwyne said, grabbing her hand and squeezing, "and would be broken-hearted if you didn't because of her."

Victoria bit her lip. Gwyne was right, of course.

"Please say yes, Victoria. Debuting at Chateau D'usse! In front of all our friends from school! I doubt anyone in our class will be as lucky."

The blue snuff box glowed brighter in Victoria's memory. Surely if there was one temptation, there would be many. "But Gwyne, GG has so many… breakables. Wouldn't she be afraid of someone knocking over a crystal vase? Or putting out their cigar in an African tribal bowl?"

Gwyne laughed. "We wouldn't be dancing in the parlor, Tory. She has a ballroom for that. My entire house could fit in that room. So, do we have a deal? Or would you rather drag poor old Mr. Pottersmith around with you on all your errands?"

It was just one evening, and one with plenty of distractions—music, dancing, tables groaning with sweets and drink, Gwyne chattering about which young man was the best dancer, had the best job, the nicest smile. And more immediately important, Gwyne would come with her on all of her errands to help Miss Lizzie. Certainly, the seriousness of this work would help her move past her childish game. She'd be older, level-headed, responsible.

Before she could answer, a little boy of about eight led a large group of fashionable young couples past them, calling over his shoulder, "Jest a few streets further now, to the lady murderer's house."

A tour guide? "Hey now!" Victoria shook a finger at him,

which he ignored.

Tapping Victoria's arm, Gwyne gently added, "Think how happy it would make your mother, Tory." Her concerned gaze melted Victoria's heart. What a good friend she was!

"Oh, Gwyne, you're right. Maybe that's just the thing she needs, something to look forward to. And it does sound wonderful." She took Gwyne's hand and squeezed it.

Just stay out of the parlor, she thought, *and you'll be fine.*

"Then you'll do it?"

Victoria nodded. Gwyne enveloped Victoria in a tight hug, hopping around and jostling them every which way. "Oh, Tory, we are going to have so much fun! Come on, let's celebrate!"

A few minutes later, the girls were on their way home, celebratory lemon sticks in hand, Gwyne listing possible themes and related food for their party. Victoria strained to listen over the roaring in her ears and thudding of her chest. It took two full blocks to loosen her grip on the stolen gumdrops. Glancing back, she saw the dots of red and green nestled in the dirt along the edge of the boardwalk.

CHAPTER THIRTEEN

A full bladder awoke Victoria early the next morning as well as a sharp pain her cheek— her father's cufflinks she'd stuffed into her pillowcase. She rubbed the tender spot, remembering yesterday's stolen candy. "Serves you right," she whispered.

Why, oh why was it so difficult for her to stop taking things? Especially since they were things she had no use for. She didn't even like gumdrops! She dug the cufflinks out of the pillowcase and studied them. It wasn't the item itself, she realized, as much as the feeling she got stealing the item. It was as if she were a pot-bellied stove in the morning, all cinders, faintly glowing. But add a stick of kindling, a little air, and poof! A flame erupts. That's how it felt each time she pocketed something—a burst of fire in her chest.

But fire can also destroy. She'd been lucky so far, but luck only lasts so long. And how selfish, to be wrapped up in her own childish high jinks while her dear Miss Lizzie languished behind bars!

"Get busy, Victoria," she muttered. "You've got a friend to

save." Slipping the silver studs into her robe pocket, she tiptoed down the back stairs, used the toilet, then headed outside.

As usual, the shed's tang of rusty tools and baked dirt brought on the delicious, secretive feelings of her childhood, but this time, she fought it. *It's just a shed, Victoria. With a box full of junk.* Outside the mottled windows, birds flitted about in the misty morning, and the sky seemed indecisive about which color it should be: pink, orange, or yellow. Miss Lizzie's strong alto voice came to mind, singing, *Morning has broken, like the first morning...*

Eyes burning, Victoria dug up the hatbox, skipped the three kisses and secrecy pledge, and dropped the cufflinks in. "Last time," she whispered, hastily kicking dirt back over the lid before slipping out the partially open door. She'd only taken a few steps when she heard her name whispered. She froze.

A figure stepped out from behind the low hanging tree branches, making her yelp. "Declan!" She pulled the lapels of her robe close to her neck. "What are you doing here?"

Declan ran his hand across his tangled curls, eyes full of concern. "Very sorry, miss. I didn't mean to frighten you. I was up in the Bordens' barn, checking out Miss Lizzie's alibi and—"

"This early?" Victoria interrupted. She took a few steps, trying to distance herself from the shed.

"It's the best time to think," Declan said, "without Father at my elbow, giving me his opinions. Anyway, I saw you running from the house and thought there might be trouble. Is everything okay?" He leaned to the side and peered around her to the shed.

"Oh, yes, fine, fine." Her mind raced. "I was just... that is, I thought I saw Gwyne's cat, Mousie. She's been missing and Gwyne's been worried sick about her and..." She shook her head and took a few more steps toward the house. "Mother would be horrified if she knew I'd come outside in my dressing gown."

Declan pointed at the dilapidated shed. "So, was the cat inside? Do you want me to—"

"No!" Victoria smiled, trying to appear calmer than she felt. "Thank you, no. As soon as I went in, Mousie slipped out, so there's no need. Please," she said, "go back to your investigation and help Miss Lizzie."

With one last glance at the shed, Declan nodded reluctantly. "I'm trying, but as I told you yesterday…"

"I am so sorry if I got you into trouble. I just didn't know who else to ask."

Declan shook his head. "Nothing I can't handle, miss."

A flickering light caught Victoria's eye. Penelope's third floor window, which was open, glowed with faint candlelight. She would soon be down in the kitchen. Victoria silently pointed to the window and then held a finger to her lips.

Nodding, he added in a whisper, "If you really want to help your friend, you need to see if she'll open up to you. She is tight-lipped with us, and it's not helping her case at all. In a few weeks, Judge Blaisdell will decide if there's enough evidence to bring her to trial and right now, all the evidence is against her."

"What happened to 'innocent until proven guilty?'"

"That's for the jury trial. The preliminary hearing is just to establish probable cause. If she could provide something—anything—that would point to her innocence, or to someone else's possible guilt, she might be able to have the charges dismissed. If her defense can show there's at least a fifty percent chance she was not involved, she will walk. Otherwise..." He shook his head.

Victoria pictured the foul-smelling police department. "I tried to visit, but the awful man at the desk told me visits were for family and lawyers only."

He nodded. "They've given her a private cell now, her being a Borden and all. I'll make sure your name is on the visitor's list." The twinkle in his eye made Victoria's heart skip. "A real list this time."

Victoria couldn't hide her smile. "Add my friend Gwyne Jacobsen's name too. She'll be accompanying me."

"Will do. Let me know if you learn anything useful. And I'll pass it on to her defense team." With a tip of his hat, he turned and jogged off toward the Bordens.

It was decided then. She would visit Miss Lizzie, who could probably stand to see a friendly face. Hopefully, she would be back to her old self and Victoria would be able to find out something that would help prove her innocence and set her free.

THE *FALL RIVER Gazette* headlines that morning paper shouted, "Who Wrote Mrs. Borden a Note?", the contents of which rattled Victoria so much, she began slicing the breakfast sourdough for Penelope just to give her hands something to do. The dining table bell tinkled.

"Good mornin', sir," Penelope said, poking her head out the door. "I'll have your tea out quick as a cricket."

"Good morning, Father," Victoria called from the kitchen. "I'll join you in a minute."

"Don't bother, dear," came her father's reply. "I just have time for a cup of tea. Your mother is waiting for her breakfast, so see to her. And don't make any plans for today because Penelope is meeting her sister's ship."

Victoria widened her eyes at Penelope. "Your sister! I'd completely forgotten. Good for you!" But what about her visit to Miss Lizzie? "Father? Perhaps you could stay with Mother for a bit? I have an appointment."

"Break it" was his reply. "I've got piles of work to catch up on in town."

Maybe if you stayed in town, you'd be all caught up. "But Father…"

Penelope, wrapping the end of her apron around her hand and lifting the steaming tea kettle, gave her a sympathetic look. "Sorry," she whispered. "I'd stay if I could." A stream of hot water bubbled from the spout, filling the silver teapot.

"Don't be selfish, Victoria," Father called. "You need to do your share."

My share? She stared at the steaming teapot and imagined emptying it over his head.

Penelope shook her head in a *don't listen to him* type of way.

"And by the way," Father added, "where's today's newspaper?"

Glaring at the wall that separated them, Victoria snatched the *Fall River Gazette* off the table, tore out the Borden article and stuck it into her apron pocket.

"The paper?" Silently, she opened the stove door and shoved the *Gazette* into the flames. Penelope's eyes shot open but Victoria put a finger to her lips. "I have no idea."

THE DAY WAS long, hot, and tedious, made worse by her urgent wish to visit Miss Lizzie. The longer she spent locked up, the more guilty she would appear. Time was a wasting!

Half-past four, Victoria found herself seated at her mother's bedside. Wiping the perspiration off her mother's damp face, Victoria turned the page and read aloud the final poem.

"I never lost as much but twice,
And that was in the sod;
Twice have I stood a beggar
Before the door of God!
Angels, twice descending,
Reimbursed my store.
Burglar, banker, father,
I am poor once more!"

Frowning, Victoria sat back. "I'm not sure I understand. Is Miss Dickinson saying that her own father robbed her, along with the banker and the burglar, or is she saying she's actually died twice—knocked on God's door—and got a second chance?"

Mother stared at her, not blinking. She had small wet curls plastered to her temples.

"Sorry," Victoria said, shaking her head. "That was two questions." She tried to arrange her thoughts into a question her mother could answer with a yes or no but found the late afternoon heat had drained her last ounce of energy. "I think," she said, setting the book aside, "I will check to see if Penelope has left us anything in the larder for supper. If not, I'm afraid you will be suffering my questionable culinary skills."

As she stood and stretched, she thought she saw, for just a moment, Mother's lips curve upward.

"Mother! Did you just begin to smile?"

Too-large eyes stared back at her, blankly, then blinked twice. No.

She straightened her mother's blanket. "Never mind. I'll see what I can rustle up for us to eat."

As she descended the back stairwell, Dr. Appelbaum's admonishment to her mother swirled in her mind. While he was wrong about Mother, that Freud fellow he'd mentioned had an interesting theory. That your mind could shut down your body because of something you couldn't or didn't want to remember... Interesting but far-fetched. Perhaps it was something like Aunt Frieda breaking out in a rash when she ate strawberries, but with Mother, whatever she ate made her muscles stiffen up.

There was nothing in the ice box but ice, so Victoria chipped off a few chunks and added them to a glass of water, which she took out onto the front porch. *Just for a few minutes,* she thought, lowering herself into the wicker rocker. *A little time to myself.* Forced cheerfulness was exhausting.

Hoarse from reading aloud, Victoria relished the icy water soothing her throat, and her ears welcomed all the sounds that were not her own voice: tinny clanks of hammers upon horseshoes, rocks spewing out from rattling carriage wheels, shouts of children playing down the street, dogs barking. How differently this pleasant din would sound from inside a jail cell.

Finally, the mill whistles hooted their dissonant five o'clock chord. Time to put together something for supper. As she stood, she saw Declan and his father coming down the sidewalk from the Bordens. Quickly, she pinched her cheeks and smoothed her hair and began fussing with the potted geraniums, pulling off the dead blooms and fishing out cigar butts left from the crowds. When Declan called out a greeting to her, she feigned surprise.

"Hello Master Dempsey. Detective."

Declan said something to his father and headed up Victoria's walk.

Her heart raced as she descended the steps.

"I've something for you." He reached into his jacket.

"Not another hanky, I hope, for I already have quite a collection of yours to return."

Declan laughed and pulled out a folded magazine. "Came in the mail today—the latest *Strand*." He presented it to her with a humble bow. "Complete with Sherlock's next case."

"Oh, but you mustn't!"

"Don't worry," Declan assured her. "I read it on my lunch break and it's one of Doyle's better ones. I think you'll enjoy it."

She felt her cheeks color as she accepted the gift. "This is very kind of you."

"Well, couldn't have you waiting for weeks while I had a copy right here." He glanced over his shoulder toward his father, who was flagging down Hennimen's Bakery Cart. The smells of onion and rosemary wafting on the breeze made Victoria's stomach growl.

"Did you get a chance to speak to your friend today?"

Victoria ran her fingers down the spine of the magazine, her glow from his thoughtfulness dimming somewhat at the reminder of her delayed course of action. "No, I'm afraid I was detained."

Nodding, Declan said, "It's just as well, as we have a new

wrinkle in the case. I'm hoping you could ask her about it when you do visit." He explained that police questioned Miss Lizzie as to why she called for the maid instead of her stepmother when she'd found her father murdered. Lizzie claimed her stepmother had told her she'd received a note from a sick friend and was going out to call on this friend. However, no such note was found, and no sick friend had stepped forward.

Victoria frowned. "Implying she called for Bridget because she knew her stepmother was already dead, perhaps because she had been the one to kill her."

Behind them, Mrs. Bowen and Mr. Hall from the stable had joined Declan's father at the food cart, and they were all carrying on a lively conversation.

Declan sighed. "I'm afraid so. But if we could find that note or the person that supposedly wrote it—"

Detective Dempsey called to Declan, holding up a newsprint-wrapped meat pie in each hand. Declan nodded to him, then turned back to Victoria.

"Ask her about the note," he said, his voice low. "If you find out anything, flag me down and I'll find a way for us to speak. Alone." His green eyes held hers.

She could only nod, her face hot as a skillet.

AFTER DINNER, VICTORIA took a blank ledger book from her father's study, a jar of bone glue, and a pile of newspaper articles she'd been saving—including the crumpled one in her apron—and began a scrapbook of everything written on the Borden case. She was having trouble keeping the information surrounding the case straight in her mind, so laying out what the papers said plus her own handwritten notes from conversations with Declan and her own observations should help her think. As she pasted and cut and wrote, she felt a renewed sense of hope and purpose. She had a job to do, like a real adult.

And she was doing it.

FALL RIVER HERALD
Significant Disappearance

That letter of which mention was made Thursday as having been sent to Mrs. Borden, announcing that a friend was sick, has since disappeared. The explanation that was given out was that after reading its contents, Mrs. Borden tore it up and threw the pieces in the fire. Bits of charred paper were found in the grate, but not enough to give any idea of the nature of the note.

Nobody about the house seems to know where the letter could have come from; and since publicity has been given and considerable importance attached to it, it is considered probable that the writer will inform the family of the circumstances and thus remove suspicions.

CHAPTER FOURTEEN

That night, Victoria's slumber was jarred awake by a startled whinny from the barn—Admiral, Father's horse, whom he claimed was better than a watchdog.
Immediately, the cricket song dimmed.

Father wasn't just coming home now, was he? She listened for the creaking of the barn door but then remembered Father hadn't taken Admiral to town, he'd walked.

She plumped her pillow and, when no further noise reached her, decided a raccoon had spooked Admiral.

There was another whinny then, higher pitched. Wings flapped and tree branches creaked.

Victoria rubbed her eyes. Slipping out of bed, she went to the window to check.

Light flickered next to the Bordens' barn. An odd sound accompanied the light, which Victoria realized was the crunch of a spade piercing the ground, then the swish of dirt sliding off the blade. *Crunch. Swish. Crunch. Swish.*

Goosebumps prickled up her arms. Someone was digging in Miss Lizzie's yard.

A Bible verse popped to mind, one she'd heard Miss Lizzie quote more than once in her Sunday School room: "Men loved darkness rather than light, because their deeds were evil."

Evil deeds going on in the Bordens' yard—there could be no other reason to be working in the dead of night. Were they burying something or digging something up?

Victoria clutched her arms, shivering. She could sneak out, see who it was and what he was burying or digging up, and report him to Declan in the morning. Miss Lizzie could be free by lunchtime tomorrow!

Snatching her robe, she gave the flickering light one last glance and hurried out of her room.

VICTORIA CROUCHED BEHIND the Bordens' fence, her slippers soaked from the dewy grass and her whole body shaking. On the other side of thin boards could very well be the person who'd smashed in the Bordens' heads. *Fifteen times or more,* Penelope had said, *when one or two would have done the job nicely.* For a moment, Victoria considered running back to see if Father was home. *No,* she told herself, *you're already here. Just take a quick look and go.*

Carefully placing her fingertips on two adjoining fence boards, Victoria leaned forward and put her eye up to the crack. She saw not one but three shadowy forms—two of them shin deep in a hole, grunting with each stab of their shovels and the third partially obscured by a tree trunk, puffing on a cigarette, the tip glowing bright red. Hanging from a low tree branch, a small kerosene lamp sputtered, throwing jittery shadows across the ground.

The two diggers wore their caps pulled down low, making it impossible to distinguish their faces. Did the one on the right have a beard? Or maybe it was a mustache. It was hard to tell.

Cr-runch. Swish.

Cr-runch. Swish.
Cr-runch. Swish.
Thunk.

"Gentlemen, we have arrived." The smoking man dropped his cigarette and ground it out with his toe. "All right, give it here, men, and we'll check it while you fill that hole back up." He seemed to be the leader, so maybe he was the one who held the grudge against the Bordens. Maybe he'd killed them or had these other men do the killing. Victoria held her breath, waiting to catch a glimpse of his face.

The diggers did as they were told, dropping an old shoe crate at the smoking man's feet, then returned to their shovels. Victoria peered at the crate. An axe could easily fit in that box. Several axes. How she wished she could see the smoking man's face.

"Hey, Junior," the smoker whispered int the darkness. "What're ya doing, taking a nap?"

A few yards off, a dark lump Victoria had passed off as a bush unfolded itself. "I'm here," it groaned, stretching.

"Aw," said one of the diggers, "are we keeping you out past your bedtime?"

The other digger snorted.

When the figure passed under the small circle of lamplight, Victoria gasped. She clamped her hand over her mouth, but it was too late.

The smoker, the diggers, and Declan, with his unmistakable curl dangling over one eye, turned toward the fence.

"Did you hear something?" When the smoker held up the lantern, Victoria ducked away from the crack, knees quaking.

"Look." Declan's voice, in a loud whisper. "Over there."

Victoria held her breath. Her eyes began to water. She prayed they could not see her through the cracks.

"Filthy possums," the smoker muttered.

"Full a disease," the digger agreed.

Victoria let out a shaky breath.

"Come on, let's get this over with," said the third man. "We gotta get Junior here to bed."

The men laughed. There was a squeaking, the sound of a pry bar on wood. When Victoria chanced another peek through the fence, she saw the lid on the ground and Declan leaning over the box, his face aglow in lamplight. He had his hand in the box and seemed to be moving things around.

"Dress, aprons, shirt—looks like it's all here."

"Good, make a note of everything and we'll take the whole box with us."

Declan named off the items as he wrote. "Necktie, towels, sheet, napkin, rags, pillow. Even this." He lifted up what looked to be a length of yarn with a small disc at the end.

The smoker leaned in with the lantern. He had a beak-like nose. "What in the bloody hell is that?"

"Mrs. Borden's hair," Declan said, "along with a chunk of her skull."

Victoria jerked back, sickened by the sight, and lost her footing. She fell sideways, knocking the wooden fence and landing with a loud "Oof!"

"Now that there's no possum," called one man. The scuff of footsteps approached.

Scrambling to her feet, she stuck to the shadows and managed to stumble across the yards without being caught. A minute later, she was leaning against her closed bedroom door, panting. Her mind raced, trying to make sense of what she'd just witnessed, trying to think of a good, legitimate reason for Declan to be digging up the Bordens' private things with those horrible men. Kicking off her wet slippers, Victoria dug through her dresser drawers for a pair of wool stockings to warm her icy feet. With shaking hands she struggled to put them on, the wool clinging stubbornly to her damp skin.

Oh, Declan! How thrilled she'd been *just that day* when he said he wished to talk to her, alone. And now here he was, stealing! The irony was not lost on her. Surely if he'd been doing detective business, wouldn't his father have been with him, as well as a few uniformed men? And they'd be working during the day, not under a cloak of darkness.

Her heart sunk as she considered the possibility of Declan playing both sides of the law, getting information as a detective and then using it or selling it to these awful men. But what kind of information could come from some bloody clothes and rags? Victoria pulled a throw pillow to her chest and hugged it, staring across at the Bordens' dark house. She wondered who had buried the box, and why. Perhaps Miss Emma or Bridget or even Miss Lizzie before her arrest. Perhaps they couldn't bring themselves to get rid of the items, yet couldn't stand to look at them either. But to go to all the trouble to bury them? Why not stick the box in the cellar, out of sight? She quickly banished an image of her own treasure box in the potting shed.

"So," she whispered, her warm breath fogging up the cool glass, "if they weren't buried for their sentimental value, could they be worth money somehow?" She grimaced. The traveling circus came to mind, people standing in long lines and paying good money to see Allie the Alligator Boy, Armless Betty—*She Writes With Her Feet!*—the Pinhead Twins, and the worst, a stillborn baby with an enlarged head, floating upside down in a giant pickle jar. And how about that enterprising boy, earning a few pennies by leading his charges to the 'murder house'?

Yes, she decided, shivering, there probably would be someone willing to pay for such a grisly souvenir.

Victoria rubbed her toes, still cold in spite of the stockings, still numb in spite of the mild evening air. The only other possibility was if those items held incriminating evidence, and the person burying it was either the murderer himself, or someone bribing the murderer. But to bury it at the scene rather than take it with you?

And what about Declan, with those lovely green eyes and that teasing grin—the hankies, the magazines, the shared love of Sherlock Holmes?

Crawling into bed, she snuggled down like she used to in a lightning storm, covers overhead, toes touching the footboard, shaky breaths filling the small pocket of air, the darkness absolute, the same with eyes open or closed.

She had to look at the facts, like Sherlock, and not let her heart interfere. The facts were:

1. Declan was part of a group digging up the Bordens' bloody clothes—and hair.

2. They did it under cloak of darkness.

3. They carted the items away.

4. They did all this while Miss Lizzie was locked up and unable to stop them.

The only conclusion one could safely draw was that Declan and his pals were shin-deep in some sort of evil.

CHAPTER FIFTEEN

Officer Fenley, the three-fingered policeman, peered at Victoria and Gwyne across his large messy desk, a halo of dust mites dancing in the sunlight around him. A faint smell of urine and tobacco hung in the air, while officers looked up from whatever they were doing—writing, interviewing, gossiping—with expectant looks on their faces. Declan was nowhere in sight.

"Well, good morning to you again, little ladies," crooned Officer Fenley, fiddling with several puddingstones on his desk, the pebbles embedded in the sandstone like raisins in a pudding. "Still hot on the trail of our young Master Dempsey, then?" His grin revealed bits of breakfast, or perhaps last night's dinner, tucked between a few of his teeth. "Ah," he added, noticing the dishtowel-covered plate in Victoria's hands, "and bringing him his lunch! The way to a man's heart, that."

"An' if he don't want it," called a barrel-bellied policeman from the back, "I'll take it!"

A ripple of laughter passed through the room.

Victoria ignored the remark and the laughter. "I am doing

nothing of the sort," she snapped. "I am here, or, rather, *we* are here," she tilted her head to Gwyne, who gave the shallowest of curtsies, "to visit our neighbor, Miss Lizzie Borden. Our names are on the visitor list. Victoria Robbins and Gwyne Jacobsen." Victoria had only told Gwyne they were making a morale-boosting visit to Miss Lizzie, figuring if her friend knew about the diggers, she'd refuse to leave the house.

"Oooh," Officer Fenley chuckled, finding their names in his book. "Calling on a murderess, now. I'll give it to you, miss, you are a plucky one." He straightened a stack of papers and picked a medium-sized rock to use as a paperweight.

Victoria gripped the plate. "Miss Lizzie is nothing of the sort! If any of you would just take the time to listen…" Declan's handsome face floated before her, boosting her irritation. *Traitor.*

"If I were you, miss," the officer whispered, placing his three fingers beside his mouth, as if telling her a secret, "I'd stick with the folks on the abiding side of the law. You were on the right path before, chasing our Declan."

Gwyne let out a small squeak.

"*Chasing?*" Victoria gasped. "That scoundrel? You must be joking," she said, tugging on the hem of her day jacket, straightening it. "I would no more chase after Master Dempsey than I would… would… jump into the Quequechan!"

From around the room came a few muffled coughs.

"Victoria," Gwyne whispered, squeezing Victoria's elbow.

Turning, she looked past Gwyne's alarmed expression to Declan, arms crossed over his chest, his green eyes hard as jade. Heart pounding, she returned his look. How dare he look insulted. He *was* a scoundrel, hoodwinking her into believing he was on her side. The question *What were you doing last night?* circled her brain, begging to be released, but this was not the time, not in front of all these policemen who might very well be a part of it, whatever *it* was.

Declan gave her a curt nod and strode out of the building.

For a moment, Victoria stared after him, wishing she'd never seen him with those awful men, wishing she'd snuck back home before he'd come out of the shadows. Or that the boy she'd seen was not Declan at all but his identical twin, and that the real Declan knew nothing about the unearthing. But of course, that was all stuff and nonsense. She thought of Sherlock, after being tricked by a rich man posing as a beggar, said, "Better to learn wisdom late than never to learn it at all."

Her throat ached. She had to concentrate on keeping the quiver out of her voice as she faced Officer Fenley once more. "So, are you going to let us see Miss Borden or not?"

The officer tilted his head toward the door from which Declan just exited. "Tha' wasn't very nice, miss. He's a good egg, that one."

"A good egg?" Hysteria began to rise up her throat. "You wouldn't know a good egg if you sat on one!" She regretted the words as soon as they left her mouth. But it was true! He probably knew all about Declan's escapade; they probably all did.

"You'll have to forgive her, officer," Gwyne said, jumping in. "As neighbors of the Bordens, this whole ordeal has put us all on edge, as I'm sure you can imagine."

Victoria resented how her friend's words placed her in the role of the hysterical female, but after all she'd witnessed, she saw the wisdom of Gwyne's tactics.

"So if you'd be so kind as to show us the way to Miss Borden, sir," Gwyne continued sweetly, "to enable us to perform our Christian duty...?"

"Well, all right," Officer Fenley grumped, giving Victoria a sideways glance, "but you should teach your friend here some manners."

Victoria pressed her lips tightly shut, hating Officer Fenley for thinking he had gotten the last word. She placed the plate of biscuits down on the premise of straightening her hat. In picking it back up, she scooped the smallest puddingstone as well. Easy as a game of jacks.

AS WELL-DRESSED and coifed as ever, Miss Lizzie looked ridiculously out of place in the dismal cell, as did the embroidered "B" towel lying next to a rusted wash basin and the flowered oil lamp from her parlor at home. A rectangle of thin, milky light came in through the one small window near the ceiling and landed on a pair of blue silk slippers lined up at the foot of the cot. The skinny-necked police officer who had escorted them had explained her holding cell was reserved for "special" prisoners.

"Victoria!" Miss Lizzie stood up from her bunk, where she'd been reading her Bible. "What are you doing here?" Frowning, she patted her hair with one hand and held her Bible in the other, one finger holding her spot, as if she wished to continue reading.

Victoria was taken aback—she'd been expecting a much warmer welcome—but she hugged her friend anyway, grateful she looked and sounded like her old self. Up close, however, Miss Lizzie did not smell like her old self, and Victoria wondered how often prisoners were allowed to bathe or change clothes.

"You know our neighbor, Gwyne Jacobsen, don't you?"

Gwyne curtsied.

"I believe," Miss Lizzie said, squinting, "you were in my Sunday School class some years ago?"

Gwyne blushed. "Yes'm."

"It's thanks to Gwyne that we are here at all. I lost my temper with that horrible Officer Fenley, but she used her feminine wiles to gain us entry." With a flush of guilt, Victoria's fingers touched her waistband where she'd tucked the stone.

Behind them, the cell door slammed shut. The clunk of each bolt, three in all, echoed in Victoria's chest and suddenly, she saw herself alone in the cell, her secret habit known to all.

Forcing the image from her mind, she presented Penelope's

baking powder biscuits. "I hope you'll be home before you get the chance to enjoy them."

Sighing, Miss Lizzie lay her Bible aside before accepting a biscuit and lowering herself onto her bunk. "Emma always said our mother—our real mother—made the best baking powder biscuits." She chewed thoughtfully, turning the biscuit one way and then the other, examining it between bites. "These are quite good. Perhaps I should give a few to the judge. Maybe then he'll decide there's insufficient evidence for a trial." She gave a wry smile and patted the wool blanket beside her.

Hesitantly, Gwyne took a seat, but Victoria continued to stand. "I've been studying all of the articles about the case and realize the only evidence they have against you is circumstantial. You were home." She ticked off one finger. "You found your father. No one else was seen coming to or leaving your house. And there's a handless axe in the cellar that fits the wounds." She held up four fingers. "Am I missing anything?"

Miss Lizzie gave a half-hearted shrug. "I don't think so."

"Sorry," Gwyne said. "But isn't all that true of your maid as well? Except the finding your father part." She helped herself to a biscuit.

"My thoughts exactly, Gwyne." Victoria nodded. "What if—"

"Oh, Victoria." Miss Lizzie gave her a disapproving look. "Maggie would never do such a thing." She pulled a hanky from her cuff and dabbed her nose.

"I'm not saying she would, only that she could. That she had the same opportunity you did."

"No. I won't hear a word spoken against our Maggie."

"Maggie," Victoria breathed, squinting with concentration. "Hmmm."

Gwyne, brushing crumbs off her skirt, said, "You call your Bridget by her birth name? That's quite noble. Tory's family is the only one I know who doesn't just call their maid Bridget."

"Actually," Miss Lizzie said, clearing her throat, "her birth name *is* Bridget. Emma and I call her Maggie after our old childhood maid."

Victoria deflated a bit. Her mind had been racing with a hypotheis that being called the wrong name had built resentment, and then being asked to wash windows on that hot day and while ill had caused the maid to snap. But no.

"Well, if not Maggie, then who else? Not to be disrespectful, Miss Lizzie, but is it possible your father had an enemy or two?" She held back from saying how he was known for being a tight-fisted employer.

"I told the police I'd heard Father arguing with a man just the day before the murders. Father refused to lease him one of his buildings, and the man was quite upset. But since I did not catch a glimpse of this man, they seemed to dismiss it." She then spoke of hearing about a "wild faced" man seen by Dr. Handy staggering down the street the day of the murders; and another man, sighted in Steepbrook Woods wielding a hatchet and muttering about "poor Mrs. Borden." Also, a neighbor reported seeing a horse carriage parked down the block for an extended period of time the day of the murders, but the police attributed it to one of Dr. Kelly's patients.

She shook her head. "I just don't understand. There have been many leads, yet they seem to have set their minds on me."

Detective Dempsey's words came back to Victoria. *Once you have the answer you need, you stop asking questions.* It just wasn't fair!

Victoria swallowed. "Speaking of leads, I've been thinking about the note your stepmother received from her sick friend. If we could find the note or learn who it was from, that would give credence to your story. And it could point to someone else trying to draw her out of the house."

Miss Lizzie waved all these questions away with one word. "Inconsequential."

"But..."

Miss Lizzie's stern look silenced Victoria. Why was she

being so stubbornly unhelpful? Victoria's brain turned like the gears of a clock as she paced the floor of the small cell. The man in charge of the digging—could he have been the man arguing with Mr. Borden? Or the staggering man, or the bloodied man in the woods? Had there been a note or not? And how do the box of clothes fit in?

Gwyne, already looking bored, offered Miss Lizzie another biscuit and then took another herself.

"My other thought was about your uncle."

"Victoria!" Miss Lizzie looked up sharply. "How could you say such a thing?"

"I'm sorry, Miss Lizzie, but we can't afford to rule anyone out. He was there that morning. I saw him myself." Victoria pictured the tall, gaunt man with his long chin and deep-set eyes, whose visits, Miss Lizzie used to joke, always seemed to occur just as they sat down to eat. If guilt could be based on looks alone, Victoria would have put her money on him. "I understand he has an alibi, but perhaps he paid someone else to do the deed."

Lizzie shook her head. "Absolutely not. He's my mother's brother. My only living tie to her."

"Which," Victoria said, nodding, "could be his motive." She began pacing again. "What if he was jealous of your father's generosity towards your stepmother? Didn't I hear your father bought a house for her relatives? Maybe Uncle Morse felt your stepmother was getting what was due his sister, or her daughters, you and Emma? I mean, let's not forget, she was killed first."

"Impossible!" Miss Lizzie slapped her thighs. "I won't have you talking about him like this. He got along very well with my stepmother."

"Miss Lizzie," Victoria said, sighing. "I admire your family loyalty, I really do. But don't you see? We must show the judge there are other possible suspects."

Miss Lizzie straightend and raised her chin. "I will not point the finger at others in order to save my own neck, Victoria. The truth will win out."

Victoria saw from the set of Miss Lizzie's jaw that it was useless to continue in this vein. Time for a change in tactics. She sat down next to Miss Lizzie, the wooden cot frame creaking disconcertingly.

"Miss Lizzie, I have a question of a very delicate nature. And I only ask because there's a chance it might shed some light on this case."

Gwyne leaned forward, and Miss Lizzie leaned back, wary.

Victoria took a deep breath and blew it out. "Do you know what was done with your father's and stepmother's clothes? The ones they were wearing when they were, um—"

"Murdered," Miss Lizzie said. "You can say murdered."

"Yes, when they were murdered."

"I can't say as I recall at the moment." The older woman did not meet Victoria's gaze.

"They were buried," Victoria said quietly. "In a box, in your yard."

Gwyne gasped but Miss Lizzie, her mouth pursed tightly, did not move. Then she blinked, rapidly. "Of course. I remember now."

Victoria squinted at her. "And did Miss Emma know? And Bridget and your uncle?"

Again, a moment's hesitation before Miss Lizzie made a scoffing noise. "Of course. We... all did."

Did she really know? Victoria couldn't tell. Why would she lie about it?

"Why?" Gwyne asked, her nose scrunched at the thought of it. "Why would anyone bury all of that?"

Miss Lizzie bristled. "Goodness, child!" She balled up her hanky and began blotting her forehead. "I daresay that is none of your business. And now I am recalling you better," she added, scowling at Gwyne. "Didn't you spend a good deal of time in the corner of my classroom, facing the wall for speaking out of turn?"

Blotches of pink flared on Gwyne's cheeks and Victoria was taken aback by this change in Miss Lizzie's demeanor.

"Oh, Miss Lizzie," Victoria said, "please don't be upset. We're only trying to help. And understand."

Miss Lizzie did not answer. The pale yellow hanky in her fingers was twisted into a pig's tail.

Victoria lay a hand on top of Miss Lizzie's. "I'm only bringing it up because I saw someone—well, several someones—dig up the box and cart it away. I was hoping you could tell me why."

Miss Lizzie froze, her pursed look returning. When she spoke, her voice was tight, controlled. "My dears, I have not slept well since my arrival here, as you can well imagine, and at the moment, I am feeling quite worn through. If you don't mind, I'd like to take a rest."

Victoria and Gwyne exchanged glances. Murmuring their apologies, they carefully rose, the cot springs quietly groaning. While Gwyne went to the door and knocked, Victoria straightened the blanket where she'd been sitting and smoothed the lace edge of Miss Lizzie's pillow, another touch of home.

"Before I go," Victoria whispered, cringing slightly, "if I could just ask one more thing about the note. Is it possible your stepmother never—" Miss Lizzie's tight grasp on Victoria's wrist stopped her short.

"I thought you were on my side, Victoria." Her pale eyes searched Victoria's.

"I-I am," Victoria stuttered, her heart racing under Miss Lizzie's penetrating stare.

"Well, it certainly doesn't feel like it."

After a moment, Miss Lizzie's expression softened. She loosened her grip and began smoothing the cuff she'd wrinkled, gently, over and over, as if petting a bird. "I'm so sorry," she murmured.

Gwyne's look of concern mirrored what Victoria was

feeling.

Finally, Miss Lizzie released her hand and smiled. "Thank you for your visit. Please come again. Both of you."

FALL RIVER HERALD

John J. Maher was on a streetcar on New Boston Road Thursday afternoon rather under the influence of liquor. He was telling that when a reward was offered for the man [who murdered the Bordens], he could find him in 15 minutes. When questioned by an officer as to what he really knew, Maher said that a boy had seen a small man with a dark mustache come out of the house at the time of the murder and, going down Second Street, had turned up Pleasant.

Maher was locked up on a charge of drunkenness.

THE NEW YORK HERALD
EXCITED BY AN OLD WOMAN'S DEATH

Excitement in police circles ran high this evening when it was reported that an unknown woman had been found murdered in a lonely spot in South Somerset, near William's Pond. Investigation showed that Mary Gifford, aged seventy years, was dead and had been found lying in some bushes near a stone wall, her position indicating that she had fallen naturally from weakness. There were two bottles found near her, both of which smelled strongly of liquor.

Medical Examiner Dolan was in doubt as to whether or not the woman had been treated violently before death and he proposes to hold an autopsy, tomorrow or the next day.

Mrs. Gifford was well known in police circles as "Portsmouth Mary," and a dissolute character.

CHAPTER SIXTEEN

The days crawled by, during which Victoria's attempts to meet with Miss Lizzie's lawyers were unsuccessful and she was unable to discover any new evidence to help her friend. During this time, two unthinkable things happened: at the preliminary hearing, Judge Blaisdell declared Miss Lizzie's case would go before the grand jury; and twelve days later, the grand jury indicted Miss Lizzie, deciding she should be tried by a jury of her peers. No other suspects were being considered and Miss Lizzie would remain in jail until her trial was over.

Victoria knew she should go back to visit Miss Lizzie—the poor woman must be terribly frightened and lonely—but somehow she never found the time. She told herself it was because of her work with Mother and getting her wardrobe ready for school, but late at night, as she lay in bed, cold ribbons of doubt had begun to wind themselves through her consciousness. How well did she really know Miss Lizzie? Was there a side to her she never saw? Certainly, some of her behaviors lately were stranger than normal. But was it because of the stress she was under? How would she, Victoria, behave if her parents were murdered and she was thrown in jail? It was impossible to know.

Then school started, as if it were just another fall, as if Miss Lizzie's life were not hanging in the balance.

"The best part about going back to class," Gwyne said, hooking her arm through Victoria's as they walked down the sidewalk, "is seeing the Durfee High boys standing about, waiting for the doors to open."

Victoria did not respond, having bigger things on her mind. Mother was no better; Victoria hadn't seen Declan since the day she'd insulted him at the police station; and she felt guilty for stealing again. When would she stop?

"Oh, look," Gwyne whispered. "Is that Jared Winters? He must have grown a foot over the summer." She touched the back of her neck and smoothed a few stray hairs upward.

Victoria looked at the boy in question, but he lacked Declan's wavy hair and dimpled smile. Then she was irritated with herself for thinking so.

Jared and his schoolmates lifted their hats as the girls passed. While Victoria gave a simple nod, she noticed Gwyne ducked her chin and smiled coquettishly, looking like the woman in the Wunderoil advertisements. The bronze Durfee statue, gripping a book in one hand, a slide rule in the other, stared off into the distance, oblivious to the flirtations going on below him.

"I'll have to remind Mother to add Jared to the guest list," Gwyne said, squeezing Victoria's arm. "And look, on the steps. Isn't that Edward Pottersmith? He looks deep in thought."

Victoria grunted. "Probably dreaming up new ways to falsely accuse people."

Gwyne, knowing the story with Dickie, laughed.

"Which reminds me," Victoria said, "in case you didn't read the paper today, Miss Lizzie has now been formally charged."

"I heard." Gwyne adjusted her hat in a shop window as they

passed. "Don't take this the wrong way, but might you be wrong about her? That maybe your detective friend Declan was right?"

Declan. If he was in any way responsible for Miss Lizzie's indictment... "Maybe Declan was right about what?"

"Her birds!" Gwyne said. "That maybe Miss Lizzie killed her parents because they killed her birds."

"No. Of course not." But that had been one of the worries keeping her up at night. And the fact that resentment can build over time.

"Well, it made sense to me. Oh! Speaking of Declan..." Gwyne gave Victoria's arm a little tap. "I meant to tell you I saw him at Ollinger's Florals. GG, Mother, and I were there to pick out arrangements for the party, and he was at the counter, talking quietly to Mr. Ollinger." Gwyne shook her head. "I swear, your bad habits are rubbing off on me because I actually snuck behind a display of orchids and eavesdropped on what they were saying."

"Well done!" Victoria grinned.

"I hate to admit it, but it was very interesting, actually. Declan was asking about the Bordens' funeral flowers, and Mr. Ollinger said the sisters chose white roses to lay atop Mrs. Borden's coffin, which he thought was curious because white roses symbolize eternal love and he'd always heard the girls were not overly fond of their stepmother. Did you know she wasn't their real mother?"

Victoria nodded absently. "Did he say anything else?"

"So, here's the most interesting part. He'd heard one of the first things out of Miss Lizzie's mouth after the murders was that she wanted the fashionable Mr. Winward to be the undertaker. Mr. Ollinger thought it was an odd thing to be thinking about so soon after finding out her parents were dead."

A sick feeling trickled into Victoria's stomach. "Well, she... was probably in shock. I saw her the day after, remember, and she was not at all herself. Whatever Dr. Bowen had given her made her quite muddled."

Gwyne sighed. "How about when you asked her about the buried clothes? She seemed to freeze up. Then the way she snapped at both of us, remember? And then the note—she never answered you."

All points Victoria had been actively trying to ignore.

AT TEATIME, VICTORIA and Gwyne took their lunches to the big swamp oak. They spread their cloaks on the grass and used cloth napkins as plates.

"I brought fancies from Fernwood's Bakery for us to sample for our sweet table," Gwyne said, unwrapping a wax paper package and handing one to Victoria. "These," she breathed, "are divine. And the little frosting flower buds are so pretty. Oh, Susan!" Gwyne waved to Susan Lindholm. "How was your summer on the Cape?"

Susan, as pretty as she was dramatic, flounced herself down on the grass. "Boring. My grandparents don't believe in parties or dancing or anything else that might even hint at being fun. And they're sailing fiends, so we spent most days on their boat, getting sprayed by ocean waves and trying to keep our hats on our heads."

Victoria quipped, "Sun and fresh sea air? Sounds dreadful."

Gwyne laughed but Susan went on as if she hadn't heard Victoria. "And then to read about all that was going on back here in Fall River! Well, it just did not seem fair to miss out on all the action."

"Action?" Victoria almost dropped her fancy. "It's murder, Susan, not a minstrel show at the Academy."

"Oh, I know, I know," Susan said, waving her off. "But really, we are the talk of not only the state but of the country. My auntie read about it in her local paper in Texas and sent a telegram to my mother, asking if we were okay. Texas! And you must admit, it's exciting—especially with both of you living just a few houses down from the murderer!"

"She is not a murderer any more than you are, Susan." Victoria wished she could feel as confident about that as she sounded.

Glancing worriedly at Victoria, Gwyne broke off a piece of her fancy and thrust it toward Susan. "Here, you really must try this and tell me what you think of it. Tory and I are having a joint Coming Out party and we are considering these for the sweet table."

Susan popped the piece of cake in her mouth and, after a few chews, nodded enthusiastically.

Gwyne smiled and sighed, seemingly content she had derailed the conversation.

"Good choice," Susan said. "But back to the murders…"

"Can we talk about something else?" Gwyne groaned, but Susan ignored her.

"I've been thinking about it and I'm wondering if it would have been such a sensational case if the poison had worked. They could have died much more peacefully, and who knows? She might have gotten away with it."

"Poison? What poison?" Victoria leaned forward, her hand flattening the dry, prickly grass. "What are you talking about?"

"The prussic acid?" Susan looked from Victoria to Gwyne and back to Victoria. "At Smith's Drug? You didn't hear?"

Victoria shook her head. There had been nothing in the papers.

Susan, whose dream was to play Juliet in the yearly rendition of Romeo and Juliet, fluffed out her skirt and straightened her shoulders as if readying herself for the audition. "My cousin," she began, in a clear, somewhat affected voice, "works at S.R. Smith's Drug store, and a fellow employee and pharmacist, Eli, told my cousin that a woman came in the day before the murders wanting to buy some prussic acid. However, Eli wouldn't sell it to her because she didn't have a prescription. She said she only wanted to use it on the edge of her seal skin cape, but still Eli refused. The next day, the Bordens were murdered. Eli was pretty sure the woman who tried to buy the poison was Miss Lizzie."

Victoria held up a finger as she chewed and swallowed her bite of cake. "Tell me, did your cousin see her?"

"No," Susan sighed. "Of all the days to take off to go fishing, he had to choose that one!"

"Victoria," Gwyne said, "does Miss Lizzie *have* a seal skin cape?"

The frosting had left a slick, waxy taste in Victoria's mouth. "I have no idea, Gwyne. Lots of ladies have them. But even if she did, and even if it was her that tried to buy the acid, which I'm sure it wasn't, she didn't get it, so what is the point?"

"The point," Susan said, "is that the Bordens had both been sick to their stomachs the day before. Obviously Miss Lizzie found something else with which to poison them, only it didn't work, so then she had to kill them with the axe." She smiled triumphantly and popped a frosted morsel into her mouth.

Victoria could feel a rebuttal fluttering in the deep recesses of her mind.

She looked positively green, poor thing, Penelope had said.

"But they were all sick, Susan. The maid, too. Why would Miss Lizzie poison herself and the maid if it was the parents she was trying to kill?"

Susan gave her a quizzical smile, seemingly amazed at Victoria's thick-headedness. "To throw off suspicion, of course!"

Of course.

Gwyne nodded. "That *would* be the smart thing to do."

"Gwyne!" Victoria widened her eyes at her friend.

"You have to admit, Tory, the evidence against Miss Lizzie is starting to stack up."

She thought again how Miss Lizzie stuck up for her in the Dickie Houndsworth incident. It had looked bad for Victoria, especially with a supposed witness, horrible Edward

Pottersmith, claiming he'd seen her push Dickie. Sometimes things were not always as they seemed.

"This is not evidence." Victoria got to her feet and brushed off her hands. "This is one person's supposed memory, and everyone knows memories are tainted by the present. Susan said herself that he didn't remember the incident until *after* he heard about the murders. And he said he *thought* it was her, not that it *was* her. I bet he didn't even know Miss Lizzie existed until after the murders." She snatched up her bag. "Enjoy your lunch," she said, and bustled back into the school.

The classroom was empty. From her desk, Victoria could hear the rattle of easels being unfolded and the clinking of paint jars being stirred as Miss Minning prepared for art class in the adjoining room. She stared at the faded world map nailed to the wall: pastel countries floating in pale aqua oceans while cities, mountains, and rivers were labeled in irrefutable bold type. How different from the ancient map she'd seen in her history book, with toothy sea serpents raising their tentacles out of the wavy seas; giant lobsters gripping swimmers in their spiked claws, blood spurting from the swimmers' middles; and one fuzzy, green, whale-like creature, mistaken for an island by overly proud explorers poised to thrust their flag into the beast's spine. "Fear fuels one's imagination," Miss Minning had explained in reference to this map, "and ignorance allows it."

Trying to bend, in her mind, the flat rectangle of land and water into the sphere she knew it to be, Victoria decided much of what was said about Miss Lizzie came from fear and ignorance as well. People were turning an ordinary woman into a mythological, bloodthirsty beast in the same way their ancestors turned a simple river snake into a giant serpent. But just where did the facts stop and the imagination take over?

Though she hated to admit it, the poisoning theory did make sense; what better way to deflect suspicion than to take a bit of the poison oneself? Victoria thought of Mr. Borden's open torso—a sight that would surely haunt her forever. Perhaps they were testing his organs for poison. She wondered if Declan knew about this Eli person's claim and if it was part of the reason that Judge Blaisdell ordered Miss Lizzie to sit before the grand jury.

Victoria traced the inkwell hole with her fingertip as her thoughts raced in circles, only coming up with one solution: she needed to swallow her pride and apologize to Declan in the hopes of regaining his trust and obtaining information. The problem was, even if he did accept her apology, could she trust him to give her honest answers?

CHAPTER SEVENTEEN

When Gwyne came by to pick her up the next day, Victoria told her to go along without her, as she wouldn't be going to school that day.

"This isn't about yesterday, is it?" Gwyne asked. "Because I am sorry. I'm sure it felt like Susan and I were ganging up on you and I did apologize."

"Not at all," Victoria said. "My mother needs me."

It was not entirely false. Father had left for the farm that morning, so she would take care of Mother, but the truth was, cursive and crocheting seemed unimportant compared to every-thing else going on. And spotting Detective Dempsey in the Bordens' yard earlier that morning had decidedly tipped the scale. If the detective was there, she was betting that Declan wouldn't be far behind.

"PENELOPE," VICTORIA SAID, setting Mother's breakfast tray by the wash tub. "Do we have any more of those almond cookies? I thought I could bring a little plate of them over to Miss Emma. She could enjoy them herself or bring some to Miss Lizzie."

Penelope disappeared into the pantry and came out with a small tin. "Bridget might like one too."

Victoria blushed. "Yes, of course. For Bridget too." Before she could lose her nerve, she slid some cookies on a plate, put on her jacket and hat, and set out for the Bordens'.

The fall air was brisk and leaves danced at Victoria's feet. The crowds had returned to the Bordens, but in smaller numbers, and many times in groups led by small entrepreneurial ruffians who'd begun hanging out at the train depot, offering to take visitors to the Murder House for a penny apiece. Guarding the Bordens' gate was a pot-bellied police officer with a name-tag bearing the name *Owens*. The tip of his lumpy nose was pink, and he held out his hand as she walked up.

"Thank ye, ma'am," he said. "I'll be sure Miss Emma gets 'em."

Victoria's heart thrummed. She needed to talk to Declan to see if there was any truth to the poison story. Squaring her shoulders, she said, "I'd like to deliver them myself, if you don't mind."

The officer shook his head. "Sorry. Police chief's orders."

"Well, how about Master Dempsey? I thought I saw him earlier."

"What about him?" Officer Owens eyed the cookies hungrily.

Victoria plucked one cookie off the plate and held it out to him. "I'd like to speak to Master Dempsey, if I may."

A grin spread across the heavy man's face. Accepting the cookie, he yelled to the officer sitting on the front steps. "Get the Dempsey kid, will ya, Frank?"

As soon as Declan spotted Victoria standing apart from the group of onlookers, he stopped. With a frown, he came slowly down the steps. His posture was stiff, his expression guarded.

"Miss Robbins," he said. "To what do I owe this... pleasure?" Sarcasm dripped off his words.

Officer Owens looked on, eyebrows raised.

Victoria looked into Declan's eyes. Where there had been kindness and even a hint of interest a few weeks before, there was now only cold scorn. Picturing him with Mrs. Borden's hair, anger began to glow in her chest, a burning piece of coal. One drop of perspiration snaked down her spine. "I brought cookies for Miss Emma and Bridget."

"You called me away from a high-profile murder investigation to have me fetch a plate of cookies? I realize you don't think very highly of me, Miss Robbins, but I am no delivery boy." As he turned away, Victoria grabbed his sleeve.

"Listen to me," she said, noticing Officer Owens lean forward with interest. She faced him. "Would you give us a moment, please?"

The heavyset man hesitated, then glanced at the plate still in her hands.

"Oh, for goodness' sake." She held out the plate of cookies. "Here, take one more and then deliver them, please." The officer took it without hesitation and ambled off to the house, munching contentedly.

"Declan," she said, steeling herself. Her hands felt empty without the place, so she gripped them together. "I am sorry for my unfortunate words at the police station, and that you had to overhear them."

He folded his arms and glared at her, clearly not accepting her apology.

"You have no right to look at me like that," she said, abandoning her apologetic tone. "Especially since I saw you and your..." She hesitated, looked around, and then lowered her voice. "*Associates* stealing the box of clothes from the Bordens' yard." There. It was out.

Startled, Declan gave a quick glance over his shoulder, then slipped through the gate and took her elbow, drawing her off the sidewalk and toward the street. His touch was like the crackle of stepping on thin ice, branching up her arm and across her chest.

"Master Dempsey!" She pulled away.

"Sorry. Habit of the profession," he whispered. "But please tell me how you know about that."

Declan's fingertips seemed to have left a permanent imprint in her skin. She rubbed the spot. "I saw you."

"How?"

Ladies rolling prams passed with curious glances, not even trying to hide their eavesdropping. Declan put out his hand to Victoria, urging her to walk with him in the opposite direction down the sidewalk.

"My bedroom faces that way," she finally answered. "Why were you there?"

"Not that I have to answer to you," he said, evenly, "but it *was* part of the investigation."

"Why would you dig up a box of things the family obviously had buried for a reason? And how did you even know about it?"

He gave her an impatient frown. "The uncle hired a few men to bury the bloody clothes and things, don't ask me why. Anyway, it was fortunate he did, because Dr. Dolan found a new wound on the lady's back and wanted the clothing to find the matching tear."

"And I suppose the doctor made this request in the middle of the night?"

Declan sighed. "Miss Robbins. Can you imagine the ensuing chaos had we done it during the day, with half the community ogling over the fence?"

Victoria frowned. "Well..."

"Can you imagine what the papers would have done with that? The photographs they would have taken? Can you imagine your dear Miss Lizzie opening the *Fall River Gazette*, only to see a picture of us holding up her father's bloody shirt?"

Victoria pictured the eerie night scene again and shivered.

"I still don't see why they were buried in the first place."

"That," he said, shrugging, "I have no answer for."

The iceman's carriage clattered by, giving off a waft of cool, sawdust air.

"So," Victoria said, still wrestling with the sinister-seeming digging party. "You weren't doing anything... illegal?"

"Illegal?" Declan stopped in the middle of the sidewalk. "Is that what all this is about? You thought I was..." He began to laugh.

"It's not funny," she said, crossing her arms. "I was quite frightened. Especially when you held up that hair with the chip of skull attached."

His laughter sputtered out as his eyes widened. "It was you we heard! You were spying on us!"

Victoria lifted her chin. "Miss Lizzie is my friend. I will do whatever it takes to help her."

"Apparently," he said, peering at her curiously. "Spying on the police. Interrupting autopsies. Braving the Granite Street police department." He shook his head. "I guess Old Three Fingers was wrong. You're not chasing after me."

Blushing, Victoria crossed her arms. "Of course not."

"You're chasing after my job!"

Now it was Victoria's turn to laugh.

"I must say, you've got more nerve and backbone than half the police force," Declan said, the kindness back in his eyes.

"To say nothing of a ruined pair of slippers."

He grinned at her. Something made her hold his gaze just a few extra seconds before they both glanced away. They turned and began to walk back toward the Bordens', more leisurely this time. She liked walking with Declan.

"Well," he began as she said, "I guess..."

He ran his fingers through his hair. "You first."

"I heard a story about Miss Lizzie unsuccessfully trying to buy poison and then attempting to poison her family with something else. Is there any truth to that?"

"I can't speak to the truth of Eli Bence's statement," he said, "but I can tell you that the stomachs were sent to the Chemistry Department at Harvard, as well as the milk they thought might be poisoned. All came back negative."

"Negative! Good!" Then Victoria winced. "Wait, the stomachs were sent? How?"

Declan shrugged. "In jars. The same man, Professor Wood, also examined the hatchets found in the basement and the hair found on one of the hatchets."

"And?"

"Well, one of the hatchets had a spot that was suspected to be blood, but it turned out to be rust. The hair on the other hatchet was from a cow."

All of this would almost be comical if Miss Lizzie was not in jail, awaiting trial.

"Declan, a few weeks ago, you mentioned not wanting to be influenced by your father's opinions and urged me to speak to Miss Lizzie and report back."

Declan nodded. "That was before I learned of your fondness for swimming."

Victoria felt the color rise up her neck. She felt awful, now, for thinking the worst of him. "I *am* sorry for that, Declan. Remember, however, I'd just seen you sneaking around like a grave robber."

"I could see where you might have gotten the wrong impression."

"I'm wondering," Victoria said, "if you are having doubts about Miss Lizzie's guilt?"

"To be truthful, yes."

"Really?" Victoria clasped her hands together at her waist.

Declan put up his palm. "Don't go getting excited," he said. "Right now, all we have is a jumbled-up mess. Either way, Mayor Coughlin is happy to have someone charged with the murder."

"The mayor! What does he have to do with any of this?"

"Sometimes," he said, frowning, "people in high places are satisfied to have it appear like the case is solved so that the story goes away quicker. My father is happy because the mayor is off his back and the mayor is happy because it doesn't look good for a city to have a double murder case flapping in the breeze. Makes our town look dangerous, and our police incompetent."

They were in view of the Bordens' front gate, where the cookie-eating officer stood at his post. Two women posed on either side of him, having their picture taken by a third, the Kodak box held firmly at her waist. With one hundred photographs per roll of film, Victoria wondered if the ladies would even remember the significance of the photo once it was finally developed.

She pulled her attention back to Declan. "*Are* the police incompetent?"

Declan grimaced at Officer Owens. "What my colleagues fail to realize—and even scoff at, when I point it out—is the possibility of new clues still out there. More evidence. Let's just say, I would have done a few things differently, starting with sealing off the house and grounds immediately. Who knows how many clues were lost with reporters, doctors, and neighbors tramping around? Any number of people could have walked off with a vital piece of evidence and we'd never know it."

"Surely no one would take anything from the scene?"

"People do it all the time, wanting a souvenir to show their friends."

Though it hadn't been a souvenir, Victoria thought of the stone she'd taken from Officer Fenley's desk.

"Even the killer could have returned," Declan continued. "Coming back for something he dropped, something that could tie him to the murders. The possibilities are endless."

Victoria blinked, feeling like her vision of the world had suddenly sharpened. The idea that the police had not gathered all the evidence—or that the mayor might be more concerned with appearances over truth—had never occurred to her.

They were almost to the gate. Officer Owens was now at the corner of the property with the three women, talking and pointing to the back yard, apparently giving the ladies an impromptu rundown on the crime.

"Good Lord," Declan muttered. "Now he believes he's a bloody tour guide. Say, as long as I have you here, I have a few questions." They stopped by the gate, and he turned to face her, an air of professionalism dropping over him. "First, that ring she got you. Was there any packaging or tag that showed it had been purchased overseas?"

Victoria frowned. Did she still have the box it came in? She'd put the ring on immediately and hadn't taken it off since. "I don't remember. I don't think so. Why?"

"Just following up on something. And the second—"

The front door to the Bordens' house swung open and out strode Detective Dempsey. At the sight of his father, Declan stiffened.

"I was hoping you could tell me more about the day of the murders." Declan held up a hand to his father, indicating he'd seen him. "What you were doing in that alley, sneaking around, dressed as a maid?"

Victoria's chest caved in. "I…"

"You understand, I have to ask," Declan said, almost apologizing. "I wouldn't be much of a detective if I didn't. You knew the deceased." He began ticking off his fingers. "You are close with their daughter, you were dressed in a disguise, you were in a dirty alley, it was approximately one half hour after the bodies had been discovered…"

He stopped and watched her, waiting for an explanation.

Her hair suddenly felt heavy and hot, like a horse blanket across her shoulders. She fanned herself. "I was just out… for a bit of fun."

Declan remained silent.

"A lark, really," she said, forcing a light-hearted laugh. She thought of Gwyne, of the breezy, chatty air she had with boys and tried to do the same. "You wouldn't understand, being a man. We girls are like prisoners. Not allowed to go anywhere without an escort. The maid disguise allows me a bit of freedom."

Brow furrowed, Declan let himself through the gate. "You looked quite agitated when we met in the alley."

"Well, yes. I had just found out about the murders."

His nod was slow, thoughtful. "You had just found out about the murders and so you went into an alley, alone, instead of staying with the other shoppers?"

Victoria blinked. Goodness, he was good at this. "I wanted to take a shortcut home, to check on my mother. She was ill."

Detective Dempsey, on the porch, cleared his throat loudly.

Declan glanced over his shoulder and then back to Victoria. "Is there anything else I should know? Any part of the story you're leaving out?"

Mrs. Benson's phantom grip tightened on her arm. And then her last theft, right under a policeman's nose. What would Declan think of her if he knew? The back of her gown clung to her skin. "Nothing relevant to the Bordens." That, at least, was true.

Declan looked unconvinced. "Well, I best see what my father needs."

With that, he gave a quick bow, then jogged up the walk. He stopped on the stairs and called back, "If you get a chance to check where she got that ring, I'd appreciate it."

"Would finding out help her case?"

"It could go either way."

She nodded and lifted a hand in farewell, then forced herself to walk calmly and slowly back home, her head held high, as if her conscience was as clear as Sherlock's magnifying glass.

CHAPTER EIGHTEEN

"The man might have died in a fit; but then the jewels are miss-
ing," mused the Inspector, "Ha! I have a theory. These flashes
come upon me at times... What do you think of this, Holmes?
Sholto was, on his own confession, with his brother last night.
The brother died in a fit, on which Sholto walked off with the
treasure! How's that?"
"On which the dead man very considerately got up and
locked the door on the inside," said Holmes.

— Sherlock Holmes in *The Sign of Four*

M iss Lizzie's cell sported a few additional amenities from
home: two chairs, a three-legged table upon which sat a
flowered hurricane lamp and a stack of books, one wash
basin, a silver comb and brush set, a bottle of rose water and an
embroidered washing cloth. Yet the tiny room remained dank
and depressing.

"My!" Victoria tried for her cheeriest smile. "You've really made it quite cozy in here."

"Emma's doing," Miss Lizzie murmured, meekly accepting the flowers Gwyne handed her.

Miss Lizzie had lost weight, and with her hair in a loose braid, she resembled her younger self, the age she'd been when she taught Victoria to fish. A wave of love and fierce loyalty surged through Victoria. Why had she ever doubted her?

"You having to stay here is so unfair," Victoria said, sitting down in the smaller of the two chairs. Gwyne lowered herself onto the corner of the cot. "Couldn't they let you go home until the trial?"

Miss Lizzie remained standing, arranging the orange flowers. "They do not grant such freedoms to alleged murderers, Victoria. According to my lawyer."

Victoria could feel Gwyne's eyes on her but she refused to look. "But you're not a murderer, Miss Lizzie."

"Is that what you truly believe, Victoria?" Her voice was low and raspy, but it was her eyes—flat, almost vacant—that made the hairs on the back of Victoria's neck prickle. Her feelings of certainty and loyalty of just a moment ago began to falter. Quickly, she sat straighter and pressed her shoulders back, hoping to mask the shudder that just ran up her spine. "Of course I believe it!"

Gwyne nodded in agreement, but Victoria could see it was just for show. Could Gwyne—and the rest of the town—be right about Miss Lizzie? She made her mind focus on her motivation for coming in the first place—to find out about that ring.

Outside the high window, crows exchanged mournful caws. A thin column of sunlight spilled onto the chipped brick floor. The air in the tiny cell now felt suffocating.

Gwyne broke the silence. "It must be hard being inside all the time."

Another crow cawed. Miss Lizzie looked up toward the window with such a dreamy expression, it made Victoria wonder if Dr. Bowen had visited recently with his bag of medications.

"Yes, but I do enjoy hearing the birds. It reminds me of that hymn, *A Little Bird I Am*. Do you know it?" She gazed intently at Victoria, her eyes hard and inscrutable.

Victoria looked away and shook her head, but Gwyne said, "Oh, I do!" Then sang, cheerfully,

"A little bird I am,

Shut from the fields of air,

And in my cage I sit and sing

To Him who... placed... me there..."

Gwyne faltered as the words of the song sunk in.

Miss Lizzie nodded and finished the verse in her deep alto voice.

"Well pleased a prisoner to be,

Because, my God, it pleaseth Thee."

Victoria exchanged uncomfortable glances with Gwyne. Those last two lines. Did they mean—did Miss Lizzie mean—that God put her in jail? And she was happy about it?

Miss Lizzie sighed. "Funny. It had never been one of my favorites, but now I find myself humming it quite a bit." She smiled up at the window and then turned, seemingly back to her normal self. "So, girls, tell me what's going on in your life. School has started, I believe. How is it?"

Victoria blinked, her stomach churning. She was letting her emotions cloud her thinking, she knew that. *Emotional qualities are antagonistic to clear reasoning*, Sherlock liked to say. *You came here to find out about the ring,* she told herself. *Focus on that. Focus on the facts.*

"School, yes," she said with forced cheeriness. "Our last year at Miss Minning's."

Gwyne put on a playful pout. "So sad!"

Victoria shook her head. "I've had enough poetry and penmanship to last a lifetime. Oh, and needlework, which has never been a talent of mine." Normal conversation felt right. If she could keep it like this, she might be able to get the information without raising Miss Lizzie's suspicions.

"Oh yes," Miss Lizzie said. "I remember the sampler you struggled with."

Victoria rolled her eyes. "It had more knots than stitches. And the birds in the corners looked like dogs."

At Miss Lizzie's familiar laughter, Victoria's shoulders relaxed a little. Maybe she had let her imagination run away. Wasn't Miss Lizzie just the same as she'd always been?

"And we have other news," Gwyne said. Excited, she bounced in her seat and made the chains supporting the mattress squeak. "Victoria and I are having a Coming Out party, together, at my great-grandmother's on The Hill! And we're going to Anderson's on Thursday to pick out fabric for our dresses." She clasped her hands together and squeezed them to her chest.

Miss Lizzie gave a small smile. "Very nice."

"Only Gwyne is picking out fabric," Victoria corrected. "I'm just going along for the ride. As you can imagine, she strong-armed me into this extravaganza. It's not really my cup of tea."

"Well," Miss Lizzie said. "It wasn't mine, either, at your age. But now I regret not having one. I've had a lot of time to think in here and I've decided, if I get out, I'm going to throw more parties."

Victoria reached out and hesitated only slightly before patting Miss Lizzie's knee. "You will get out. I'm sure of it."

Miss Lizzie's eyebrows raised. "Hmm! Do you know something I don't?"

"Oh!" Victoria felt terrible for raising her hopes, and deceitful for planning to do Declan's bidding. If it helped her case, however, it would be worth it. "I can say I have made inroads with a detective on the force, and I've been bending his ear quite a bit about you, about your good works and such."

"That's very kind."

"Let's think of a brighter future. What's the first thing you want to do with your freedom restored? Travel? Perhaps go abroad again?" She hoped the change of subject hadn't been too obvious.

Miss Lizzie glanced up at the window, considering the question. "Maybe someday. But for now, I just want to be home."

"Would you," Victoria said, trying for an innocent air, "ever want to return to the countries you visited?"

"I'm not sure." Miss Lizzie's brow wrinkled. "I have such fond memories, and two albums filled with photographs, I'd be afraid a second visit might spoil it. That it wouldn't live up to my memories."

"I'd love to spend my honeymoon abroad," Gwyne said, sighing.

"Oh yes, me too," Victoria lied. She fiddled with the jade ring. "Remind me, Miss Lizzie, where did you get this beautiful ring? I get so many compliments on it but realized I don't know the story of how you came by it."

"Oh, goodness," Miss Lizzie said, shaking her head. "It was a four-month trip, my dear, all over Europe. I couldn't possibly remember."

She moved her hand closer to Miss Lizzie. "Oh, do think, Miss Lizzie! I'm sure it's a fascinating tale." Her insides felt oily with deceit.

When Miss Lizzie hesitated, Victoria's heart leapt. But then Miss Lizzie just shook her head and said simply, "Can't." Clapping her hands together, she thrust back her shoulders. "Now, enough about me. What about you girls, and your plans after graduation? University, perhaps?"

Victoria's neck hairs prickled again. Was Miss Lizzie purposefully avoiding answering?

"No university for me," Gwyne said. "I plan on attending as many balls and assemblies as possible."

Still thinking about Miss Lizzie, Victoria spoke without thinking. "Perhaps I could work in the new library once it's built. I do like to read."

"A job?" Gwyne laughed. "Your parents would never allow that. Why would you ever want to lower yourself in such a fashion?"

Victoria frowned. She hadn't meant to bring up the library, but she had thought a life spent among its shelves and patrons and pages would prove rewarding. "Because, Gwyne, I want to do something important with my life. Important and exciting."

Miss Lizzie lifted one eyebrow. "Important, I understand. Excitement?" She shook her head. "I've had my fill of that."

"Me too," Gwyne said, giving Victoria a dark, meaningful look. She tapped one finger ever-so-slightly against her knee, pointing in the direction of the door. Victoria couldn't blame Gwyne's discomfort—she felt it herself—but answered by widening her eyes just slightly, silently urging her to be patient for just a little while longer. Maybe she could change the subject and circle back to the ring from a different direction.

"Miss Lizzie," Victoria said, turning. "Do you ever wish you had gone to university? Or studied a trade of some sort? Had a career?"

"What I wish most right now is that I had shirked my responsibilities with the Christian Endeavor Society and gone away to the country with Elizabeth and the other girls, like I was supposed to." Her folded hands rocked back and forth on her lap as she stared, her top thumb tapping the one beneath it. "Had I gone away," she murmured, almost to herself, "none of this would have ever happened."

Gwyne shot Victoria a frightened glance. Her normally pink cheeks were bloodless.

Miss Lizzie turned to Victoria and blandly smiled.

A funny time to smile.

Victoria couldn't hide her shudder.

THE BOSTON GLOBE
Give the Girls A Chance
One of Them Thinks they Should Not Have to
Marry for a Home
by Mary Norton Bradford

The "maiden malgre," says an English editor, is becoming a very serious problem,
for it is an undoubted fact that there are
much fewer marriages among the upper middle
classes than there used to be, and how to
provide for his daughters is a question
that troubles many a man with a large, expensive family.

"Make some provision for your girls," urges
another well-known writer; and he goes on
to tell the story of an advertisement which
was answered by "women of all ages, gentle-
women, pressing in, pushing, waiting, eager
for the chance and the pay that was offered
was 5 shillings a week!"

In a higher vein comes the following commu-
nication from a girl in society, writes
from her point of view:

"Why are we not given professions as a matter of course, like our brothers?" demands
this young lady. "It is dreadfully unfair
to expect us to cajole men into marrying
us, and it is too humiliating for anything
to have the family all expecting and waiting for us to get some young man to take us
for better or worse.

"My father and brothers are fond of me, I am sure, and yet I am being constantly twitted with the want of a husband. Of course, I know with Papa it is only that he wants to see me provided for; but why cannot some other means to an end be contrived than dressing us up and 'giving us a chance,' as they call it?

"Everyone knows what going into society means: it is simply to let us be seen and, if possible, get a husband. There is no use mincing matters: we all know what it signifies. Do you suppose if it were not for that we would be allowed to idle all our time away and buy expensive clothes, while the boys are made to work?"

CHAPTER NINETEEN

How often have I said to you that when you have eliminated the impossible, whatever remains, however improbable, must be the truth?

—Sherlock Holmes in *The Sign of Four*

A nderson's Dry Goods was twice the size of Benson's, with high tin ceilings and large windows letting in white sheets of light. A fleet of sewing machines could be heard in the back workshop, clacking and whirring in noisy song, and Victoria remembered this is where Penelope's sister Olive got her job. The air was thick with cotton dust, and as Mrs. Jacobsen admired the immense selection of fabrics, Victoria and Gwyne discussed Miss Lizzie's odd manner the day before.

"You have to admit," Gwyne whispered, stopping to touch a roll of lace trim, "the way Miss Lizzie was talking yesterday, it sounded like she was confessing to killing her parents. And that hymn she likes, happy about being locked in a cage because God put her there?" She shook her head. "I'm sorry, Tory, I know we had a deal, but I can't go back there again. She gives me the shivers."

Victoria glanced over her shoulder at Mrs. Jacobsen, enraptured with a bolt of crushed velvet. "Gwyne, we've already discussed this. Miss Lizzie meant that if she were away like she was supposed to have been, she wouldn't and couldn't have been blamed for the murders. Like Miss Emma. No one's looking at her because she was out of town." Victoria really wanted—needed—this explanation to be true. It was too much to think the person she'd most admired and felt such a connection had a secret, darker side. Like herself.

Gwyne pulled out a length of lace and wrapped it around her jacket cuff. "I think you're allowing your loyalties to cloud your judgement. She said 'none of this would have happened,' and to me, 'none' means everything, the murders included. As in, 'had I gone away, I wouldn't have murdered my parents and therefore wouldn't have been arrested and wouldn't be in jail right now.' Who knows? Maybe she just snapped."

The logic of Gwyne's argument was undeniable and made Victoria jittery. Ever since she was in short dresses, she'd wanted to be just like Miss Lizzie when she grew up—baiting a fishing line with ease, raising pigeons and feeding them out of her hand, bravely sailing off to Europe with friends. And how many times had Miss Lizzie told her how alike they were? What did the possibility of her friend being a murderer say about Victoria?

"Let's not talk about this," Victoria said, taking her friend's arm. "Today is supposed to be all about you and getting your perfect dress."

Gwyne smiled. "Agreed."

"Goodness," Mrs. Jacobsen said, bustling up to the girls. "They don't call Fall River 'Spindle City' for nothing, do they?" She ran her hand across the rolls of fabric lovingly. "This store has doubled their stock since my last visit. There are just so many to choose from!"

The rapid tapping of heels on wood made them all turn. "Mrs. Jacobsen!" A tiny woman approached, holding out her arms to Gwyne's mother. "How wonderful to see you in my shop again." Her blue tailored jacket mimicked a soldier's, softened by fashionable, puffed mutton sleeves.

"It is my pleasure, Mrs. Anderson." Gwyne's mother took the woman's hands. "I had heard you'd expanded into the shop next door but never dreamed it would be this grand!"

Mrs. Anderson accepted the compliment with a gracious nod. "Yes, well, it's all thanks to loyal customers like you. And now that a certain person is in jail," she added, raising her eyebrows, "I'm sure we will prosper even more."

The bolt of pink taffeta slipped from Victoria's arms, and she grabbed it before it could touch the floor. "You mean, because of all the visitors coming to town? To see the Bordens' house? They stop and shop here?"

Mrs. Anderson seemed to notice Victoria and Gwyne for the first time. "I'm sorry," she said, somehow looking down her long, thin nose at Victoria despite being shorter. "I didn't realize I was speaking to you."

Victoria blushed.

"Forgive me, Mrs. Anderson," Mrs. Jacobsen gushed, "I should have introduced you. This is my daughter, Gwyndolyn, who is making her debut and would love a dress made."

Smiling, Gwyne curtsied.

"And this is her friend," Mrs. Jacobsen added, her tone dropping an octave, "Victoria Robbins."

Laying the bolt aside, Victoria curtsied and kept her gaze at the floor.

"Charming to meet you, Gwyndolyn. And to answer your question, Victoria, yes, there has been an uptick in business from out-of-towners, but I was referring to the merchandise I will no longer be losing. Because not only is Miss Lizzie Borden a murderer, she is a thief as well."

A thief? Victoria's head felt weightless, empty, a hot air balloon threatening to lift off her shoulders.

"Gwyne," her mother said, giving Victoria a worried glance, "why don't you and Victoria go look at... buttons for the cuffs and neck?"

Gwyne nodded and took a step, but Victoria did not move.

"I don't believe I heard you right," Victoria said, her voice cracking. She glared at the shopkeeper, straight into her metal gray eyes. Never had she hated a person so fiercely.

Mrs. Anderson gave a disbelieving huff. "A thief, I said, and I meant it. Every time she walked into my shop, something came up missing. And if you don't believe me, go ask Mrs. Gunner at the jeweler's. She says it happened so often, she'd just send Mr. Borden the bill." She leaned forward, hands clasped in front of her. "Which, I might add, he *paid.*"

"Come," Gwyne said, pulling Victoria like a spaniel on a leash. "Let's go find my buttons."

Head swimming, Victoria let herself be led to the end of the aisle, to a vast array of buttons sorted into trays according to size and material: wood, metal, pearl, shell, colored glass.

Gwyne squeezed Victoria's hand. "Don't listen to her," she said under her breath. "Like you said, now that Miss Lizzie's been accused, everybody's got a story to tell. She's no different than that pharmacist fellow, saying he saw something just to get people's attention."

"Oh, Gwyne..." Victoria looked at her best friend through watery eyes. "Do you really think so?"

Gwyne patted her hand. "Of course. Now help me pick out some buttons."

Victoria stared down at the piles of buttons, just inches from her fingertips.

The shopkeeper's words rang in her head. *Not only a murderer, but a thief.*

And then she saw Miss Lizzie's dreamy expression. *You remind me of me.*

The buttons shimmered with an otherworldly luster. She imagined sweeping an armful into her purse and walking out the door, relief showering upon her like a sparkling waterfall.

A murderer. And a thief.

A thief and a murderer.

"I'm sorry," Victoria gasped. "I really need to get some air."

And with that, she rushed out the door.

With an anchor button clutched tightly in her fist.

WHEN GWYNE AND her mother came out of Anderson's an hour later, they wore matching frowns. Behind them, in the window, Mrs. Anderson peered out suspiciously, making Victoria glance down at her décolletage to check on the button stashed between her breasts. Still woozy from the horrible woman's accusation, Victoria rose from the bench and pasted a cheerful smile on her face. Neither Gwyne nor her mother looked at her as they began walking down the sidewalk.

"So," Victoria said, hurrying to catch up. "Which material did you decide on?"

Mrs. Jacobsen gave a miffed grunt.

"If you were interested," Gwyne said, staring straight ahead, "you would have come in and seen for yourself."

What Gwyne didn't understand was Victoria could not risk going back inside Anderson's. She had gotten to the point where she couldn't trust herself; she'd lost all control. And if what Mrs. Anderson said about Miss Lizzie was true, and if they were so alike, well then... She shook her head, not allowing herself to follow this train of thought.

The sidewalk was crowded with shoppers, yet Gwyne and her mother made no attempt to make room for Victoria, forcing her to go around people and hurry to catch up. When they turned at the Freedom Bank on Maple Street, she feared losing them and quickened her step. But as she rounded the corner, she ran straight into the chest of a man, her nose painfully colliding with his chin.

She felt hands on her elbows to steady her and a deep voice sputtered, "Oh, miss, I'm so terribly sorry…"

Stepping back, hand to nose, eyes watering, Victoria dipped into a curtsy and upon rising, found herself face to face with Edward Pottersmith.

Of course it would be Edward, put on earth for the sole purpose of irritating her.

He stared for a moment, blinked, and then stepped aside, extending his arm to allow her to pass. "My apologies," he mumbled, touching the brim of his top hat.

Victoria gave the smallest nod of acknowledgement as she bustled past to catch up with Gwyne, who had stopped with her mother to admire a display of beaded purses in the window of Filbert's Finery.

"Gwyne," she said, out of breath, "I *am* interested, I was just feeling ill. You heard what she said about Miss Lizzie." Gwyne did not respond.

Suddenly Victoria remembered Declan asking about her ring. *He didn't think…*

She touched the jade stone, her heart pounding.

INSTEAD OF GOING in her own front door, Victoria slipped around back to the shed, with the button wrapped in Declan's hanky. Once inside, she dug up the box, her eyes burning with tears. *You remind me of me.*

What if it were true? What if they really were alike in good ways—and bad? Because if it was true about Miss Lizzie being a thief, what could also be true—about both of them? Sickened by the sight of her "treasures," Victoria kicked the box back into its hole and hurried out.

WHEN VICTORIA LET herself in the back door, Father was there, teacup in hand, leaning against the kitchen cabinets.

Her heart lurched. "Father! I thought you were at the farm." She quickly turned away and busied herself with hanging up her jacket.

"I came back an hour ago." His tone was cool. "Tell me, what were you doing out in the yard by yourself?"

Victoria blinked. "I… was checking on Penelope's garden. Seeing what was still growing. To make suggestions for dinner." She shrugged. "Like Mother used to do." She hated playing the pity card, but she could not let him find her treasure box in the shed.

Father set down his teacup and crossed his arms. "You weren't meeting someone back there, were you? A boy, perhaps?"

"A boy?" she scoffed. "Of course not." Her skin tingled with relief at how far from the truth his presumption had been.

"Because you looked guilty, the way you hurried back to the house."

She laughed, faking an ease she did not feel. "I was cold and wanted to get back inside."

"Well," he said, studying her, "you just mind your Ps and Qs. Just because I'm not home all the time does not give you free rein to act immorally. Remember, you are a young lady now, on the brink of formally entering society. Your good name is the richest jewel you possess."

Her hand went to the jade ring on her finger. "I know, Father," she said, giving it a turn. "You and Mother have taught me well."

THE BOSTON BUGLE
Differing Stories

Just what was life like inside No. 62 Second Street? It depends upon to whom you speak! Bridget Sullivan, the maid in the Borden house for over two years, says the family got along "jest fine, same as most families." She admitted they had their differences but that these were no different from those of any other household she'd worked in over the years. A friend of Miss Sullivan, however, claimed Bridget had wanted to return home to Ireland but Mrs. Borden begged Bridget to stay, claiming Bridget was the only one in the house that treated her kindly. Along those same lines,

Mrs. Hannah Gifford, seamstress, said she'd heard Lizzie call her stepmother a "horrid old thing" last spring, and John Morse, Lizzie's maternal uncle, admitted there had been ill feeling between Mrs. Borden and her step-daughters. However, Miss Borden has won the full support of the *Boston Herald*, which claims Lizzie is above suspicion, stating, "From the consensus of opinion it can be said: In Lizzie Borden's life there is not one unmaidenly nor single deliberately unkind act."

Lizzie Andrew Borden

So, normal, everyday family? Or one with secrets to hide?

CHAPTER
TWENTY

"I know, my dear Watson, that you share my love of all that is bizarre and outside the conventions and humdrum routine of daily life."

—Sherlock Holmes in "The Red Headed League"

The next morning, Victoria was reading Dickinson to Mother when Penelope poked her head in.

"Caller for you in the parlor, miss," she whispered, smirking.

Who is it? Victoria mouthed, standing and straightening her skirt.

"See for yourself" was her maid's cheeky answer.

Walking into the parlor, Victoria's stomach did a little flip. Declan looked quite dashing in his brown sack coat and grass-green waistcoat the exact color of his eyes. Truly, the Durfee

High boys in their fussy tailcoats and posh toppers were no competition. Her pleasure at seeing him was mixed with trepidation, however, with Mrs. Anderson's accusations still fresh in her mind.

Declan bowed, sending his unruly curl toppling onto his forehead. "Hope I'm not interrupting, miss."

She gave a quick curtsy. "Not at all, but please tell me you have some good news about Miss Lizzie. I've had enough bad lately."

Declan frowned. "I'm afraid not, miss."

"Oh." Victoria's shoulders sagged. "Well, still, I am pleased you are here."

His smile made Victoria feel like she had melted butter running through her veins.

Declan gestured to Father's tufted armchair. "May I?"

Victoria hesitated. Father had left for work and Mother was, of course, unable to chaperone the visit, but surely it was acceptable to receive a detective on official business. The silver taper candles on the fireplace mantle flickered gaily, the mirror behind them doubling their merriment and giving the burgundy fleur-de-lis wallpaper an almost romantic glow. But Penelope was here, Victoria reminded herself, and they weren't doing anything improper. Declan would be long gone by the time Father returned.

"Please do." Lowering herself onto the side of the crushed velvet love seat nearest his chair, Victoria suddenly felt self-conscious. She fluffed the skirt of her gray muslin day dress and could already hear Gwyne's admonition: *Tell me you weren't wearing that dreary gray thing when you received him, Tory. I keep telling you—you have to look your best at all times!* For once, Victoria saw Gwyne's logic and wished she had chosen her red taffeta that morning.

Penelope swished in with the silver tea tray and set it on the low table in front of them.

"Oh no." Declan held up a hand in protest. "Please. I don't want to be a bother."

"Nonsense," Victoria said. "A detective has to eat." Having watched her mother on innumerable social visits, she knew the routine by heart. Tea first, then sugar and milk offered. Stir back and forth, not around in a circle. Plates. Tarts, letting the guest serve himself.

Relenting, Declan took a large bite of blueberry tart. "So," he said after chewing and swallowing, "I just came with a few questions, the first being have you learned anything about your ring yet?"

Victoria shook her head, remembering Miss Lizzie's inability—or unwillingness?—to recall where she'd bought it. To be fair, it *had* been over three years ago. And she'd visited many countries and probably bought numerous gifts. She also was in jail with more pressing matters on her mind.

"Right. Okay, next, had you ever heard of the Bordens being robbed?"

"Robbed?" She listened with interest as Declan told her how the Bordens had been robbed one day the past June while the parents were out but Lizzie, Emma, and Bridget were home. Someone had broken into a locked desk in the parents' upstairs bedroom and stolen the stepmother's jewelry, money, and a few horse car tickets, all without being detected. The tickets were later found and traced to "a certain unnamed person," according to the report.

Declan sat back in his tufted chair and rested his saucer on his knee. "Perhaps most curious is that when learning of the findings, Mr. Borden told the officer to drop the case, with no explanation."

Victoria felt sick. This story lined up with Mrs. Anderson's about Mr. Borden paying the jeweler for items Miss Lizzie had stolen. She did not want to believe either. Avoiding his gaze, Victoria busied herself making more tea, taking the smaller teapot and pouring hot water into the larger. She would not add fuel to the fire by sharing Mrs. Anderson's accusations. They were only hearsay, after all.

Declan sat forward, cup and saucer in hand, elbows on his knees. His jacket cuffs showed two thin lines where the sleeves, like his pants, had been let out twice. "Just like with this murder case, there was talk at the time that Miss Lizzie was the thief. A few of the older officers have told me."

Even though she knew this was where his story had been heading, dread still squeezed her ribs. She had to concentrate on logic. Facts. "But why steal from her own parents, Declan? She didn't need the money." Father had mentioned that Miss Lizzie, by herself, had an account larger than Victoria's family's.

"Seems crazy, I agree, but people don't always steal out of need, Miss Robbins."

Cheeks flushing, she looked down at her seat cushion and ran her hand across the crushed velvet. "How strange," she said, trying to sound only mildly interested. "I've never heard of such a thing."

"A handful of officers say they've responded to shopkeepers' complaints about her stealing in the past, but there's no paperwork to prove it. Our best guess is that Mr. Borden paid off the shopkeepers. Now, if this is true, it would jive with Mr. Borden dropping the robbery case, because of course he would not want the arrest of his own daughter."

"If," she said, "it actually was Miss Lizzie that broke into the desk in the first place."

"True. If it was her that stole the items from her stepmother's desk, it would show a history of discord between them and, lumped with Mr. Borden killing her pigeons, strengthens the revenge motive." Declan pressed a fingertip to a few crumbs on his plate and then to his lips and for one brief moment, staring at his lips, Victoria forgot all about Miss Lizzie.

"Furthermore," he continued, "Mr. Borden had signed over one of his properties to his wife a year or so ago. It seems his daughters made such a fuss, he gave it to them and gave his wife a different house."

She remembered her father mentioning something about this when it happened, but she hadn't paid much attention. Miss Lizzie certainly never spoke of it. Teapot in hand, she refilled their cups, holding the handle tightly to keep her hand from shaking. "So the matter was resolved. What's the problem then?"

"Perhaps she was mad her father gave it to her stepmother in the first place. She was jealous. Remember that ring she gave her father?"

Victoria nodded, suppressing a shiver at the autopsy memory. "He was wearing it when he died."

Declan's nose wrinkled. "Don't you find that rather odd? He wore it on his pinky finger, but it reminded me of a wedding band. Like she was trying to claim him. Perhaps she was jealous of his affections for her stepmother?"

Victoria looked at her own ring. That gift to Mr. Borden *had* always struck her as odd.

"But if revenge was her motivation, as you suggest," she mused, "wouldn't she have taken the ring off his finger, and kept it, or even thrown it out? I mean, if you were mad enough to kill someone, surely you'd want the symbol of your love back. Or at least off their hand."

"Maybe." Declan frowned. "Or maybe it would be satisfying for her to see him wear it to his grave, proof she'd won, if you could call it that."

Victoria squeezed her eyes shut. "I can't believe I'm even speaking this way about her. She *didn't* do it. She *wasn't* jealous. Or vengeful. She is innocent!"

"Are you sure," he said, placing his teacup back on the tray, "you're not holding back information about this? Or about anything else that might incriminate your friend?"

Mrs. Anderson's story was only gossip, and Declan was already aware of the rumored stealing anyway. "No," she said. "Nothing."

He stared absently at his empty cup and then sighed. "Forgive me," he said, looking up, his green eyes searching hers. "But my gut still says you are not being entirely truthful about what you were doing in that alley."

Oh, why wouldn't he let it go? His stare backed her into a corner, tied her tongue. For a moment, Victoria pictured telling him everything, her secret life spilling out like greasy dishwater tossed from the wash bucket. But then those eyes, those emerald eyes, would never smile at her again.

Summoning Gwyne's coyness, Victoria attempted an exaggerated mysterious expression. "You remember what Sherlock said about women—we are naturally secretive."

Declan's disappointment seemed to radiate from him as he looked down at the faded floral carpet. "Miss Robbins, my father has no time for me and my ideas. Each time I attempt to speak, he cuts me off, saying 'Listen and learn.' He's got the whole force doing it. And so I decided to speak with you. You're biased, yes, but clever too, and I felt like I could trust you."

The word "clever" rang in her head like a church bell. Had anyone ever called her that?

"I trust you," he repeated. "And I wish you would trust me with whatever it is you are holding back."

She stared at the flickering candles on the mantle, so easily snuffed out with a single breath. His trust would be just as easily extinguished. If she were truthful with him, he would no longer trust her, and the only way to keep his trust was by continuing to hide the truth. "I—"

The front door slammed, cutting her off. *Father.*

Holding her breath, she prayed he would bypass the parlor and go straight to the sitting room. But he strode into the room, declaring, "I've got the whole afternoon off!" His cheerful expression clouded over when he saw Declan.

Declan stood while Father scowled at Victoria. "What is going on here, Victoria?"

She took a deep breath. "Father, I'd like you to meet Master Declan Dempsey, detective in training."

Declan put out his hand but Father ignored it, continuing to glare at Victoria. "Since when has it become acceptable to entertain a young man without the presence of a chaperone, Victoria?"

Declan colored but still gave a respectful bow. "Official business, sir, I assure you. The Borden case goes to trial next week and my father and I are still investigating. I had some follow-up ques—"

"Well, young man, official or no, your question session is over." He stepped to one side, allowing a clear path to the doorway.

Declan gave a slight incline of his head. "Of course, sir." Victoria was amazed at his continued good manners, for she was shaking with humiliation.

"Father," she began, but Declan turned to her.

"Miss Robbins," he said, pulling a small notebook from his chest pocket. "If there's anything else you can think of that might be useful..." He scribbled something onto the top paper. "This is where you can reach me." As he handed her the folded paper, her eyes locked with his, but she could not read the emotions in their flecks of green. She felt her cheeks flush.

He bowed one last time to her and then to Father and took his leave.

At the sound of the front door closing, Father stalked over to the window and squinted at Declan's retreating figure. "Is this who you were meeting in the backyard this morning? This... Irishman?" His mouth curled as if the word tasted foul on his tongue.

"No! I wasn't meeting anyone. I told you, I was checking for vegetables."

He narrowed his eyes. "And what vegetables did you find?"

Victoria swallowed. *Think. Fall vegetables.* "S-squash, brussels sprouts... rutabaga." She forced a disinterested shrug. "Nothing appealing."

Father stared at her, as if trying to see into her heart. "This is my house, don't forget. What goes on inside and outside it affects my reputation."

"We were merely discussing Miss Lizzie's case. What is the harm in that?"

He made a sour face. "Don't be ridiculous, Victoria. Trust me, that young mick was not here to get your opinion."

She sat up straighter. "Yes, he was. He respects what I have to say." *Unlike you*, she wanted to add. "And don't call him a mick."

His eyes bulged at her impertinence but before he could say anything, Penelope rushed in. "I'm sorry, sir, I wasn't expectin' ya for supper. If ye give me a minute, I'll fix you a plate."

Father nodded stiffly. "Thank you, Penelope, that would be fine."

Penelope gave a quick apologetic glance to Victoria and disappeared back into the hallway.

"Don't you be getting any ideas," Father whispered, pointing at Victoria. "He is a mick and I will not have him sniffing around this house." With an angry huff, he blew out both candles on the mantle and walked out.

Face burning, heart aching, Victoria sat motionless, clutching the folded paper in her fist. She closed her eyes and willed herself back to the beginning of Declan's visit, wanting to relive every minute of it. Never had she felt so alive and intelligent—*clever, he had called her*—and intrigued, like the deliciousness of reading a Sherlock Holmes story for the very first time, but better. Father was wrong. Declan *had* wanted her opinion. He'd said so. At the same time, she hoped Father was correct about the way Declan looked at her. Did Declan feel the same leap in his heart she felt when looking at him? She tried to hold on to the image of Declan's gaze as he handed her the note.

The note. She unfolded the paper in her hand, which read *221b Baker Street, London*

She smiled. Sherlock's address.

Below it, he'd added, *In case you change your mind.*

She ran a thumb over Declan's writing, back and forth, as if by doing so, she could summon him like a genie from a bottle. But then again, if he started hounding her about that day in the alley again, she just might have to stuff him back inside.

HAVING NO DESIRE to sit at the table with her father, Victoria fixed a supper tray for her and Mother to share upstairs. The quiet would also help in processing what Declan had confirmed—that Miss Lizzie was a thief. Just like her.

It was too much. Too close. Unless she changed, she would no longer be fit for society. Every promise she had made to herself, she had broken. It was time to get serious. And so, with each step up the stairs, Victoria promised God she would steal no more.

No. More. No. More. I. Promise.

"Good afternoon, Mother." Full of false cheer, Victoria strode into her mother's dim bedroom. "Let's get some daylight in here, shall we, before it's all gone?" She went from window to window, hooking braided cords around the peach chintz curtains, leaving the lace sheers to hang, already worrying about the promise she'd just made to God. She'd been stealing since she was eight, when she walked out of this very room with those nail clippers hidden in her pinafore. Could she really just stop, for good? Maybe she shouldn't have been so hasty. A promise to God was no schoolyard pinky swear.

"So, Mother," she said, brushing a gray ash off the curtain fringe, "I've got some of Penelope's good sourdough and... Mother!"

Her mother was half-sitting up—slouching really—but she had moved! And she was smiling! Bursting into tears, Victoria rushed over and enveloped her mother's bony body in her arms, which felt meaty by comparison, and for once she did not mind the smells of stale skin and unwashed hair. Her mother was improving! Questions bubbled out like water from a teapot left over the flame.

"How are you? When did this happen? What can you move? Does anything hurt?" Mother managed a tiny shake of her head, and her mouth, still pulled to one side, uttered a slurred, "Noooo."

Mother's thin body shook with laughter, and then Victoria was laughing too, laughing and crying. After pulling gently from their embrace, she jumped up and ran into the hallway. "Father! Come quick! It's Mother—she's better!"

In seconds, Father was at the base of the stairs, staring up. "Truly?"

"Well," Victoria said, grinning and wiping her wet cheeks with the back of her hand, "not all the way, but she's starting!"

Father took the steps two at a time, and Penelope was close behind him, calling out, "Saints be praised! Saints be praised!"

Victoria stood in the doorway, watching Father kneel at her mother's bedside, taking up her hand and kissing it. Penelope huddled close to Victoria, warm and smelling of maple syrup.

"It's a miracle," the maid whispered. "A true miracle. God has heard our prayers."

Victoria blinked. Prayers. Her throat was so swollen, she could answer with only a nod. Had God been waiting on her all this time?

CHAPTER TWENTY-ONE

Dear Miss Lizzie,

I hope this note finds you in good health and good spirits. You must be anxious for the trial to get underway. I wish I could have visited more these past weeks, but I've been quite busy with Mother's care.

Which brings me to my good news—Mother has recovered from her latest spell! She's improving by the minute. I'm hoping this is a sign of more good news to come—that you will be quickly acquitted and home in time to attend my Coming Out party. We can celebrate our stepping into (and back into) society together.

Please know that I am thinking of you more than you know.

Sincerely yours,

Victoria

A FEW HOURS later, delicious smells of smoked herring, rosemary potatoes, and leek and mushroom pie filled the candle-lit dining room. Victoria sat at the table in her second-best gown, the navy silk. She'd loaned Mother the red taffeta, as Mother had lost too much weight to fit into any gowns of her own, and the red reflected some color onto her pale skin. Father, in his ascot and tails, raised a glass of wine and smiled warmly at his wife.

"To Joanna," he said, "for returning to us!"

Angry as she was with her father, Victoria couldn't help but smile and lift her own glass. "To Mother. May I never again have to read aloud another Dickinson poem!"

Mother's eyes glimmered in the candlelight. As quickly as the paralysis had frozen her body, it left the same way, evaporating like a puddle in the sunlight. Still weak, her hand shook slightly as she held up her wine, but she'd insisted on eating at the table with them.

"It's good to be back," she said, enunciating her words carefully, a foreigner practicing a new language. "Be-lieve me."

"Drink up," Father urged her. "You need to regain your strength. I hear we have a Coming Out party to host." He winked at Victoria, as if their earlier argument had never occurred. For Mother's sake, Victoria gave him a half smile, one that said she had not forgiven him but did not want to ruin Mother's special dinner.

The door to the kitchen thumped open, and out came Penelope, backside first, holding a tray of steaming bowls. "No more clear broths for you, ma'am," she said, placing a bowl before Mother. "Queen Victoria's calf's feet soup *a la Windsor* tonight!"

Mother smiled. "I feel like a queen. So lucky and…" She swallowed, her eyes getting watery again. She looked down at her lap and smoothed her napkin. "I hope you know, I d-didn't mean to get sick. That horrible Dr. Appelbaum..." Her voice broke.

Victoria could feel her own eyes beginning to water, remembering the way the doctor had shook Mother's rigid feet and yelled as if she were hard of hearing as well as paralyzed, accusing her of malingering.

Mother shook her head. "I would never do that to you." She lifted her head and looked at each of them, Penelope included, one at a time. "To any of you. I promise."

"Of course, dear," Father said, fiddling with his spoon. Victoria hoped he felt silly for his confidence in the doctor's assessment.

She looked at her mother. "Can you tell us about it, Mother? What was it like?"

Mother held her hand above her steaming bowl of soup, palm up, and slowly curled her fingers into a fist and then, just as slowly, unfurled them, like a flower blooming. "Trying to move," Mother began, studying her hand as it opened and closed, "is like... trying to push a tree to the other side of the yard. It's impossible. Frustrating. Terrifying. It helps I've been through it twice before. I know I have to be patient and wait it out. But this time it was so much longer, and I was really starting to worry I wouldn't come out of it. So, I tried to keep my mind active, building a mental list of things I want to do upon my recovery."

She smiled and sighed, as if her little speech had tired her out. "At the top of my list this time was to help plan your Coming Out party, Victoria. So, your turn. Tell me what's been arranged while I devour Penelope's delicious soup!"

Victoria, who could not stand the idea of eating a soup featuring a pig's foot, was happy to push her bowl aside and tell all she knew, describing the flowers Gwyne had chosen—roses, smilax, and mountain laurel—the furnishings to be scattered about the hall for fatigued guests, the dance programs with Gwyne's and Victoria's monograms stamped upon the front, the famous orchestra that was to play, etc. She answered questions all through the main course, during which she carefully avoided eye contact with her father as well as the entire subject of the Borden murders.

By the time Penelope served the cocoa flummery, Victoria was actually getting excited about the party. She thought about Gwyne and how much time she'd put into planning everything, down to which style of napkin to use at the coffee table. *I really should help her, now that Mother's better. She could use the assistance and I could use the distraction.* Victoria took a big spoonful of her favorite dessert and nodded, sealing the deal with herself.

"And what about the guest list?" Mother smiled, lifting one eyebrow. "Is there anyone special you would like to invite? Any young man who has caught your fancy?"

Victoria's heart sped up and she could feel Father's glare drilling into her temple. Although she knew it was impossible to invite a member of the working class like Declan to her debut, she was not willing to admit defeat. Not yet. "I'm still thinking," she said, and gave a vague, innocent smile.

"Well, I have one," Father said, surprising both Victoria and her mother. "Edward Pottersmith, Old man Pottersmith's grandson."

There was a clattering of pots in the kitchen.

"Oh, Father, not Edward."

"Why not? He's the sole heir of the family fortune."

"He also accused me of pushing Dickie Houndsworth down the church steps." Victoria grimaced. "And not to be impertinent, but what fortune? Mr. Pottersmith's home seems to be crumbling about him and his chair."

Father wiped his mouth and sat back, looking smug. "I happen to know Edward will one day be as rich as Mr. Pottersmith appears to be poor. That old bird hasn't touched a lick of his principal in the bank, and believe me, it's substantial."

Edward—as blond as Declan was dark and as cold as Declan was kind. Victoria scowled. "All the money in the world cannot make up for Edward's dreadful personality."

"Victoria." Mother frowned. "There's no harm in inviting him, and I believe Mr. Pottersmith would be touched. You don't need to *marry* him."

"Fine," Victoria sighed. They could invite him, but they couldn't make her dance with him.

CAUGHT UP IN thoughts of Edward, Declan, her upcoming party, and Mother's recovery, Victoria abandoned her attempts to sleep and sat wrapped in a blanket on her window seat. Tree branches shook angrily in the wind, dark purple clouds slithering across the moon. Was Miss Lizzie also awake, gazing out at the same night, the bars in her window dividing the sky into violet rectangles? And if so, what was going through her mind? Was she searching her memory for old family enemies as possible suspects? Or was she recalling how the axe felt slicing into her parents' skulls? While Victoria still could not imagine her friend lifting a hand—let alone an axe—to anyone, she'd also have bet her life she was incapable of stealing as well.

Fear dug into her chest. Her own stealing had progressed from lifting worthless bits of bric-a-brac from home and school to brazenly stealing from stores right under the noses of others. Why couldn't she stop? Mag had become a tyrant, pressing her into more and more dangerous situations.

There is no Mag, she reminded herself, glaring at her own reflection in the window. *It's just you.* This made her feel worse—how powerless she was over her own actions. While her mother had described trying to move was like trying to push a tree across the yard, for herself, trying to resist Mag's—*her own*—urgings was like trying to hold up a chopped tree: heavy, impossible to balance, and such a relief to let go.

Victoria shivered in the darkness, wondering what would

happen at Miss Lizzie's trial, just two days away. Eventually, a decision regarding her guilt would be made. Miss Lizzie would either return home, celebrated by all, or...Victoria drew her knees up to her chest. Up until that moment, she'd never allowed herself to think about what would happen if Miss Lizzie was found guilty.

In the state of Massachusetts, the sentence for murder was death by hanging.

A strong gust of wind rattled the window, shaking twigs out of trees and setting the rooster atop the Borden's barn spinning around and around and around.

CHAPTER TWENTY-TWO

"I, for one, am happy to have your mother back in charge," Penelope said the next morning, coming in from the outside kitchen with a bushel of apples. She kicked the back door closed and it shut easily, no longer swollen from August's humidity. "I'm tired of planning the meals and shopping on top of the cooking and cleaning."

Victoria picked out a pink-and-gold-speckled apple and began peeling it with a paring knife. "Wouldn't you think she'd ease back into it, though, instead of coming at us with a list as long as a chimney brush?" The past night's foreboding worries were still with her, making her happy to be with Penelope in the coziness of the kitchen.

Penelope heaved the basket onto the worktable. "Like yer mother says, she had a load of time to think. And she's doing it for your own good, ye know. You're gonna be marrying age soon, so you've gotta know how to run a household."

"I already know how to make applesauce. And wash a window."

Penelope shook her head but couldn't hide her smile. "Such cheek. Nothin' wrong with a little hard work." She sorted through the apples, picking out dried leaves and twigs. "Speaking of marriage, I think I made a mistake letting in that young detective yesterday."

Victoria flushed. "Not at all. Father overreacted and was terribly unkind. It wasn't like Decl—Master Dempsey had come for social purposes. He is investigating a double murder, which does not necessitate a formal introduction, nor a chaperone listening to every word we say." A peel had stuck to her knife, and it took her several shakes before it finally dropped to the floor. "Honestly," she said, bending to retrieve it, "the way Father carried on, you'd think he'd caught me prancing around the parlor in my undergarments."

The apple in Penelope's hands spun like a bobbin, the peel coming off in one long ribbon. "Don't be toying with that boy's heart now, miss," she said. "It's not right."

"Penelope! I'm doing nothing of the sort." Picturing Declan's handsome face, her heart skipped a beat.

"I seen the way you two got all fluttery in each other's company, and it's best you put an end to it. Facts is facts, miss. He's Irish and your father would never allow it."

Had Penelope really seen that in him? Her pulse quickened, yet she kept her expression neutral. "By 'not allowing it,' you mean marriage?"

"Marriage, courtin', simple conversation, anything. I don't know where that boy comes off, thinking he has a chance with you, but he is sorely mistaken."

Victoria chopped her apple in half, and juice spotted her apron. "Not that I agree with your assessment of Master Dempsey's intentions, because I do not, but I don't think it should be up to my father whom I marry. If all marriage comes down to is money and property, why do poets and composers wax lyrical about love?"

Penelope made a face. "Because poets are fools. Trust me, after the glow of passion dies down, no debutante would want to live on a policeman's salary, or worse, be forced to take on work herself to make ends meet."

"You don't know that." Victoria sniffed. "I might like to have a job."

Penelope leveled her gaze at Victoria. "I'm serious, miss. If you really care for the boy, you'll tell him he's barking up the wrong tree."

Victoria shook her head and reached for another apple. "You have misread the entire situation, Pen. He visited only to discuss the case."

"Hmph," Penelope grunted. "Since when are you an expert in murder cases?"

"I'm an expert on Miss Lizzie."

"In your discussions, then, did he mention anything about bloody rags in the basement?"

Victoria looked up from her peeling. "What?"

Penelope sighed. "Men. Anything even looks like it involves lady's monthlies and childbirth, and it doesn't exist."

Shocked, Victoria looked over her shoulder to make sure Mother was not within earshot. "Pen," she whispered, "what are you talking about?"

"I'm talking," Penelope whispered back, "about manners taken too far. Sissy went out to empty her slop pail this morning and heard two officers at the Bordens talking about that first night after the murders. She's a flirt, that Sissy," she added, a hint of admiration in her tone, "and got the whole story outta them.

"Just hours after the murders, when it was dark, Miss Lizzie and Miss Alice went down to the cellar to use the privy. One of the men had been on guard duty and saw the lamp light through the basement window. Crazy that Miss Alice had agreed to stay over, just hours after the murders, don't cha think? I'd have thought they'd both have stayed at Miss Alice's."

Nodding, Victoria kept her blade to the apple and turned it slowly, imagining the scene. Dark, cold basement. Strange shadows, cast by the oil lamp, dancing against the brick walls and all the doorways behind which someone could be hiding— the coal room, storage room, pump room, privy.

Shivering, she asked, "What happened?"

"The ladies finished their business and went upstairs. Fifteen minutes later, the guard noticed lamplight in the basement again. It was Miss Lizzie, come back, but this time by herself. He peeked in the window and saw her stooping over something in the washing room. Turns out, this was where her parents' bloody clothes were being soaked."

The same clothes that had been buried and dug up? The apple's red peel slid over Victoria's hand like a snake, making her shiver again. "And?"

"Her explanation, when questioned, was that she was adding her womanly rags to the bucket. When the officers heard that, they acted like she'd added a tarantula. Nobody would go near it. For fear of being indelicate, I suppose." She snorted. "Indelicate. The police had no problem looking at the Bordens' heads used as chopping blocks, but the mere mention of a woman's monthly rags scared them away."

"Indeed." She distinctly remembered her mother teaching her to secret her own rags in a pail underneath the washing tub, out of Father's sight, and to rinse the water daily until laundry day. "I suppose Miss Lizzie was too embarrassed to take care of her items in front of Alice. And where else to put them but in the same bucket?"

"Think about it, miss," Penelope said quietly. "Would you be comfortable going, all by yourself, into your cellar at night, in the house where your parents had just been murdered, with the murderer not found? And on top of it, touching the bloody, shredded clothes of your dead parents? Since nobody bothered checking, who's to say it wasn't something else Miss Lizzie had been washing? Her own dress, even."

"Penelope!" Victoria dropped her knife, the handle banging onto the table. "You don't believe that."

Penelope gave an exaggerated shrug. "I'm sorry, miss, but with all the things we're hearing about her, I might. Crazy's in the blood, ye know. You know about the other Borden lady who tossed her children down a well—killed two of 'em good, then killed herself."

Victoria had known that story since childhood and had even played a game on the playground where if you were tagged, you were "thrown in the well" until someone freed you. But *crazy's in the blood*? She thought of her shared sin with Miss Lizzie. Was that in the blood too?

"Well, if we're looking into backgrounds," Victoria said, tossing her apple slices into the large black pot, "what about Bridget? All her family is back in Ireland. Maybe she comes from a whole line of killers."

The skin on Penelope's neck exploded with red splotches. "How dare you say that? Bridget is my friend."

Victoria glared back. "Well, Miss Lizzie is mine."

Penelope picked up the pot and turned her back to Victoria as she set it on the stove. An angry silence brewed as they continued to peel, slice, and drop apples into a second pot. Victoria was just reaching for the last apple when Mother rushed in.

"I just heard the bell from Hennimen's Bakery Cart and I'm dying for a lamb pie." She fished a few coins out of the cracked honey server. "Victoria, be a dear and get us two."

A tiny ray of sunlight split through Victoria's dark mood. "How could you hear that little bell?" she asked, hanging her apron on its hook by the door. "With all the windows closed?"

Mother held open Victoria's cloak. "When all you can do is listen, you'd be surprised how much you can hear."

Outside, charcoal clouds lined the sky, hiding the sun and chilling the air, blowing the warm, cinnamon-y kitchen air out of Victoria's cloak with just one puff. Mr. Pottersmith, sitting in his chair by the window, raised his clawed hand in greeting, which she returned as she hurried past, coveting the blanket on his shoulders. She could just make out Hennimen's Bakery Cart at the end of the long block. The wagon had a large open window and wood plank counter where Mr. Hennimen stood, his savory pies stacked behind him. As she approached, a delicious rope of aroma began to unravel into its individual threads: musky rosemary, robust red wine, onion, beef, bacon. But not even the thought of biting into her favorite lamb pie could distract Victoria from what she'd learned about Miss Lizzie's activity in the cellar.

A young voice pierced through her thoughts. "Lizzie's dress now in question as she heads to trial!"

The newsboy, ears sticking out of his flat cap, stood on his stack of papers to keep them from blowing away. He held a few issues in his reddened hands and called out the headlines, his thin voice cutting through the clomping of horse hooves and rattling of carriages. Victoria gave him her coin, then joined the line at Hennimen's cart clutching the paper, still mulling over Penelope's story.

While the question of what Miss Lizzie had added to the soaking clothes seemed answered by the fact Declan had listed "rags" in the group of items buried in the box, what bothered her was how Miss Lizzie could have been brave enough to go down in the cellar alone.

Sherlock might point out that Miss Lizzie could have felt safe for any number of reasons: the large number of police guarding the house, the thorough house search, how she had just been down there with Miss Alice.

And? a voice in her head prodded, and she pictured the very first illustration in "A Study in Scarlet," with Sherlock seated in his chair by the fireplace, looking at Watson with an expression of patient superiority. *Victoria,* she could almost hear him say, *you are ignoring the most obvious possibility.*

Sour dread pooled in the back of her throat.

Perhaps Miss Lizzie had nothing to fear because she herself was the killer.

The line moved forward.

Fine, she told the imaginary Sherlock. A possibility but not the only one. Miss Lizzie was not your average woman.

With that, she scanned the paper she'd bought, only to find more bad news. Nosy Mrs. Churchill's recollection of the dress Miss Lizzie was wearing on the day of the murders did not match the one Miss Lizzie turned in to the police for examination, which had been found free of blood. Not one officer had noted what Miss Lizzie had been wearing that day, and she'd not been asked for her dress until two days after the murders. Once again, sloppy police procedure working against Miss Lizzie. Last night's ominous mood returned with a vengeance, filling Victoria with a cold, damp dread.

Something knocked into Victoria's arm, making her drop the newspaper.

"Sorry, miss!" Brownie—or perhaps it was Thomas—bent into a deep bow, snatched up the baseball at her feet, then took off with his cohort.

"Honestly!" Dusting the dirt off her paper, she called, "Don't you boys have homes or chores or anything?" Faint laughter was their only answer.

It seemed to Victoria that the whole world was in a sloppy, chaotic mess, where little boys ran wild in the streets and incompetent police endangered the lives of the citizens they were sworn to protect. The unfairness of life made her eyes burn.

"G'day, missy," barked a cheerful Mr. Hennimen. "What'll it be then?" His grin was wide, blinding, making her resentful of his happiness.

"Lamb, please." She sniffled. "Two."

"Comin' right up!"

She watched his fingers, thick as sausages, grab the pies, wrap and tie them up with precision, then cut the twine with his rusty knife and set all on the wood plank counter. Her eyes stayed on the knife. Something about it promised relief from the terrible ache creeping up her throat.

"Ten cents, miss."

Ears beginning to roar, knees starting to quake, Victoria handed him the coins. She could taste the metal in her mouth, feel the weightless, free feeling of being taken over by Mag, a wave lifting her, propelling her up, up, up. Seconds away from imminent rapture, she remembered Miss Lizzie's thievery and her own vow to stop.

Mag is not real, she reminded herself.

The roaring in her ears got louder; the swirling in her chest sped up.

Stop. God is watching. You promised!

But she was already sweeping up the package and knife together, murmuring "Thank you," and stepping away. Inside, her chest sparkled and swelled so tightly, she had to fight to keep from closing her eyes in ecstasy.

"Hey!" Mr. Hennimen yelled.

Victoria halted, stomach heaving.

"Jim, ya rascal. Where's that pint ya owe me?" His laugh was raw and wet.

Looking over her shoulder, Victoria saw that Jim was none other than the horrible three-fingered Officer Fenley. She quickly turned away but thought he may have recognized her.

"Soon as yer wife let's ya outta the house," Fenley called back, laughing.

Rattled, Victoria turned to rush off, but bumped straight into a man who smelled of cheap cologne and horse sweat.

"Pardon me," she said, looking up to see Lizzie's Uncle Morse staring down his long nose at her.

Heart slamming against her ribs, Victoria hurried away, ears straining for yells of "Thief!" that never came. At the corner of Second Street, she chanced a glance back.

And did not see Mr. Morse or Officer Fenley anywhere.

She slipped the dirty knife into her purse and willed her burning eyes not to overflow.

BOSTON DAILY GLOBE
The Adams-Nervine Asylum

A good many people besides the doctors are beginning to realize that nervous diseases are alarmingly on the increase. To use that abominable word which nowadays parades all newspaperdom, nerves are the most "prominent" complaints of the nineteenth century—at least, on this side of the water… And so long as… people will persist in leading lives that keep every nerve in their bodies in constant tension, just so long shall we need such institutions as the Adams Nervine Asylum at Jamaica Plain.

At One Fell Swoop

The statistics of the asylum show that of those admitted, unmarried women are in a great majority. Chiefest among the causes mentioned by the doctor as giving rise to this state of things is the fact that many of these women have worn themselves out working for and waiting upon others—daughters upon whom have devolved the weight of household cares and the nursing of invalid parents or relatives, and who have no one to fall back upon when their own strength fails. They and similar cases are the ones who appear in the report of the asylum as having "no occupation"—a statement calculated to lead one who doesn't read between the lines into serious error.

CHAPTER TWENTY-THREE

rriving home, Victoria was relieved to find Mother in the front hallway, clutching a dust rag and facing the open study door. *Thank goodness.* Breaking her promise to God had not—as yet, anyway—sent Mother back into paralysis.

Then Father's voice boomed from inside the study. "There's no other explanation for it, Joanna. I've suspected her off and on for years."

Victoria's stomach tightened.

"Don't be ridiculous," Mother said. "I have spent much more time with her than you have and I'm telling you she is *not* a thief."

Victoria stopped breathing, feet frozen to the entry rug. The purse strings around her wrist pinched from the weight of Mr. Hennimen's knife, and she swore she could smell all the food it had ever cut—lamb, beef, onions, yams, leeks, red-skinned potatoes.

"Pray tell, then," Father argued, "what other explanation is there?"

Sighing, Mother shook out the dust rag. "You must have misplaced them. Or a breeze came and..."

"A breeze does not blow two silver cufflinks into the great beyond, Joanna."

The silver cufflinks. In her box. In the shed.

Mother folded the cloth and absently ran it over the door frame. "Well, what about the farm then?"

Victoria chanced a peek into the study and saw her father's back as he faced the window, hands on his hips. He was coatless, in his shirtsleeves and vest, and his unsecured cuffs bagged about his wrists like those of a colonist's ruffled shirt.

"What about the farm?" He said, giving the smallest of shrugs. Or perhaps it had been a twitch.

Victoria took the opportunity to sneak past, through the sitting room and into the kitchen.

"Maybe you lost them there." Mother sounded as if she were explaining something to a child.

Victoria set the pies on the stove to keep warm and stood in the kitchen, hesitating. Should she dash out to the shed and grab the cufflinks? Would she have time? What if Mother caught her coming back in—what would she say? Not willing to risk it, Victoria tip-toed up the rear steps, her parents' voices echoing through the floorboards, the vibrations buzzing the soles of her feet.

"And what about my pipe tamper?" Father bellowed. "Shoe horn? Mustache comb? They've been missing for ages! She's no good, I'm telling you."

Father's words struck Victoria like a hundred needles, and she had to pull herself up the last step. She'd finally been discovered. Hadn't she known all along it was bound to happen? Eyes burning, she clutched her purse to her chest and hurried into her room, the tip of Mr. Hennimen's knife poking her rib. Good. She deserved it. Who steals a knife, heavy, sharp, and dirty, from a good and cheerful man like Mr. Hennimen? A man just trying to earn a living, probably cooking his pies before she is even awake every morning? And, even worse, who breaks a promise to God after He has just healed her mother?

Father was right. She was no good.

The sounds of thumpings on the front carpeted steps stirred panic in Victoria's chest. Her parents were coming upstairs. Did they know she was up here? Dashing to the corner of her bedroom, she stuffed the purse between the dresser and the wall. Then she hurried to her window seat, grabbed the closest *Strand Magazine*, and sat.

What should she do? Admit she'd stolen the cufflinks and everything else? But how could she stand to see the disappointment in their eyes? Should she claim innocence?

"They're all the same," Father said, his voice muffled through the walls.

Who? Victoria thought. Daughters? Women? Thieves?

Mother's voice, shrill: "I *forbid* you to fire her."

Victoria gasped, squeezing the magazine in her hands. *Penelope.* He was blaming Penelope for all the things she herself had stolen. Hurrying to her door, she peeked out to see Mother at the top of the front stairs, blocking Father's ascent, so she dashed down the hall and ducked into the attic stairwell. There, at the top, surrounded by a halo of daylight from her room, stood Penelope, leaning against the door jamb, one hand gripping the unvarnished wood as if she might faint. Victoria's earlier anger at her maid vanished.

"Forbid me?" Father roared. "Since when do you forbid me anything?" His heavy footsteps resumed.

"There are plenty of things I should forbid you to do, Jonathan, but I do not."

Penelope's sniffles were like thorns to Victoria's heart and she climbed the remaining steps to be with her, keeping to the edge of each stair to avoid its creaking. Penelope did not look at her, nor did she move to the side to make room for Victoria. After an awkward few seconds in the cramped stairwell, wondering if she should take Penelope's hand or reach up to pat her shoulder, Victoria decided to sit on the treadle at her maid's feet.

Mother's voice again, less shrill, more resolute. "Penelope has been a godsend to me in my illness and has looked after Victoria all these years as if she were her own."

Drawers screeched open, slammed closed. "Well, tell her to look after my cufflinks as if they were mine. And find the blasted things. If she finds them," he declared, "she can stay."

Hope sputtered inside Victoria. She could get the cufflinks, return them somehow.

"But if they're not found," he grumbled, "she's finished."

Victoria twisted around just in time to see Penelope, stifling a full-out sob, slip into her room and silently close the door. Victoria continued to sit on the step and listen to her maid's sorrow, penance for being the one who'd caused it.

"DID YOU CHECK between the sofa cushions?" Mother asked an hour later. They were in the sitting room, their latest search underway.

"Yes," Victoria said, sighing. "Honestly, Father gets an idea into his head and there is no budging him. I bet you're right, Mother. I bet he left them at the farm." She tried to keep up normal dialogue while guilt stewed her gut.

"He likes to nap in the lounger," Penelope called from the corner of the room, peering under a corner of the oriental rug. "Check in the crevices."

"It's a bumpy road to the farm," Victoria said, heading to the fainting couch. "They're probably in a ditch somewhere or ground into the dirt road."

Mother said nothing, yanking open a drawer in a nearby side table.

Victoria glanced at Penelope, on her knees, squinting under

the chifforobe, and felt terrible. It was too late to suddenly "re-member" she had them. But going to the shed to retrieve them risked being seen. "And really, what on earth would Penelope want with his old pipe tamper or mustache comb?" At this she felt herself blush.

Penelope shook her head. "I wouldn't, miss, I swear."

"Of course not," Mother snapped. "We know that, Pen. That's why we're helping you."

"I suppose," Victoria continued, "I could understand the cufflinks, because of their value, but even then, where could Penelope sell them? Every pawn shop in town knows you're our maid."

"You're preaching to the choir, miss." Penelope groaned as she pushed herself to her feet. "Well, that's it for the sittin' room. Kitchen is next."

"The kitchen?" Victoria straightened and rubbed her back, sore from bending over so long in her pretend search. "Father never goes in the kitchen."

Mother pulled a few loose tendrils of hair back and re-pinned them to her bun. "We are leaving no stone unturned, Vic-toria. Every room, every cupboard, every drawer, no matter how unlikely the spot. Although..." She lowered herself onto the fainting couch and sat back. "I think we need to be done for to-day. It's nearly dinnertime."

"But ma'am," Penelope said, voice small, "I can't have Mr. Robbins thinking what he does of me."

"No, we can't." Victoria pictured the cufflinks, resting atop her pile of treasures.

"He will think even less of you," Mother said, "if his dinner is late. Although I have half a mind to..."

Penelope, dusting off her apron, paused.

Victoria raised her eyebrows. "To what, Mother?"

Mother's bony shoulders sagged and there was a thin gray sheen under each eye. Was she getting sick again?

That knife! She never should have stolen that knife.

Mother leaned back into the couch and closed her eyes. "Never mind," she said, giving a weak wave of her hand. "Dinner."

Penelope sighed. "Yes'm." As she turned to leave, she glanced at Victoria and something menacing flickered in her eyes—suspicion? Accusation? Betrayal? Or just a trick of the waning light?

As soon as Victoria had the house to herself, she would fetch those cufflinks and hide them somewhere they hadn't searched yet. But what on earth would she do with Hennimen's knife?

DINNER WAS AN uncomfortable affair: Father and Mother barely speaking, Penelope wordlessly serving the dishes, eyes cast downward, mouth a taut line. Had Victoria not gone into Father's room that day, she wouldn't have seen the cufflinks and none of this would have happened.

None of this would have happened. Victoria's heart sputtered. It was the same thing Miss Lizzie had said, wishing she'd gone away with friends instead of staying home. Banishing the thought, Victoria slowly unfolded her napkin and lay it across her lap, smoothing the white linen flat, tracing the embroidered white R.

"Father," Victoria said, looking up, "don't you think it's time we tell Mother? About…" She widened her eyes meaningfully.

Caught mid-chew, Father raised a finger. He finished, took a sip of wine, and squinted at his plate, as though looking for the right words among the applesauce and gravy.

"If you're talking about the Borden murders," Mother said, dabbing a corner of her mouth, "I already know."

Penelope almost dropped the decanter of sherry she was carrying, and Victoria exchanged shocked looks with her father.

"What? How?"

Mother gave an arched smile and shook her head. "I keep telling you. When all you can do is listen, you can hear quite a bit—conversations in the house, in the yard. On a particularly quiet night, I heard two policemen discussing the case, which is how I have come to believe Mr. Morse, the uncle, had something to do with the murders."

Victoria stared at her mother. "Uncle Morse? Why?" Uncle Morse's look of contempt when she'd bumped into him at the bakery cart loomed. She'd never liked him.

Penelope went around the table, pouring the sherry slowly, almost drop by drop.

"Their cigarette smoke woke me up," Mother explained, nodding her thanks to Penelope. "The smoke, as well as their voices, drifted directly to my window. One was complaining about having to stand guard night after night, just to stop people from taking bits of siding of 'the lady murderer's house.' And the other one said something about the bits being worthless once the 'real murderer' was named."

"And he said it was Uncle Morse?" Victoria clasped her hands together.

"Not the murderer per se," Mother said, "but the one who was behind it, who paid off a few men to do the dirty work, is what he said."

Father stopped buttering his piece of bread. "And what was his reasoning?"

Penelope had given up all pretense of serving and stood transfixed by the sideboard, gravy boat in hand.

"At one point the policeman asked his friend, 'Who has an air-tight alibi?' And his friend hemmed and hawed and finally came up with Miss Emma, which made the first man laugh, saying, 'That old bird? Think again. Who else?' And the second man finally came up with Uncle Morse."

"Darling," Father said, "perhaps you don't understand what an airtight alibi is. It means—"

"I know what it means, Jonathan, and his point, which I was getting to, was, if you were going to murder someone—two people—wouldn't you make sure you were seen by as many witnesses as possible, as far from the murder as possible?"

Father sat back. "Go on."

Victoria, wide-eyed, didn't give Mother a chance. "That's true. Uncle Morse left right after breakfast—*I* saw him. He went to the post office, called on some relatives, and then was very specific about which streetcar he took home—didn't he even know the number? And the conductor's badge number too? I think I read that somewhere."

"The interesting part," Mother added, swallowing her sip of water, "was how he acted when he came back. According to this man, even though there were police outside the house, Uncle Morse didn't stop to ask why they were there, but walked right past them, into the back yard, picked a pear, and ate it."

Penelope gave a small huff of disbelief, then, remembering herself, put the gravy boat aside and brought the platter of pork around for seconds.

Victoria waved away the offer of meat. "Goodness. Well then, by the same token, if Miss Lizzie was the murderer, why wouldn't she give herself a better alibi than going to the barn for a reason she couldn't remember? I mean, she would have had over an hour between the murders to make up a story. She could have said she'd seen a stranger running from the yard. She could have knocked some things around in the house to make it look like a break in, or sliced herself up a little to look like she'd been attacked too."

Mother nodded as she speared a piece of pork. "Pen, may I have more gravy?"

"Of course, ma'am."

Victoria was suddenly ravenous. Savoring a spoonful of cinnamon applesauce, she wondered if Declan had ever questioned Uncle Morse's airtight alibi. Had he ever considered the uncle a suspect?

Father drummed his fingers on the table. "I guess we'll find out soon enough. Joanna, do you feel well enough to attend the trial tomorrow?"

Nodding, Mother watched Penelope ladle gravy over her pork and then signaled for her to stop. "I wouldn't miss it for the world."

The awkwardness and anger between her parents was gone, the silver cufflinks forgotten for the moment. But then Victoria saw Penelope, at the sideboard, fussing with candlesticks and the decanter of sherry, worry pulling down the corners of her eyes. Penelope had not forgotten. And neither could she.

The cufflinks or the knife.

CHAPTER
TWENTY-FOUR

"One thing that hurts me inexpressibly, and causes me to weep when I am alone, is the malignity that is directed against me. I have never knowingly harmed any human being. I have done much good to many persons who now desert me. In my own home there are hands stretched out against me that I have loaded with favor in the past."

—Lizzie Borden in a letter to Mrs. Mary A. Livermore

The courtroom was more crowded than church on Christmas morning, the mood just as festive—women in towering fall hats and lace gloves greeting one another excitedly, men patting backs and exchanging firm handshakes, and everyone talking, whispering, joking, speculating, asking after one another's families. Had there been stained glass windows in place of the double-hungs and an alter instead of the judge's towering bench, the effect would be complete. Below the bench stood the evidence table, with Miss Lizzie's blue dress laid out and a few other items covered by a large sheet of paper.

The subject of all this excitement, Miss Lizzie herself, sat behind the rail with her stiff back to the crowd, black brocade stretched across wide shoulders, single brown bun topped with a black poke hat, the wide rim fanning out—a style, she'd once told Victoria, that softened her strong, square face.

Victoria spotted Gwyne across the room seated with her mother, both in burgundy satin, but saw no sign of Declan, though he could easily be hidden within the mass of bodies. Father, along with a great deal of other men, lined the back wall, their voices sounding like distant thunder, a low, sustained rumble hinting at a coming storm.

The twelve male jurors answered as their names were announced, one by one. Not one woman. Was it even legal for a woman to serve on a jury? Probably not. Then the clerk called out, "Prisoner, Miss Lizzie Andrew Borden," and the crowded courtroom silenced, as if the judge had slammed his gavel and banished breathing. The spectators all leaned forward, anxious to see the woman charged with her parents' brutal murders, to hear her voice, listening for any hint of guilt or innocence.

As Miss Lizzie pushed back her chair and stood, Victoria caught a glimpse of her face, and though her friend looked pale, her lips especially, she saw no other evidence of fear or worry. She could be standing in her own kitchen, for all her expression showed.

"Present," Miss Lizzie answered, her voice low, firm. The plume of blue feathers on her hat flickered as she gave one decisive nod.

The entire room exhaled, shoulders settling against the backs of benches, heads tilted together in quiet whispering, hand-fans fluttering like so many bird wings. Then, as Miss Lizzie bent to take her seat, Victoria saw her hand, reaching for the arm of the chair, shake, betraying the fear beneath her mask of calm.

The trial had officially begun.

Victoria was surprised to feel her mother's fingers suddenly grip her own, her palm moist. "Pray for justice to be done, Victoria," she whispered. Victoria nodded, then stopped her silent prayer almost immediately. If Miss Lizzie did commit the murders, a prayer for justice would be for a guilty verdict, and she certainly did not want to be part of pushing her friend up the galleon steps. Not that God would be listening to her prayers anyway.

"Gentlemen of the jury," the clerk, a balding short man, said, "hearken unto an indictment found against the prisoner at the bar by the grand inquest of this county."

The word "prisoner" reverberated in Victoria's mind, and while the clerk nattered on, she saw herself in Miss Lizzie's spot, her basket of treasures on the judge's desk with Mr. Hennimen's knife and the silver cufflinks balancing on top. The clerk calling out: *Prisoner, Miss Victoria Margaret Robbins.* Her parents in the front bench Miss Emma occupied, Mother's hand gripping Father's, Penelope beside them, arms crossed, glaring.

The knife is what they'd focus on. Of all the things to steal, a knife! How would she ever make them believe it meant nothing, that she had no nefarious plans to use it, that it was as random a prize as the anchor button or the spool of thread? Who would believe she hadn't planned on stealing it, that it was in her hand almost before she knew it? They would laugh, call her crazy, a liar.

Crazy's in the blood, Penelope had said.

And all the doctors seemed to think Mother was missing a few marbles herself.

Clearing his throat, the clerk leaned heavily on the wooden rail penning in the jurors, concluding his address with "To each count of which indictment Lizzie Andrew Borden, the prisoner at the bar, has heretofore pleaded and said that thereof she is not guilty, and for trial puts herself upon her country, which country you are. You jurors, are the country's representatives for this case and are now sworn to try the issue. If she is guilty on either or both of said counts, you are to say so, and if she is not guilty on either or both of said counts, you are to say so, and no more. Good men and true, stand together and hearken to your evidence."

Mr. William H. Moody, one of the prosecutors along with Hosea M. Knowlton, scraped back his chair from behind his table at the front of the room and stood.

"Victoria," Mother whispered, "loosen your grip, you're hurting my fingers."

Mr. Moody, a young man with short, reddish hair and matching trimmed mustache, surveyed the entire room dramatically, as an actor might collect his accolades at the end of his performance. He was well-known for his courtroom skills.

"Upon the fourth day of August of the last year," he finally began, his voice clear and strong, "an old man and woman, husband and wife, each without a known enemy in the world..."

Not true.

"...in their own home, upon a frequented street in the most populous city in this county, under the light of day and in the midst of its activities, were, first one, then after an interval of an hour, another, severely killed by unlawful human agency. Today a woman of good social position, of hitherto unquestioned character, a member of a Christian church and active in its good works, the own daughter of one of the victims, is at the bar of this court, accused by the grand jury of the county of these crimes."

Moody made a grand sweeping gesture toward the accused. Miss Lizzie's black lace finger touched the flowered broach at her throat, as if checking it was still there, then lowered her hand to her lap.

Grabbing both lapels, Moody continued, swinging back to the jury men. "There is no language, gentlemen, at my command, which can better measure the solemn importance of the inquiry which you are about to begin than this simple statement of fact."

He went on in laborious detail of Mr. and Mrs. Borden's family histories. Peeking between the puffed sleeves and lace-adorned necks in front of her, Victoria caught another glimpse of Miss Lizzie. She appeared only mildly interested, as if he were speaking of a couple she had briefly met on holiday some years back. How was she able to remain so stoic? More of Dr. Dolan's medicine?

Moody went on to discuss the Bordens' marriage, their finances, and the happenings the day before the murders, including their stomach illness, Eli Bence's claim of Lizzie attempting to buy poison, and Miss Lizzie's visit to her good friend, Miss Alice Russell, the night before the murders. Moody paused, his eyebrows raised, swiveling on his heel to make sure he had the room's full attention. He certainly had Victoria's. She hadn't heard about this.

"Lizzie Borden told Miss Alice many things that night. She mentioned overhearing her father arguing with a man about renting out one of his buildings," boomed Moody, raising one finger. "Told her about another time," he said, raising a second finger, "when she'd noticed a man lurking around their house at night. She brought up the family's recent illness and proposed they were all being poisoned. She even said she wouldn't be surprised if their house was one day set afire as a result of her father's troubled business dealings."

Victoria was confused. Wasn't the prosecutor supposed to prove Miss Lizzie's guilt? Instead, he seemed to be suggesting other possible suspects.

"All this," Moody said, waving his hand with four fingers raised, "Miss Borden told her friend Alice, the night before the murders! Coincidence? I'd say not."

Ohhh.

He turned and gazed indulgently around the room, satisfied by the smirks, the tittering and whispering and poorly contained laughter. Victoria glared at Moody but his gaze slid right past her on to more approving folk. She saw now how Miss Lizzie's story sounded contrived, as if she were laying the groundwork for the following day's murders. Without missing a beat, Moody went to the evidence table, below the judge's podium, and held up Miss Lizzie's blue silk dress. He told the courtroom what Victoria had read in the paper—that it did not match Mrs. Churchill's description of the one her friend had been wearing that day.

Moody tossed the blue silk aside, inadvertently dislodging the large paper covering his other pieces of evidence. As the tissue blew off, there was a collective gasp, and Miss Lizzie cried out and slumped sideways.

Staring out at the crowd were two human skulls. The remains of Andrew and Abigail Borden.

Miss Lizzie's lawyers and a few others jumped to her aid. Someone called for smelling salts. The clerk ran for a glass of water. Hand fans were offered over the rail and her lawyers began waving them at Miss Lizzie's face. Victoria's mother hid her eyes behind her fan, but Victoria could not stop staring at the skulls. Why hadn't they been buried with the bodies? She thought again of the heads bobbing around in an enormous pot of water, as described by Declan.

Half the room was on its feet, some for a better look, some in outrage, some to comfort their overcome wives or friends. The perspiring Moody scrambled to re-cover the skulls, then ran his fingers through his red hair as he pretended to look through his notes. Judge Blaisdell scowled and banged his gavel, demanding quiet.

Order was eventually restored, but Moody had lost his audience. He spoke a bit longer, then in closing cited three reasons pointing to Miss Lizzie's guilt: no money or valuables had been taken (thus removing robbery as motive), no signs of a struggle in either murder, and lastly, Miss Lizzie had been heard speaking ill of her stepmother. Mr. Moody probably meant this to be the culminating moment of his speech, something newspaper-men would highlight in their articles and jurors would have in their minds' eyes as they deliberated the case. However, if these men and women were anything like Victoria, they would only remember those skulls sitting atop the wooden prosecution table, their hollow eyes forever holding the secret truth of their brutal demise.

"JOANNA!" MRS. KETTLESON, the church organist, de-scended upon Victoria and her mother as soon as they stepped into the frigid air outside the courthouse. Her considerable girth and trademark voluminous, layered skirts cut a wide swath in the exiting crowd, and as usual, she was unaware of the disrup-tion and dirty looks she left in her wake.

"I haven't seen you in ages," she trilled. "How are you?"

With her mother cornered by Mrs. Kettleson, Victoria was free to wave down Gwyne, just stepping outside the courtroom.

One of Gwyne's hands gripped her cloak to her neck, the other shaded her eyes. Spotting Victoria, Gwyne wove her way through the crowd.

As she waited, Victoria could feel the cold dust kicked up by the crowd sticking to her damp forehead and upper lip, and her neck ached from the unnatural position she'd held in order to see Miss Lizzie through the heads and hats blocking her view. Gwyne, extra rosy-cheeked in the autumn air, began talking while still a few steps away.

"Oh Tory," she said, out of breath. "We sent out the invita-tions yesterday—eighty in all!"

"Gwyne," Victoria said, incredulous. "I cannot believe that's the first thing out of your mouth."

"And I cannot believe our party is the last thing on your mind!"

Guilt pricked at Victoria. "Yes. You're right. I'm sorry,

Gwyne. I promise to be more involved."

Gwyne gave a haughty little nod of acknowledgement. "Oh, and your father came over the other night to make sure Edward Pottersmith was on the guest list, which he was, of course. One of Fall River's most eligible." She batted her eyelids playfully.

Victoria's nose crinkled. "And most horrible."

"Who's horrible?"

Victoria spun to find Declan smiling and tipping his hat in greeting. The tip of his nose was pink—he must have been outside a while but, truly, his smile could melt an iceberg.

"No one," Victoria answered, at the same time Gwyne whispered, "Edward Pottersmith."

There was a moment of uncomfortable silence that Gwyne broke, adding, "He's Victoria's father's choice of suitor for her."

Why would she say that? She knows I have feelings for Declan.

"He's a lucky man." Declan's smile dimmed, which made Victoria's heart lurch.

Shaking her head, Victoria countered, "My father lives in the dark ages, apparently thinking arranged marriages are still en vogue."

The sputter of an engine momentarily drew their attention to the road, where a motorcar chugged past, the driver looking jaunty in his driving cap and the woman by his side with a blanket on her lap, gripping the edges of her seat.

"Edward's grandfather is very wealthy," Gwyne announced, as if she hadn't heard Victoria, "and Edward's the sole heir."

Victoria gave her friend a wide-eyed glare, then turned to Declan. "You'll have to excuse my friend and her loose tongue—you remember Gwyndolyn Jacobsen, from... the cemetery."

Gwyne gave a shallow curtsy. The motorcar's puttering faded, drowned out by distance and the more familiar sounds of squeaking carriage wheels and clopping horse hooves.

"I'm… afraid the trial has affected my friend's good sense, talking in such an indelicate manner."

"No harm done," Declan said, his tone somewhat clipped. "She was just being honest. I admire that in a woman."

Victoria chose to ignore this jab.

"See?" Gwyne grinned. "There's no harm in speaking the truth, Victoria."

"Of course not," Declan said, "and it's never too late, either." His meaningful look made Victoria's pulse quicken. "In this trial, for example, people can come forward with information up until the second the foreman reads the verdict."

"Oh my." Gwyne looked up from admiring her lace gloves. "Has anyone done so?"

Declan clasped his hands behind his back. "Let's just say there are a few surprises in store. A few people whose consciences have been bothering them." He stared at Victoria and she looked away.

"A bigger surprise than today's?" Gwyne asked.

"Don't tell me you were bothered by seeing those skulls, Miss Jacobsen, after seeing what you witnessed at Oak Hill?"

Gwyne blushed, the skin around her rouge turning a different shade of pink. "Only the thought of the bodies being buried without them—can they really rest in peace? Will they be floating around Heaven, headless and—"

"Master Dempsey," Victoria interrupted, "is there new evidence against Miss Lizzie?"

"I'm sorry, miss." Declan tilted his head. "I'm not at liberty to say. You know us detectives…" He shook his head with fake regret. "We are naturally secretive."

Her own words being used against her. But worse than that, there was no teasing in his voice, no twinkle in his green eyes. He knew she was hiding something and his disappointment shamed her. There was no way to convince him it had nothing to do with Miss Lizzie without telling him what it was, and she could not possibly tell him about Mag.

"And now, if you ladies will excuse me..." With a tip of his hat and an exaggerated bow, he headed in the direction of his father holding court with the mayor and other distinguished gentlemen.

Victoria watched him stalk away, her heart aching. Of all the people to run into in the alley that day, why, oh why did it have to be him?

Another Joke! Bicyclers Emulate the Taunton
Spirit

SEE FUN IN A MURDER

A company of young men with reputed good
sense have entered into a conspiracy
against the fair name of the city. It was a
thoughtless movement at the start, and citizens who have the good reputation of Fall
River at heart hope that they will abandon
the idea when the foolishness is pointed
out. It happened this way:

The enthusiastic bicyclers who recently attended the convention of the Massachusetts
division of wheelmen at Cottage City wanted
some sign which should be peculiar to Fall
River riders. By an inconceivable method of
reasoning—or, more probably, without any
reasoning at all—it appears to somebody
that an axe, suitably inscribed, would be a
cute little badge for the Fall River wheelmen.

Acting upon this idea, some of the riders
had a pin made of silver and wore it on
their uniforms. It was something like this:

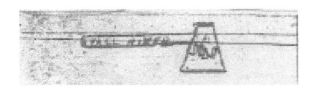

The Cute Badge

Not content with this inconspicuous souvenir, the Fall River riders bore a banner in
the parade which was inscribed thus:

A Bright Idea

CHAPTER
TWENTY-FIVE

U pon arriving home from the courthouse, Victoria found
the family's winter clothes hanging near open windows.
In addition to airing out the coats, Penelope had spent her
day baking something sweet that smelled divine. *Trying to get
back into Father's good graces.* Well, she could help with that.
As soon as Mother, Father, and Penelope were settled into their
own duties, Victoria dashed to the potting shed.

Squatting above her box of treasures, Victoria thrust her
hands deep into the jumble and closed her eyes. Waves of peace
poured into the crevices of her soul, filling up the empty spots.
She took a deep breath and let it out slowly, the vapor coming
out in lacy, white wisps. How would she be able to part with any
of them? Blinking her eyes open, she gazed at her treasures in
the flickering candlelight and smiled. *Magpie's Treasure Nest.*
She'd felt so clever coming up with that name. With a fingertip,
she lovingly stroked a shoelace, mustache comb, toothpick,
piece of chalk. The silver cufflinks, snuggled next to the chalk,

winked at her, reflecting the candle's flame.

Mine, Mag whispered.

Her heart pinched.

Beside her on the splintered shed wall, the shadow of herself hunching over her hatbox resembled a witch peering into her cauldron. Pushing aside that image, Victoria picked up the cufflinks and cupped them in her hand. They'd been the first things of real value she'd taken. The next thing she'd stolen was the knife, a weapon. Going from bad to worse. Her hand began to tremble.

My debut, she thought, clutching the cufflinks to her chest. *My debut will change me.* What was that quote Miss Minning had them copy for Handwriting? *When I was a child, I spake as a child, I understood as a child, I thought as a child: but when I became a man, I put away childish things.*

I am a full-grown woman and it is time to put away my childish things, my childish habits. Beginning this very moment.

Gritting her teeth, Victoria tried not to notice how good the cufflinks felt nestled in her palm. *It's for Penelope*, she reminded herself. Before she could change her mind, she jumped up and kicked the box back into its hole, shoved the pile of dirt over it, and slipped out of the shed.

Back inside in the upstairs hallway, Victoria played *eenie-meenie-miney-moe* with the jackets, spread out to air.

"Moe," she panted, pointing to Father's black wool tailcoat. She breathed in its faint odor of mothballs, her fist poised above the pocket, a lump of hot coal burning in her throat. Her fingers would not loosen.

Ridiculous, she told herself, blinking away the hint of tears. *Ridiculous and immature.*

Downstairs, the door to the cellar thumped shut and something metal clanked—a pan upon the stove. Behind Mother's bedroom door, floorboards creaked. No time to dillydally.

Pulling open the jacket pocket with one hand, Victoria slowly uncurled her fingers. She tipped her hand and watched the cufflinks tumble into the soft, dark opening.

Good-bye, she thought, hating the lump thickening in the back of her throat. *Good-bye, good-bye.*

That night, Victoria dreamed she went out to the potting shed and pulled out her treasure basket. But instead of treasures, it was filled with blood, Mr. Hennimen's knife floating on top.

HAVING NEVER ATTENDED any court proceedings, Victoria was finding out how long and tedious they could be—how a trial could drag on for days, how the lawyers would ask the same questions, in different ways, over and over. The prosecution seemed to find as many opportunities as possible to show how the blade of the handle-less axe fit perfectly into the skulls of the deceased. And they could belabor a seemingly insignificant point until Victoria wanted to jump up and shout, "Get on with it, man!" It wasn't just the prosecution, either. Miss Lizzie's own lawyers, Jennings and Robinson, hammered away with their own repetitive questions, attempting to show contradictions in the testimonies of state witnesses.

Every day, the number of reporters grew, as did their rudeness, taking up more and more of the seats. Gwyne chose to return to school rather than attend the rest of the trial, and Declan, seeing Victoria's father keeping a close eye on her, kept his distance. At least, that's what Victoria told herself each day he managed to be somewhere other than where she was.

And every day, Victoria brought Mr. Hennimen's knife with her, wrapped in several hankies, secreted in her purse, in the hopes of passing his cart. She had yet to see any sign of him. Illogically, she felt like his absence was her fault, that he had gone out of business due to losing his knife. But surely a baker would have more than one knife. Mother's strength had continued to improve, so perhaps God knew of her intentions and was granting her an extension to carry out her plan. However, familiar with Old Testament stories of floods and desert wanderings and people turning to salt, Victoria did not want to press her luck, and kept a sharp eye, and nose, out for the baker's cart.

Day after day, Miss Lizzie sat at the rail, well dressed yet not overly so, remaining poised and impassive as she listened to friends, acquaintances, and even strangers tell their versions of the truth. Whispers about her cold heart were countered by claims of her clear conscience, and while Victoria had witnessed Miss Lizzie being a no-nonsense Sunday School teacher, she still marveled at her ability to maintain her composure through all the ups and downs of the testimony. At times, Victoria's heart swelled with pride at her friend's strength and other times, goosebumps of doubt tip-toed up her spine. And always, always, the cold lump of their shared sin sat heavily in the pit of her stomach.

Twice Miss Lizzie laughed. Once when Bridget was on the stand and mentioned the leftover mutton Mr. Borden insisted she serve for breakfast that morning. Mother covered her smirk with a gloved hand, as did others familiar with Mr. Borden's stingy—or as Mother called it, *frugal*—nature. The second instance of laughter was when Bridget described Mr. Borden's apparent annoyance at his inability to unlock his own front door the morning of the murders.

"I heard someone at the door," Bridget testified from the witness stand, "pushing at it, trying to unlock it. It was Mr. Borden back from his morning errands. I unbolted it and turned the key and said, 'Oh pshaw' and I heard Miss Lizzie upstairs, laugh."

There, sitting at the defense table, Miss Lizzie laughed again, out loud, and shook her head, and Bridget smiled across the courtroom at her, the two women sharing amusement at the old man's grumpy impatience.

But it felt off, this levity. The grumpy old man at whom they were laughing had been entering his home for the last time, his mutterings the last words he would speak, his steps the last he would take, bringing him closer and closer to his own demise. Victoria could hear people's whisperings, see their alarmed expressions.

"Miss Lizzie was upstairs where?" Mr. Moody's tone was all innocence, overly so, which instantly put Victoria on alert. If she had learned one thing so far, it was how sneaky lawyers could be.

Bridget shrugged. "Either in the entry or the top of the stairs, I suppose, I couldn't tell."

Moody nodded. "Wouldn't that be just outside the spare bedroom?"

"In the hallway, yes."

"So, the accused was laughing... just outside the spare bedroom where, according to our expert's opinion, Mrs. Borden lay, dead?"

The gasps and mutterings of the spectators drowned out Jennings' objections. Victoria's thoughts raced. Mrs. Borden had been found on the floor, on the far side of the bed. Could Miss Lizzie even see the body from the hallway? Surely it would have been out of sight.

Moody continued to question Bridget but he needn't have. He'd scored an enormous point for the prosecution by searing into everyone's mind the image of a laughing Miss Lizzie, just steps away from her dead stepmother.

THE EIGHTH DAY started off with good news for once, when the judge ruled pharmacist Eli Bence's testimony inadmissible. His claim of Miss Lizzie attempting to buy prussic acid was deemed irrelevant to the case since poison was not found in the Bordens' systems. This drew audible outrage from one corner of the courtroom but it pleased Victoria greatly. *Finally. Something going our way.* Victoria wished Mother hadn't stayed home today, as she would have enjoyed hearing this news.

Then Inspector William H. Medley took the stand. Squeezed between two pungent newsmen, Victoria had been preoccupied with elbowing herself a little breathing room when the man on her right leaned forward.

"Hey Jim," he whispered to the man on the other side of her. One of his front teeth was gray and sat at an awkward angle. "This is the star witness we heard about."

Inspector Medley had a long nose, floppy ears, and a bushy mustache. It took quite a few minutes of tedious questioning by prosecutor Moody before his replies became worrisome.

"After you went into the barn, Mr. Medley," Moody asked, "what did you do? Describe in detail."

Puffing out his chest, Medley began his speech. "I went up-stairs until I reached about three or four steps from the top, and while part of my body was above the level of the floor, and I looked around the barn to see if there was evidence of anything having been disturbed." He mimicked looking around. "Nothing seemed to have been disturbed, and I stooped down low to see if I could discern any marks on the floor of the barn having been made there. I didn't see any, and I reached out my hand to see if I could make an impression in the dust on the floor of the barn, and I could." Here he placed his hand upon the stand and pre-tended to peer closely at the surface, one eyebrow hooked in exaggerated inquiry.

Victoria wrung her hanky, sickened by the insinuation. His whole story felt rehearsed. Had someone put him up to this? Medley went on to describe how he then walked along the edge of the dusty floor, then came back to the steps, walked down a few and examined the floor again.

"And did you, Mr. Medley," Moody asked, "see any other footsteps in that dust than those which you made yourself?"

"No, sir. Mine were the only ones visible."

Across the courtroom, men and women burst into excited whispers and newspapermen scribbled, all gleeful with this new information: if there were no footprints, then Miss Lizzie could not have been up in the barn at the time of the murders, as she had claimed. Victoria glared at Inspector Medley. He was all but calling Miss Lizzie a liar. Two rows ahead, a grinning Mrs. Kettleson spoke into her sister's ear, and Victoria was fairly certain she wasn't discussing which hymns she would play at church that Sunday.

The gray-toothed newspaperman to Victoria's right leaned forward. "Guess it's a moot point whether she was up there for a bit a screening or for some iron for her fishing line, eh, Jim?"

Jim, on her left, snorted as he continued writing. His mustache was so thin it appeared to have been drawn on with a shard of coal. "Never believed that story from the get-go," he mumbled. "What kind of rich lady climbs up a dirty, old barn ladder in all her fancy clothes?"

"I'll tell you what kind," Victoria muttered. "That kind." She nodded toward Miss Lizzie, sitting tall and unmoved in her wooden chair. "Because that's exactly the type of *rich lady* she is."

Victoria had been only five or six when Miss Lizzie first brought her up into the barn loft. *A full-grown woman*, she remembered thinking, *liking wild animals!*

"Would you like to feed them?" Miss Lizzie had held out a bucket of seed and a wooden scoop. Victoria's chest felt near to bursting, given such an important job, but the birds' hopping and flapping for food frightened her.

"They're not after you," Miss Lizzie had assured, waving away the birds. "They just want the best seat at the table."

Victoria had pictured the birds eating in a formal dining room and laughed.

A loud throat-clearing brought Victoria back to the present. Mr. Robinson, one of Miss Lizzie's lawyers, was holding up a finger. He took a sip of water, coughed twice more, then began his cross examination of Officer Medley. Many questions with nothing to refute Medley's testimony. After the inspector stepped down, the judge called the lawyers up to the bench to discuss a procedural point.

Worried, Victoria took a deep breath and sighed. The news-paperman on her right grinned.

"Pretty exciting stuff, eh?" Mr. Gray Tooth whispered. "Think she did it?"

"Of course I don't. This isn't a freak show, sir."

"Beg pardon, miss, but"—he waved his pencil at the crowd—"sure looks like one to me." When he laughed, Victoria decided his tooth was gray from someone punching him in his obnoxious mouth.

"Personally," Mr. Mustache, Jim, whispered, "I hope they find her innocent."

"I am glad to hear you say that, sir. I doubt many people here share your wish."

"Nah, these folks want blood. A cautionary tale to tell their grandchildren." He shook his head. "Not me."

"That's commendable."

"Yep," continued the mustached man. "See, if they say she's guilty, she hangs and that's the end of it. But if they find her not guilty..." He shrugged. "Well, then she'll be a news story the rest of her life. Now, that's what I call job security."

Victoria inhaled sharply. "You, sir," she choked out, "are a pig."

"I'm sorry, is she a friend of yours?" Mr. Mustache rolled his pencil between his fingers. "Would you... care to make a statement?"

"Yeah," chimed in Mr. Gray Tooth, flipping his notebook to a fresh page. "How does it feel to know your friend might hang?"

Before she could dwell on the thought of Miss Lizzie, her brown, square-toed shoes kicking the breeze, Victoria stood. "This discussion is over." She excused herself all the way down the row, not caring how many newsmen's toes she trod upon.

Outside, a blast of cold air made her eyes water even more. Parked carriages crowded the street, along with tied horses and even a few motorcars, all waiting for their owners to spill out of the courthouse and claim them. She would love to know which horse or rig belonged to those horrible reporters—she'd untie it and send it off down the street. Maybe she would wait for them to come out and then confront them and—

The courthouse door banged open and out jogged Declan, eyes sweeping the yard before stopping on her.

"Miss Robbins," he said, striding over. "Are you sick? Do you need help?"

Though her first instinct was to throw her arms around him for support, she grabbed a nearby hitching post instead. "Sick with worry, Master Dempsey. That Medley fellow is all but calling Miss Lizzie a liar!"

"Don't worry, Victoria. There are still lots of other witnesses to be questioned. Dr. Handy will be testifying about the strange man in the light suit—"

"Whom no one has been able to track down."

"True, but there's also that ice cream peddler who claimed to have seen a woman fitting Miss Lizzie's description walking from the barn about the time she said she did—"

"A peddler who didn't come forward for two days and the police never bothered to check his story." She'd been reading both morning and evening editions of three different newspapers and had all the facts on her fingertips. "How valuable a testimony is that?"

Declan opened his mouth to say something and then, frowning, shut it. His dark curl dangled in front of one eye and he did not move to brush it away. "I don't know what to tell you," he finally said. "We have to let each witness speak."

"But isn't there anyone else? Anyone who could refute this… Meddling Medley's claim? I bet he made the whole thing up!"

Crossing his arms, Declan asked, "And why would he do that?"

"To make himself look good, of course. You heard him—he

was a lowly patrolman last year but now suddenly he's an inspector? Don't you think this very public, detailed account of his
meticulous, methodical inspection is just what the bumbling Fall
River police force needs to regain the public's respect? Don't
you think it's possible he was put up to this?"

Declan's fingers drummed against his arms. "I will admit, it
was a boost for morale in the department…"

"Yes, see? There must be a way to refute his claim! Are you
sure he was even there that day?"

"Oh, he was there all right, him and a hundred other people.
But all of them were interviewed. I've gone over their statements myself, and I've found no contradictions—to Medley's
account, at least."

"His is the only one that matters. This evidence—if we can
call it that—is the first real blow to her alibi. It will make or
break her case. Do you consider Medley's report true?"

Declan sighed, kicked the dirt. "Personally, no. I'd only
consider it fact if I'd seen it for myself. But I'm guessing the
jury will."

Whether from cold or fear, Victoria's chin began to quiver.

"She is my friend, Master Dempsey," she said, her voice
cracking, "and she might hang." A choking feeling took over
and she ran a finger around the inside of her collar to help her to
breathe.

"Believe me, miss, I am not anxious to see an innocent person, woman or man, hang. Just between you and me…" He
paused to glance around the empty yard, then lowered his voice.
"I feel like I'm the only one in the department who feels that
way. Well, me and Lupin. This detectiving business…" His
shoulders sagged. "Well, it's not how I pictured it would be. But
I promise, even if I have to sneak behind my father's back, I will
go over every statement and see if there is anything missed." He
lifted his hand, as if taking an oath.

Staring at the lines crisscrossing his palm, Victoria was reminded of Miss Lizzie's hand, holding out a mound of corn and

barley, the pigeons pecking the food right out of it, their irides-cent necks changing from green to purple to azure and back again. She was so gentle with them. Surely those gentle hands, which had fed God's fragile creatures so lovingly, were incapa-ble of doing evil.

And then the hand was Declan's again, with a pink scar on his thumb she'd never noticed, so shiny she was tempted to reach out and touch it. She looked up and found him staring at her. He glanced, once, at her lips, then took a step back, clasping his hands behind him.

"I should get back," he said, his voice catching.

Victoria couldn't answer.

"Your father will be looking for you, and perhaps that Pot-tersmith fellow will be as well."

Victoria blinked, then shook her head. "Edward Pottersmith has no interest in me, I can assure you."

Declan's forced smile faded and Victoria realized he may have misconstrued her meaning, that she cared for Edward and regretted her feelings were not returned. Of course, nothing was further from the truth. She considered clarifying, but worried she'd only make it worse.

"Wait, I wanted to ask you…" Her mother's comments from dinner a few nights prior had occurred to her. "Uncle Morse—I know you said he had an airtight alibi, but I heard he walked right past the police at the house the day of the murders and didn't even ask what was going on."

"That's true," Declan said, nodding. "His manner was defi-nitely odd, but he could account for every minute of his morning."

"As a horse trader, he probably knows lots of undesirables who'd be happy to kill a few old folks for money. Maybe his alibi is so good because he is, in fact, guilty."

"I actually thought the same thing but never found any solid leads." He hesitated, then put out his elbow. "Shall I… walk you in?"

Victoria considered his arm, the cuff of his coat sleeve frayed, a small spot of neat stitches mending a hole. How wonderful it would feel to take his elbow, but she then considered the rest of it—the crowd, the reporters, not to mention her father's horror were he to see them together.

"No. Thank you. I think I've heard enough for one day."

"As you wish," he said, giving a smart bow.

She watched him walk away, his shoulders squared, his hair tousled by the wind, and she imagined calling him back. Imagined him striding over, taking her hand, pulling her toward him, enveloping her in his arms, his breath warm in her hair.

He hurried up the courthouse steps and went inside, closing the door firmly behind him.

He has not been willing to say much for publication heretofore, but today he consented to tell the *Herald* his full story. He said: "I returned to Fall River from New Bedford on Wednesday afternoon; and after a drive to Swansea and back came to Mr. Borden's house and stayed that night. The next morning, I had breakfast about seven o'clock and at a quarter to nine I left. Mrs. Borden was upstairs. I hadn't seen her since eight o'clock. Mr. Borden left me at the door, asking me to come home to dinner. I went to the post office and several other places about town and finally to Daniel Emery's, at No. 4 Weybosett Street. I stayed there until between quarter after and half-past eleven, when I started for home by streetcar. It was twenty minutes to twelve when I got home and heard of the murders. The house was full of policemen and people. That is all I know about it."

"Mr. Morse," I said, "it has been asserted that when Lizzie Borden was away the week before the murder, she went to New Bedford to see you."

"That is not true," said Morse vehemently. "She did not see me. I didn't get any letters from her either, though I heard she was at Marion."

Mr. Morse admitted that there had been ill feeling between Mrs. Borden and her step-daughters but he would not discuss that matter further. Lizzie, he said, was a peculiar girl, often given to fits of sullenness. His statement about his whereabouts during the morning of the murder has been fully corroborated, and persons who were on the streetcar with him when he went home testified to that fact. Perhaps it was only Mr. Morse's furtive and unhappy manner when he talked that directed any suspicion toward him.

VIEW OF THE VICINITY OF THE MURDERS.

I. Borden house.
II. Borden barn.
III. The well.
IV. Fence with barbed wire on top.
V. Side entrance.
VI. Churchill residence.

VII. Dr. Bowen's house.
VIII. Dr. Chagnon's house.
IX. Kelley house.
X. Yard from which officers watched the Borden house.
XI. Kelley's barn.
XII. Pear orchard.

CHAPTER
TWENTY-SIX

"It has long been an axiom of mine that the little things are infinitely the most important."

—*Sherlock Holmes in* A Case of Identity

The next day was Saturday, and the dining room had never been cleaner—the etched globes in the chandelier glowed brightly, the gleam of the silver candlesticks and tea service on the sideboard reflected doubly bright in the spotless mirror behind. As Victoria nibbled her toast, waiting for Father to finish the morning paper, Penelope came in and out of the dining room half a dozen times, refilling Father's coffee cup, brushing toast crumbs from the table, offering more pork sausage, checking that Father had enough cream and sugar for his coffee, and asking if he wanted more toast. Victoria could not bear to look at her, at the fear and supplication in her eyes, and wished Father would be kinder in his refusals.

When the kitchen door swung open once more, Victoria expected Penelope again, and was surprised to see Mother with an annoyed look on her face. Her navy silk hung about her ribcage like a dressing gown and when she thrust her hand out toward her husband, her sleeve cuff bagged around her thin wrist.

In her hand lay the silver cufflinks, looking lonely and out of place. Victoria had to fight the urge to snatch them up.

"They were in the pocket of your tail coat," Mother said, her tone icy.

Father, who'd been drinking his coffee, stopped mid-sip and stared at the cufflinks, his brow furrowed.

"I haven't worn that coat in ages! Yet I wore the cufflinks just a few weeks ago—I'm certain of it."

Dread shot up Victoria's spine. How foolish she'd been! The tailcoat was a winter weight fabric, which was why Penelope had been airing it in the first place.

"Perhaps all of your back-and-forthing to the farm is wreaking havoc on your memory," Mother said dryly. "Among other things." She dropped the squares unceremoniously onto the dining room table, one tumbling under the edge of Father's saucer with a tiny clink. "You owe Penelope an apology," she added, then stalked out.

Father opened his mouth to reply, then with an angry sigh, shut it. He glared at the offending cufflinks, as if this unpleasant exchange were their fault.

Victoria kept her eyes on the specks of grain in her bread and pretended not to notice Father's huffs, head shaking, and paper-rattling. Part of her felt bad for causing his anguish, but another part felt he deserved that and more for making Penelope cry and for being so rude to Declan.

Finally, tossing his paper aside, Father stood and straightened his vest. When he looked up and saw Victoria, his face softened and he came over and kissed the top of her head.

"Sorry for the unpleasantness, Pidge," he said.

She watched his fingers close around the sparkling squares and hated the pinch of sadness this caused.

"Me too," she replied.

VICTORIA WAS JUST finishing the depressing article that covered Medley's testimony when Mother returned to the dining room.

"Victoria, we still haven't gotten a dress made for your debut and it's only two weeks away!" She frowned at the silver candelabra on the sideboard and moved it one inch to the right. "I thought we'd go to Anderson's today and get us both measured. Mrs. Jacobsen raved about their fabric selection, and their turnaround time was impressive."

Anderson's? The buttons. That horrid woman.

"Oh, Mother, no, not Anderson's. The owner is frightful and said some very unkind things about Miss Lizzie. Please, let's just have Mrs. Gifford come to the house. I would hate to give Mrs. Anderson our business."

"We are going to Anderson's and that is that. Now, get your hat and cloak. I expect they will not be open much past noon."

MRS. ANDERSON, IT seemed, had been called away on "family business" for which Victoria was greatly appreciative. Sherlock had instructed Watson that in certain cases, instead of looking for fresh evidence, one needs to sift through details already collected, so Victoria spent the entire fitting time doing as she was told by the seamstress while inwardly picking through the particulars of the murder day as best as she could recall: Feeding Mother. The workers in the Chagnons' backyard. Mr. Borden in town. Mr. Clegg. The announcement in Benson's. Stealing the thread. Declan in the alley. Tearing her coat on Mr.

Pottersmith's bushes. The chaos in the Bordens' yard, as seen from her bedroom window. The police. The reporters. The neighbors. All this she re-imagined as she stood obediently, arms stretched out like a scarecrow, while the silver-haired clerk measured and murmured and pinned.

There had to be something.

Mrs. Plover was just marking the hem length when the jingle of the front door sounded, followed by muffled snorts and giggles. Across the store, Victoria immediately recognized the impish duo from her neighborhood.

"I'd like to buy..." said Thomas in a warbly falsetto.

"A corset!" finished Brownie.

They dissolved into laughter and became a tangle of arms and legs in their attempt to get out the door before the other. The bell jangled again and the boys were out on the sidewalk, giggling and pushing each other between the shoppers.

"Like a couple of bad pennies, those two," Mrs. Plover mumbled around the pins in her mouth. "Always turning up."

Victoria nodded in agreement, and then stopped. *Always turning up.* She pictured the chaotic scene in the Bordens' yard again. The police, the reporters, the neighbors. The boys weaving in and out. They had been there that day!

"Excuse me. You're finished, right?" Victoria didn't wait for Mrs. Plover to answer and yanked the length of pinned fabric over her head. "I'm so sorry, but I have to..."

"Victoria!" Her mother's shocked voice.

"I'll... be right back," she said, grabbing her cloak. "Or as soon as I can."

Pulling on her cloak, she rushed in the same direction Thomas and Brownie had headed. "Stop! Stop those boys!" she yelled.

The boys, frightened, began to run.

"Help!" she called louder, and then, because they were getting away, added, "They've stolen my purse!"

Her purse, of course, was back at the store with her mother.

With the knife inside. She prayed her mother would not discover it.

When Victoria finally caught up with the boys, they were in the grips of Officer Lupin, the thin policeman who'd tipped Victoria off about Oak Grove Cemetery all those weeks earlier. Both boys appeared to be on the verge of tears, one looking defiant, the other more fearful.

"Hello again, miss," Officer Lupin nodded. "I don't see your purse anywhere, so they must've ditched it. Is that what you did, then, boys?" He gave the defiant one's arm a tug.

"We didn't steal nothing!"

"It wasn't us, I swear it!"

"You know," Victoria said, peering closely at Thomas and Brownie, "now that I see them up close, Officer, I'm not sure it was these two. Would you mind if I asked them a few questions?"

"Be my guest, miss. Now listen up, young sirs," he said, giving them both a shake, "and give the lady your honest answers."

The taller boy jutted out his chin. The other boy merely nodded. People passing by gave the boys dirty looks and one woman in a gray hat *tsk-tsked* loudly.

"All right then, boys," Victoria said, keeping her voice low. "Why don't you start by telling me where you were the day the Bordens were murdered?"

"HONESTLY, VICTORIA," Mother whispered as they left Anderson's together. "I've never been so embarrassed in my life! Such a scene you created! What will Mrs. Anderson think of us when Mrs. Plover tells her what happened?"

A tongue lashing from Mother could not spoil Victoria's mood. Straightening her jacket and tucking her purse firmly under her arm, she felt an inexplicable surge of love for every stranger that passed them on the footpath. She'd caught the boys and had arranged for Officer Lupin to deliver them to Miss Lizzie's lawyers to tell them what they saw. Also, her knife had not been discovered.

"Frankly, Mother," she said, smiling at a gray-haired gentleman shuffling by, "I do not care one whit what Mrs. Horrible Anderson thinks of us, and if I have to wear my dusting dress and apron to the ball, I will."

"Don't be ridiculous, Victoria, but now you must tell me— what was the emergency? Had you witnessed a crime? Spotted the president's carriage? What?"

Victoria thought for a moment. "I would say it was more a matter of preventing a crime. I hope." She hooked her arm through her mother's. "I pray."

Mrs. Livermore Makes Another Statement
About the Prisoner

*Sane and Remarkably Level-Headed, She Found
Lizzie Borden to Be*

Mrs. Mary A. Livermore was seen by a repre-
sentative of the *Boston Post* Monday evening
and was asked her opinion of the current
rumor of mental weakness in Miss Lizzie
Borden. She announced her absolute disbelief in the report and said, "She seemed
not only rational but remarkably level-
headed—so much so, in fact, as to surprise
me not a little, ill as she was and under
such a dreadful strain. When she was taken
to New Bedford for arraignment, she caught
a bad cold, which was attended with some
fever… In this physical condition, she surprised me by the clearness and vigor of her
mind. She received me with evidences of
deep emotion, but never for a moment was
there the least sign that her mental poise
was not perfect. Some of her reasoning it
would puzzle the government lawyers to answer, as for instance when she said:

'Had I purposed to murder my father and
mother, should I have done it at mid-day,
with the house all open? How easily might I
have arranged it in the night. Father and
Mother were both heavy sleepers, and one
blow to each would have finished the dreadful business. Then how easy for me to have

counterfeited the evidence of a struggle in the apartment, thrown an outside door suspiciously open and left the morning light to pin the crime to some unknown outsider?'

"This is certainly not the reasoning of an insane person," continued Mrs. Livermore.

CHAPTER
TWENTY-SEVEN

O n the tenth morning of the trial, the prosecution retired
their last witness and presented their exhibits, including a
map of the neighborhood, the handle-less axe, the blue
dress Lizzie claimed to have worn that day, and, of course, the
skulls. *Finally.* Victoria was beginning to think Miss Lizzie's
lawyers would never get a chance to present their side. White-
haired Andrew Jennings, with his stern eyebrows and stiff countenance, took his time rising from his seat. Would this old man
be any match against the young prosecutors? He adjusted his
cuffs and nodded graciously to the judge.

"May it please your Honors, Mr. Foreman, and gentlemen
of the jury," Jennings began warmly, as if chatting with old
friends by the fireside. "I must preface this opening by stating
that one of the victims in this heinous murder was my client and
close friend since boyhood, and I have similarly known the accused all of her life."

Was this something to which one's solicitor should admit—

a built-in bias? Not a particularly strong position from which to begin.

"Therefore," Jennings continued, "if I manifest more feeling than you think necessary, you will ascribe it to that cause. The counsel, dear sirs, does not cease to be a man when he becomes a lawyer."

Miss Emma, sitting behind Miss Lizzie, reached out and touched her sister's shoulder in a comforting way. Miss Lizzie turned, and Victoria sat up, hoping to catch her eye, but Miss Lizzie's gaze passed right over Victoria.

Jennings spoke for only forty minutes before beginning to call his witnesses, making Victoria worry. What if he ran through his list before her young scamps arrived? Would he wait for them? What if they'd gotten away from Officer Lupin and never gave their statements? With each testimony, her nerves grew tauter, her palms, sweatier. Several witnesses claimed to have seen suspicious men outside the Borden home the day of the murders, but all the descriptions were vague, the identities of the men unknown, and none of the accounts matched. Hymon Lubinsky, the ice cream peddler, was the only witness to testify seeing Miss Lizzie walk from the barn to the house, but even then, he could only say it was a woman in a dark dress and that it wasn't Bridget. His English was shaky and during their cross examination, the prosecution made him look foolish.

"You ask me too fast," Hymon complained, which was probably just what that bully, Knowlton, intended.

"Poor man," Mother whispered.

By the time the matron of the Fall River police department stepped down, Victoria felt the whole case was a muddied mess, with not one strong voice the jury could believe. Studying Jennings' disheartened face, his jowls sagging, eyes drooping, Victoria wished Miss Lizzie had chosen a younger man to represent her, someone with fire and passion, not this old coot who looked like he was late for his afternoon nap.

A sudden scuffling at the back caught the room's attention

as the rear doors flew open, revealing Victoria's young witnesses. Finally! Almost unrecognizable, their faces were scrubbed pink, and hair combed so fiercely the skin between the slicked-down rows looked burned. An officer of the court led the boys to a bench in the front, shooing a few reporters out of their prized spots.

Everett Brown—Brownie—was called to the stand a few minutes later. As he shuffled forward, there was quiet laughter, a few dismissive shakes of heads. Several reporters lounged back and began doodling in their notebooks and a few left the room. Victoria bit her lip and glanced back to Declan, whose father seemed to be grilling him about these new witnesses. Had she gotten him in trouble again?

"This boy is who I was chasing," she whispered to her mother. "Him and his friend. Let's hope it was worth it."

Everett Brown sat on his hands and swung his legs until catching sight of his mother, and promptly clomped his shoes together. With each question Jennings asked, the noises that belong to a crowded room—feet shuffling, throat clearing, rustling of skirts, coughing—lessened.

"Tell us what you did," said Jennings, "when you got to the Bordens' that day."

Everett straightened, knowing this was the important part. "We went in the side gate and up along the path to the door, tried to get into the house, and Mr. Sawyer wouldn't let us in. He was at the door."

"Did you see Officer Medley there at that time?"

"No, sir."

"Do you know Officer Medley?"

"Yes, sir."

Everett Brown continued answering the prosecutor's questions, saying he and "the party that was with" him went directly to the barn and stood inside a minute to see who would go up into the loft first, his friend balking because "somebody might drop an axe on him."

Victoria could only see the back of Thomas Barlow, the brasher of the two friends, and was amused to see the tips of his ears turning bright red.

"So we went upstairs and looked out of the window on the west side, and went from there over to the hay, and was up in the barn loft about five minutes." He explained they'd kicked the hay around, looking for someone hiding within, but finding no one, they left the barn, went to the house, and tried to look in the windows. When this proved unsuccessful, they returned to the barn.

"Then we saw Officer Fleet arrive."

Gasps erupted from those who'd been paying close attention to the case, and they whispered to the less astute that Officer Medley testified he also saw Officer Fleet arrive a minute after he arrived. *Before* he went into the house and looked around. *Before* he questioned Miss Lizzie. And much before he made his way to the barn and supposedly saw no footprints and nothing disturbed.

If Everett and Thomas had been in the loft before Medley, which apparently they were, the floor would have been covered in their footprints and scattered hay, not undisturbed as Medley had claimed. The crowd was so noisy, Judge Blaisdell had to bang his gavel five times to obtain quiet.

Thomas Barlow was called to the stand next and his testimony echoed Brownie's. He went on to say that after Officer Fleet arrived, he and Brownie were "put out" with everyone else from the back yard, and hung around the front yard until supper, around five o'clock. Then they came back and stayed until midnight. Now the ones blushing were Thomas's grandmother and Everett's mother, who had allowed their young imps to roam the streets until all hours with a murderer on the loose. Victoria wanted to hug them both for their years of negligence.

"Your honor," Jennings said. "The defense rests."

"See, Mother?" Victoria swished her skirts as she strode out of the courthouse. "My scene-making was well worth it, don't you think?"

With an expression a mixture of admiration and bewilderment, Mother held up her hand to block the peach rays of autumn sunlight and peered at Victoria. "But how did you know those boys had been up in that barn, Victoria?"

Victoria smiled, her eyebrows arched. "You can thank Arthur Conan Doyle for that." She scanned the crowd for Declan and found him in a group on the far side of the yard, being dressed down by an unhappy Mayor Coughlin. Though sorry for Declan, Victoria was happy to see the mayor upset—served him right for pressuring the police to make a quick arrest. And Declan wouldn't be able to explain the presence of the witnesses, for Victoria hadn't had time to talk to him and Officer Lupin must not have mentioned it.

"Arthur who?" Mother asked.

Victoria took her mother's thin arm—too thin, she needed to eat more—and walked her down the sidewalk. "The author of those 'crass whodunits,' as you call them, in the *Strand*. His main character, Sherlock Holmes, solves mysteries by looking at the facts."

Mother's foot slipped on a wet leaf and Victoria tightened her hold.

"Thank you, dear. Now, you'll have to elaborate because I am not following."

"Well, I knew I had seen those boys in the Bordens' yard that day—that's one fact." Though Victoria had imagined explaining this to Declan, it still felt good to share it with her mother. She was quite proud of the way she'd put it all together, and though she hadn't yet solved the mystery of who murdered the Bordens, at least it gave credence to Miss Lizzie's story.

"I also knew," she continued, "from seeing these two around town, that they are irrepressibly curious, as well as brash and impulsive—another fact. I then imagined what two curious, brash, and impulsive boys might do in a yard where a murder has just been committed—they'd go looking for the killer, hoping to get a reward! And where would they look?"

Mother smiled and nodded. "In the barn."

"Exactly! I also guessed that the police saw the boys only as nuisances and wouldn't think to interview them, even though they were some of the first on the scene." Victoria gave a pinecone a victorious little kick and watched it tumble down the walk before them. "That I learned from Sherlock too. He paid his Baker Street Irregulars—street urchins, really—a guinea apiece for an important clue."

"Victoria! Did you pay those boys?"

"Of course not!" They stopped at the curb to wait for a break in the carriages. "I just threatened to tell their parents about their shenanigans in Anderson's if they didn't talk about what they saw that morning." Victoria laughed. "Suddenly, they were more than happy to speak up."

She felt very clever for a full five seconds, which is when her own shenanigans in Anderson's popped to mind. *But you're done with that*, she reminded herself. *You're going to be a debutante. A different person. Mature. Self-controlled. You'll be fine.*

She tightened her grip on her purse, the knife still inside, and pushed her lips into a smile. Her heart, however, did not follow.

THE NEW YORK TIMES
Lizzie Borden's Remarkable Coolness

The most remarkable feature of the trial
has been the demeanor of Lizzie Borden.
From start to finish she has manifested no
feeling of weakness and has listened to the
recital of the most cold-blooded and shocking details of the crime with a perfectly
impassive and unmoved countenance. The description of the wounds by the medical
examiner, his gory tale of how the skull
was forced into the brains of the aged couple a dozen times, his recital of how the
skulls were sawed from the bodies under his
direction and the removal of the flesh from
them-all these and other similarly ghastly
stories the young woman heard and was apparently unmoved. Three or four times she
enjoyed a hearty laugh: for instance, when
her attorney, desirous of ascertaining the
space occupied by the body of her stepmother as it lay upon the floor compared the
aged lady's physical proportions to those
of the solidly built District Attorney.

Those who believe her insane consider this
good evidence of that fact, but there is no
apparent insanity in the clear blue eyes
which look up now and then with apparent
interest at the half a hundred busy press
correspondents.

CHAPTER
TWENTY-EIGHT

O n the way home from the trial, Victoria suggested they
    call on the Jacobsens. Mother, anxious to learn all the
    details of the Coming Out party, happily agreed. Out of
habit, Victoria and Gwyne headed to the sitting room.

"Girls!" Mrs. Jacobsen stood outside the parlor door. She'd
applied too much rice powder to the left side of her face, giving
her an unbalanced look. "It's high time you began joining us in
the parlor to practice the fine art of conversation."

Victoria knew from experience that Mrs. Jacobsen's "fine
art of conversation" meant listening to bragging and name-
dropping and mentioning GG's father-in-law *the Duke*. So, before her mother could agree with Mrs. Jacobsen, Victoria
slipped her arm through Gwyne's and gave her friend's mother
her warmest smile. "Just once more, for old time's sake?"

Mrs. Jacobsen relented and, as soon as they were safely behind the closed sitting room door, Victoria told Gwyne her
whole victorious story.

"You do realize," Gwyne said, not looking up from her needlework, "that it comes down to an inspector's word against that of two delinquent boys?"

Victoria frowned. "Gwyne, please. This is the first time I've felt hopeful in weeks. Don't spoil it."

"Fine, we'll change the subject." Gwyne said, putting down her embroidery, a hanky by the looks of it, edged in yellow and green French knots. "Let's talk about *boys*."

Victoria had to laugh, and immediately her heart filled with thoughts of Declan: his eyes crinkling as he smiled, his dimple, that loop of hair that practically begged her fingers to set straight.

"Who are you hoping for your first dance partner at the party, Victoria?"

Declan in a tuxedo, holding out his hand for her to accept, warm candlelight from the wall sconces making his eyes shimmer… She shook her head. The only way Declan would be allowed into her debut was if someone committed a crime there. "No one special."

"Oh, come on." Gwyne scooted forward in her chair conspiratorially. "There has to be someone. My secret choice is Jared Winters."

Victoria laughed again. "That's not a secret. You've been babbling on about Jared all summer."

Gwyne blushed. "Fine. I'm not the secretive type. Not like you! Sometimes I wonder if you'll disappear one day, and I'll find out you were a German spy or a visitor from a distant planet or a secret mistress of Buffalo Bill's."

Although Victoria knew Gwyne was kidding, her comment struck a little too close to home. This was not the first time her friend had accused her of being secretive.

"Well," Victoria admitted, "there is one boy who has caught my eye, but he's not on the guest list."

Gwyne inhaled deeply as her eyes widened. "See?" she said. "I had no idea! *Who*?" She practically bounced in her armchair.

"He's not from Durfee, or church. Not really in our social circle." But he was so much *more* than any of those boys.

Gwyne frowned in concentration. "The only boys I know that aren't in our social circle are all working class—gardeners, piecers, stable boys, farm hands—and of course they'd be out of the question…"

Victoria felt the heat in her cheeks and Gwyne gasped, her hand flying to her chest. "Oh Tory! It's not that detective fellow, is it? The one from the cemetery?"

"Shh!" Victoria glanced toward the doorway, hoping their mothers hadn't heard, though of course, the door was closed. Then she nodded, whispering, "Yes." There, she had admitted it, to her best friend, and it felt as though a whole garden of flowers had just burst into bloom in her chest. She, Victoria Robbins, was in love with Declan Dempsey.

"Well, that's ridiculous." Gwyne laughed. "You are always such a contrarian! Resisting a Coming Out party. Preferring mysteries to poetry. Defending a woman the entire town believes is guilty. Honestly! Leave it to you to snub all the eligible men for a young man you could never marry. Why do you pretend to be so different?"

The garden wilted instantly as shame and anger washed over Victoria. "I am not pretending, Gwyne. You asked who I fancied and I told you." A pair of sewing scissors near Gwyne's elbow caught her eye—small, shaped like a stork, its beak the two blades.

She felt a slight throbbing behind her eyes.

Gwyne blinked, surprised. "Goodness, Tory, you look positively ashen. Maybe you shouldn't be going to the trial every day. I think it's taking a toll on you." She picked up her embroidery and started back on it.

"It's not the trial, Gwyne. It's your condescending attitude. Declan Dempsey is a perfectly respectable young man, and handsome too. You said so yourself."

"Fine," Gwyne said with an impatient sigh. "He's handsome but a completely inappropriate choice. Is that better?"

The scissors glinted in the lamplight. "No."

Another sigh. "I just want us to have fun at our debut, and you won't if your head is filled with that boy and this whole thing with Miss Lizzie."

"*Thing*? You mean her trial, which will decide if she lives or dies?"

"I'm sorry, Victoria, I've tried to be a good sport about all this, but Miss Lizzie is all you think about! All you *talk* about. You don't seem to give a whit about me anymore." She slipped a folded hanky from her cuff and dabbed her nose. "When we went dress shopping, you couldn't leave fast enough. Then when you went for your dress, you didn't even think to invite me. When we sampled the sweets for the party, you never commented on which we should serve. Do you realize you've never made one decision or even one suggestion about the party? Every time we're together, you seem to wish you were somewhere else!"

Her voice cracked on the last words and her cheeks were two pink splotches.

Victoria felt horrible. Everything Gwyne said was true. But how could she explain her rudeness without giving herself away? She hated herself, hated her weakness, hated constantly covering her tracks, hated all the lying. It was humiliating.

The stork scissors at Gwyne's elbow throbbed temptingly.

No, Mag. I'm done.

"It was just terrible timing, with our debut coming at the same time as the trial."

Gwyne shook her head. "It's not just the trial, Tory, it's… you. You're different. Guarded, even more than you used to be. I can even see the disinterest slip over your eyes sometimes, lowering like window shades. You try to cover it up, but it's painfully obvious you'd rather be somewhere else. Anywhere else."

"Oh, Gwyne, no." Victoria pressed her folded hands to her

ribs. "That's not true."

"Well, what is true? I'm never really quite sure when it comes to you." Gwyne folded her hanky into a smaller square.

The stork scissors were slightly open, laughing at her.

"After this trial is over, I promise things will get back to normal. I'll be a better friend—a new me. That's what I'm hoping for." She glared at the scissors. *I don't want you.*

Gwyne frowned at the stitchery in her lap, absentmindedly pulling the edges straight. "I'd settle for the old you, Tory. Like you were when we were little. Remember Madam Fi Fi and Sir Pierre?"

Madam Fi Fi and Sir Pierre were acorns, so named because of their beret-like caps, and she and Gwyne spent many afternoons tapping them along the ground, up and down branches, in and out of hidey-holes, and going on adventures that usually involved a lava pit and a winged horse. Part of her childhood before she'd started stealing.

Laughing, Victoria said, "That's right! And their baby. What was his name?"

"Frére Jacques!" Gwyne gave a watery grin. "Don't you remember how we'd sing that song when we'd put them to bed under their leaf blankets?"

A deep, pure happiness, surged through Victoria, warm as a long drink of hot cocoa. She'd forgotten what that felt like, joy with no shadows lurking behind it. No worrying. No covering up. No hiding.

It would be nice to be that free again.

Victoria reached out to her friend and Gwyne took her hand. "I really don't deserve you and I promise I'll make it up to you."

Her friend gave Victoria's hand a gentle squeeze. "Just be yourself, Tory, your old self, and I'll be happy."

Smiling at her friend, Victoria tried to hold the smell of honeysuckle and dirt in her mind, to feel the innocence, the simplicity, the honesty of her earlier life. She would re-set herself back to her true self, to the person she was before she began to steal. She would be that pure person but grown up. She would be the friend Gwyne deserved.

"I will, Gwyne."

When Victoria pulled her hand back, her purse slipped off her lap and hit the oriental rug with a loud thump. Her heart fell with it.

Gwyne frowned. "Wait. It's torn. There's something sharp poking out."

The tip of Hennimen's blade had cut through the material and was sticking out.

Gwyne blinked. "It's a knife." Eying Victoria warily, she leaned back ever so slightly. It was the same look Victoria had seen on so many faces in the courtroom as they watched Miss Lizzie enter and exit. Now was Victoria's chance to be honest. She could tell her everything. *Gwyne,* she could say, *I have something to tell you.* Or *I know this is going to sound crazy but...*

"We needed a knife to cut our snack of apples and cheese at the trial. We don't dare leave our seats for lunch, with all those reporters waiting to swoop in. What did you think?" She forced a laugh, feeling miserable.

Gwyne just stared back at her.

THE NEXT DAY, the prosecution asked for a rebuttal in light of new evidence. When they called Alice Russell's name, Victoria's hands clenched. Miss Alice took the stand without glancing once at her old friend. What was going on?

Moody reviewed Miss Alice's history and friendship with Miss Lizzie from the first time she'd testified, adding that there was one important detail she hadn't felt comfortable disclosing. He asked about Sunday, three days after the murder—after breakfast but before noon—and what it was she saw when she entered the kitchen. The way he said it, pausing slightly, enunciating the words so carefully, made the hairs on Victoria's neck prickle. Whatever came next was not going to be good.

Miss Alice swallowed. "I saw Miss Lizzie at the other end of the stove..." Her voice was so quiet, Moody put his hand to his ear, signaling her to speak up. She nodded and continued, louder. "I saw Miss Emma at the sink. Miss Lizzie was at the stove and she had a skirt in her hand and her sister turned and said, 'What are you going to do?' and Lizzie said, 'I am going to burn this old thing up; it is covered with paint."

"Go on."

Her gaze flicked from Mr. Moody to Miss Lizzie and back to Mr. Moody. "Miss Lizzie stood up toward the cupboard door—the cupboard was open—and she appeared to be either ripping something down or tearing part of this garment."

"What part?"

"I don't know for sure: it was a small part. I said to her, 'I wouldn't let anybody see me do that, Lizzie.'"

"Did she do anything when you said that?"

"She stepped just one step farther back up toward the cupboard door."

Like a flock of started seagulls, the crowd erupted with gasps and muffled cries of "Burned the dress!" Several journalists jumped up and scooted down their rows, off to contact their head office. Others stayed in their seats, writing furiously, the sound of their pencil scratchings grating upon Victoria's ears. The judge banged his gavel for quiet. Moody, fighting a smug smile, continued his questioning.

"The next day, you spoke to her about the dress. What did you say?"

Miss Alice studied her clasped hands, one thumb tapping the knuckle of the other. "I said, 'I am afraid, Lizzie, the worst thing you could have done was to burn that dress. I have been asked by the police about your dresses.'"

"And what did she reply?"

"She said, 'Oh, what made you let me do it? Why didn't you tell me?"

"Miss Russell." Moody's voice was low and steady, and a smile tugged at one corner of his mouth. "Will you tell us what kind of a dress—give us a description of the dress she burned."

"It was a cheap, cotton Bedford cord."

"And tell us, what was its color?"

The pencil-scratchings of the reporters ceased. Heads snapped up. Even Mrs. Kettleson stopped whispering to the painfully thin woman next to her. One older woman elbowed her husband, who snorted awake.

Victoria gripped her pig-tailed hanky. *Please don't say...*

"Light blue ground," Miss Alice announced, "with a dark figure—small figure." Victoria knew that dress. The dark figures were little diamond shapes. Or perhaps fleur-de lis?

As people around Victoria gasped outwardly, she groaned inwardly. Mrs. Churchill had testified that on the morning of the murders, Miss Lizzie was wearing a blue and white groundwork dress with a deep navy diamond figure.

But she said it was calico or cambric, Victoria thought, not a Bedford cord. Would the difference be enough?

Both Miss Alice and Mrs. Cunningham testified in cross-examination that they'd seen no traces of blood on Miss Lizzie's dress or hands or face while they fanned her that day, and that her hair had still been perfectly arranged. But as she sat through the rest of the day's proceedings, hope leaked out of Victoria like water from a cracked bucket.

Finally, court was adjourned for the day. Tomorrow, both sides would make their closing arguments, and then it would be up to the jury to decide if Miss Lizzie would walk or if she would hang. Victoria caught Miss Lizzie's eye as she was led out of the courtroom by a baby-faced police officer. Victoria gave her an encouraging smile, but Miss Lizzie's lips didn't move, set like two pencils bound together.

ON THE WAY home, Victoria spied Mr. Hennimen's cart—*finally*—and the delicious smell was all the help Victoria needed to convince Mother to buy several for supper. While Mother exchanged pleasantries with Mr. Hennimen, Victoria, heart pounding, turned away and pulled the wrapped knife from her purse, keeping both low and close to her cloak. An untidy stack of paraffin papers sat on the counter, along with another knife and roll of string, and when Mother pointed at the pies she wanted and Mr. Hennimen turned, Victoria stepped forward, pressed her belly to the counter and slipped the knife bundle under the edge of the messy papers. For one panicked moment, she was not sure she could let go of her prize. But she did, and when she stepped back, she wrapped her purse strings around her fingers, tight as a tourniquet.

THAT NIGHT, VICTORIA could not sleep, her mind a carousel going round and round with different facts of the case popping up and down. The burned dress—had it been the one she'd been wearing? And though the story of the prussic acid had been ultimately thrown out, were the jurors truly capable of ignoring it? Then there was Medley's testimony about the barn floor. And Thomas and Brownie's contradicting account. The handle-less axe. The hour between the two murders. The missing note. Thank goodness the allegations of Miss Lizzie being a thief never surfaced.

And then there was that blasted Coming Out party coming up—in GG's house, overflowing with valuable trinkets and every young man but the one she wanted. Where was Declan, anyway? The last time they'd spoken, he had made that comment about "her" Edward Pottersmith. Perhaps he had given up on her and maybe it was for the best. Gwyne certainly seemed to think so, to say nothing of her parents. Even Penelope voiced her doubts earlier that night as they tidied the kitchen together.

At least she'd been able to return the knife. At least she had that in her favor.

The sky was beginning to lighten as she finally fell asleep, and after what seemed like only a moment, Penelope was shaking her shoulder, telling her she'd be late for the trial if she didn't get up.

CHAPTER
TWENTY-NINE

The cherry-paneled courtroom was the most crowded it had ever been. Victoria's father was able, after some cajoling, to elbow out a spot in the back large enough for the three of them to stand. The judge called for quiet and the defense began their closing remarks. Mr. Jennings proclaimed the state had not one shred of evidence against Lizzie—no murder weapon, no witnesses, and no blood on her person. Using the state's own timeline, he pointed out that had Miss Lizzie been the murderer, she would have had only eight to thirteen minutes between her father's murder and calling out to Bridget Sullivan, to wash blood from her face, hands, hair, clothes, murder weapon, possibly change her dress, then break the handle off the axe and dispose of it so cleverly, it was yet to be found. When he finished, it took everything inside Victoria to keep from jumping to her feet and cheering.

Unfortunately, Mr. Knowlton had the advantage of being the last to speak, and speak he did. Victoria had only attended the theater twice in her life, but neither performance held a candle to the mastery that was Knowlton's closing argument. He spun a tale of an embittered and hateful woman who finally gave in to her murderous intentions against her stepmother, brutally attacking her from behind, exacting eighteen blows into her skull, neck and back. Then, surprised by her father's early return, she felt it necessary to kill him too, lest he discover her terrible deed, even going so far as suggesting he lie down on the sofa to take a rest so she could later kill him in his slumber.

Knowlton reminded the jury of Miss Lizzie's prediction just the night before the murders of someone exacting revenge upon her father. Then he went on to discredit her "absurd and impossible" claims of being in the barn, of burning a paint-stained dress, of the mysterious note received by her stepmother—"No note came; no note was written; nobody brought a note." Worst of all, he hit upon the one thing Victoria felt the most unease over: the fact that, upon discovery of her father's body, with his blood still flowing, Lizzie was not frightened out of the house, fearful the murderer might still be within, but remained inside, calling for others to come in instead. Then later that same night, she felt comfortable enough to visit the cellar, a disquieting and gloomy place on the most normal of nights, and she went down not once but twice, the second time alone, into the very same room where her parents' bloody clothes soaked.

Victoria shook her head, attempting to clear it of the morbid story Mr. Knowlton told. It wasn't true! It couldn't be true. But what was the truth? Sherlock boils everything down to the facts, but the facts can be interpreted different ways. A burned dress could be an innocent way to rid oneself of a paint-stained frock, or a conniving method of destroying evidence. A negative remark about one's stepmother could be the casual words of a woman blowing off steam, or evidence of murderous intent from a spiteful heart. Canceling a trip to the country could show dedication to one's civic obligations or premeditation for murder.

How could each side's argument could be so completely

different yet make such complete sense? As Knowlton summed up the prosecution's evidence, Victoria stared at the men of the jury—the fleshy, impassive face of this one; the intent, rat-like eyes of that one; the one in the back fighting to keep his chin from hitting his chest in slumber—and silently willed all twelve to declare Miss Lizzie innocent of her parents' murders, therefore severing her own march toward the gallows.

FEW PEOPLE IN the courtroom moved more than standing to stretch, not wanting to give up their spots and miss the jury's return. Cigarettes and pipes were lit. Hand fans fluttered. Beside her, Mother looked so pale that Father led her out in search of a place to sit and rest. Victoria's stomach growled and her neck was damp with perspiration. She thought she glimpsed Declan's tousled black head across the room but couldn't be sure. She caught glimpses of Susan from school, whose cousin worked with Eli Bence of the prussic acid fame. Mayor Coughlin. The kindly Officer Lupin who helped her with Brownie and Thomas. Hundreds of other faces, familiar and not, all bunched together like so many marbles in a pan. Miss Lizzie was somewhere behind this mass of humanity and Victoria ached for what she must be feeling.

In one of the front rows, a young boy was sick into his father's bowler cap. There was quite a lot of shuffling and rearranging as father and pale son made their way down the row. The sight of so many hankies pressed to noses brought Victoria back to the day after the murders, standing in Miss Lizzie's crowded hallway. Some of the very same people, assembled then to give Miss Lizzie comfort, were now, just a few months later, ghoulishly witnessing her possible demise.

If only she could go back to that day, knowing what she knew now, she could... well, what *would* she do? Not trust the police to do a thorough job, to begin with. Maybe she and Declan could have done their own investigating: asking Miss Lizzie for her dress that very day instead of a week later. Gone through her closet meticulously, seen the paint-smudged dress for themselves. Followed up on other leads rather than just focusing on Miss Lizzie. Told the doctor not to give her so much morphine so she'd be more lucid. Gone through the pile of bloody rags instead of avoiding them all together.

A window screeched open, letting in a ribbon of cold, industrial air to combat the smell of vomit. *If only*, Victoria thought again. If only she could go back to the day of the murders and have not gone to town, but instead stayed home and read at her window seat, for then she would have seen Miss Lizzie going to the barn, been a witness, and known for sure if she was telling the truth. She'd have seen it with her own eyes. Instead, she'd followed the devil inside her, for hadn't she known, deep down, that she'd steal that day?

If only she hadn't gone. If only she hadn't stolen that thread. If only she'd never stolen anything, ever. For an hour and a half, Victoria's thoughts traveled this circle, her legs throbbing from standing, her stomach woozy with fear, her heart heavy with regret, as if her stealing had been the root of all that had gone wrong. A punishment. Mother and Father returned, and Victoria blushed, as if they could read her guilty thoughts.

It seemed an eternity until the door swung open and the jury men filed in. The men took their seats, straightening their jackets. The crowd's excited murmuring was replaced with loud shushing. Victoria scanned the jurors' faces for any indication of what decision they'd reached but had no idea what she was looking for. The sleepy man looked alert. The rat-eyed man was frowning. Her stomach roiled and she wondered, briefly, if she'd have to use her own father's hat in which to be sick.

The clerk stood and read off the names of the jurors, each of whom responded as their name was called. Then he turned and faced the defense table. "Lizzie Andrew Borden, stand up."

There was a quiet scrape of chair legs upon wood floor.

Victoria could just barely see a slice of Miss Lizzie through all the bodies in front of her. The tip of the feather in her hat stood at attention.

"Gentlemen of the jury," the clerk continued, "have you agreed upon your verdict?"

The foreman nodded. "We have."

Victoria could feel her heartbeat throbbing in her ears. Mother gripped her hand.

"Please return the papers to the court."

An officer took the papers from the foreman and handed them to the clerk.

"Lizzie Andrew Borden, hold up your right hand. Mr. Foreman, look upon the prisoner; prisoner, look upon the foreman."

The foreman. *His eyes. They look sad.* Victoria felt the bile rising in her throat.

Oh God, no. Please, no.

The clerk took a deep breath. "What say you, Mr. Foreman?"

THE NEW YORK HERALD
Open War on Mrs. Borden

The Borden household must have been a rather grim sort of a place. Mr. Borden himself, though perfectly respectable and upright, was not particularly cheerful, and between his wife and stepdaughters there was open war. The elder daughter, Emma, is described as of a mild and gentle disposition, but there was little mildness about Lizzie, seven years her junior.

Mr. Borden was worth half a million dollars, and, though penurious as a rule, was inclined to be generous to his household. But Lizzie resented his liberality toward the stepmother. Her own mother died in giving birth to her and she has been odd all her life. She grew up to be much of a recluse. She is far from homely, though not particularly handsome, but she never had a lover, she has avoided the company of young men and has never gone into society. She has her defenders, who say she has an amiable disposition. The allegations to the contrary may be mere ill-natured gossip.

One thing is certain. She has wonderful self-possession. When with Dr. Bowen she stood by her father's body, when her stepmother was discovered murdered, at the time of the funeral, and on all other occasions since this story began, she has manifested, they say, almost unshaken calmness. She is a masculine-looking woman, with a strong, resolute, unsympathetic face. She is robustly built; thirty-three years old and of average height. Her voice has a peculiar guttural harshness. Her hair is brown and long, her eyes blue and steady. Her self-possession is expressed in her looks. I do not think she is afraid of many things.

CHAPTER THIRTY

The courtroom was silent as a tomb as lawyer, spectator, and prisoner alike held their breath, waiting for the foreman to deliver the jury's verdict. Victoria stared at the foreman, at his lips, waiting for them to form the words, and all around her, reporters stood at the ready, pencils poised on notepads. From the open window came the sound of pigeons cooing.

The foreman swallowed. Nodded.

"Not guilty, on both counts."

Miss Lizzie cried out and dropped into her seat, and the room exploded. Shouts, cries, gasps, exclamations of shock and disbelief, the judge banging his gavel, the defense attorneys laughing and slapping each others' backs, jurors scraping their chairs as they rose, reporters shouting, "Excuse me! Excuse me!" as they pushed their way to the doors.

For a moment, Victoria sat, stunned, taking in the scene but not comprehending.

Not guilty, the foreman had said.

Brownie and Thomas had hoisted themselves up onto a deep windowsill and were watching the crowd, swinging their feet, boot heels kicking the plaster wall. Mrs. Kettleson, the organist, waved a hanky in the air like a flag at a parade; Dr. Chagnon circled his wife's shoulders as she hid her face in her hands; and nosy Mrs. Churchill had somehow, in a matter of seconds, made her way down the row to Alice Russell and was yelling earnestly in the younger woman's ear, her hat brim tapping against the side of Miss Russell's head.

Victoria blinked. Not guilty. *Not* guilty! She was afraid to believe it.

Mother patted Victoria's shoulder. "Well done, Victoria. You helped free your friend."

Victoria had almost forgotten her mother was there. "Yes," she answered, dazed. "I suppose I did."

Miss Lizzie was not a murderer.

Suddenly, weeks of aching worry spilled out in hot tears. *It was going to be all right. Everything was going to be fine.* Pressing Declan's hanky to her streaming eyes, she breathed in its comforting scent. *Miss Lizzie is not a monster,* she thought. *And neither am I.* She cried harder. The judge banged his gavel, the officers held up their hands, patting the air for quiet but the crowd was long in quieting.

"Gentlemen of the jury," the clerk called out, "you upon your oaths do say that Lizzie Andrew Borden, the prisoner at the bar, is not guilty?"

"We do," answered several jurors.

The clerk nodded. "Lizzie Andrew Borden?"

Victoria heard the chair scrape again and could only see the top of her cap, it's black feather quivering.

"The court orders that you be discharged of this indictment and go, thereof, without delay."

THE EXCITED CROWD pushed toward the doors, talking, adjusting their hats, fanning themselves, calling out to people ahead of them—like opera-goers at the conclusion of the show, their minds already on the meal or brandy or soft chair awaiting them at home. Her own parents got caught up in their own conversations—Father with Reverend Buck and Mother with Mrs. Liverpool—giving Victoria the chance to slip away, unnoticed.

When she got to the outer hall, Victoria spotted Declan and her joy doubled. Not even the presence of his father by his side could keep her from pushing past others to get to him.

"We did it!" she exclaimed. Though her impulse was to throw her arms around him, she settled for grasping his hand and squeezing. Immediately, she knew she'd made a grave error. Detective Dempsey's mouth bunched tight, and Declan widened his eyes at her.

"I am happy," Declan said stiffly, "you feel your friend received the appropriate verdict, Miss Robbins. But of course, my father and I only collect the data."

"Oh, I see now," Detective Dempsey said, nodding. "This is why you've been fighting me about the case. Trying to impress a young lady."

Fear squashed Victoria's happiness as she saw humiliation color Declan's face.

"No—" Victoria started.

Declan interrupted, his voice tight. "That's not it at all, Father. I keep telling you, I am merely after the truth."

Detective Dempsey snorted. "I'll give you a truth, son: this high society miss has used her pretty manners to pull you off her friend's trail, and now that she's gotten what she wanted, she will have no use for you."

"That's not true." Victoria felt herself pushed sideways by a reporter squeezing through the crowd. Frowning, she pushed back, giving him an elbow for extra measure. "Your son is my friend."

"Oh really?" Detective Dempsey's eyebrows arched in exaggerated surprise. "I saw the announcement in the paper about your debut, Miss Robbins. Did you invite my son, your *friend,* to attend?"

Shame burned her cheeks. She turned to Declan to explain, but he beat her to it.

"I apologize for my father's rudeness, miss." His jaw was set and he gave a curt bow. "And now, if you'll excuse me, I have some matters I must attend to."

"Declan..." She reached for his sleeve, but the fabric slid out of her fingers as he disappeared into the crowd.

Detective Dempsey gave her a satisfied smirk. "There. I just did your dirty work for you. You're welcome."

A good slap in the face—his hateful, splotchy face—was what this horrible man deserved.

She pushed past him, making sure to grind her heel into his big, fat foot.

He grabbed her arm. "A word a warnin', miss," he whispered. "Not only should you keep your distance from my son, you'd also be wise to stay away from that lady friend a yours. Not guilty does not mean innocent. Just means she got lucky."

WITH THE TRIAL over, all Mother could talk about was the debut party—the food, the band, the dance cards, the decorations—but Victoria could not rid her thoughts of the expensive baubles and trinkets Mag would be tempted to snatch. Every day that passed, more worries surfaced, more doubt crept in, souring her stomach and disrupting her sleep, until she was as gaunt as her mother had been at her sickest.

To make matters worse, Mother would not permit Victoria to visit Miss Lizzie, saying their neighbor would be overwhelmed with visitors and needed time to adjust to being home. But from Victoria's careful watch, it seemed Miss Lizzie and Miss Emma had very few callers and very many curiosity-seekers sneaking by in whispering, snickering packs. Reverend Buck, Mrs. Liverpool, and the grocery boy were the only ones who stepped inside. No Declan, of course, as he had no need to visit anymore.

Every day, Mother had a new excuse as to why Victoria could not call on Miss Lizzie, and every day, Victoria grew more agitated. The not-guilty verdict should have put Victoria's heart to rest, but for some reason, it had had the opposite effect. The story had no ending, the mystery was still unsolved, and a gaping hole yawned in her chest where the truth should rest. *If Miss Lizzie hadn't done it, who had?*

True to her promise, Victoria called on Gwyne daily, which improved Gwyne's mood and, hopefully, her opinion of her, but the never-ending debut talk escalated Victoria's growing anxiety. Then, on Thursday, two days before the party, the dance cards were delivered to the Jacobsen's.

"Ooooh!" Gwyne lifted a gold-embossed booklet from the box. "Look how perfect!" The cover of the little booklet showed an elegant couple dancing under the moonlight, with the girls' names and date of the party in gold script below. From the top left corner hung a loop of fine white ribbon, with a small pencil attached.

"Look!" Gwyne slipped the ribbon around her wrist and picked up the pencil, hovering it just above the open booklet. Putting on a very coquettish look, she batted her eyelashes and said, "I'm so sorry, young man, what did you say your name was? There are far too many of you to remember!"

Victoria laughed. Then, playing along, answered in a deep voice, "Jared Winters. Put my name down for all twenty-four dances."

Gwyne's mouth dropped. "Can you imagine? Wouldn't that just be divine?"

Opening one of the booklets, Victoria looked at the order of dances—waltzes, reels, lancers, and more—and imagined *Declan Dempsey* written next to each. Twelve dances with him before supper, twelve after. That *would* be divine and would certainly keep her out of trouble. Sadly, names of other, less intelligent, less attractive, less interesting boys would fill her book, making for a very long night. After the final dance were the words "Home Sweet Home" and the picture of a retreating horse-drawn carriage. She'd officially be a debutante then, riding home with her parents. Would it work? Would she be different? No longer a thief? Her heart fluttered, but from fear or excitement, she couldn't distinguish.

And then, in what felt like two blinks, it was debut day. When she brought her gown upstairs, Victoria noticed someone in the Bordens' yard, beating a rug on the line, and for one confusing moment, she thought it was old Mrs. Borden, for beating out the dusty rugs had always been her job. Then she recognized Miss Lizzie's brown hair and broad shoulders. Her hunched stance, however, was definitely her stepmother's, and it was as if Miss Lizzie had stepped into the old woman's shoes left at the back door and transformed into the old woman herself. Pity mixed with frustration swirled in Victoria's chest. She needed to know the truth, and now that the trial was over, maybe Miss Lizzie would confide in her, no matter what the truth was. Without a second thought, she grabbed the afghan off her bed and wrapped it around her shoulders as she hurried down the rear stairs, through the screened summer kitchen, and onto the back stoop.

"Miss Lizzie!" she called and waved, but Miss Lizzie did not turn around. Undeterred, Victoria hurried across the yards, frozen bumps of ground biting through her thin-soled shoes. She tried to picture her neighbor's joyful reaction upon seeing her, how she might cry out or laugh or envelope her in a tight hug. Perhaps all three.

Arriving on the other side of the fence, Victoria found Miss Lizzie still thumping the oriental runner with a vengeance, each whack accompanied by a deep grunt of effort and throwing up another puff of dust into the hazy cloud around her. For a dizzying moment, Victoria saw a hatchet in place of the carpet beater, blood droplets in place of dust particles.

Stop, she told herself. *You're welcoming her home.*

Reaching out, she touched Miss Lizzie's shoulder, the cotton material warm and damp. "Miss Lizzie?"

Miss Lizzie spun around, eyes fierce, the wicker carpet beater raised.

Heart racing, Victoria stumbled back.

"Oh, Victoria," Miss Lizzie sighed, arms dropping to her sides. "You gave me a fright!"

"I'm so sorry. I tried to get your attention." Victoria gave a limp wave toward her house. "I saw you from my window and wanted to come out and welcome you home."

Nodding, Miss Lizzie drew a rag from her apron pocket and blotted her forehead, leaving the skin there whiter than the rest of her face, still speckled gray with carpet dust. "It's partly thanks to you that I am home. Quick thinking, using those boys." Her bun was askew, with silver hairs joining the brown drifting about her face, and she had two new frown lines, deep fissures between her brows. But her eyes were back to the clear blue Victoria remembered from her childhood.

Victoria took her hand, giving it a warm squeeze. "Will you come tonight? To my debut?"

Miss Lizzie shook her head. "My presence would only be a distraction. Also, I have much to do. We are moving. We bought a house on The Hill." She pointed the rug beater like she was still teaching Sunday School with a yardstick as pointer to show the Holy Lands on the map. Her smile was the same as well— tight, intelligent, matter-of-fact.

Victoria's stomach dropped. "No! You can't!"

"I am destined to live my remaining days in relative isolation, Victoria, as is my sister, because of me. As such, we might as well be comfortable, in a more luxurious house, with modern conveniences, and," she added with a raise of an eyebrow, "pets. I will finally be able to have a cat or two for company. My father, as you know, did not share my love of animals."

Victoria pretended not to notice the resentment in this last sentence. "But Miss Lizzie, I'll never see you!"

"Precisely." Miss Lizzie gave the brown grass at her feet a final swipe with the carpet beater. "And I shall not invite you to visit. For your own good, you understand. I will not allow a friendship with me to blemish your reputation."

Reputation. The word, Father's word, turned her stomach. "But I want to stay friends."

"You say that now, Victoria, and I'm sure you mean it, but nothing in my life can go back to the way it used to be, including our friendship. There would always be a big question hanging over our heads—did I or didn't I?—and pretending it wasn't there would, frankly, be too exhausting."

So? Did you or didn't you? The question circled Victoria's mind, daring her to pose it.

Then Detective Dempsey's words joined in: *not guilty does not mean innocent.* Victoria found herself trembling and squeezed her elbows to stop.

"I think it's better we part friends now, Victoria, while we still have fond memories of our time together."

Memories. Of pigeons. Picnics. Fishing. Lemonade in the parlor.

A gust of wind kicked up, knocking drops of old rain off tree branches, pricking Victoria's face and hands, and sending a shiver down her arms. Miss Lizzie presented her palm, then raised her eyebrows in a light smile. Reluctantly, Victoria took her hand.

"You have a sharp mind, Victoria, and a good and kind heart, standing by me when others did not. But now I would like to free you from the obligation of our friendship so you can start your new life fresh, with no ties to an accused murderess."

Shame pressed hot and wet at the corners of Victoria's eyes at the undeserved praise. She tried to think of something mature and kindly to say but feelings of loneliness and abandonment overwhelmed her efforts. "Don't leave me, Miss Lizzie."

A pitiful, childish plea.

"Oh, no tears now, Victoria." Miss Lizzie looked down at their clasped hands and noticed the jade ring on Victoria's finger. Her own eyes misted over as she straightened it gently. "I wish you a long and happy life, my dear," she said, her voice barely a whisper. "And I will always be grateful for your belief in me."

CHAPTER
THIRTY-ONE

The foyer of Chateau D'Usse, already impressive in its own right, had been transformed into a spectacular ivy and flower-filled bower. Strategically placed electric lamps directed at the crystal chandelier sent a dizzying array of reflections dancing across the walls and leaves and marble floors. Seeing so much green in one place, after the grays and browns of autumn, was a shock to the system that almost made it possible for Victoria to forget Miss Lizzie's good-bye.

A pointy-nosed footman stepped forward and held out his arm for their wraps. Victoria followed Mother's lead, giving the servant a small nod as she handed him her beaver stole, regretfully, as she was chilled with nerves. Father handed over his coat and then leaned close to them and murmured, "I see you two were not exaggerating. This is quite a place."

A flower-wrapped arbor stood a few feet away, with Timms on the other side, waiting to escort them to the ballroom. It all looked so... magical. Out of nowhere, tears sprang to Victoria's eyes. She didn't deserve such beauty, such royal treatment, didn't deserve the proud smiles and encouraging nods from her parents, didn't deserve a friend who would plan and share this extravagant party with her. Certainly, she didn't deserve to be celebrated for being well-off and sixteen—there was no feat in it. Meanwhile, the boy she cared about had most likely written her off as a shallow and manipulative society girl, and her friend who had just escaped the hangman's noose sat home alone.

She looked up at the glittering chandelier to keep the tears from spilling down her cheeks. She should have insisted Gwyne invited both Miss Lizzie and Declan. Neither would have come but would have appreciated to have been invited.

Mother gently squeezed Victoria's wrist. "Ready?"

Victoria blinked away the last of the tears. "Not really."

"Oh, I was nervous at my debut as well," Mother whispered. "Don't worry. You look beautiful and Miss Minning says you're a fine dancer. You'll have your pick of suitors."

If only Mother knew how little Victoria cared about any of that. She gazed at the beautiful woman next to her. It was almost impossible to reconcile with the frozen, twisted body she had cared for. The thought of her mother's recurring illness pricked her insides: another mystery, unsolved. *This is her night,* Victoria thought, *as much as it is mine. Enjoy it for her.*

Pressing her lips into a smile, she took a deep breath and used Miss Minning's posture technique—imagining being pulled upward by a string attached to the top her head.

"Okay, Mother. I'm ready."

Passing under the flowered arch was like stepping into springtime—a magical start even without birdsong. A second encouraging sign was Timms leading them in the opposite direction of the parlor—with its snuffboxes—down a long hallway, past closed door after closed door, portrait after portrait, gas lamp after gas lamp, finally arriving at a wide staircase descending into the ballroom. At the far end of the grand room, under "trees" of tightly bundled branches woven with flowers, stood the Jacobsens, GG, and Gwyne, who looked stunning in her white satin gown. More groves of flowered "trees" dotted the room, with crushed velvet chairs and love seats nestled beneath, and all under a glittering, blue-domed ceiling.

With nasal formality, Timms announced their arrival.

"Miss Victoria Robbins, of Fall River, and the Mr. and Mrs. Jonathan Robbins, of the same."

"We know, Timms," GG called out, her thin voice half-absorbed by the flora. "They are the other hosts!"

Holding back a laugh, Victoria looked at Gwyne as she descended the stairs, waiting to exchange a secret look, but Gwyne's smile was too tight, her eyes too staring.

"You're nothing short of a princess, Gwyne," Victoria said, arriving at her friend's side. "Truly, seeing you in that dress, I wouldn't be surprised if you fielded several proposals by the end of the night."

Gwyne's eyes welled up, her bottom lids a bright pink.

"Gwyne!" Victoria quickly took her friend's elbow and led her away from the adults. They stopped near a large, skirted platform where tuxedo-clad musicians were setting up. "What is it? This is the night you've been dreaming of and it's perfect."

Sneaking a hanky from her cuff, Gwyne dabbed at her dripping nose. "I... I..." She swallowed, blinked. "I've been thinking. Maybe... I shouldn't get married. Maybe I'd be better off a spinster."

Choking back her surprise, Victoria said, "What are you talking about? You've spoken of nothing else but marriage for months. Years, even."

Sniffing, Gwyne nodded. "I know, but on the way here tonight, Mother and Daddy bickered in the carriage. That's nothing new, of course, but the way Father was looking at her, so sour, so disgusted, as if he had a nose full of limburger and I... I..." Tears trickled out of the corners of Gwyne's eyes, which she deftly swiped and then gave a quick check over her shoulder. "Oh, Tory, it suddenly hit me. Maybe I don't want to marry if that's the way marriage is."

Victoria stared at her friend, at the way she was biting her lip to stop it from quivering, at her shaking hands pressing the hanky to her cheeks to absorb the tears without smearing her powder.

One of the musicians walked by them carrying a small case. He was a thin gentleman with slicked back hair and when he met Victoria's eyes, he paused. "Hello ladies. May I offer my congratulations?"

It took Victoria a moment to recognize Officer Lupin, the maligned policeman who tipped them off about the cemetery and who'd helped her collar Brownie and Thomas.

"Officer Lupin." Victoria extended her gloved hand. "I had no idea you were a musician."

He gave a little bow over her hand, revealing a small, freckled bald spot. "If I could support myself playing the clarinet, I'd quit the force tomorrow, miss." Giving a nod to Gwyne, he stood. "Enjoy your night, ladies."

Gwyne sniffed. "Thank you," she said, a crack in her voice.

Giving a gracious smile to Officer Lupin, Victoria turned back to Gwyne and took her arm, leading her in a circuit about the room. "Listen to me, Gwyndolyn Marie Jacobsen. Our mothers were told who they could and should marry, but the world is changing. Soon, we're going to have the right to vote, so we should have the right to marry whom we wish, for love and not for prestige or money or family loyalties."

They stopped at a bank of French doors, their ghostly reflections mirrored back at them, the blazing electric lights making the outdoors just a sheet of black. The air filled with sounds of the musicians warming up—a harpist plucking experimentally at her strings, two violinists playing a scale, the reedy whispers of clarinets, oboes. Victoria waited while Gwyne regarded the hanky in her hands.

After a moment, Gwyne lifted her head and spoke to Victoria's reflection. "I'm sorry I was so horrid about your Irish fellow."

Declan. Victoria sighed. "It doesn't matter. You were right. It never would have worked out."

"What?" Gwyne half-laughed, dabbing the corners of her eyes. The beads and gold threads of her dress shimmered in the glass reflection. "You just said we should marry for love!"

"True," Victoria said, fixing a tendril of Gwyne's hair that had fallen. "Unfortunately, it only works if the person you love loves you back. Now," she said, forcing Declan's image from her mind and pressing her lips into a cheery smile, "I am absolutely certain that every young man who walks into this room tonight will become instantly besotted with you, so you only need to determine which one pulls at your heartstrings as well."

Gwyne sniffed, her smile shaky. "You really think so?"

"Of course I do! You are a vision of beauty and smart as a whip to boot! And if any of these men don't fit the bill, you've got a year of parties at which to meet more."

Gwyne patted the last of her tears away and let out a deep sigh. "Thank you, Tory."

Warmth spread through Victoria's chest. With renewed energy, Gwyne linked her elbow in Victoria's and led her across the ballroom toward their parents.

"I cannot believe I actually said the word spinster referring to myself," whispered Gwyne, her nose wrinkling.

Victoria laughed.

"Don't you dare tell a soul, Tory! I mean it!"

She squeezed Gwyne's arm to her side. "Don't worry. I'm terrific at keeping secrets."

THE LINE OF eligible young men to greet seemed endless. Some Victoria recognized from the grounds of Durfee High, including the especially shy Jared Winters and the horrid Edward Pottersmith. She made sure to give Edward the grimmest of smiles and shallowest of curtsies. The rest were strangers to Victoria, though she recognized several of their last names from the society pages. Around the edges of the room, in small, giggling groups of dark satin, were the classmates Gwyne had invited. Their looks of envy at both debutantes made Victoria feel more like a fraud than ever, and she had to turn away.

By the time the last guest passed through the receiving line, her dance card was full, and the band struck up a tune reminiscent of the Queen's March. Victoria's heart drummed, racing ahead of the music. This was it—her announcement. Father, handsome in his black tailcoat, stepped away from his wife's side and gave Victoria his elbow. He winked at her and she saw a tiny cut on his chin where he'd nicked himself with his razor. On the opposite end of the line, Mr. Jacobsen and Gwyne were similarly preparing. The guests made their way to the edges of the room, forming an enormous circle. From the bandstand, Lupin raised his eyebrows encouragingly at her from behind his clarinet.

"Presenting," Timms called from the top stair, "Miss Gwyndolyn Ruth Jacobsen, daughter of Mr. And Mrs. Harold T. Jacobsen of Fall River."

Gwyne and her father processed slowly in a wide circle as the guests stood on the outer rim, looking on admiringly. As Gwyne passed by, her eyes locked with Victoria's in a brief exchange of secret excitement. She was back to her old self. *You're next*, her look said. They completed their walk in the middle of the circle where Mr. Jacobsen lifted Gwyne's hand and she gave a deep, perfect curtsy. Upon rising, Victoria could see Gwyne struggle to maintain a cool exterior, suppressing her natural wide smile.

Polite applause.

"Also presenting," Timms continued, "Miss Victoria Anne Robbins, daughter of Mr. and Mrs. Jonathan H. Robbins of Fall River."

Father patted her hand encouragingly and then it was they

who were walking the circle, Victoria giving small nods of gracious acknowledgement as her mother had instructed. Twice she thought she saw Declan's head of wavy hair, but of course she was wrong. Finally, Father led her to the center of the circle where Gwyne and Mr. Jacobsen waited. Carefully resting her fingertips in Father's, Victoria dipped into a perfect curtsy of her own. When she stood and heard the applause, she felt a fleeting sense of well-being, of normalcy.

Then she danced. First with her father, and then with the long list of young men on her dance card. Quadrilles, two-steps, waltzes, lancers, Portland Fancies, and on, one young man after another in an endless parade. As she stepped, skipped, turned, and clapped, Victoria found herself comparing each new partner to Declan.

Eyes not as engaging.

Smile not as warm.

Conversation dull.

Hands sweaty.

Even handsome young men were too handsome, friendly young men maddeningly so.

Stop, she finally told herself. *Think of something else.* And so her mind went back to Miss Lizzie.

Taking her partner's freckled hand and stepping right and right, then left and left, Victoria pictured Miss Lizzie wielding the carpet wand—how fierce she'd looked! And then her sad good-bye.

Turn and turn and switch hands.

Funny how she felt she'd known Miss Lizzie's life so well, only to find out so many things: Mr. Borden killing her pigeons, Mrs. Borden being her stepmother instead of her real mother, their house robbery and, of course, the stealing.

Victoria's dance partner, with hair the color of a new penny and an expression of a lovesick basset hound, had his eyes trained on her, waiting to be acknowledged. Out of guilt, she gave him a small smile, which seemed to energize him as he dropped her right hand and picked up her left. They repeated the dance on the opposite side with extra gusto, his spirited feet nipping her toes at times.

Right and right, left and left. Turn, bow, step up, step back.

And all those worries Miss Lizzie had shared with Miss Alice about her father having enemies. To Victoria, she'd always waxed poetic about her father, talking about what a clever businessman he was and how he'd earned his wealth the hard way, unlike some of the other, higher brow Bordens. Which was the truth?

The answer hit her just as the music stopped, the last chord drawing out the obvious conclusion: *She didn't really know Miss Lizzie.* She was fifteen years younger. Just because she had told Miss Lizzie all her childish worries and woes did not mean Miss Lizzie had shared her own. Now she wondered if she had been a nuisance to Miss Lizzie. Perhaps Miss Lizzie had only pretended to enjoy her company all these years out of politeness. Perhaps Miss Lizzie's final good-bye had been a welcome excuse to be finally free of their supposed friendship.

Humiliation pressed in on Victoria's chest.

The red-haired boy had bowed and was now staring at her. "Are you alright, miss?"

"I'm sorry, yes," she said, flushing and dipping a curtsy. Pushing against the growing ache, she thanked him for the dance before hurrying off, in search of Gwyne or Mother or some other woman with whom she could escape to the lady's resting room. This new vision of Miss Lizzie, of their unequal "friendship," made her feel the floor was tilting under her feet. She needed a private place to sit and pull herself together.

She was waving, trying to pull Gwyne's attention away from Jared Winters, when GG's voice rang out from the top of the steps.

"Supper will now be served!"

As hostess and new debutante, it was Victoria's responsibility to help lead the guests to the dining room. The Jacobsens took their place on the first stair, Victoria's parents behind them. When Gwyne and Jared Winters followed, panic seized Victoria. She was supposed to have asked one of her partners to be her escort. Now what would she do? Then she felt a warmth at her side: some poor gentlemanly sort, no doubt, coming up from behind to her rescue. *Thank goodness.*

She turned and found Edward Pottersmith, face stern, elbow offered. Stunned, she took it, hating herself for being so out of sorts she had to hold on tightly. Gritting her smile, she proceeded up the stairs into the candle-lit dining room, where they paraded to the music, past table after table of meats, cheeses, breads, candied and fresh fruits, cookies, cakes, Mr. Fernwood's fancies, and other powdered confections. Between the wonderful food and the hours since she'd last eaten, she should have been famished, but images of Miss Lizzie flashed by—feeding the pigeons, in her jail cell, putting a worm on her fishing hook. Victoria heard Detective Dempsey's words: *she just got lucky.*

On the last table sat two ice-carved swans, beak to beak, their curved necks forming a heart, making her suddenly very aware she was still holding the arm of horrid Edward Pottersmith.

"Thank you," she said and started to remove her hand from Edward's arm, but he placed his hand atop hers and pressed down. His white-blond hair seemed to glow, his serious eyes an icy blue. The music had stopped, and the guests were busy mingling and talking and filling their plates.

"I'd like a word, Miss Robbins."

She was incredulous. Edward Pottersmith had spoken to her only once since accusing her of pushing Dickie Houndsworth down the church stairs when they were children, and that was to mumble an apology for their sidewalk collision just a few weeks ago. Now, when all she wanted was a moment alone, he wished to have a conversation? If she wasn't feeling so fragile, it would have been funny.

"Edw—Master Pottersmith, I'm really not feeling…" She

tried again to remove her hand, unsuccessfully.

"Please," he said, quietly. "Just a word."

With an angry huff, she nodded. He had, after all, stepped up as her escort and saved her from embarrassment.

Edward led her from the tables crowded with hungry guests to the French doors overlooking the rear gardens. Curiosity and irritation added to the emotions swirling inside her, and out of hearing of the others, she couldn't help speaking.

"What is it, Master Pottersmith? Are you going to accuse me of something else now—kidnapping you, perhaps? Let me point out it is you holding fast to me, not the other way around."

Edward only faced her calmly. "First," he said quietly, "I must tell you, I did not petition to be invited to your debut. I did not want to come, but your father insisted."

Victoria widened her eyes. "Well, thank you for taking this time to tell me," she sputtered, trying to pull away.

He held firm. "I did not want to," he repeated, "because I knew you would not want me here."

"You would be correct," she whispered. "Please release my hand."

"I just wanted to say…" He took a deep breath. "I'm sorry." He let go of her, and she took a half step back, staring at him. "I was a foolish boy who did a foolish thing, and once I did it, I could not take it back. My false accusation must have caused you a great deal of pain and for that I am deeply sorry." He gave her a small bow.

When Victoria could not find any words, he went on. "You see, at first I thought Dickie was faking, going for the big laugh. But when I realized he was really hurt, I panicked and didn't know how to take my words back. I felt terrible for getting you into trouble, and that night promised myself I'd confess in the morning. But then Dickie woke up and was fine and admitted he'd been clowning around, which let you off the hook, so I stayed mum, hoping people would forget what I said. And everyone did. Except you."

286 · BEVERLY PATT

His blue eyes were no longer icy. They were just... blue.

"All this time..." Victoria shook her head. So every time he had seen her and he had looked away—it wasn't snobbishness. What was it, then? Guilt? Embarrassment?

"I was... trying to get your attention." A sheepish look pulled at the corners of his mouth. "Like I said, foolish."

Get her attention as in fancying her? Edward Pottersmith?

The hatred she'd held for him all these years sat like a trunk of someone else's clothes left on her doorstep. She had nowhere to go with it.

"Anyway," he continued, "this being the first grown-up affair, if you will, to which I've been invited, I thought it appropriate to finally act like an adult and tell the truth. I don't expect you to forgive me, Miss Robbins but I hope, with time—"

"Tory!" Gwyne bustled up, cheeks rosy and eyes bright. She looped her arm through Victoria's and started pulling her toward the front of the room. "We're going to have a toast! You'll excuse us, won't you, Master Pottersmith?"

"Of course." He bowed to them both. "A pleasure talking with you, Miss Robbins."

"Yes," Victoria said, looking at him with new eyes. He wasn't pure evil. He'd actually fancied her. And though she felt no spark when meeting his gaze, she did have a newfound respect for him.

"*You're welcome*," Gwyne whispered, hustling her away.

With her thoughts jumbled, Victoria could not respond.

Champagne was poured and distributed, and when glasses were lifted in the girls' honor, Victoria saw the Durfee High boys back together in their usual group, smirking and whispering to one another. Edward, however, was not among them. After toasts to the girls' health and future, the band started tuning up again. All the comfortable love seats and couches were occupied by old ladies and pot-bellied men, and Victoria felt like lying down in the middle of the floor and never getting up.

Five minutes. She needed five minutes to sit and breathe

and collect herself to make it through the night. Five minutes to stop her world from turning and tilting, to reset people in their new, proper positions in her mind. Unfortunately, Gwyne was having a special moment with Jared Winters, their heads tilted together in shy conversation. Mother and Mrs. Jacobsen were deep in what looked to be hostess issues, discreetly pointing to the food tables and ticking things off on their fingers, and GG was busy drinking tea with other white-headed ladies, fielding compliments on her beautiful house and party. Victoria watched helplessly as the servants passed in and out of the service door, reminding her of the freedom her maid's costume had afforded her in the past.

It did not make sense that a servant had the freedom to go where they pleased while a debutante did not. The suffragettes were fighting for a woman's rights—certainly one of those should be the right to walk to the resting room by oneself. She followed the maid and found herself in the kitchen. The cooks and maids did not seem surprised to see her inside the kitchen, and one sinewy woman with a mole on her cheek paused in her ladling to point to the far side of the enormous, tiled room.

"Through that door, left and then right and you'll be in a quiet spot ta catch yer breath."

Victoria gave her a grateful smile and followed the instructions. As she closed the final door behind her and leaned against it, she found herself in GG's dimly lit parlor, complete with the etagere of beautiful snuffboxes standing in the corner.

CHAPTER THIRTY-TWO

O f all the rooms to have ended up in, GG's parlor was the worst. And yet, as she slowly made her way across the darkened room, she did not feel the pull of the blue snuffbox she'd been so drawn to on her last visit. Squinting down at it in the fuzzy light, she was shocked to see how plain and unremarkable it now appeared, no worse but certainly no better than any of the others surrounding it.

She touched the smooth blue enamel lid lightly with her fingertip, testing, as one might a caterpillar to see if it's alive, but felt no surge of excitement, no thrilling desire. It was just a small, pretty snuffbox, one of several. Did she dare pick it up? That would be the true test, how it felt in her hand. Taking a deep breath, she reached out, placed her fingertips around the cool edges and lifted.

Nothing.

She turned the box over in her hand. Still nothing. Perhaps becoming a debutante *had* changed her, cured her. She looked at the box in her hand, the same hand that held Miss Lizzie's earlier that day. The good-bye now seemed symbolic: their tie, their shared sin, broken, and now Victoria was free of her habit for good. Placing the box back, she fumbled her way through the darkened room to GG's chair by the cold, hollow fireplace.

Her life—she couldn't imagine what would it look like without the urgent desire to pocket something. The potting shed would now be just a potting shed, a shopping trip just a shopping trip. Who would she be if she weren't a thief? In the darkness, Victoria could smell the spicy, exotic presence of Lord Thorton's eerie artwork: leering tribal masks, carved swords, paintings of staring needle-beaked birds, all making her feel as if she'd wandered into a strange land. Suddenly, she was desperate to be back in the crowded, noisy ballroom, back with her best friend, back to her role as debutante, where she'd be distracted with music and dancing and slick-haired boys on their best behavior.

Jumping up, she hurried out of the parlor, her toes sinking into the carpet's plushness, quietly closing the door behind. In the hallway, several identical doors stretched down the hallway. Unsure, she tried one. Locked. The next, a closet. Oh dear. They'd be wondering where she was. Turning to get her bearings, her gaze snagged on a black porcelain vase sitting on a narrow hall table, about the length of her forearm, with hand-painted pink and white peonies on its front, and two scrolled, gilt handles on its sides.

Her heart began to race.

A metallic tang filled her mouth.

"No," Victoria whispered. "Not here." But even as she said the words, she felt them float away from her lips. Hard balls of pressure, like plums, pressed against the backs of her eyes, pinpointing her vision on the vase. Her hands ached to cradle the soft belly of the vase, to rub each painted petal, trace each carved swirl. To have it for her very own.

Very weak, as if straining to keep from being pulled underwater, came the thought, *No, you can't...*

But in the next second, the vase was cradled in her arms, and she was running, back into the parlor, her ears roaring, chest exploding, skin on fire. Inside, over to the French doors. Opening one door, the outside air chilling her bare neck and shoulders. Thrusting the vase beneath the scratchy bushes. Snapping the door shut, racing from the parlor, back down the hall, this time finding her way without thought.

Descending the steps into the ballroom, blood racing, cheeks flushed, Victoria could still feel the exquisite weight of the vase against her chest, and suddenly, all the young men surrounding her were handsome, the ladies beautiful, the dancing hypnotic, the night perfect. It wasn't until she was in a circle of eight, all holding hands aloft, that she noticed a line of blood trickling down her arm, pooling in the crease of her elbow, a scratch from the bushes no doubt, and the truth of what she had done pierced her heart.

"GOOD NIGHT, DEAR," GG said, her bony hand squeezing Victoria's as they all stood in the grand foyer. The last of the guests had finally departed, their laughter and calls of good health to friends just barely audible from the open door. "You made a delightful deb," GG continued, "and you have a full year of exciting parties and balls ahead of you!"

"Yes," Victoria said, forcing her lips into a smile. *Dear GG.* "Thank you so much for everything."

"Oh, my darling girl, you don't need to thank me, it was my pleasure!"

Victoria's glance strayed down the hall to the table where the porcelain vase had sat, the sight of the empty spot causing a hollowness in her stomach. After returning to the dance, she'd waited for a servant to rush in and report the stolen vase. Each time the kitchen door bumped open, her heart leapt. Now the evening was finally, blessedly, over. If she could make it out the door, she would go home, crawl under the covers and never come out.

Mother and Father thanked GG as well and bid her good night. As they stepped out the front door, Victoria took a quick look toward the bushes and thought she caught a glint from one of the vase's golden handles. Blood drummed in her ears. Mother said something to Father and pointed toward their waiting carriage.

A succession of terrible options flipped through her brain: running and grabbing the vase; pretending to notice something in the bushes and alerting Timms; leaving and hope the gardener would discover it. She could not come back for it; the distance was too far.

It's OURS, Mag cried. *Go get it!*

Mother tugged at her arm. "Come along, dear. You must be exhausted."

Sickened by her cowardice, Victoria allowed herself to be led to the carriage, looking once over her shoulder, now seeing nothing but dark fuzzy branches. Once seated, she closed her eyes, which were beginning to water. Her life was over. She was still a thief. She'd lost Miss Lizzie as a friend, and Declan thanks to his horrible father, and now she'd lose Gwyne once the vase was traced back to her. It wouldn't be too difficult a mystery to solve, for the kitchen help had sent her that way themselves. GG would tell Mrs. Jacobsen, who would then tell her parents, and that would be it. She'd have brought shame upon the family, ruining their reputations, exactly as her father predicted, but not for the same reasons. What would they say once they found out? What would they do with her?

Pulling the brim of her hat low, Victoria leaned her head against the side of the carriage as it bumped down the street, accepting the discomfort of her forehead knocking against the cold glass, for she deserved that and so much more. Tears, held back for hours, finally flowed from the hard knot in her throat, hot sorrowful tributaries trickling down her cheeks, no doubt making streaks of white through her face powder, but it did not matter. Not anymore. She was a criminal, not fit for society. Her future was over. As her parents discussed the evening in hushed tones, Victoria saw the gold-gilded vase tucked beneath the bushes and poor GG hobbling around inside in search of it. She wondered how long before it was discovered missing.

Victoria swallowed the lump in her throat.

You're fine, whispered Mag.

But she wasn't fine. She'd just tried to steal something the size of a ham from GG's, where she was the guest of honor. She was crazy and impulsive. And if her impulses were getting bigger and bolder, what would be next? She could not help but picture Miss Lizzie, rug beater raised overhead, and the other Borden woman who threw her children down the well.

That was it. She should not continue to live at home, putting her parents and Penelope in danger. Neither should she marry. Or have children. She could not trust what she would do next, what she would feel compelled to do. She needed to be locked away, where she couldn't steal, couldn't find out what more awful acts she was capable of. Here she was supposed to be starting her new life, a good and pure life, and she'd already destroyed it. Miss Lizzie's face swam in Victoria's mind. Once people knew about Victoria's habit, she would be shunned, avoided, just like Miss Lizzie. Maybe Miss Lizzie's words were prophetic in a way: *you remind me of me.* Maybe she too would end up living the rest of her days in isolation. Maybe she should choose isolation now.

"I was thinking," Father said, interrupting Victoria's inner turmoil, "as long as Admiral is already hitched up, I should just keep on going, out to the farm, after dropping you ladies off, and Mr. Flint of course. After so many days in a dinner jacket and necktie, my skin begins to chafe."

Victoria, eyes still closed, heard her mother's sharp exhalation. "Tonight," she whispered, "on the heels of your daughter's debut?"

But Victoria understood, even envied her father. She, too, wished to stay in the warmth of the cozy carriage, with its worn leather seats and heavy velvet curtains, rocking down the cobbled road, away from home, away from town, away from stores, people, debutantes, and parties, on and on, never stopping.

"The party is over, darling," Father answered, "and look, our debutante is already asleep. If I get out to Swansea tonight, I can get a full day's work in tomorrow."

"Hmph," Mother sniffed, "is that what you call it?"

No other city gentleman worked so hard on his own farm as her father did.

Her parents were silent the rest of the ride home, while Victoria, pretending to be asleep, became more and more awake. The answer to her problem was right before her: the farm. She would go with Father to the farm and stay there, with no one to steal from but the cows and the pigs and the chickens and the horses. Even though Mother had forbade her going, it would be harder to leave once Victoria was there. Maybe she'd stay a few years. Or forever. After all, Miss Lizzie was moving, Gwyne would be swept up in a year's worth of debutante balls, Mother was healthy, and Declan wasn't speaking to her anymore. What was keeping her home? Father could bring her clothes and food and her magazines too, so she could keep up on Sherlock Holmes's adventures.

The carriage, nodding up and down over the rocky road, seemed to agree.

When they arrived home, Victoria, acting exhausted, said good night and trudged upstairs to her room. Once the door was closed, she sprung into action, changing into her house shift, stuffing a few dresses and underthings into a bag, and writing a quick note to her mother so she wouldn't worry. She would write a longer letter from the farm the next morning, and one to Gwyne, and maybe Declan too, explaining how she'd changed her mind about being a debutante, and how she'd always wanted to live in the country, which was half truthful. No one need know the whole truth.

Opening the door, she gave one parting glance to her room, her sanctuary for sixteen years. What would her bedroom be like at the farm? A tiny window, just inches off the floor was all she could remember of the room she'd stayed in as a girl. She would dearly miss her window seat.

Her parents' voices rumbled. She had to hurry. While her father changed, she snuck down the back stairs and out to the carriage, crouched on the floor, and covered herself with the musty wool lap blanket. Moments later, the kitchen door slammed and the carriage rocked as her father climbed onto the driver's bench. With a jangle of reins and the clicking noise Father made to urge Admiral forward, they were off.

AS THE MILES wore on, Victoria made her way off the floor and onto the leather seat, and with her clothes bag as a pillow, she watched the shadowed landscape pass by. Her thoughts drifted back to the party, so beautiful, so magical, yet not magical enough to transform her into someone else. Edward Pottersmith's apology had been a surprise, as had been his admission of prior admiration.

But Edward, even with his kind apology and family money, was not the man for her. There was no one for her, there couldn't be. She was a liability to any man. Declan's horrible father had, in a way, been right. He'd saved her from having to lie to Declan, saying she had no feelings for him. Better he think her snobbish and upper crust than a thief and potential murderer.

Declan swam before her eyes. And because she was leaving her whole life behind, she allowed herself one indulgence— imagining herself back in GG's ballroom, with Declan as her dance partner, one hand resting lightly on her hip, the other cradling her fingertips, his green eyes staring longingly into hers, stirring that place inside that made her shiver.

CHAPTER THIRTY-THREE

A sudden jolt woke Victoria, and for a moment, she thought she was back in the darkened parlor at GG's. Then Admiral whinnied and she remembered, bolting upright. She wondered how her father would react when she revealed herself and if he'd believe her lie about hating city life and wanting to live in the country. Would he be pleased to have his daughter there to keep him company?

The carriage squeaked as Father jumped off his perch and Victoria scooted close to the window, watching for the right time to surprise him. In the moonlight, steam floated off Admiral's neck like a halo, dissolving into the starry night sky. Goodness, what a lot of stars there were. And the farmhouse—so quaint and cozy, nestled in its stand of trees which had been mere saplings the last time she'd been there. Taking it all in, she felt a feather-light peace settle over her heart. Here, away from all temptation, she would have the best chance of giving up her habit and blossoming into the person she truly wanted to be.

A lantern flickered on in the house and then a window glowed golden, spewing pale yellow gauze across the gray ground, a welcome path to her new home. Victoria smiled. It was an omen. She had made the right decision.

The back door opened. Out from the light stepped a woman, all in shadow, holding a large sack over her shoulder. The cook?

Father stopped. Admiral snuffled.

"Finally," the woman called. Her voice was like honey in the darkness. "I think he has a fever."

The woman took another step forward and Victoria saw it was not a sack she held, but a child. A tousle-haired boy.

Confused, she watched her father drop the reins and stride toward the pair. She watched him place a practiced hand on the little boy's forehead.

Then Father's other arm slid around the young woman's waist.

Was Father kissing her hair?

No! This was Father! Her father. Married to Mother.

Mother, who hated the farm. Who forbade Victoria to visit. Who made snide remarks about all the work Father did at the farm. Victoria clutched at the leather loop alongside the carriage door to steady herself. Father. Cavorting with another woman. Fury burning in her chest, Victoria watched, frozen, as Father ushered the woman and child into the house, talking quietly, stroking the boy's hair. The glow of candlelight faded as it receded into the house, reappearing in a second-floor window, where it hovered for several minutes before floating downstairs again.

The door snapped open and Father came out alone, his approaching footsteps on the frozen grass crunching like a knife scraping toast. Victoria gripped the carriage handle, her heart racing. When he was just three steps from the carriage, she dropped to the floor and yanked the blanket over her body.

The carriage jerked into motion, rolling across the yard, then stopped. Reins clanked, barn doors creaked open. Her shaky breaths filled the small wooly space, magnifying the smells of mildew and dust. More stopping and starting. Then the patting of hand on flank. More creaks. A clank. Some swishing of hay. Then the carriage rocked.

And the door opened.

Victoria froze. Held her breath. The muscles in her arms started quivering and she could not make them stop.

She needed air. So hard to breathe without moving.

Then a grunt and the snap of the door shutting. Victoria took a deep breath of humid, musty air. Her arms shook madly.

Long after she'd heard the barn door scrape shut and Father's footsteps fade, she stayed hidden, trying to piece together the truth of the past eleven years. Her parents would argue, many times about the farm, her mother wanting him to sell it and Father saying it brought in extra income. Usually, Victoria would grab her *Strand* magazines and disappear to the furthest room, reading out loud to drown out their angry voices. Soon she'd be walking down a foggy, dangerous London alley or sitting in Sherlock's cluttered, cozy flat, puzzling with John Watson over seemingly unrelated details that Sherlock would then line up into an astounding series of clues.

Certainly she, such a mystery lover, should have picked up on the clues in her own house. Every time Father left for the farm, he'd admonish her, "Take care of your mother." Did he know she felt responsible? And while she was wiping her mother's chin and bottom, he was at the farm with his *mistress.*

Father must pay. She imagined all sorts of revengeful scenarios as she sat on the floor of the carriage—charging into the house screaming, throwing pots and pans, breaking every dish in sight, stomping up the stairs and ripping the blanket off her father and his mistress, yelling, "How dare you?" Suddenly, it became very important she collect the proof for herself, first-hand proof of this relationship. Her frustration over Miss Lizzie's case boiled over and she would not deny herself the opportunity to know at least one thing for certain, one thing that could not be argued or explained away.

And so, when even the crickets had gone to sleep, Victoria crept out of the carriage.

STEPPING INTO THE kitchen, the smells of smoke and fried bread opened a tiny door deep inside her, unleashing the thinnest waft of something warm and happy from long ago. She knew this room, had forgotten she knew it. Next to the fireplace, the wicker basket stored sheep skins to lay on and blocks to stack— her special playing spot. She tip-toed over and knelt, running her hand through the soft wool. This must be the little boy's spot now. His rug. His blocks. *His father*.

She noticed the glass jam jar stuffed with feathers on the mantle. Frowning in the darkness, Victoria picked up the jar— Father had made a game of seeing how many feathers she could find. She remembered chicken feathers didn't count and flicked through them until she found a pigeon feather. She scraped the edge softly across her neck, back and forth, the way she did when she was little, trying to tickle herself. The feel of it made her throat ache, and her eyes water. They had been happy once. They had been happy, and Father ruined it.

Clutching the cold jar to her bosom, Victoria made her way quietly across the kitchen to the stairs. She placed one slippered foot on the first step, and then slowly shifted her weight forward.

At the top, she saw two of the three bedroom doors were closed, so she headed toward the one open door, praying it was her father's and keeping close to the wall to avoid the squeakiest boards. One peek inside and her heart dropped. The bed was empty, untouched. She tried to remember which of the closed doors had been her parents', but she couldn't remember. Holding her breath, she clutched the doorknob of the closest and slowly, slowly, twisted until it would turn no further, then pushed the door open a quarter of an inch at a time. She had to take a few steps into the room before she could make out the figure of the little boy asleep in his bed, and when she did, she immediately turned away, not wanting to see his face. She wanted to hate him. Seeing his face might spoil that.

Creeping across the hall, she opened the final door in the same quarter-inch-by-quarter-inch fashion and stepped inside. There lay her father, not three feet away, with his mistress beside him, her arm thrown across his chest, a thin silver bracelet dangling from her wrist. A rush of tears surprised Victoria, and she realized the proof she'd been hoping for deep down was proof of her father's innocence. Proof she'd made a faulty deduction. Proof he was still her father, alone.

But here was the undeniable truth. Her father was an adulterer.

A haze of moonlight lay across the bed like an additional quilt and Victoria could see the mistress's private items on the bedside table her mother had once used—a book, a tiny picture frame, two small bottles of lotions or tinctures, a milk-glass lantern and…

Victoria squinted, leaned forward. Next to the lantern was a small glass jar—of pigeon feathers.

Gripping her own jar to her chest, Victoria glared at her father's sleeping face, at his slack jaw and peaceful expression, at the small triangle of stubble on his cheek where his razor had missed. She could kill him. Really, actually kill him, right now. In his sleep. She could hold this jar over her head and bring it down with the force of her rage, crashing so hard upon his unlined forehead, it would crack his skull into pieces. No one would blame her. *Cheat. Liar. Philanderer.*

She stared at her hands gripping the jar, the hands that seemed to have a will of their own. Strange. They were shaking but she couldn't actually feel them shake.

She blinked. Were they really her hands? Maybe they belonged to someone else. All these years, maybe they'd been controlled by another being. What a relief that would be!

She lifted her arms, watching the hands with the jar as they rose before her.

Up.

Up.

Up.

She couldn't feel her fingers on the jar, but she could feel the tears on her cheeks, streaming down, dripping off her chin. The feathers in the jar quivered, the tallest one suddenly reminding her of Miss Lizzie's hat at the trial. And then she thought of Declan, his smile, that curl. How he'd called her clever.

She was clever.

Clever enough to know she was acting crazy. That the only one who controlled her hands was herself. That no matter how similar she was to Miss Lizzie, she was herself first.

Victoria lowered her shaking arms and fled the room.

BACK IN THE barn, she tossed the jar of feathers aside and put on Father's dungarees and work jacket, still hanging on the same hook by the barn door, over her clothes, stuffing her skirts down the pant legs. A woman on the road alone was certain to attract attention; a man would not.

She saddled up Admiral, led him out of his stall and carefully, quietly, closed the stall door. *Back to my old ways,* she thought ruefully, grabbing Father's hat off the nail in the wall. She had to unpin the twist of flowers from her hair in order to make his hat fit and then stood for a moment, staring at the tiny bouquet, hating to part with it. She'd planned on pressing it between the pages of a book but then, looking up, realized she had a much better place for it. Smiling, she stepped forward, pressed it to her nose, then slipped the flowers through the stall latch. Father would come out to feed Admiral the next morning and find only her bouquet, like a calling card, left behind.

Him and his reputation be damned.

The night was much colder than she'd realized, and her fingers grasping the reins quickly felt frozen to the leather. Pulling her father's long cuffs over her hands helped, but the bagginess of his coat allowed rivulets of cold inside, chilling her torso. Admiral was in a feisty mood, having been put into service when he'd rather have bedded down, and fought to veer and turn around at every opportunity.

Victoria patted the horse's neck. "We're going home, Admiral," she said with the same false cheer Mother used to use to get her to eat rutabaga. "Don't you want to go home?"

Apparently, Admiral didn't, any more than she did.

"We have no choice," she said, sighing. Because, truly, there was nowhere else she could go. It was fantasy to think she could set off on her own, to a strange town, with no money, no skills, no decent clothes or even a hairbrush. Equally as naive was the idea of heading off into the wilderness to live like John the Baptist, sleeping under a tree and eating bugs and bark and fish caught by hand. Besides, now that she knew about Father, she realized Mother needed her now more than ever.

Trotting down the deserted road, Victoria found the scenery shifty and menacing, with every tree, bush, and shed suspect for what, or who, it could be hiding. She thought of animals that only came out at night to feed. All hiding. All secret. Even herself, sneaking back home in the dark. Back to the home where a whole hatbox of secrets awaited. Secrets she was so tired of keeping.

Admiral snorted and pulled on the reins.

She lay forward onto Admiral's warm neck and ran her fingers across his smooth coat, feeling his muscles shift as he walked along. Secrets. Did everyone in the world have secrets squirreled away in their hearts? Father's secret was his mistress; her own, of course, was the stealing. Mother's was her strange illness. And Miss Lizzie was the only one who knew of her innocence or guilt.

Admiral stopped, ears perked. After a few seconds, Victoria heard what the horse had already picked up on—hoofbeats. Coming toward them. She glanced around. No farmhouse or barn to head to, nothing but spent corn stalks.

"Git!" Victoria whispered, trying to kick his ribs with her evening slippers, which she'd forgotten to change. *Stupid.* "Git, Admiral! Git!"

The approaching horse and rider were coming very fast. Victoria dug her heels into Admiral's flanks and nudged the reins to the side, trying to make him move and make room for the rider at same time. Hopefully, he'd just fly past.

She gave her hat a yank, pulling the brim lower over her face, and then flicked Admiral's reins. "Come on, Admiral," she pleaded. "Git!"

A leisurely trot was as fast as Admiral would go.

Closer now. She peeked up but only saw a black blur of horse and man, coat tails and horse tail flying.

A stone's throw away and he was not slowing. *Good. Go past. Leave me be.*

The rider touched his hat brim, and she gave a barely perceptible nod.

He passed in a whoosh of wind, dust and horse sweat.

She exhaled, patted Admiral. "Good boy. Good boy. Come on, now, keep going."

Then a yell, echoing into the night. "Victoria?"

Admiral flinched, veering again. It was Declan's voice. Declan, come to arrest her. GG had figured it out.

"GO!" She dug her heels into Admiral's ribs again and again, but the horse could smell her fear and began snorting and side-stepping. Hoofbeats. Declan coming back.

"Victoria! Stop!"

Her eyes burned. This was not how her night should have ended.

Or maybe it was exactly how it should have ended.

Declan pulled his horse up right next to hers and took the

reins from her stiff fingers.

"Didn't I tell you," he said, panting, "that if you're ever going to disguise yourself, you've got to change your shoes?"

Still kind, still joking, even when she didn't deserve such treatment. "Declan." Her voice was raw, broken. "What are you doing here?"

Declan's horse shook his head and side stepped, but Declan kept him under control. "I'd been at the station, cleaning out my things, when your maid—Penelope is it?—came rushing in, asking for someone to go after you. That you'd run away. They gave me the address of your farm."

"Goodness," Victoria said, wrapping her father's barn coat more tightly around her. "You must think me a petulant five-year-old." So he wasn't sent by GG. Maybe the vase hadn't been discovered missing. Yet.

"Actually, five-year-olds only get to the corner before they get hungry or scared. I'd say you sound just like what you are, a sixteen-year-old young woman who, I dunno, maybe felt overwhelmed or scared for some reason?"

Admiral stepped toward the road's edge and bit off a big chomp of grass. Victoria watched him chew, his massive jaws clenching. The vase. The stealing, getting worse. Her secret. Her horrible, despicable secret. Which she'd rather die than discuss.

Shivering, Victoria shook her head. "Did I hear you correctly? Did you say you were clearing out your things?"

Declan frowned. "It's a long, boring story." Reaching behind his saddle, he unbuckled his blanket roll and handed it to her. "Now, your maid was insistent someone leave right away and stop you before you got to your farm. I'm guessing I was too late?"

Wrapping herself in the blanket, she gave him a grudging smile. "So, what were your clues, Sherlock?" They began riding side by side, Admiral perfectly obedient.

Declan gave a short laugh. "Well, to begin with, you weren't in a carriage, like your maid said you'd be. Second, you are riding away from the address she'd given me, which I suppose could mean you turned around before you got there. But then third…" He glanced over and his voice softened. "You look like you've been crying."

Victoria swallowed.

"Your big party was tonight. Did something happen?"

Picturing the beautiful vase laying in the dirt, and Father embracing the young woman—and his *son*—Victoria's eyes burned. She could only nod.

For a moment there was only the sound of the two horses walking in unison, their hooves clumping the dirt in a steady rhythm, the occasional swish of a tail adding an extra beat.

Then Declan asked, "Would you like to tell me about it?"

The story was there—tonight's theft and all her past thieving, poised on her tongue, ready to spill out. But she couldn't let it ruin this moment. She'd been missing him her entire party, and here he was right beside her, so kind and handsome, just the two of them together in this vast space. He'd find out about her soon enough. The theft of a valuable vase at GG's house would certainly make the papers, even if it was found.

"Tell me about you," she managed to say around the lump in her throat. "Tell me what you meant by clearing out your things."

Sighing, Declan patted his horse's neck. "I decided I'd had it with being a yes-man to my father and the mayor. The way the department bungled the Borden case, I was ashamed to be associated with it. So I'm going out on my own, to pursue the truth in each case, no matter how messy or ugly or inconvenient."

She smiled. "Very admirable, Declan." So much more admirable than herself, or her own cheating father who had called him a mick. Fury tingled through her again, thinking of all his nonsense about upholding the family name while he lived half his days with a mistress and son.

"What if," Victoria said, staring straight ahead into the black, "you discover the truth about someone and it's bad? Horrible even?"

Out of the corner of her eye, Victoria saw Declan turn to her and then, seeming to think better of it, returned to facing forward. "Well," he said, choosing his words carefully, "knowing the truth, at least I'd know where I was with that person. I'd have a place to start. Even if it's a very low place, it's at least solid ground, not floating around in uncertainty."

The sound of crickets, more apparent now that they were walking at a slow speed, rose and fell, making a whirling roar in her ears.

Floating around in uncertainty. Victoria combed her fingers through the closest bit of Admiral's mane. "Miss Lizzie said something similar to me just yesterday. She broke off our friendship, saying I'd always wonder about her guilt."

"Do you think you would?"

Victoria tried to picture them together now, fishing, picnicking, having tea in her new house.

"I want to say no, I wouldn't wonder, but there were so many conflicting testimonies at her trial. So many inconsistencies and unanswered questions. I thought I knew her because I'd spent time with her. But how someone acts with one person is not how they act with everyone." The image of her father kissing his mistress's hair swam before her. She shook her head. "People can surprise you."

They rode along in silence, the night breeze stirring the few remaining leaves on the trees, the horses' steady clomps marking the seconds. Then Declan reached over and took her reins and pulled both of their horses to a stop.

"Miss Robbins," he said, his expression now serious. "Do you trust me?"

She stared into his eyes and felt as if she were falling into a warm emerald lake. The sprig of hair falling over his forehead waited for her fingers to smooth it back.

"Yes," she said, her voice hoarse.

"Then tell me, what is it that you're hiding?"

Her eyes began to water. "If I told you the truth," she said, looking away, "you would never speak to me again." A small stone, loosened by Admiral's hoof, rolled off the edge of the road. She watched it tumble into the darkness of the ditch.

"I'd rather know the truth. You've been tying me in knots, Victoria. Let's get to some solid ground."

His quiet, intense tone made her throat ache. "What if that solid ground is a weed patch, ugly and overgrown and hideous?"

Declan just smiled. "One man's thistle is another man's rose."

Hot tears pressed at the corners of her eyes. Victoria felt her lifetime of secrets swelling inside of her, like one of those far-off waves she'd seen at the beach, gathering speed and silently growing in girth, threatening to crash.

"I'm afraid," she said, her voice barely audible. "There's too much. It's too awful."

Declan sidled his horse closer. "How about just one thing then? Start with just one."

He reached out and put his hand on hers. So warm, and comforting, and heartbreaking. *Remember this,* she told herself, *remember how this feels.* Looking down at his hand on hers, she traced the scar on his thumb and said, "Tonight, a valuable vase was stolen from Chateau D'Usse during my debut ball."

Declan said nothing. His hand on hers tightened.

She swallowed. "I know this because I was the one who stole it. Well, almost stole it. It's sitting under some yew bushes. Outside the parlor windows."

His voice was low, soft. "You had a change of heart?"

The tears she'd held off now came dribbling down her cheeks. She shook her head and kept stroking his scar. "I never have a change of heart until it's too late. And the crazy thing is—I don't want a vase. I don't need one! But this feeling comes over me and suddenly…" A sob escaped, unleashing a gush of tears. "I can't help myself."

Declan took a deep breath and let it out. She could not look at him.

"Does this have anything to do with the time we met in the alley and you were dressed as a maid?"

Crying harder, she nodded.

"So all your nervousness when I pressed you about it had nothing to do with the Borden murders? You weren't trying to hide something, to protect Miss Lizzie?"

"No," she sobbed, wiping her rough jacket sleeve across her face. "I was telling the truth about that. When we met, I had a spool of thread in my bag. From Benson's."

The wind blew, hissing through tree branches, rattling dry corn stalks. The horses nudged noses and flicked their tails.

Finally Declan asked, "Is there anything else I should know?"

A vision of Miss Lizzie wielding the rug beater morphed into her laughing outside the bedroom where her stepmother lay dead, bringing Victoria a fresh wave of tears. "Only that I am scared... of what I'll do next."

Declan gave her hand a last pat and then held out her reins, his expression unreadable. "Thank you for telling me. Let's go home."

THEY RODE THE rest of the way to Fall River in silence. At first, all Victoria felt was regret and shame, but as the miles wore on and the sky did not fall, she sensed something else deep within herself, something new and strange, a solid feeling—acceptance. Peace. Her secret was out—at least to Declan—and her relationship with him was officially over, as it had to be. It was a sad ending but an ending just the same. No more floating around in wonder and worry, and there was a certain lightness that went with that. Declan had been right.

From a block away, they could see Victoria's house glowing, every lamp in the house lit, and before they even got to her driveway, Mother and Penelope were running down the front steps, calling to her. Victoria slid from Admiral's back and gratefully accepted their hugs and admonitions.

"Young man," Mother said, reaching over Victoria's shoulder and taking hold of Declan's bridle. "Please come in and warm up with a cup of tea. It's the least we can do."

Dark shadows hung beneath Declan's eyes. "Thank you, ma'am, but it's been a long night. I think I best just head home." And with a tip of his hat and a fleeting glance at Victoria, he turned his horse and rode off. Victoria stood for a moment, hoping he'd look over his shoulder, just once. He wouldn't even have to smile or say anything, just catch her eye. But he did not, and the darkness absorbed the silhouette of horse and rider until only the distant tip-tapping of hooves on cobblestone were proof of the duo's existence.

Mother and Penelope prattled on in loud whispers as the three of them walked Admiral toward the carriage house, yet Victoria heard none of it. Her face and fingers were numb with cold and the hoofbeats of Declan's horse echoed in her ears. "You two go inside and start the tea," she said. "I just need a few minutes alone. I'll get Admiral settled."

Penelope began to protest, but Mother gave Victoria a discerning look and pulled the maid inside. Grateful for the time to process, Victoria unsaddled Admiral and gave him some extra oats for his trouble. Stroking his side, she thought of everything and nothing. The rhythmic stroking warmed her hand and quieted her thoughts until there was only one thought left. The last act in this sad drama, the period at the end of the sentence. Nodding, she gave Admiral one final pat and strode directly to the shed.

Digging her box of treasures out from under the shelf, she proceeded to squeeze it and then herself out the door and over to the rubbish bin, into which she unceremoniously dumped the entire collection. After a moment's hesitation, she dropped the hatbox in too.

CHAPTER
THIRTY-FOUR

"Mother," Victoria said, warming her fingers on her steaming mug a few minutes later, "you do know what I found out there at the farm, don't you?"

They were sitting at the little kitchen table, a gas lamp lighting their faces and throwing shadows on the cabinets and hanging pots and pans. Penelope had fixed them all hot cocoa instead of tea, to better help them sleep, and then, carrying her own mug, excused herself to bed.

Pain flitted across Mother's pale features. "I was hoping the officer would overtake the carriage and warn your father you were inside, but when you came back on Admiral, I suspected you'd seen everything."

"Why wouldn't you tell me? A mistress and a son? All while he's lecturing me on our family's reputation?"

In the soft lamplight, with her hair down in a long side braid, Mother studied the steam rising from her cocoa. "I was... ashamed."

Victoria lowered her cup abruptly, spilling hot chocolate onto her knuckles. "You have nothing to be ashamed of. Father is the one who should be ashamed." She pulled Declan's hanky out from her pocket and dabbed her hand with it. She would not return this hanky, one precious memory of something given to her instead of stolen.

Mother took up her spoon and touched the tip of it to her drink, slowly stirring the cluster of bubbles on top. "I wanted to be strong and independent, like the suffragette ladies are always harping on us to be, but what could I do? Having been nothing but a wife and mother all my life, I have no marketable skills. And with my spells, I'd never be able to hold a job. We'd end up in the Poor House. We—I—needed your father's money." Her smile was sad, apologetic.

"Fine," Victoria said, leaning forward, "but why let me think Father was the pillar of righteousness, when all the while he's carrying on with another woman, committing adultery?"

Mother sighed, a deep resigned sigh, then took a sip of cocoa. Finally she said, "A girl should honor and respect her father."

The lamp flickered and she saw the figures of Father and his mistress in her mind's eye, the woman resting her head on Father's chest. Victoria shook her head. "Respect has to be earned." Declan left his job because he did not agree with the work done by his father or the force. He was going out on his own *to pursue the truth in each case, no matter how messy or ugly or inconvenient.* Now that was worthy of respect.

Mother eyed Victoria. "What started all of this? Whatever would make you do something so rash as to run away to the farm? "

The old guilt, which had been temporarily set aside in her anger at Father, fell back onto Victoria's chest, a bag of wet sand, gritty, heavy, immovable. It had taken all her strength and courage to tell Declan about her stealing, and then to suffer through the humiliating silence that followed, she really did not think she could do it again. Not so soon.

"I promise I will tell you, Mother, but not tonight."

Mother lifted her chin, looking as if she might demand an answer, but then, perhaps remembering her own secrets, merely nodded.

TWO DAYS LATER, Victoria sat in her window seat, gluing the latest articles about the Borden murders into her scrapbook. The sky was bleak, smeared with threatening gray clouds, and giving off the lonely feel of dusk, a day already over, instead of the late morning it was. Since the trial, the majority of articles favored Miss Lizzie and the jury's verdict, the most extreme being the *New York Times* calling the Fall River police department "muddleheaded," "ignorant," and "untrained." However, the Borden house remained buttoned up, with very few callers coming and going, giving credence to what Miss Lizzie had predicted.

Blowing on the page to help the bone glue dry faster, Victoria realized, with a stab of regret, that she'd just added the very last article she'd ever put into this scrapbook. Though obviously happy with the outcome of the trial, she was going to miss the mystery, keeping track of facts and theories, coming up with questions to ask Declan, slipping through town to the jail, the cemetery, the courthouse. Now it was back to normal life, but worse. No mystery, no case, no Miss Lizzie, and no Declan.

Not only that, she couldn't help feeling there was also no… *her*.

Confessing her stealing habit to Declan was like Sampson cutting off his hair, the one thing that gave him his power. Now that she'd broken her secret wide open, she felt like a shriveled pea shucked of its crisp, green shell, a mealy apple stripped of its bright red peel. Ugly, disappointing, worthless.

The world, too, seemed to have changed since her confession, somehow stripped of its allure and excitement, and though Victoria had no second thoughts about dumping her treasures, she still worried about her habit. Since Victoria's return, Mother had not pressed her to talk, and had even stepped back from her usual demands, giving Victoria time alone to brood and solidify her conclusion that with her affliction, she was unfit for friendship, marriage, and motherhood. Continuing to charade as a debutante was out of the question, for no man, no matter how horrid, deserved a thief for a wife. She felt stuck and rudderless and more than once wished her mother's strange illness upon herself, a relief and an excuse for living a meaningless life.

Miss Lizzie had once spoken of a young girl who'd had "the troubles"—which Victoria assumed meant pregnancy out of wedlock—and found refuge in a convent. Victoria wondered if becoming a nun might pay for her past sins. But she still had Mother to worry about. Finally, tired of her own melancholy, Victoria posted letters of inquiry to one convent in Boston and two in Connecticut. Though it didn't seem like the perfect solution, it did feel good to at least take some kind of action.

She'd also written several heartfelt notes of thanks to GG and to Gwyne's parents, having to rewrite each twice due to guilty tears blurring the ink. Gwyne had left a calling card in the mail slot, apparently embracing the formality of being a debutante to the hilt, but added a handwritten note on the reverse side regarding the upcoming balls she hoped Victoria would attend with her. Gwyne deserved a better friend than Victoria.

Still no word regarding GG's vase. Thank goodness. And no word from Declan, though that was not a surprise. The fact he hadn't had her arrested was something for which to be grateful.

Setting her scrapbook aside, Victoria pulled Declan's hanky out from her cuff, laid it across her bent knees and rested her chin on top. His earthy scent had disappeared, but she imagined she could still smell it. Staring out the window, watching the bare tree branches bend and sway in the autumn wind, she wondered what Declan might be doing right at that moment.

Would he find a cozy apartment like Sherlock's, with a fine fireplace and a landlady who brought him puddings? Or maybe a small storefront near the edge of town with his name painted on the window in crisp, black letters. Perhaps once she heard, Victoria could convince Mother to walk by it with her, to try to get a glimpse of him through the window or, even better, see him coming out, on his way to investigate an important case. Wouldn't it be ironic if he ended up renting the empty shop that Mr. Borden had supposedly refused to lease to that other man? (Another suspect never followed up with by the police.) The building must be owned by Miss Lizzie and Miss Emma now, she supposed.

And just as she thought of Miss Lizzie, there she came, out of the back door, wrapped in a black cloak, heading to the barn to use the privy, most likely. Her new home on The Hill would probably have an indoor toilet, unlike the basement pot which needed to be emptied or the smelly barn loo. Victoria shook her head. Of all the scenarios she'd imagined about life after the trial, Miss Lizzie ending their friendship was not one of them. The thought of never seeing her neighbor again—the fact she would never again be able to just stroll over and chat with the one adult who took her seriously and treated her equally—gave Victoria a burning lump in her throat. It was for Victoria's best interests, Miss Lizzie had said, but it didn't make it hurt any less.

Miss Lizzie stopped before she got to the barn and looked back at her house, where Uncle Morse was just coming out the back door. He hurried forward and they had a short discussion, ending with him placing his hand on her shoulder and then walking back toward the house and out of the yard. Miss Lizzie did not move, but watched him the whole way, her cloak flapping about her, reminding Victoria of an enormous blackbird. She shivered.

"Miss?" Penelope knocked on Victoria's open door. "Someone here to see you."

Startled, Victoria stood and quickly stuffed Declan's hanky back in her cuff, then straightened her dress. Now that she was officially "out," it could be any number of callers. She glanced back outside, but Miss Lizzie was gone. She had the strangest sudden image of her flying over the rooftops in her long black cloak, soaring in the direction of The Hill.

"Thank you, Pen," she said, "I'll be right down."

Declan, cap tucked under his arm, stopped pacing the parlor as soon as Victoria entered. Penelope had lit the mantle candles, but they did little to cut through the dreariness of the gray day. Declan was dressed in a new suit, the hem of which his fingers plucked at self-consciously. He bowed. "Miss Robbins." His tone was very formal.

Victoria's heart lifted and then sank. Ever the gentleman, he must have come to say a final good-bye. Another good-bye. Well, she was an adult now and would accept it like an adult.

She curtsied. "Master Dempsey. Would you care to sit?" She motioned to a chair. His chair, not her father's. She thought of the last time Declan had sat in it, how happy their exchange had been, how they'd gotten on so well discussing the points of Miss Lizzie's case. From that chair, he'd declared her "clever." She would never forget that as long as she lived.

"Actually," Declan said, clearing his throat, "I can't stay long. I just came by to tell you I have secured a room from which to operate my new business." In his hand, he held out a small white card.

She took it and read aloud, "D. Dempsey Detective Agency. 141 1/2 12th Street." She forced a gracious, mature smile. "Well! Congratulations are in order."

"Yes." He cleared his throat again. "Thank you. Yes. So." He swiped the errant curl off his face, but it bounced back down.

Her heart was breaking. He was so nervous, trying to be kind in saying good-bye, to find a way out of this mess of truth he'd asked for. She'd warned him, hadn't she? Best to get it over with as quickly as possible.

"Good luck to you then, Master Dempsey. I'm sure I'll be reading about your exploits in the papers one day." She extended her hand.

He didn't take it, however, and reached into his pocket instead.

Embarrassed, she dropped her hand, the hand responsible for so much stealing. Of course he would not want to touch it.

"Thank you, Miss Robbins," Declan said, "but I wanted to ask you something. I wanted to ask…"

As Declan pulled out a pen and small notebook, there was a loud slamming and stomping coming from the kitchen, and Father's voice, bellowing Victoria's name.

"How dare you." The voice was getting louder as he made his way through the house. "Leaving me with no horse, no way to get around the farm, no way to get home…"

He burst into the parlor, vest askew, hair matted, his eyes bulging when he saw Declan. Footsteps tapped overhead: Mother and Penelope, making their way to the stairs.

"And you! Mick!" Father stabbed the air in Declan's direction. "Didn't I tell you to leave my daughter alone?"

"Stop right there, Father." Victoria squeezed her hands into tight fists.

Mother rushed into the room, but father and daughter did not acknowledge her presence, their eyes locked in a mutual glare.

Victoria stepped between her father and Declan. "How dare *you*," she said, her throat constricted with rage. "How dare you lecture me on reputation while you have been dragging Mother and me through the mud behind you all these years? Carrying on with other women? Having children with them? What's wrong with *us*, Father? Were we not enough for you?"

She remembered the way Father had placed his hand on his son's head. Soft, tender. *A son.* Bitter tears lodged in her throat.

Father blinked, momentarily stunned. He opened his mouth to speak, then rubbed his hand across his lips and chin, back and forth, making a scratching noise. He hadn't shaved.

"Victoria," he finally said, "this is a private matter, between your mother and myself. It does not concern you, and it certainly does not concern this..." He jutted his jaw at Declan.

Victoria placed her fingertips to her breastbone and adopted a look of innocent surprise. "Oh, but Father, if my behavior could reflect badly on you, surely your behavior could reflect badly on me. I mean really, I have a reputation to uphold."

Recognizing his own words being used against him, Father dropped his hands to his sides. "No one but the people in this room—and the *parties involved* at the farm—know about my... situation."

Victoria crossed her arms. "Yet." Behind her, Declan shifted his feet. Mother stared at her, transfixed. The grandfather clock ticked menacingly.

"What do you propose I do, Victoria? Send them packing? Sell the farm? Promise to uphold my wedding vows?" He gave a scornful laugh. "You have much to learn about the way the world works, young lady."

"The world is changing, Father. Soon, women will have the right to vote—"

"Never," he scoffed.

"And we will start making other choices too."

"You already do! You chose that dress to wear. Your mother picked out these curtains, this wallpaper, all the furniture you see here."

Victoria searched for the right words, the words to explain what she'd been feeling these last few months—the gnawing dissatisfaction, the deep hunger for something, something base, primal, necessary for survival.

"I want to be in charge of my own life. I want to choose what I do and where I go and with whom I associate."

"That's ridiculous. You are young and immature."

"I'm mature enough to recognize an adulterer when I see one."

Father grunted, rubbed his whiskered face again.

Mother looked down at her hands folded in front of her.

"So go ahead and run your life the way you chose, but you best sing our praises as Mother and I run ours."

"Sing your praises?" Father barked.

Victoria smiled. "Think of how enlightened everyone will consider you, Father. Especially your boss, Mr. Roberts, whose wife heads the Right to Vote committee. It would be a shame if he found out about your—what did you call it?—situation."

Father, red-faced, squinted at her. "What's happened to you, Pidge?"

A lot had happened to her, too much to explain. "I've grown up. I'm a woman now."

Father grunted. "Well, I don't like it." And with that, he turned and stalked out.

There was a minute or two of discomfort: Declan asking if he should leave, Mother assuring him he should not, Penelope offering tea and Declan declining. Finally, Victoria raised her eyebrows at the two women, and they hurriedly excused themselves and left them alone in the parlor.

Declan, still holding the notebook and pencil, shook his head. "That was most impressive, Miss Robbins. Though I guess I should not be surprised. You've shown your gumption from the moment I met you."

Victoria blushed, remembering her terrible Irish maid impression. "You were about to ask me something," she said, "when my father burst in."

"Yes." Declan nodded, looking down at the notebook in his hand. "But first, I have a confession. Hearing what you said to your father made me realize I haven't been entirely truthful with you, either."

Oh dear. The red fleurs-de-lis on the wall began to waver. Victoria reached back for the arm of the love seat and lowered herself into it. He'd taken out his notebook, looking like he was here to arrest her. For GG's vase. Maybe for all her thefts. She was going to take Miss Lizzie's place in jail. Declan took the cap out from under his arm and, placing it atop his notebook, bent both of them together. "The thing is, miss, I knew about your father, about his situation, several months ago, and I never let on."

"You..." Victoria stared at the crumpled cap in his hands, then raised her chin and met his gaze. "How?"

"Right after the murders, we headed up to Swansea, Father and me, to check out the workers on the Bordens' farm to see if any of them could be suspects." Declan shifted his weight, scuffing his new shoes across the flowered carpet. Because their farm was just down the road from the Bordens', Victoria suspected she knew what came next. "When we went asking around to the neighbors about Mr. Borden and how he got on with his help, well, I saw him. And her. And the little boy." He shrugged. "I didn't make the connection until we came to your house to interview you. Actually, my father is the one that pointed it out."

Victoria flashed back to that interview, Detective Dempsey's hulking frame on Mother's little writing chair and the way he reacted when he'd heard about Miss Lizzie's cancelled plans. They both had known the whole time they were interviewing her that her father was committing adultery. And after that, when her father kicked him out of the house.

Victoria shook her head. "You never said anything."

Declan ran a hand through his dark hair. "I thought maybe you knew, thought maybe these kinds of things were different in your level of society, like in England when a king had... young ladies so he didn't have to bother the queen."

Victoria winced at the implied vulgarity.

"But the minute I saw you on the road home from the farm," Declan continued, "I knew you'd had no idea, and I felt horrible."

Victoria gave a sad laugh. "I'm not sure whether to be insulted or embarrassed."

"Neither," he said. "You cannot be held responsible for the

actions of your father. So, now that I've unburdened myself with that, I still have something to ask you." He held out his hand.

Uncertain, Victoria touched her fingertips to his palm, and he helped her to stand.

"Miss Robbins." He tucked his cap back under his arm. "I was going to ask…" He paused to take a calming breath. "Ask if you would care to be… my Watson."

Victoria blinked. "Your Watson? As in Sherlock's sidekick?" A blast of wind rattled the windows. The candles flickered.

"No, no, not sidekick," Declan assured her. His green eyes held hers. "Partner."

Victoria's insides swirled faster and stronger than any spool of thread had spun them. The red flowers on the wallpaper danced in the flickering candlelight.

But.

"Declan, you couldn't possibly want me for a partner. Have you forgotten? I'm a..." She glanced over her shoulder. "Thief," she whispered.

"Yes, you are," he said, giving a little shrug. "But you are also a loyal friend, a devoted daughter, a dogged investigator, an extraordinarily clever and beautiful young woman. And, according to Officer Lupin, quite a fine dancer as well."

Victoria laughed. His dimpled grin made her legs wobble.

"I think we make a great team, Miss Robbins. As Sherlock says, 'Nothing clears up a case so much as stating it to another person.'"

He placed the pen and booklet in her hand and closed her fingers around them, just like he had so long ago with his hanky. "You can take your notes with this hand," he said, "and I," he looped her free hand around his arm, "will take care of the other. How does that sound?"

"I think," she said, her breath almost leaving her, "that sounds like a wonderful idea."

From the hall, Penelope's suppressed glee drifted toward

them.

And because it was the truest, smartest, strongest urge she'd ever had, Victoria leaned forward and kissed him, square on the mouth, and the resulting explosion inside her chest put every last thieving thrill to shame.

Goodness, she thought, staring into her new partner's eyes. *There just might be a cure for me yet.*

EPILOGUE

On a sunny November morning, two months following the trial, as the smell of burning leaves wafted through the air, Victoria stood on the wide porch of Miss Lizzie's new home, Maplecroft, waiting for Miss Lizzie to answer her knock. The case of who killed the Bordens had not been neatly wrapped up like her beloved Sherlock Holmes mysteries, but she was learning real life is not fiction. What had Penelope said as they gazed down upon the chaos in the Bordens' yard after the murders? *Real life is messier.* Yes, messier. And complicated. And imperfect. But also beautiful, and full of opportunities for love and hope.

The door swung open and before Miss Lizzie could even say hello, Victoria spoke.

"I know you said it was best for me to cut ties with you, but I am making my own decisions now, and I've decided we should stay friends."

Miss Lizzie, clutching a shawl to her neck, blinked. A caramel-colored cat wound itself around her skirts. "Victoria? What are—"

"I don't care what other people think of me," Victoria interrupted, "just like you. In fact…" She smiled up at her old friend.

"You remind me... of me."

Miss Lizzie stared and then gave a quiet laugh. Reluctantly, she opened the door. "Enter then, if you dare." One eyebrow arched and a hint of a smile played at her lips.

Victoria hesitated only briefly before giving her a gracious nod.

And walked in.

POSTSCRIPT

Lizzie and her sister Emma lived together in their new Hill home, Maplecroft, for twelve years. After forming a friendship with actress Nance O'Neil, Lizzie threw many parties there, which included Nance and her theater friends. Reportedly unhappy with these gatherings, Emma eventually moved to Providence, Rhode Island. After "finishing her season in the east," Nance moved away as well. A "poor correspondent," Nance did not stay in touch with Lizzie.

Among Lizzie's closest companions over the years were two of her chauffeurs, Norman Hall, who worked in her employ for five years, and Ernest A. Terry. Both Norman's and Ernest's children lovingly referred to Lizzie as "Auntie Borden" and received frequent visits, gifts, and letters from her throughout their lives.

In the spring of 1927, Lizzie's health began to decline. Just hours before her death on June 1st, she summoned Ernest Terry and gave him a blank check to cover the repairs on his home. He tried to refuse the gift, but she insisted. She breathed her last at 8:30 that evening. She was sixty-six years old. Emma died just nine days later of "chronic nephritis," or kidney disease.

Lizzie remained an animal lover throughout her life, leaving the majority of her money (approximately $30,000) to the Animal Rescue League of Fall River. The remainder of her wealth went to cousins, servants, and friends, after first setting aside $500 for the care of her father's burial plot. Lizzie was buried next to her father, under a tombstone reading "LIZBETH." This tombstone, as well as Emma's and the rest of the Borden family's, still remain in the Oak Grove Cemetery. The original Borden home, where the murders took place, has been restored and is currently a bed and breakfast bearing Lizzie Borden's name.

The mystery of who killed Andrew and Abigail Borden has never been solved.

AUTHOR'S NOTE

Setting out to write a book about Lizzie Borden, I knew I wanted my main character to have a secret flaw that would make her sympathetic to Lizzie's plight. I chose kleptomania for its fascinating disconnect—otherwise "moral" people unable to stop themselves from stealing items they neither need nor want. There were few lone—and lonely—first-person accounts of sufferers, and I wondered if I could write about such an unknown condition.

When I came across an obscure article about Lizzie Borden being an alleged thief, however, it was too big of a "coincidence" to pass up. And so I wrote Victoria's struggle with kleptomania as true to the descriptions of real-life sufferers as I could find: the recurring intrusive thoughts, the failure to resist the impulse to steal, and the great relief of pressure following the act, as well as the consequences of guilt, remorse, anxiety, and social segregation. The rest came from my imagination.

From what I can gather, had Victoria been a real person, she would have struggled with kleptomania her entire life. We have come a long way from the 1890s, however, and today there are a wide variety of treatments including cognitive therapy, behavior therapy, psychotherapy, and systematic desensitization, in addition to medications for mood and anxiety. My heart goes out to those in the grip of this—and all—psychological struggles.

Please know you are not alone. There is help out there, but the first step starts with you. Please reach out and tell someone.

As for her mother's "hysterical paralysis," the American Psychiatric Association refers to it as a conversion disorder, and some cases are thought to be brought on by psychological stress or trauma.

The majority of the newspaper articles in this book are excerpts from actual articles. All images and the associated newspaper articles can be found at www.phayemuss.wordpress.com, as listed in the Works Cited. However, *The Boston Bugle* article, "Differing Stories," is fiction, based on historically accurate details, written for the purposes of this story.

While many of the characters in this story were actual people, much of their dialogue is fictional. A few facts were altered for the sake of the plot. For instance, the jail Lizzie stayed in was not in Fall River but in the nearby town of Taunton, and her trial did not take place in the fall but almost a year after the murders, concluding on June 20, 1893.

ACKNOWLEDGMENTS

First and foremost, I'd like to thank editor Robin Benjamin, with whom I began this long journey at Marshall Cavendish, oh so many years ago, when this story was still in its infancy. Next thanks go to past agent Clelia Gore who took me on and had the smarts to query Owl Hollow Press. Also to agent Adria Goetz who took the baton from Clelia, negotiated the sale and kindly supported me through the whole publishing process.

My amazing writing group deserves huge kudos and many lemon squares for reading and critiquing untold versions and chapters and revisions and re-revisions of this story, including: Marlene Donnelly, Jude Mandell, Janet Nolan, Sharon Porter-field, Sarah Roggio, Sara Shacter, Ruth Spiro and Beverly Spooner.

I am indebted to Northwestern professor and gifted writing coach Fred Shafer for his guidance, as well as the dedicated members of his writing class for their valuable input: Delia O'Hara, Mary Hutchings Reed, David De Jong, David Pelzer, Jen Lawrence, Joan Loeb, Bill Kennedy, Virginia Smiley, Laura Cole, Lois Barliant, Lee Prusik, Mary Herlehy, Joan Parks.

And of course, where would I be without the awesome folks at Owl Hollow? Huge hugs to Emma Nelson and Hannah Smith for picking my manuscript and wanting to make it their own; to the amazingly talented editor Olivia Swenson, who gave me just the right amount of structure and insight to raise this story to a higher level; to the aforementioned Hannah for cleaning up and tightening the final version; and to Caroline Geslison and Elise Meyer who worked their online magic promoting MORE THAN A THIEF in ways I'd never know how to do no matter how many "Marketing for Boomers" books I might read.

Finally, unending gratitude to my hubby, Jer, for supporting me and this ridiculous passion of mine for all these years. And thanks to my kids, who fill my life with love.

ABOUT THE AUTHOR

Beverly Patt is the author of *Best Friends Forever: a WWII Scrapbook,* a story of friendship for readers seeking to understand the roots of racism in our society.

She has a master's degree in special education and taught at a school for abused and neglected children. Because of the wide age range in her classroom, Bev realized the one activity her students could all do together was to listen, so she made a point of reading to them every day, and then began writing stories herself.

When not writing, Bev plays and coaches tennis, knits badly and reads obsessively.

You can learn more about Beverly Patt and her thoughts on writing at www.beverlypatt.com.

WORKS CITED

Doyle, Arthur Conan. *The Original Sherlock Holmes.* Castle
    Inc, 2004, Secaucus, NJ.

Linder, Douglas O. *The Trial of Lizzie Borden: Selected News
    paper Articles.* Famous-trials.com, UMKC School of
    Law, 2018.

Martins, Michael and Binette, Dennis A. *Parallel Lives: A So-
    cial History of Lizzie A Borden and Her Fall River.* Fall
    River Historical Society, 2010, Fall River, MA.

Musselman, Faye. *Tattered Fabric: Fall River's Lizzie Borden.
    Musings, Reflections, and Sharing on This Enduring
    Fascination.* phayemuss.wordpress.com, 2007.

Widdows, Harry. *Trial for Lizzie Andrew Borden*, Volumes 1
    and 2. LizzieAndrewBorden.com, 2001.

Printed in the USA
CPSIA information can be obtained
at www.ICGtesting.com
LVHW050353310823
756645LV00004B/632